The Shadow Earl

STELLA RILEY

Copyright © 2023 Stella Riley
All rights reserved.

ISBN: 9798397511094

Cover by Larry Rostant
Typography by Ana Grigoriu-Voicu

CONTENTS

	Page
Prologue	1
Chapter One	9
Chapter Two	21
Chapter Three	35
Chapter Four	50
Chapter Five	63
Chapter Six	74
Chapter Seven	85
Chapter Eight	96
Chapter Nine	108
Chapter Ten	122
Chapter Eleven	135
Chapter Twelve	146
Chapter Thirteen	157
Chapter Fourteen	171
Chapter Fifteen	182
Chapter Sixteen	193

	Page
Chapter Seventeen	204
Chapter Eighteen	215
Chapter Nineteen	226
Chapter Twenty	239
Chapter Twenty-One	251
Chapter Twenty-Two	263
Chapter Twenty-Three	276
Chapter Twenty-Four	287
Chapter Twenty-Five	296
Chapter Twenty-Six	306
Chapter Twenty-Seven	319
Chapter Twenty-Eight	329
Chapter Twenty-Nine	342
Chapter Thirty	354
Chapter Thirty-One	363
Epilogue	374
Author's Note	378

PROLOGUE

Athens 1777

A large map spread over the table in front of him, Christian Selwyn, Lord Hazelmere, traced a particular route with his left hand whilst making a neat list of notes with his right.

Behind him, his cousin leaned against the window-frame, ogling the doe-eyed beauty on the balcony across the street. Not until the lady disappeared from view did he turn and say testily, 'Please tell me you're finding our best way home from this fly-plagued oven of a city.'

Silence.

'Kit?'

The tawny-gold head lifted slightly.

'Sorry. Did you say something?'

'Yes. I've had enough of this place and, whether you have or not, it's time we were heading home. Isn't that why you're studying a map?'

Laying down his pen, Christian sat up and, with an apologetic smile, said, 'Not exactly.'

Basil scowled at him. 'Go on.'

'I thought ... since we're so close and getting there will be easy ... it seems a pity to turn back without spending a few days in Constantinople.'

'*What?* No. Absolutely not.'

'But – '

'No! Are you *insane?* More heat, more damned mosquitoes, more peculiar food and undrinkable wine – and in a country where they aren't even *Christians?* No.' Basil stalked over to glare down at him over folded arms. 'Surely to *God* you've had enough of sight-seeing by now? Personally, I've seen enough paintings and tramped over enough ruins to last a life-time.'

For possibly the umpteenth time, Christian wished that at least one of his friends had been free to make the Tour with him. But none of them had been ... so here he was, stuck with his cousin.

Close in age though he and Basil were, they had little or nothing in common. *He* had soaked up the culture and art of Florence and marvelled at the ancient ruins of Rome and the amazing discoveries being uncovered daily at Herculaneum; Basil had grumbled and yawned through all of it and constantly mourned the wine and women they'd left behind in Venice. Getting him as far as Athens had been like pulling teeth. It looked as if getting him to Constantinople would require more of the same; and Christian didn't think he had either the patience or the energy to go through it all again. On the other hand, he wasn't going to miss a chance to see the minarets and domes of the great city on the Bosphorus where Europe met Asia.

He said mildly, 'What's a few more days? A pleasant cruise across the Aegean and through the Dardanelles to the Sea of Marmara, then on to Constantinople. A week there – no longer than that, I promise and – '

'No.'

'But we'll never get another opportunity like this. Surely you can see that?'

'I don't care. And our return will be overdue as it is,' Basil pointed out. 'You agreed to a Grand Tour of two years and it's already been almost that even *without* the endless slog of getting home.'

'The return journey will be quicker. And – '

'What will Miss Kelsall think? More importantly, what will her *father* think?'

This, Christian knew, was a valid argument. At the time he'd asked for Sophia's hand, he'd been a couple of months shy of twenty-two and she, a mere seventeen. Sir Joseph Kelsall's reluctant response had been grudging agreement to an informal betrothal *only* if followed by a long separation to test the strength of their attachment. And he wouldn't have even gone *that* far if it had not already outlasted everyone's expectations.

Christian had a sudden vivid memory of the day he'd said goodbye to her.

* * *

Had it been left to Sir Joseph, they wouldn't have been allowed to say their farewells in private. But Lady Kelsall's opinion of the situation was entirely at odds with that of her husband. He *was* adamant that Sophia would not marry the first man to come her way. She *had* decided that only over her own dead body would an earl slip through her daughter's fingers. So here Christian was with Sophia folded as close in his arms as was humanly possible whilst still fully dressed.

For a time, neither of them had spoken. But finally, trying to sound cheerful, she said, 'It's a shame you have to travel with Basil.'

'It is. But it can't be helped.'

'*Can't* any of your real friends go with you?'

'No. Benedict's brother has sent him north to manage the dukedom's most distant estate; with Anthony's father only dead these three months, his mother and sisters wept buckets at the mere thought of him going away; and Daniel's family simply can't afford the cost of it.'

'Neither, it seems,' muttered Sophia aridly, 'can your Uncle Eustace.'

'He probably could — but doesn't see why he should if he doesn't have to. As for Daniel, he's too proud to make the trip at my expense.'

'Unlike Basil.'

'Yes. Unlike Basil.' Christian sighed. 'Are we *really going to* waste these last precious minutes talking about my cousin?'

'No. It just … it's just safer.'

'Than what?'

'Saying the things that matter.' She tilted her head to look up at him out of delphinium blue eyes swimming in tears she'd so far refused to shed. 'Two years is so long. You … you might forget me … or meet someone else in Florence or Venice.'

'So might you, love – right here in London.'
'I won't. Of course I won't!'
'Then why would you think I might?'
'Your situation is different.'
'Only geographically. But here's the thing, Sophie-Rose. I could meet a dozen other girls anywhere in the world ... and not one of them could compare to you.'
'You can't know that.'
'I can. Can't you in reverse?'
'Yes.' She burrowed into his throat. 'Of course I can. I'm sorry. I'm being foolish. It's just that I - I'll miss you so much.'
'I know. I'll miss you, too.' Christian paused and said the thing that had been in his mind all along. 'I don't have to go. I only agreed because your father has made it a condition and following orders now seemed the surest way to eventually get what we want. But there's still time to change my mind. Shall I?'

Seconds ticked by before, her voice muffled against his cravat, she said, 'No.'

'No? Are you sure? It's no real sacrifice, you know. I'd rather be here with you.'

'Except that you won't be. They'll find other means to keep us apart.'

He frowned. 'They?'

But she went on without hearing him. 'I don't want you to give up the Grand Tour – or anything else - for me, Kit. In time, you'd come to regret it. We both would. Also, the reason we agreed that you would go hasn't changed. So although I'll miss you horribly, you should go.' Sitting up and, despite the tears which had finally defied her, fixing him with a resolute gaze, she said, 'Go. Visit all those wonderful cities, see all the sites and enjoy every minute of it. Promise you'll do that?'

'If you'll promise you'll be doing the same here; accepting invitations, dancing with the best-looking fellows and walking in the park with the most charming ones – all of whom I already hate. Will you?'

Sophia made a sound that was part laugh and part sob.

'Yes. At least, I'll try. And as long as you don't forget to write to me.'

'I won't. From everywhere I go and in the minutest detail,' he vowed. *'I'll write so much you'll wish I hadn't.'*

'Never. And when you come back ... if you still feel the same --'

'If we both still feel the same,' he interposed firmly.

'All right. If we both do ... you can speak to Papa again. But otherwise not. I shall not regard you as bound to me and – and you should not either.'

Christian smiled and gathered her closer, tipping her chin up with one finger.

'Think of it as you choose, sweetheart – and so shall I. But I've been yours for a long time ... so although you can set me free, it doesn't mean that I'll fly.' And he kissed her, long and very sweetly.

* * *

Coming back to the present, he said firmly, 'Sophie trusts me. She knows I love her and that I'll come back. She'll wait. So will her father.'

'Oh – I daresay they will,' drawled Basil cynically 'Sir Joseph isn't about to pass up his daughter's chance of becoming a countess, is he? But that's not to say that either of them will *like* it.'

'Can we stick to the point, Basil?'

'Which was?'

'A round trip of three or four weeks from here to visit Constantinople.'

'Those same three or four weeks would see us back to Italy and the road home.'

There was a long silence. Finally, Christian came to his feet and said, 'Go, then.'

Basil stared at him. 'What?'

'We're not joined at the hip. You've had enough and want to go back. I understand that – so go. I'm not stopping you and I'll follow in due course. I doubt I'll even be very far behind you.' Then, because he suspected it might be the crux of the matter, he added, 'Naturally, I'll leave you with sufficient funds.'

Throughout their travels, it had been Christian who'd defrayed all the costs – which was why, although he'd claimed it was for their safety, Uncle Eustace had decreed that the cousins should make the Tour together. Christian didn't mind the money. He'd even felt a niggling sense of obligation to do something for the cousin whose circumstances were very different from his own. He just wished he liked him better.

Christian's father had died while he was still at Oxford and a year short of his majority. Inevitably, his uncle had been named his guardian and trustee. So far so good. But Uncle Eustace and his father had been twins ... and Christian's father was the elder by some ten minutes. Consequently, it was Christian who had become the Earl of Hazelmere, inheriting numerous properties and a very comfortable fortune. Uncle Eustace and therefore Basil were doomed to remain untitled and substantially less well off. There was, Christian had come to realise, some understandable but unfortunate resentment about that which he preferred not to ponder too deeply.

As usual, he pretended to take everything at face value and waited for Basil's reply. Eventually, his cousin said moodily, 'You can't go haring off to the Ottoman Empire on your own. You don't know what you'd be facing. *Anything* could happen to you.'

Christian refrained from observing that facing the unexpected was one of the points of making the Grand Tour and said instead, 'Anything could have happened to either of us at any time since we left Dover. However ... are you saying you'll come with me?'

'Not a chance.'

'Fine. Then stay here. Alternatively, take a ship to Palermo and wait for me there. Getting onward passage to Marseille shouldn't be difficult.' And carefully, after a slight pause, 'As I said, money won't be a problem.'

Basil's mouth tightened at that. 'No need to rub it in.'

'I wasn't. I'm just looking for a mutually acceptable solution.'

'There isn't one! *Turkey*, for God's sake! You don't even speak the bloody language.'

'There are bound to be guides here in Athens who do.'

'That's no answer. You could be robbed, beaten and dropped overboard in the middle of the Aegean. The possibilities are endless.'

'So you already said.' Weary of the argument, Christian turned back to the map thus missing the peculiar expression that flitted through his cousin's eyes. 'It's true that something bad *could* happen along the way … but equally true that it may *not*.'

Basil expelled a long, slow breath.

'And if it does, what the hell am I going to say to Father?'

'You'll say you did your best to stop me but I wouldn't listen – except to your point about the risk of robbery. You're right about that. So I'll leave the bulk of our funds with you, taking only sufficient to get me comfortably to Constantinople and back, then onwards – '

'If something happens to you, Father will blame me for not going with you.'

'Then onwards to Palermo,' finished Christian as if he hadn't spoken. 'If we're agreed on that course. Are we?'

'Oh God. I must be as mad as you are.'

'*Are* we?'

'Yes. All right. Palermo it is. Anything's better than remaining here.' Basil fell silent, staring through the window. Finally, he said, 'If you're absolutely sure about this, you'd better let me seek out a reliable and reputable dragoman to accompany you.'

'Covering your back with Uncle Eustace, Baz?' asked Christian on a note of laughter.

'What do *you* think? But that's not the only reason. You can't go alone.'

'I know that. And I'll appreciate your help.'

'Good – though you'd do better to change your mind about the whole thing.'

'You've made that plain. Can we please not go through it again?'

'Fine. A dragoman, then. Anything else?'

'Well, I suppose that, in the unlikely event I don't arrive in Palermo within the month, you might send someone to look for me?' He sent a fleeting, persuasive smile over his shoulder. 'Meanwhile, stop worrying. It will be perfectly fine. You'll see.'

* * *

When he'd said the words he had no way of knowing how often and for how long they would come back to haunt him; or that they would carry with them a bone-deep hunger for revenge.

CHAPTER ONE

London, two years later

Four gentlemen sat in one of the private card rooms at Sinclairs. Bottles and glasses littered the table but two unopened decks of cards had been pushed aside in favour of maps and a neat sheaf of papers from which one of them was briskly reminding the others of things, most of which they already knew.

Three of these men had been friends since Eton, throughout university and beyond.

Tall, dark-haired and severely handsome, Lord Benedict Hawkridge was a younger brother of the Duke of Belhaven. Son of a viscount, the Honourable Daniel Shelbourne was also tall and almost equally good-looking; and less imposing than either of these, Anthony, Baron Wendover's countenance usually reflected his easy-going nature. At present, however, all three gentlemen wore expressions of grim determination.

Alone of the four, Gerald Sandhurst had not attended Eton and nor did he have aristocratic connections. He'd met and become friends with the others at Oxford and, since Christian Selwyn had inherited his earldom and they'd left university, Gerald had served as his private secretary. As usual, however, his tone remained professional and his face gave nothing away while he enumerated such facts as he had.

'After we recalled the other searchers six months ago, Penfold stayed on but to little or no effect,' he said dispassionately. 'As we already knew and as Basil Selwyn maintains, the two of them parted company in Athens when Christian left for Constantinople. When he didn't arrive at Palermo as planned, Selwyn claims to have sent someone to locate him and only returned to England himself when they failed to do so. Penfold has found no trace of the dragoman Christian engaged for his journey – or, interestingly, the men Eustace Selwyn supposedly despatched to search for him when Basil returned alone.'

'No surprise there,' muttered Daniel. 'There's a murky pit of jealousy and resentment in Basil – and possibly Eustace as well – that I don't think Kit is remotely aware of.'

'He knows,' said Benedict. 'He just doesn't care to explore the depth of it.'

'Quite.' Gerald reached for the next page and went on with his report. 'There was a possible sighting of Christian in Çanakkale on the Dardanelles some weeks later. After that, nothing other than a rumour of a fair-haired Westerner among the retinue of one of the viziers in a province outside Constantinople. That might be anyone, of course. The Turks take captives throughout eastern Europe, even Russia.' He looked up. 'Basically, we're no nearer finding him than we were a year ago. All we can be *sure* of is that he would have returned if he could. So either he's too ill or injured to travel or …'

'Or someone is preventing him doing so,' finished Benedict grimly. And then, 'We've let this slide far too long.'

'I agree. Sending men to search was all very well at the time,' replied Anthony. 'But when they found nothing, we should have gone ourselves – not all of us, perhaps, but two at least.'

'Can't we just kidnap Baz Selwyn and choke the full story out of him?' suggested Daniel. 'I wouldn't put it past him to have had a hand in Kit's disappearance. At the very least, he knows more than he's saying.'

'We *believe* he does,' corrected Benedict with a wry smile. 'Unfortunately, we can't prove it.'

'Which is why,' insisted Daniel, 'we should force him to admit it.'

'He won't.' Gerald straightened his papers, removed his spectacles and faced his friends with an apparent detachment he was far from feeling. 'He and his father are behaving more and more as if Christian was dead – though they can't categorically declare that he *is* dead without admitting knowledge they claim not to have. But they live in his house, spend his money and treat the earldom as if it was their own.

Eustace is stepping far beyond any rights he had as Christian's trustee during his minority. Quite frankly, given what they're up to, I'm amazed they didn't dismiss me long ago.'

'They'd do it fast enough if they knew you were in league with us,' remarked Benedict. 'So ... we can be fairly sure Kit reached the Dardanelles. What we don't know but need to find out is whether or not he got as far as Constantinople. Has Penfold sought help from the Consulate?'

'He tried but he said they weren't much interested.'

'Not *interested?*' echoed Daniel. 'In the disappearance on foreign soil of an English earl? *Seriously?*'

'Not interested in taking Penfold's word is probably nearer the mark,' said Gerald. 'I think Anthony is right. Two of us should have gone in search of him a year ago – and still should, even now.'

'Agreed.' Benedict leaned back in his chair and toyed idly with his empty glass. 'The Consul won't be able to ignore *us* so easily. But not you, Gerald. You are more valuable here, watching the usurpers and keeping us informed.'

'And not you either,' came the swift retort. And with something resembling a grin, 'Your role, amongst other things, is to help fund the mission – '

'How kind. Thank you.'

' – because, in addition to the cost of the search, if someone *is* holding Christian against his will, it's likely to take money to free him.'

For a moment or two, they all looked at each other in silence. Then Daniel said, 'Well, then. It looks as if it's you and me, Anthony. What do you think?'

'I'm game if you are,' shrugged his lordship. 'How soon can you be free to leave?'

'Within the week. You?'

'The same. And I suggest we start by trying to retrace Kit's steps from Athens.'

'Good idea,' nodded Benedict. 'Come to Dover Street tomorrow and I'll give you a banker's draft towards expenses. We can discuss your best and quickest route at the same time.'

'Wait,' said Anthony. 'There's something else you and Gerald need to be aware of while Dan and I are away.'

Benedict sank back into his seat. 'Go on.'

'Sophia Kelsall.'

'What of her?' demanded Daniel.

'According to my cousin, Drusilla, the two additional years of Kit's absence and his unknown whereabouts have resulted in the suggestion that Sophia might marry Basil instead.'

All three gentlemen stared at him. Then Benedict said, 'Eustace's idea or Basil's?'

'Basil's probably. But Sophia's mother is also apparently in favour of it.'

'Damn!' muttered Daniel. 'Stealing Kit's betrothed as well as everything else? But Miss Kelsall *adores* Kit. Surely she's not willing?'

'Drusilla says not. And perhaps her father might veto the idea if he wasn't still incapacitated from the apoplexy he had a few months ago. But since he is, Lady Kelsall is holding the reins. As she sees it, if Sophia can't marry an earl she can at least marry the *heir* to one – which is what Basil will be if Kit is either found dead or not found at all. And her ladyship is an overbearing female used to getting her own way. So it all depends on how long Sophia can stand firm ... and on locating Kit.'

'Well, you and I will do our best on that score,' said Daniel. 'But you should keep an eye on the Kelsall situation, Ben – and be prepared to take counter-measures if necessary.'

'Quite,' agreed Benedict crisply. 'To that end, I'll continue reminding the polite world that, despite Eustace Selwyn's behaviour to the contrary, there is nothing to indicate that Kit is dead – and that we four believe he'll be found alive and well and *will* return.'

'Perhaps you can also encourage His Grace, your brother, to use his influence in the Lords and elsewhere to raise – if not questions – then at least *doubts* about Eustace Selwyn's free and frequent use of the Hazelmere money,' added Gerald. 'It could be helpful.'

'There won't be any difficulty with that,' retorted Benedict on a note of sardonic laughter. 'Vere's opinion of Eustace was never very high and has recently sunk considerably.'

'Good.' Daniel reached for the brandy and poured each of them a stiff measure. 'We have a plan of sorts. Let's drink to it, gentlemen. Here's to finding Christian.'

Glasses were raised. 'Finding Christian!' they echoed. And drank.

* * *

A short distance away in Charles Street, Miss Kelsall was enduring another of her mother's determined attempts to make her see reason.

'Hazelmere has been gone for over four years, Sophia – four *years*, for heaven's sake! And for the last two, no one's seen hide nor hair of him. I do give him the credit to accept that he would not leave you hanging in this way voluntarily. But, however it has come about, he has left you betrothed and yet not. It cannot go on. I know that you do not wish to accept it … but the only logical conclusion after so long is that he will never return because he is – '

'Don't say it! *Don't!* Kit is *not* dead. If he was, I'd know. I'd *feel* it. He's alive and he *will* come back.'

'If he could,' snapped her ladyship irritably, 'he'd have done so by now. Face it.'

Sophia shook her head. 'I can't. I won't. His friends are searching. Lord Benedict and Mr Shelbourne and the others. Drusilla says Lord Wendover has been considering setting out himself, even now. He still believes they'll find Kit. *All* of them do.'

'They have been searching for over a year to no avail. Their tenacity and their faith are admirable. One cannot fault them. But if Hazelmere *could* be found someone would have found him. No – please do not argue. The situation is extremely unfortunate but we must start looking to the future. If, God forbid, your father dies and Cousin George inherits we'll be left with a mere pittance and perhaps, if we're *very* lucky, the dower house at the Grange. Security for all of us lies in you being settled before then – particularly for poor Julia, whose handicap means that she will almost certainly never marry.'

Seventeen-year-old Julia had been born deaf and, for the first twelve years of her life, had never had any reliable method of communication. But around the time Christian departed for his Grand Tour, Sophia – having learned about a school for the deaf and dumb which taught reading, writing and sign language – had waged a constant war until she and Julia had been allowed to take the classes. That was when they had discovered that Julia was dumb as well as deaf for, had she not been, Mr Braidwood's academy could also have taught her to speak.

'So you have said before – though I don't see why she shouldn't. But – '

'There are no buts. You will be twenty-two on your next birthday and should be married by now. I am hopeful that Gwendoline will receive an offer from Lord Chillenden in the very near future, though that is by no means certain. Do you *really* want to see her married before you?'

'That doesn't matter,' said Sophia impatiently. 'What *matters* is marrying the right person. And for me that will always be Kit.'

Lady Kelsall stared coldly at her eldest child; loveliest of her three daughters, but also the most stubborn and thought back to how it had all begun.

* * *

At the time, it seemed fortuitous that Sophia had been invited to spend that summer five years ago in Dorset with the family of her friend Drusilla Barclay; the same summer Drusilla's cousin, Lord Wendover, had also been invited along with his university friend, Lord Hazelmere. The young earl had only recently inherited his title and still had one more year at Oxford; but from the moment he and Sophia met, neither had eyes for anyone else. They had both been ridiculously young, of course. Sophia not yet seventeen and Hazelmere barely twenty-one ... so no one had expected it to last. Yet, against all the odds, it had. And a year later, immediately after he'd left

Oxford, Lord Hazelmere had arrived in Charles Street to formally request permission to pay his addresses.

Sir Joseph Kelsall promptly infuriated his wife by refusing to see the manifold advantages of his eldest daughter making her debut already betrothed to an earl. And not just any earl. Christian Selwyn was young, handsome, wealthy ... and besotted. But all Sir Joseph could see was the couple's extreme youth. He sent Lord Hazelmere away, telling him to enjoy the pleasures London had to offer and come back in a year or so if he still felt the same; and when Sophia pleaded with him to at least allow them to be betrothed, he told her she needed to meet some other young gentlemen before he'd let her settle for the first one to cross her path.

At this point, Lady Kelsall had informed her idiotic spouse that he was throwing away, not the only chance Sophia would have perhaps, but certainly the best one. He was also not considering the future of Gwendoline and Julia ... for how were they to afford the expense of a Season for one and lifetime care for the other? They couldn't, of course. But Hazelmere could – and would if he was married to Sophia.

Meanwhile, Sophia made her curtsy along with Drusilla Barclay ... and Christian made a point of attending the same parties she did. He danced with her at balls and – always seemingly by accident – took her up in his carriage for a circuit of the park. Lady Kelsall pretended not to notice and left her husband in the dark. Within a month, however, society was in no doubt that an announcement was imminent ... a fact finally brought to Sir Joseph's attention at his club.

Thoroughly incensed, he made his feelings known to both his wife and his daughter. Lady Kelsall waited for his temper to cool and for him to begin seeing things her way as, surely, he must. Then Mr Eustace Selwyn, Hazelmere's uncle, paid an unexpected call.

'Please don't misunderstand,' he'd said. 'If Christian was a little older ... if, indeed, he'd completed his education by making the Grand Tour ... in those circumstances, I'd be delighted to see him settling into married life. But that is not the case, is it?

And I can't help but feel that both he and your charming daughter still have some growing-up to do.'

'So I've told them,' replied Sir Joseph. 'But have they listened? No.'

'Young love,' sighed her ladyship. 'We had thought the attachment would fade with time as these things usually do. But it has not. It has lasted over a year and, if anything, seems stronger than ever.'

'But they're still far too young,' he snapped back impatiently. 'He's twenty-two and she's not eighteen yet. If I'd had my way, she wouldn't have made her come-out until next year – and the pair of them wouldn't have had the chance to virtually live in each other's pockets which, it seems, is what they've been doing.'

'Quite,' agreed Mr Selwyn. 'Unfortunately, they have raised … expectations in a good many quarters.'

'I know that, blast it. If you have a suggestion about how to mend matters, feel free to make it.'

'I do, as it happens. I imagine we are agreed that the best course of action is to put some time and also, if possible, distance between them? A chance, shall we say, for them to mature a little and to find out if this … this all-consuming passion of theirs is real and strong enough to last.'

'As I said,' interposed Lady Kelsall, 'it has already weathered the separation of Hazelmere's final year at Oxford.'

Ignoring this, Sir Joseph continued to look at Mr Selwyn. 'Go on.'

'Perhaps you might agree to an informal betrothal upon certain conditions. Miss Kelsall continues with her Season; and Christian … Christian departs on the Grand Tour with his cousin as originally planned. That might solve the problem, don't you think?'

'No!' said her ladyship instantly. 'Young men rarely return from their Tour in under two years. That is far too long.'

'Forgive me, ma'am, but I disagree. In two years, Christian will be twenty-four and Miss Kelsall still only nineteen. Much better ages on both sides to begin married life … assuming, of *course, that they are still of the same mind.' He smiled pleasantly. 'If you can persuade your daughter, I will undertake to convince Christian. It would be much the best solution all round, I feel. So ... shall we try?'*

* * *

Well, thought Lady Kelsall wryly, they'd tried and they'd succeeded. And here they were, four years on rather than two, with no idea at all where the Earl of Hazelmere was or even whether he was alive and Sophia still clinging to the forlorn hope that he was going to come back and marry her.

It's an utter mess. And if I'd known then what I know now ... but one never does, more's the pity. I just wish to God I hadn't let Eustace Selwyn talk Joseph around to his point of view. Had I not done so, Sophia would be a countess by now.

Returning to her original point, she said, 'Face facts, Sophia. Hazelmere is not coming back. But even if he arrived on the doorstep tomorrow, he will not be the man you knew. He isn't just four years older. He will also have been changed by whatever his experience has been – particularly in the last two years. I cannot begin to imagine what has happened to him during that time and thus prevented his return. But I very much doubt that it has been ... pleasant. You cannot expect him to come back as he was.'

'I don't. I'm not stupid, Mama. I know he'll be different in some ways. But –'

'And if one of those ways is that he no longer wants you?' asked her mother brutally. 'What then?'

Sophia winced and briefly shut her eyes. Then she said firmly, 'I'll only believe that if he says so to my face. And he won't. He won't because, inside, he'll still be Kit.'

Lady Kelsall sighed. 'Oh Sophia. Why can't you accept that he's gone?'

'Because in my heart I know he isn't. And people don't just disappear without a trace, do they?'

'They do in the Ottoman Empire. Compared to *some* of the things that go on there, making an Englishman vanish is probably child's play. If the stories one hears are true, some of the Sultans drown their predecessor's concubines in the Bosphorus, for heaven's sake!'

Sophia had read that story and others, no less barbaric. It was apparently the custom for the Sultan's heirs to be confined in apartments which, spacious and comfortable though they might be, were known as the Cage. It was the reason that, by the time they inherited, some Sultans were wholly insane. The idea that Christian might be shut away somewhere like that, served only by mutes, made her shudder. And even though common sense assured her that there was no possible reason for this to happen, she couldn't quite banish the image from her mind.

She said staunchly, 'Horrible as that is, it has nothing to do with Kit.'

'No. But it says something about the mentality of the people in the place he went to visit. However ... let us move on. Despite the fact that your betrothal to Lord Hazelmere was an informal one, far too many people seem to believe it to be binding. I will not ask how that happened. I will merely point out that, with one exception, the result is that no other gentleman will offer for you until, or unless, it is declared null.'

Knowing what was coming next, Sophia pounced.

'Please stop, Mama. I will not marry Basil Selwyn.'

'So you have said. He, however, knows perfectly well that you were never formally contracted to Lord Hazelmere – as does his father. And that makes Mr Selwyn your only viable prospect. Fortunately, he is not merely willing but eager to pay his addresses –'

'Yes. I daresay.' Sophia's tone was bitter. 'He and his father have taken everything else that belongs to Kit. Why not me as well?'

'That is a very unbecoming sentiment, young lady, and one you should be wary of repeating,' came the sharp reply. 'Basil is perfectly eligible. Hazelmere has been missing for four years –'

'He's been *gone* for four years. He's only been *missing* for two of them.'

'Please stop interrupting. In due course, the likelihood is that his uncle will take steps to have him declared dead. Then *he* will inherit the earldom and Basil will be heir to it. This, I grant you, is not the match I would have preferred but it will still make you a countess one day which is the best you can hope for now.' Lady Kelsall rose, indicating that the conversation was over. 'I suggest you begin accepting reality and make up your mind to it.'

* * *

Two thousand miles and a world away from his life as it should have been, Christian was completely cut off from English society or anyone who might help him and had learned two lessons the hard way. Escape from his current situation was impossible; and any attempt to do so resulted in severe punishment. Using his signet ring, he had bribed a servant to take a message to the English Consulate. The man had been caught and bastinadoed. Christian's penalty had been different but no less brutal.

Somewhere at the back of his mind, he understood that his situation could have been much worse. He was well fed and his prison was a luxurious one with terraces overlooking the Sea of Marmara. Neither was he required to do anything either arduous or shameful. It was true that Ibrahim Pasha had a fondness for pretty young boys but Christian, at the age of twenty-four, wasn't young enough to qualify – for which he thanked God daily.

Unfortunately, however, Ibrahim also liked men of culture and education, particularly foreign ones – and here Christian *did* qualify. His duties consisted principally of conversation to perfect Ibrahim's English and that of his sons; of providing a window on the cities he had visited across Europe and particularly on the world he'd been born into and which was now so very far away... that of the English aristocracy.

But after two years, robbed of both his freedom and his name, he was no longer sure who he was any more. He tried to hold on to the knowledge that people would be searching for him; not Basil, of course – but the four friends who were as close to him as brothers. They would leave no stone unturned to find him. He knew that. But they'd search in Constantinople – not in a city seventy miles away. And now, after two years, what chance did they have? The trail, if there had ever been one, was utterly cold.

He had forced himself to stop thinking of Sophie some time ago. There was no point and it was too painful. More recently, he'd also stopped thinking of the outside world and the home he was beginning to believe he'd never see again.

Christian Randolph Selwyn, Lord Hazelmere, didn't exist in the household of the Governor of the Tekirdağ province. He didn't exist anywhere. He'd been replaced by a fair-haired foreigner called Ismael; and Ismael was no one.

CHAPTER TWO

London, 1780 ... eight months later

Watched by her sisters and her mother, Sophia stood before the mirror in her bedchamber and stared listlessly at her reflection.

Her expression worried, Julia tapped her arm and, using her hands, said, 'You look beautiful, Sophie. The gown is lovely – quite the nicest one you've ever had.'

'You can have it,' Sophia signed back. Then, almost but not quite under her breath, 'In fact, you can have this entire evening and everything it represents.'

'That's enough!' snapped Lady Kelsall. 'Hazelmere has been gone for nearly five years – and that is quite long enough to go on moping for him. How many times must I say it? He is *not coming back* – not *now* and not *ever*. You've finally agreed to accept Basil's offer rather than dwindle into an old maid and it will be announced at tonight's ball. So let that be an end to this foolishness. And for heaven's sake, pinch your cheeks and put a smile on your face. You look as if you're going to a funeral.'

I am, thought Sophia. *Hope is dead and tonight I'm burying it.*

'Mr Selwyn's not so bad,' said Gwendoline. 'Not as handsome as Lord Hazelmere, but not ill-looking either. And he's young. You could do worse.'

Sophia said nothing because there was nothing to say. She stared at herself in the mirror; at the exquisite delphinium figured silk gown and the intricately arranged dark hair ... at the pale face and into stark, lightless blue eyes. She had no more tears to shed and hadn't had for a long time. Kit was gone. He wasn't coming back. She would never see him again. And his loss was a black void inside her that no one either understood or wanted to.

Turning abruptly back to her mother, she said, 'Very well. I'm ready. Let's go.'

Her ladyship subjected her to a searching stare.

'You'll behave as you ought – and as people will expect – I hope?'

'I won't run away screaming, if that's what you mean,' replied Sophia. 'For the rest, I'm doing what everyone wants, am I not? Let that be enough for you.'

* * *

In the carriage, and staring blindly through the window, she contemplated the evening's crowning irony. The ball at which her betrothal to Basil Selwyn was to be announced was being held in Christian's house on Berkeley Square – where his uncle and cousin had taken up residence less than six months after he'd failed to return. At the time, more than a few eyebrows had been raised at this unseemly haste. But a year on, no one seemed to find Eustace Selwyn's decision to redecorate the main reception rooms of any particular interest.

It was her friend, Drusilla – now Lady Colwich – who had told her that Cousin Anthony and Mr Shelbourne had set off to conduct their own search. After that, since Sophia no longer attended society events, Lord Benedict Hawkridge had found devious ways of letting her know that he and Kit's other friends had not and *would* not give up hope. Then one day four months ago, he'd brought her a travel-stained packet from Mr Shelbourne explaining that, having drawn a blank in Constantinople, he and Lord Wendover were working their way back along the European shore of the Sea of Marmara towards Çanakkale, town by town and village by village, seeking any word of a foreigner with tawny-gold hair and silver-grey eyes.

'If Kit's there to be found,' Lord Benedict had said, 'they'll find him.'

Meanwhile, life in Charles Street became unbearable. Papa hadn't ever recovered from his apoplexy, thus leaving Mama in total control; and Mama never stopped nagging her to accept Basil Selwyn while he was still prepared to have her. Then, when Lord Chillenden failed to come up to scratch,

Gwendoline had joined in the campaign. Sophia, they made it clear, was the only one who could save the family from the dismal fate of closing up the London house and retiring permanently to Wiltshire where they could live more cheaply.

Since the letter from Mr Shelbourne, Lord Benedict had brought no further news. And then, three weeks ago, he'd suddenly disappeared without a word, leaving Sophia feeling as if her last link with Kit had been severed.

It was the final, bitter blow.

She'd held firm throughout the three long years since Kit had left Athens. Now, she abruptly gave in to her family's demands because, with nothing to hope for and no one to offer even the smallest grain of support, there seemed to be nothing else she could do.

* * *

Hazelmere House was ablaze with lights; candles within and flambeaux illuminating the façade. There was even a red carpet from the place where the carriages stopped at the imposing front door. No expense, it seemed, had been spared. Eustace Selwyn was clearly intent on making this night one of the great events of the Season.

Mr Selwyn being a widower, Lady Kelsall had been invited to act as his hostess, so she and her two older daughters arrived early. Eustace and Basil met them on the threshold with smiling bows and compliments on their beauty and elegance. Something acrid lodged itself in the back of Sophia's throat and her face felt frozen but she curtsied and murmured some sort of banal response.

Both Selwyn men were extravagantly clad – Eustace in a purple coat embroidered in silver thread and Basil in claret, laced with gold. Offering his arm to Lady Kelsall and talking all the time, Eustace led the way up the grand staircase to the modest-sized but lavishly decorated ballroom which occupied the full width of the house to the rear.

Leaving Gwendoline asking for directions to the ladies' retiring room, Basil placed Sophia's hand in the crook of his elbow and said, 'You're particularly beautiful tonight, Sophie. I am undoubtedly the most fortunate man in London.'

She glanced up at him and then away. He bore sufficient resemblance to Christian to mark them as relatives but in Basil it was muted ... his hair merely light brown, his eyes an unremarkable medium grey and his smile lacking in charm. She said, 'I am happy for you. But I would prefer you to call me Sophia.'

The smile dimmed briefly and something flickered behind his eyes. Then he said, 'As you wish. I hope you will honour me with the first dance?'

'Of course. Given the reason for tonight, people will expect it.'

'No one *knows* the reason. Certainly, neither Father nor I have spoken of it. We wished the announcement to be a surprise this evening.'

'Oh dear. Perhaps you should have made that clear to Mama.'

Basil muttered something under his breath which she didn't quite hear. Then laying his free hand over hers, he said, 'Ah well. It's only natural that your family should be pleased and excited, my dear. This day has been long in coming, hasn't it?'

Resisting the impulse to snatch her hand away and thinking, *This day ought never to have come*, she said, 'You must excuse me. My loyalties aren't so easy to shrug off.'

That silenced him for a few moments. But as they entered the ballroom, he tugged her slightly to one side and, in a hard undertone, said, 'You think I've forgotten Kit? I can assure you that I haven't. If he'd listened to me and agreed to turn back after Athens, he'd be safe at home. But he didn't – so here we are. And life has to go on.'

'So it does,' agreed Sophia. And thought, *It was going on very nicely for you and your father before Kit had been gone a twelve-month*. Turning her head to look him squarely in the eye for the first time, she said, 'Are you aware that Lord

Wendover and Mr Shelbourne are currently searching for him in person?'

He looked at her for a long moment before saying slowly, 'No. I didn't know that – and can't imagine what they hope to discover after so long. Where are they?'

'Somewhere in the region of Constantinople when last I heard. But they've been gone some months and may even be on their way home by now.'

'I ... see.'

'Do you? Only think, sir. If they –'

'*Sir?*' he echoed. 'We are betrothed. Can you not use my given name?'

'If you like,' she said impatiently. Then, sticking to the point, 'If they *were* to learn something or, better yet, find Kit –'

'They won't.' He bit the words off, as if instantly regretting them and added quickly, 'As I said, it's been too long and this is hardly the first search, is it? My father sent four men immediately he learned that Kit had vanished. If my cousin was going to be found, it would have been then. And now I suggest that we talk of happier things.' He smiled. 'After all, tonight is supposed to be a celebration.'

'So it is.' From below came sounds of the first guests arriving. 'Mama says your father has invited what she calls the *cream* of society.'

'Indeed – this being the first large event we have held here. And the vast majority have accepted.'

'How gratifying.' She wondered if either of Lord Benedict's older brothers would be present. The Duke of Belhaven was unlikely to attend but Lord Oscar might. If she had a chance to speak to him she might find out what, if anything, was behind Benedict's abrupt disappearance. 'But your father is signalling for you to join him at the receiving line and I would like to check that my hair is in order – so please excuse me.'

* * *

She found Gwendoline still primping in the room set aside for the use of the ladies. Sophia ignored her in favour of staring blankly through the window. She probably ought not to have told Basil that Kit's friends were in Turkey but she'd been unable to help herself. She had, however, managed not to add that there would be no wedding until she knew the outcome of Lord Wendover and Mr Shelbourne's quest. Even now, when all had seemed lost and she'd given way to the pressure surrounding her, it seemed that she still couldn't quite let go of that tiny, lingering possibility, however unlikely it was, that there might still be a small shred of hope.

By the time she followed Gwendoline back to the ballroom, it was beginning to fill up with other guests, many of whom she knew but had not seen since the Season before last. Sophia exchanged greetings with a number of people ... some clearly pleased to see her, others apparently not sure quite what to say ... and gave away dances to those gentlemen who asked. For the rest, she kept her smile firmly in place and avoided potential awkwardness by keeping on the move.

Some half hour later, she found herself face to face with Lord Oscar Hawkridge. He grinned at her and said, 'Miss Kelsall! This is an unexpected pleasure. Where have you been hiding yourself all this time?'

Nowhere, she thought. *I just don't go out much these days.* But said vaguely, 'We spent a few weeks in Wiltshire.'

'Really? Well, London has missed you.'

'I doubt that, my lord – though it's kind of you to say it.'

'Nothing of the sort.' His eyes, not quite as green as his brother's, softened. 'The mystery surrounding Kit Hazelmere hit Ben hard – and you no less so, I imagine.'

She nodded. 'It's the – the not knowing what became of him. Of probably *never* knowing. But Lord Benedict kindly did his best to keep me informed of Kit's friends' latest attempt to trace him.'

'Wendover and Shelbourne? Yes. He told me about that. But now Ben's gone haring off somewhere himself – and with not a word of explanation. Vere isn't pleased. It was Ben's turn for the quarterly duty visit to Great-Aunt Alice but he didn't go and Vere's been the recipient of auntie's displeasure.'

'You don't know where he's gone? Or why?'

'No idea. He just told his valet to pack, then took off in his travelling chaise.'

'Will he …' She stopped and gestured to the ballroom. 'Do you think he knows about this?'

'He does. The invitations went out seven or eight weeks ago.'

'Did they?' This was interesting. Eustace had planned the ball weeks before she had finally agreed to marry Basil. Their own invitation hadn't arrived until after she'd done so. 'I hadn't realised.'

'Vere didn't accept, of course. Then, when he realised Ben wasn't going to be here, he told me to come – which I'd intended to do anyway.' Oscar smiled at her. 'Do you have a dance to spare for me?'

'Yes. The supper dance, if you would like it.'

'I would. Very much. Thank you.' He glanced around them. 'Basil Selwyn is heading this way and it looks as if the dancing is about to start. Has he stolen a march on the rest of us?'

'Yes.' She tried to keep the sudden sinking of her heart out of her voice. 'Privilege of the host, I suppose. But it's been a pleasure meeting you again, my lord, and I shall look forward to our dance.'

'As will I.' He bowed over her hand, tossed a casual nod of acknowledgement at Basil and sauntered away.

Watching him go, Basil murmured, 'It's a pity his older brother had a previous engagement. Father was hoping he'd be here.'

'I'm sure.' Taking the arm he offered her, Sophia allowed him to lead her on to the floor. 'But Belhaven is renowned for rejecting as many invitations as he accepts, is he not? So I daresay he disappoints a good many hosts and hostesses.'

'Probably. Ah – I meant to tell you. Father will make our announcement at the end of this dance so you and I should make our way to the dais in readiness for it.'

The music began. He bowed and she curtsied. It was a quadrille, which was unusual. But since this meant she would not be trapped in conversation with Basil for the duration, Sophia could only be grateful. Her friend, Drusilla Colwich, was in the same set, partnering Lord Keswick's brother and smiling at her. Sophia tried to smile back but, thanks to the chill created by Basil's off-hand remark, wasn't sure she succeeded.

Other sets of eight occupied the rest of the floor; small groups of gentlemen stood chatting at the edges, while older ladies and chaperones watched from the comfort of chairs. Not having danced for a considerable time and her nerves far from steady, Sophia had to concentrate on the figures and steps. It wouldn't do to make a fool of herself. She was still concentrating when, the dance no more than half over, she became aware of a change in the ballroom.

Conversations gradually stopped; ladies craned their necks or rose from their seats and some of the dancers nearest the double doors were halting mid-figure. All of them were staring in the same direction ... at something Sophia couldn't see due to the people in between. Bit by bit, more and more sets stilled until no one was moving and, realising this, the orchestra also dwindled to an untidy halt. Suddenly, there was an airless silence broken only by the soft wind song of the chandeliers.

Then, eerily like the parting of the Red Sea, people fell back opening a path to whatever or *who*ever was holding everyone's attention.

Three latecomers had entered the room.

Lord Benedict Hawkridge, Baron Wendover and the Honourable Mr Shelbourne.

They stood a little apart from each other and looked unsmilingly first at Eustace and then at Basil. There was something coldly dangerous in the way they neither moved nor spoke. And then, still in silence, Mr Shelbourne moved aside, allowing a fourth gentleman to step forward.

A tall gentleman in black ... a gentleman with tawny-gold hair and eyes like frost.

Time stopped. The air in Sophia's lungs evaporated and she froze, paralysed first by shock and, an instant later, by the terrible fear that her eyes were deceiving her. Then a spectral gasp broke the hush ... someone said incredulously, 'Good God! *Hazelmere?*' ... and a sunburst of joy exploded inside her. *Kit.*

'Indeed.' Christian awarded Eustace an ironic bow. 'Good evening, Uncle. I could almost suppose you were expecting me ... but of course you weren't, were you?'

More silence. Avid eyes swivelled in Eustace's direction. He opened his mouth but no sound came out. The same eyes looked for and found Basil. Like his father's, his face was completely bloodless.

In those first seconds, Sophia stood frozen, scarcely breathing and unaware of Basil's grip numbing her fingers. Then her free hand crept to her mouth and she managed to whisper, 'Kit?'

He didn't hear her. As yet, he hadn't seen her either.

She tried unsuccessfully to drag her hand free of Basil's. He merely stood like a stone, gaping incredulously at his cousin.

'Let *go* of me!' she hissed, pushing at him but not letting her gaze stray from Christian. 'Let go – *now!*'

He saw her then. She watched it happen ... watched something she couldn't identify pass rapidly through those silver eyes ... and then, even as Basil finally released his grip, watched him empty his face of all expression and halting her with a bow before she could take more than two steps in his direction.

'My apologies, Sophie,' he said politely. 'I am somewhat tardy, am I not? Suffice it to say that the circumstances that delayed me were ... beyond my control.'

She stared at him. Was that all he was going to say?

Finally recovering his wits, Eustace managed a smile and, approaching his nephew, hand outstretched, said with an attempt at heartiness, 'You must forgive our shock, my boy. This – having you home at last – is the miracle we'd no longer dared hope for. Where have you ...? But no. The questions can wait.'

Christian made no move to take the offered hand. He stood perfectly still and let his gaze drift past his uncle to encompass Basil; then he watched with gentle interest as his cousin turned blotchily red.

Around the ballroom, a number of gentlemen were beginning to interpret the lost earl's peculiar reluctance to take his uncle's hand. Whispers started and, over them, Lord Oscar Hawkridge said clearly, 'Don't just stand there leaving us all to guess, Ben. Where did you find him?'

'I didn't. Anthony and Daniel did,' replied Benedict evenly. And, deciding they'd provided enough of a side-show, 'Mr Selwyn ... perhaps this might be best conducted in private?'

Eustace nodded, still seemingly poleaxed with shock, 'In private. Yes. Of course. Please everyone ... continue to enjoy the evening. Christian, Basil ... the library, I think. I'm sure Lord Benedict and his friends will excuse us.'

'*They* might,' said Christian. 'I won't. Gentlemen?' He indicated that he wanted them to follow, pausing to add, 'Benedict ... escort Sophie, will you? As my almost-*fiancée* she has as much right to be present as anyone.'

And seeing Eustace hovering as if about to show him the way, he stalked past saying, 'I know where the library is, Uncle. This is still my house, if you recall – though some parts of it are radically changed since I saw it last.' And to the orchestra, 'Forgive the interruption, gentlemen. Do please continue.'

He walked out, trailed by Eustace and Basil. As soon as the three of them vanished from sight, the ballroom erupted into a buzz of shocked chatter.

Sophia found herself struggling with a sense of unreality. He looked like Kit and the voice was Kit's voice. But the chilly composure, the words, sharp as blades and sheathed in ice ... those belonged to a stranger.

Clutching Lord Benedict's arm, she said, 'This is ... I hardly know what to say. When you left town, I thought – '

'I know and I'm sorry. But Wendover and Shelbourne sent for me when they reached Paris. Kit needed a breathing space – and clothes since he'd nothing of his own. I'd have told you except that Kit was adamant no one outside the five of us should know.'

'Five of you?' she asked, confused.

'Gerald Sandhurst, Kit's secretary. But enough of that now. I don't know what Kit intends other than that he won't be telling the full story. Yet. So the best thing is not to ask questions and let him do this in his own way.' He smiled at her. 'Come. He's had a … difficult … time but he's home and he's in one piece – which is all that matters right now. Everything else can wait until he's ready.'

Her brain scarcely functioning and feeling as if she was sleep-walking, Sophia let him lead her in the wake of the others. Over the years, she had imagined Christian's return in a thousand different ways. None of them had resembled this.

Inside the library, Christian faced his uncle and cousin across the hearth while, behind him, his friends looked on over folded arms. All of them remained standing. Benedict handed Sophia to a chair and took up a position directly behind her. No one spoke.

Finally, as if unable to bear the silence any longer, Basil said, 'Where the *hell* have you been all this time?'

'Clearly, not where it was intended I *should* be,' came the cool reply.

'What is that supposed to mean?'

Christian's brows rose. He said, 'Are you certain you want to ask that now?'

Another silence yawned about them. Into it, Eustace said, 'Perhaps we might all sit down? I'm sure Christian has quite a story to tell and, while he does so, allow me to offer everyone a glass of brandy – or sherry in your case, Sophia.'

Words seemed beyond her so she merely shook her head.

'Not for me, either,' drawled Daniel, speaking for the first time. 'Though it's jolly decent of Selwyn to offer Kit a drink in his own home. What do you think, Anthony?'

'Oh yes. *Jolly* decent.'

Eustace flushed. 'This is scarcely helpful, gentlemen. I recognise what Christian's return means – of course I do – and naturally, no one is more delighted to see him than I. But please allow my son and me a *little* time to – to adapt.'

'By all means,' drawled Christian. 'And if you feel brandy will help speed the process, please help yourself. We – my friends and I – won't be staying long.' His eyes returned to Basil. 'You asked where I've been. That is easily answered. I have been the house-guest of the Governor of the Tekirdağ province in Turkey. Ibrahim Pasha found my company so compelling that he was very reluctant to lose it.' He paused, letting the words sink in. 'However, the *real* question is not where I've been but how I got there. And that is a much longer story for which this is not the time. Right now, there is a question I would like to ask *you*.'

'Ask it, by all means,' invited Eustace. 'We will – '

He stopped as the door burst open. Lady Kelsall whirled into the room in a flurry of burgundy taffeta and came to an abrupt halt, staring at Christian.

'So it's true,' she said. 'Out there they are saying – but I could scarcely believe it. Why was I not informed?'

Having waited a moment for someone – presumably Christian – to answer this and then realising he wasn't going to, Sophia said tonelessly, 'It wasn't necessary that you should be, Mama. Neither should you be here now, uninvited.'

'I *beg* your pardon? Not *necessary*? And I *ought* to have been invited! You can't be here unchaperoned and – '

Glancing over his shoulder, Christian said, 'Anthony. Would you mind?'

'Not at all.' Lord Wendover crossed the room and offered her ladyship his arm. 'If you please, ma'am? Miss Kelsall is quite right. You don't belong here just now.' And while she was still too affronted to say another word, he escorted her through the door and remained standing in front of it to prevent further interruptions.

'Now ... where were we?' mused Christian. 'Ah yes. I was about to ask the significance of the ball currently under way in my house. Uncle?'

Shooting a warning glance at Basil, Eustace said repressively, 'Surely that is of little consequence at the moment.'

'Really? So it is not, in fact, to celebrate my cousin's betrothal to Miss Kelsall – who was, and therefore technically still is, my *fiancée?*'

Neither Eustace nor Basil answered.

Drawing a long breath, Sophia murmured, 'Only technically, Kit?'

'As things stand, yes,' he replied. And then, 'I'm sorry.'

Her smile was bitter. 'So you said. You aren't alone in that.'

He shook his head. 'No. I imagine not.' Then, turning back to his uncle, 'There is only one further thing I want to say at this stage. During my absence, you and my cousin have taken up residence in my home. Now that I'm back, I would be grateful if you removed to your own house with immediate effect.'

'Wait a moment,' protested Eustace. 'There's no need for haste. We are family – '

'For which reason, I'll allow you a week's grace,' continued Christian imperturbably. 'I shall stay with Lord Benedict in Dover Street for the time being. Shall we say that you will be gone by noon on Monday next?' And without giving them time to reply, he turned to Sophia, saying, 'I will call on you tomorrow if that would be acceptable?'

She nodded, aware – despite the fog filling her head – of a howling disappointment tinged with rising anger. 'Of course.'

'Thank you. I'm told that Sir Joseph is still indisposed so I will not trouble him. But you and I need to speak privately – a fact which I shall be making plain to your mother.' And once more to his uncle and cousin, 'I believe that is everything – for now, at least – and I'm sure you are as eager to return to your guests as they are for you to do so. There is no need to summon Fallon to show us out. I know the way.'

CHAPTER THREE

'Well,' said Daniel when, having been joined by Mr Sandhurst, the five of them were sharing a bottle of brandy in Benedict's lodgings, 'that didn't go too badly, all things considered. Eustace's face was a picture when you told him to get out of Berkeley Square.'

Christian managed a faint smile but said nothing. That hour – surely it had been no more than that? – the first he'd spent in his own home for five years, had exhausted him. The effort required to say no more than was strictly necessary and to control the wolf that howled inside him when he'd clapped eyes on his cousin had left him physically and mentally drained.

Or perhaps, he thought wearily, it wasn't *just* that. Perhaps it was a combination of tonight and everything that had gone before it. The gradual growth of despair during those three years of captivity; the almost unbearable resurgence of hope when one of the palace gardeners whispered that two Englishmen, accompanied by an official from the Consulate in Constantinople, were asking about him in the city; and then the terror that nothing would come of it – that whoever was out there would go away without finding him and that he'd be trapped here forever.

Then had come the time he'd been confined to his rooms with guards posted at the door and no one would tell him what was happening. His nerves at full stretch, he'd swung between a very frail thread of hope he was afraid to trust and absolute dread. If these Englishmen, whoever they were, had traced him to the palace but Ibrahim convinced them that they were mistaken and persuaded them to leave, Christian was fairly sure that his immediate future wasn't going to be pleasant.

But they *hadn't* given up. They and the Consulate official had questioned Ibrahim and his sons repeatedly between dire threats of what the English government would do should it learn that an English aristocrat was being held against his will by a Turkish citizen. And so, eventually, Christian had been summoned to the Divan with no idea what awaited him there.

When he'd seen Daniel and Anthony, relief had sent him to his knees ... and when they'd drawn him to his feet and into their arms, he'd cried.

He'd learned later that a large sum of money had also been instrumental in obtaining his release – but he could repay that. What he couldn't ever repay was the faith, determination and love of the men without whom he'd have grown old and died in Tekirdağ.

Passing a hand over his face, he realised that he hadn't thought beyond this evening and had no idea what came after it. What, for example, was he going to say to Sophie? Somewhat distantly, he supposed he hadn't made the best possible start. What had he said? Something along the lines of *'Sorry I'm late'*?

Brilliant, he thought, inwardly cringing. *The perfect way to greet the girl I wanted to marry but haven't seen in five years ... and absolutely guaranteed to earn her forgiveness.*

But the truth was that, in order to get through the encounter with Eustace and Basil with any semblance of dignity or composure, all his focus had been on them; nuance had been beyond him ... and his behaviour towards Sophia had suffered accordingly. Tomorrow, somehow, he'd have to put that right – though God knew how he'd do it.

He couldn't tell her what those missing years had been like or what had happened during them; not even as much as he'd told his friends and *that* was by no means everything. He also had a strong suspicion that he wasn't mentally fit to plunge back into a betrothal, let alone matrimony. So what the hell *could* he say to her?

Dragging his mind back to the present and something that had plagued him earlier in the evening, he said, 'Do you think Eustace knows ... or did Basil give him the same version of events he gave to the world?'

'Good question,' remarked Anthony. 'Eustace didn't put too bad a face on your sudden resurrection. Basil looked as if he wanted to be sick.'

'As he should,' growled Daniel. 'He must be praying to every deity there is that Kit doesn't know what he did.'

'And what *did* he do?' asked Gerald sharply. Having been unable to meet the others since their return three days ago ... unable, in fact, to do anything but send an urgent note informing Benedict that Basil's engagement to Sophia Kelsall would be announced at the ball if Christian didn't do something about it ... Gerald had a great deal to catch up on and had been listening to Benedict's account of that evening's events at Hazelmere House. Now, his question was met with silence while everyone looked at Christian. 'Well?'

Finally, Daniel said, 'Tell him, Kit. Or if you prefer, I'll do it.'

'No.' Christian sat up and met Gerald's eyes. 'Throughout our travels, we used ordinary guides but, for Constantinople, I needed a dragoman; a fellow who had all the usual skills but who also spoke Turkish. Basil volunteered to find someone and I let him. As it turned out, that was ... a mistake.' He paused; no one prompted him and, after a moment, he continued tonelessly, 'The fellow had all the right credentials. He seemed ideal. We left Athens and crossed the Aegean towards Turkey. And part-way there, he ... sold me. To a slaver.'

Gerald swore under his breath. 'And?'

'He told the slaver that the man who paid him wanted me sent to the galleys. The slaver said he could get a better price elsewhere – and what difference so long as I was never seen again?' Christian shrugged. 'You know the rest.' And thought, *Or as much of it as I'm ever likely to tell you.*

There was another long silence.

Finally, Gerald said, 'And Basil doesn't know you know that?'

'No. I doubt the dragoman went back to Athens to deliver a report.'

'Good.' Gerald looked round at the others. 'Something solid we can make use of.'

'When we have a plan,' agreed Daniel. 'And while we work on that, it will do Basil no harm to sweat a little.'

'We need him to do more than sweat,' remarked Anthony grimly. Then, changing tack, 'Tell me to mind my own business if you wish, Kit ... but what are you going to tell Miss Kelsall? Anything ... or nothing?'

'I don't know. For preference, as little as possible. Probably just that I've been helping a man and his sons to speak good English and educating them on manners, morals and social behaviour in Europe – enlivened with descriptions of European cities.'

'And you didn't come home because you were enjoying yourself too much?' suggested Daniel caustically. 'Oh yes. I'm sure she'll swallow that.'

Christian sighed. 'No. She'll ask questions I can't answer.'

'There's no disguising the fact that you *couldn't* leave,' said Anthony bluntly. 'In fact, you've already told her – and everyone else within earshot – as much. But I suppose you can paint Ibrahim as a jolly family man and his sons as your new best friends ... something like that, anyway.'

Christian stared down at his hands and said nothing.

Having taken little part in the conversation while noting Christian's obvious exhaustion, Benedict came to his feet saying, 'Time to call it a night, gentlemen. Gerald ... evaluate the mood between Eustace and Basil, if you can. The rest of us can reconvene at White's tomorrow afternoon to discuss strategy. But enough for now.'

When the others had taken their leave, Benedict poured both himself and Christian another measure of brandy and said, 'Drink that and go to bed. You look like a corpse.'

'Thank you.' Christian managed a smile and then, as it faded, said, 'What am I going to do, Ben?'

'About what?'

'Everything. But mainly, Sophie. In a few hours' time, I have to present myself at Charles Street. And I've no idea what to say to her. It's been five years. I'm ... different. She probably is, too.'

'Naturally. She was a young girl when you left. Now she's a woman.'

'Yes. And as you say, that's natural. The changes in me are not.' He hesitated before adding awkwardly, 'There are things inside me now that I ... that I don't recognise. And neither would Sophie if she saw them.'

A frown entered the green gaze. 'What are you talking about?'

Christian drew a long breath and said flatly, 'Anger. And violence. This evening, when I laid eyes on Basil, I wanted ... I wanted to put my hands around his throat and squeeze until his eyes popped out. I don't know how I stopped myself.'

Bloody hell, thought Benedict, shocked. This from a man who, in the twenty years he'd known him, had never raised a hand in anger to anyone; who, even when provoked, had defused the situation with patience and humour.

He said, 'But you *did* stop yourself.'

'Yes. This time. But I can't trust it. I'm afraid of what I might do if I lose control.'

'You won't. If you didn't do it tonight when you had every reason – '

'But I *might* have.' He paused, running a hand over his face, half-inclined not to say anything more in case he revealed the thing he couldn't even confess to Benedict. The nameless, gut-clenching fear that existed alongside everything else. 'Perhaps Sophie no longer wants to marry me. That might be for the best, really. I'm not fit for marriage – not now, the way I am. It wouldn't be fair to her.'

'To either of you.'

'No. But I can't tell her that, can I?'

'Why not? It might be the most useful thing you *can* tell her. If it's honour that is stopping you – '

'It is, though not *just* that. I asked her to marry me and she said yes. Our betrothal may not have been announced to the world but it was real enough to *us*. And I've already left her in limbo for years. If I don't fix that by offering a speedy wedding – '

'Stop it, Kit. You already have more than enough to deal with. The last three years were bound to leave a mark and that won't vanish overnight. Take time to pick up your life again and give yourself a chance to recover.'

'I can't.' His voice was growing increasingly agitated. 'If I don't do *something* her position will be even worse than it's been these last years.' He leaned his head back against the chair and shut his eyes. 'On the other hand, for all I know, perhaps she *wants* to marry Basil.'

'Don't be an ass. Of course she doesn't. Her mother and middle sister have been nagging her to take him for a year or more and she's been refusing.'

'Perhaps that was because she thought she owed it to me.'

'I doubt it. And regardless of whatever flaws you think *you* have … knowing what we know of Basil, can you honestly want her anywhere near a piece of dung like him?'

'No.' Christian rubbed weary hands over his eyes. 'Not in a million years.'

'Good. Because you're the one who can stop it happening. And if you don't know what she thinks, I suggest you find out,' said Benedict, coming to his feet. 'Talk to her. Ask how she feels before you start pressuring yourself to mend matters. And then, if it turns out that the two of you still want each other, agree to a wedding in a few months' time. You can use the excuse that, after such a long absence, there are a great many matters demanding your attention – particularly at Hazelmere. Go there and hibernate for a little while. It will do you a world of good.' He drained his glass, set it down and added, 'Take Gerald with you. And invite the rest of us to visit.'

'You don't need an invitation. None of you do. Ever.'

'Good. Now … for God's sake finish your brandy and go to bed. Everything will still be there in the morning, after all. And you're not the only one who needs sleep.'

* * *

At a little after eleven on the following morning, Christian was admitted to Kelsall House and shown immediately up to the drawing-room. He was correctly attired in a suit of pewter brocade, his hair neatly tied at the nape with narrow, black ribbon. He caught sight of himself in the mirror above the fireplace and was relieved to see that he looked perfectly composed despite the snakes writhing in his stomach.

The door opened and he turned, half-expecting to see Lady Kelsall ... but it was Sophia, even lovelier than she'd been five years ago and a few steps behind her, little Julia who, when he'd last seen her, had been twelve.

'Kit,' said Sophia, coming towards him, hands outstretched.

Five years ago, he'd have pulled her into his arms and held her, his face buried against her hair. Today, he accepted her hands, bowed over them and immediately stepped back, saying formally, 'Thank you for receiving me.'

'Of course.' Her next words were accompanied by a swift and complex series of hand movements. 'You remember Julia, don't you?'

'I do.' He managed a smile for the other girl. 'Though I almost didn't recognise her.'

Sophia's hands translated his words to her sister and then Julia's reply.

'She says welcome home. It's wonderful to see you again.'

'Please thank her for me.'

Sophia's hands spoke again. Julia nodded, tripped forward to brush a tiny kiss on his cheek and left the room with a graceful little wave.

Feeling ridiculously thankful for an unexpected topic of conversation, Christian said, 'That was sign language, wasn't it? I've heard of it but never seen it before. How did you learn it?'

'Just after you went away, I heard about an Academy for the Deaf and Dumb, newly opened in Hackney. I harangued Papa until he allowed Julia and me to go there two days a week. I had to learn as well – or what would have been the good of Julia knowing? When, after a month or so, Mama said she couldn't spare the carriage so often, Mr Braidwood recommended one of his former students – a Miss Grayshott. She came here three afternoons a week until Julia and I were both fluent.' Sophia's mouth curled slightly. 'Julia can also read and write – and I should warn you that we both lip-read as well.'

'I'll bear that in mind. And your Mama and Gwendoline?'

'They've picked up a handful of basic signs. Generally, they rely on me to translate.'

'I see. Well, it's a remarkable achievement. It must open the world up for Julia.'

'It does.' Suspecting that, if she didn't take charge, Christian would continue avoiding the real issue between them, she said, 'Last evening was quite a ... surprise.'

'Yes.' He swallowed and added weakly, 'I'm so very sorry, Sophie.'

She was half-inclined to ask exactly what it was he was sorry about.

Greeting me after an absence of five years as if we'd never been more than distant acquaintances, perhaps? That would be a start, she thought.

But she swallowed the words. Doing her best to hide both her uncertainty and the unexpected anger from last night which seemed reluctant to melt away, she gestured to a chair and took the one facing it. 'You apologised last night. And you're home now. That's all that matters.'

He remained standing. 'Is it?'

It wasn't, but with constraint already clouding the air, she knew better than to say so. So she evaded the question with one of her own, saying lightly, 'You didn't stay away by choice, did you?'

'No. I was ... detained.'

'Against your will?'

'Yes.' He wasn't ready to discuss that yet, so he grasped the first alternative that came to mind. 'But I am remiss. How is your father?'

She opened her mouth, then closed it again. It was a perfectly proper enquiry, of course ... but he was asking this *now?* She said, 'The apoplexy happened eighteen months ago. He has not recovered as well as we hoped. His speech is much impaired and the right side of his body is paralysed, so he keeps to his rooms.'

Christian inclined his head and said, 'I'm sorry to hear it. That must be very ... difficult ... for all of you.'

'Yes. It is.' Again, she waited for a moment in the hope he'd return to the point at issue and then, when he said nothing, did it herself. 'I realise this is awkward – for both of us. But won't you sit and tell me *something* about what happened? I don't understand anything at all and I ... well, you can't be surprised that I need to do so.'

For a moment, she thought he was going to refuse. There was a coldness in him that she'd never seen before, coupled with a tension that alarmed her.

Then he took the chair she'd indicated and said, 'The basic situation was as I described it last night. I was well fed and comfortably housed by Ibrahim Pasha but I was not permitted to leave. I tried, of course – but without success.'

'He held you prisoner? For *three years?*'

Christian inclined his head but said nothing.

'Why?'

'Because he could.' Something that wasn't quite a smile touched his mouth. 'The Turkish attitude to foreigners is ... singular. For example, the Janissaries – or army, if you like – are recruited from among Christian children taken as slaves and then converted to Islam. The same is true of the concubines in the harem. The theory is that this prevents Turkish families from assuming undue importance.'

'Fascinating as that may be,' she retorted tartly before she could stop herself, 'what did this man, Ibrahim, want of *you?*'

'My education and experience, both of travel and as an aristocrat. He was also eager for his sons to speak fluent English with a good accent.'

She stared at him. 'I'm sorry. I can't understand that. At all.'

'No. How should you?'

It occurred to Sophia that there were a lot of things she didn't understand – such as why Kit was behaving as if he couldn't wait to leave. Had he changed so much? Had those three missing years obliterated everything that had been between them before he'd left England? And what was it that he was so obviously not saying? There *was* something, wasn't there?

She thought back to the previous evening and then said slowly, 'When Basil asked where you'd been all this time, you told him that it was not where it had been intended you *should* be – which seems an odd way of putting it. What did you mean?'

'Simply that I never made it to Constantinople.' He looked down at his hands to veil his expression from her. 'What else could I have meant?'

Suddenly, she knew he was lying. Why? He'd never lied to her before. He'd always talked openly and freely with her about anything and everything. He'd even – because she'd insisted and despite his embarrassment – explained some of what happened between a man and a woman in the bedroom.

Sensing that something was very wrong, she persevered.

'You also said that the real story wasn't the time you spent in Ibrahim Pasha's home but how you came to be there in the first place. So how *did* you get there?'

Christian silently damned himself. He *had* said that – and wished he hadn't.

'Forgive me. That isn't something I'm prepared to talk about. Later, perhaps – but not yet.'

Sophia gripped her hands together in her lap, feeling suddenly cold. Their reunion ought to be have been joyful. Instead, there was that little knot of anger simmering inside her and Kit was holding her at arm's length, distant as any stranger. She didn't know how to bridge the gulf that had opened up between them ... and, sickeningly, was beginning to suspect that he didn't want her to.

This time, the silence was a long one. Christian wondered what she'd say if he told her how he felt. If he said that his skin no longer seemed to fit him; that sometimes he wasn't even sure he was physically present at all but merely a sort of shadow, watching the scene around him like a ghost. If he did that, she'd think him insane.

Finally he said remotely, 'Had I not miraculously reappeared last evening, would you have gone ahead with your betrothal to Basil?'

The question hit her like a punch.

'Yes. What else was I to do?'

He nodded. 'If you wish to continue down that road — though perhaps not with Basil — I will not stand in your way. *I* can't cry off, of course. But you can.'

And suddenly, quite without warning, her anger stopped simmering and boiled over. Coming to her feet, she said, 'If I *wish* to continue down that road? How *dare* you ask me that! I agreed to wait while you completed the Grand Tour. Do you think I waited a further three years for you just for *fun?*'

'No. But — '

'Or that I had the remotest desire to marry Basil — or anyone else, for that matter?'

Since she was standing, he rose too.

'I wasn't implying that. I was merely asking — '

'You shouldn't have *needed* to ask — you should have *known*! But since you didn't, here's how things stand. Lord Chillenden didn't offer for Gwendoline as Mama had hoped, so her best prospect now is the doctor who comes to attend Papa. If Papa dies, his Cousin George will inherit virtually everything. As for Mama, she says it's quite bad enough that *I'll* end up on the shelf without my selfish obstinacy forcing the same fate upon Gwen. It's all I hear, day in and day out — along with the constant litany from the pair of them about how you were n-never going to come back because you were d-dead.'

Christian looked back at her, his face perfectly white. 'I'm sorry.'

'So you've said – several times. So you *should* be.' Pressing her lips together, Sophia pulled herself together with a visible effort. Then, keeping her spine very straight and looking him in the eye, she said, 'If your feelings have changed – and I suspect they may have – just say so and have done with it. But don't pretend you're doing it for my sake or that it's *I* who wants to be free because neither is true!'

He shut his eyes for a moment and then, opening them, walked away to the window so he wouldn't have to look at her. Struggling to find not just the right words, but any words at all, he said quietly, 'Throughout the time I was ... away ... I couldn't allow myself to think about you. After a while, I stopped thinking about other things, too ... home, friends, the future. There was no place for – for emotions of that sort. But now I'm finally free, I'm *battered* by feelings – most of which I neither want nor understand – and none of them the ones I shut away for so long. *Those* seem lost. The truth is that I scarcely recognise myself any more.'

All her anger fell away. She wasn't the only one who was hurting. He was, too – and perhaps in worse ways. She said softly, 'How long is it since Lord Wendover and Mr Shelbourne rescued you – if rescue is the right word?'

'It is. And it's been eleven weeks.'

Behind him, Sophia's hand crept to her mouth. *Eleven weeks after three years of captivity? No wonder he's still in emotional turmoil. How could he not be?*

'It took eight weeks to get to Paris, travelling non-stop,' continued Christian, expressionlessly. 'Anthony said I wasn't ready to face everything here – and wearing clothes borrowed from Daniel. So they found rooms near the Palais Royale, summoned a tailor and sent for Benedict.'

'When did you get to London?'

'The day before yesterday. There was a letter from Gerald telling us to go to Eustace's ball. And why.' He drew a long breath and turned slowly to face her. 'I suppose your mother has changed her tune since yesterday.'

'Somewhat.' A glint of dark humour lit her eyes. 'If you were to open the door, she and Gwen would probably tumble through it.'

He smiled faintly. 'Tempting ... but premature, since we've reached no decision.'

Sophia returned to her chair and waited for him to do likewise. Nothing about their reunion was as she'd expected it to be and she was beginning to realise that there were complex reasons for this; reasons that suggested Kit might not be himself for quite some time. Sighing inwardly, because what had to be done was the very last thing she wanted, she said calmly, 'And we're not going to – certainly not today and probably not for a while.'

'We're not?' he asked cautiously.

'No. Last evening was the first time we've seen each other in almost five years. Even under normal circumstances, we'd both change during that time – and your circumstances have been far from normal. I *believe* I still feel the way I did when we parted but the truth is that I don't know who you've become. And as you've just said, at the moment, neither do you.'

'I'm hoping that is ... temporary.'

'As do I. But I've merely been marking time while you've been gone. *You* have endured something that is beyond my comprehension and which will have affected you in ways I can't imagine – though you've given me a glimpse of some of them. So we can't just pick up where we left off, can we? We need to get to know each other again.'

Christian didn't *want* her to know him as he was now – didn't want her to discover all the dark places inside he hardly dared examine himself. He said uneasily, 'And if we do?'

'We'll make our decision then. For now, you need time – quite a lot of it, I suspect. Time to resume your old life; time to get Eustace and Basil out of your house so you can live there yourself; and time to at least *begin* putting these last years behind you,' she replied, doing her best to sound more positive than she felt. 'Also, you'll need to go to Hazelmere. On top of redecorating the London house, there's no saying *what* Eustace has been up to there. I imagine your friends have told you that he's been spending your money with a lavish hand?'

'Yes. Gerald says he has kept a record – though I haven't seen it yet.'

'Well, then. You have plenty to keep you busy, don't you?'

'I do.' Even as he felt a lessening of the tension inside him, his conscience prompted him to say, 'But what of you, Sophie? Your mother isn't going to be happy about a further delay, is she?'

'No. But she can scarcely force us to the altar, can she? And if, in the end, we decide to – to part company, there isn't a great deal she can do about that either.'

Christian was silent for a long time. Eventually, he said, 'You know, I hope, that if there was anyone I could conceivably marry at this time, it would be you?'

'Well, that's a good start, isn't it?' She gave him a too-bright smile and stood up. 'I'm going to let Mama in now. Brace yourself.'

Lady Kelsall sailed in, pennants flying. 'Well? Have you settled matters?'

'Good morning, ma'am,' said Christian … and watched the shot fly harmlessly over her bows. 'Yes, we have decided to allow ourselves time to become reacquainted before making any irrevocable decision. There is also the matter of my taking the reins of the earldom into my own hands. I'm sure you'll appreciate the – '

'But you'll formalise your betrothal immediately, will you not?'

Christian and Sophia exchanged glances. He said, 'That would rather defeat the point, wouldn't it? But we will spend time with each other and be seen doing so before I leave for Hazelmere and –'

'That is not at all satisfactory,' declared Lady Kelsall. '*More* waiting – after all this time? What will people think?'

'What they think is immaterial,' said Sophia calmly. 'Kit and I are aware that the years apart have changed both of us in different ways. We're not who we were then.'

'Quite,' agreed Christian, before her ladyship could demur. 'Also, Benedict tells me that you have stopped going about in society, Sophie. Perhaps, now I'm back, you might start doing so again?'

'That will depend on whether or not she receives any invitations,' cut in her mother acidly. 'There have been precious few in the last year.'

'Society's curiosity will change that.' He turned to Sophia and took her hand. 'Those who invite me will almost certainly invite you as well ... thus providing some of those opportunities for us to meet and be seen together that I spoke of. But now I have another appointment and must take my leave. If I can persuade Benedict to lend me his phaeton, will you drive with me tomorrow afternoon?'

'With pleasure,' she said. 'Thank you.'

Christian bowed. 'Until tomorrow, then.'

* * *

Outside on the pavement, he drew in a lungful of air and waited for his heartbeat to settle. Why was it so damned difficult to simply appear *normal?* In most respects, Sophie had made it undeservedly easy for him. But allowing her to know some small part of the damage inside him had made him feel sick, sent sweat trickling between his shoulder blades and made him afraid that the constant howl in his chest would finally escape.

Oh God, he thought despairingly. *Perhaps I am mad.*

CHAPTER FOUR

Initially, the meeting at White's that afternoon achieved little other than an agreement that, unless subjected to pain, Basil Selwyn wasn't going to admit he'd engineered Christian's disappearance.

'Just give me the chance,' begged Daniel, 'I have no problem with hurting him.'

'None of us would,' sighed Benedict. 'But aside from the how and where it could be done, I'm not sure that confession under torture is acceptable evidence these days.'

'Do you *have* to be so pedantic?'

'One of us ought to be, don't you think?'

There was a long silence into which Anthony eventually said, 'If Basil won't admit what he did ... perhaps we can lure him into betraying himself some other way.'

'How?' demanded Daniel.

'I don't know. I'm simply saying that there must be more than one way of looking at this.' He thought for a moment, then added slowly, 'Here's an idea. Since we already *know* what he did – and Kit can testify to it – do we actually *need* a confession?'

'That would depend on whether Kit's willing to bring a case against him,' said Benedict. And to Christian, 'Are you?'

Christian, who had been lounging in his chair and letting the talk flow past him, gradually realised they were all looking at him. 'Am I what?'

'Willing to take legal action against Basil for sending you to what could, very easily, have been your death,' replied Benedict patiently. He had quickly realised that, even here among his closest friends, Christian sometimes closed himself off – as if he'd slipped away behind an invisible wall. 'It would be public and messy ... but it would be the quickest way to get the required result.'

'No.' Christian stared into his glass, shoulders hunched and jaw tight. 'He'd probably talk his way out of it, anyway.'

'He might,' agreed Anthony. 'But the mud would stick.'

'That's a good point,' began Daniel. 'We could – '

'*No!*' exploded Christian, slamming his glass down on the table. 'It wouldn't be just *Basil's* part that came out, for Christ's sake! The whole sordid mess would become public property as well. I won't – I *can't* have that. So *no* – and let that be an end of it!'

His friends stared at him in faintly stunned silence. Then Benedict said quietly, 'You're right, of course. A court case is out of the question. We'll need to give this a lot more thought before we can decide how best to proceed ... but let's leave it for now. Are we allowed to ask how it went with Sophia this morning, Kit?'

'What?' Christian blinked and slumped back in his chair. 'Oh. Well, I suppose. Better than I'd expected. We've agreed to renew our acquaintance over the next few weeks while I move into Berkeley Square and before I go down to Hazelmere.' He paused. 'I'm taking her driving tomorrow – if I may borrow your phaeton, that is?'

'Of course. But speaking of Berkeley Square ... I assume Gerald is overseeing the removal of Eustace and Basil?'

'I expect so.'

'If you'll take a word of advice – and Gerald hasn't already thought of it,' remarked Anthony a shade grimly, 'the inventory of the house should be checked *before* they move out and again after it. Given how freely Eustace has been digging into your coffers, I wouldn't put it past him to accidentally pack a few easily overlooked valuables. One or two pieces from your father's jade cabinet, for example.'

'Lord, yes!' said Daniel. 'Any of those would fetch a pretty penny.'

Benedict re-filled his glass and pushed the bottle across the table, saying mildly, 'Not that I disagree with you ... but perhaps we could stop or at least *suspend* guesswork on the various ways Kit's uncle and cousin might steal from him? I'm sure he's not enjoying listening to it and there are other things to discuss – such as the Ellingham assembly tomorrow evening. After what happened last night at Selwyn's interrupted ball, speculation will be rife – so it would be wise for us to put in an appearance. Not you, Kit; you can exchange greetings with a few people in the park tomorrow where you needn't be trapped in lengthy conversation. That will be enough to begin with. Leave fielding the initial barrage of questions to the rest of us.'

Christian summoned a smile. 'Thank you.'

'Just so we're all singing in unison, what is the official line?' asked Daniel.

'The one Kit gave last night. He was the honoured guest of a Turkish governor – a family man of mature years, so no one gets the wrong idea. He and his sons were so enjoying Kit's company that they continually delayed his departure. Don't embroider unnecessarily and do *not* get side-tracked by questions about half-naked Turkish dancing girls and the like.'

Daniel grinned. 'Just out of interest, Kit ... *were* there any of those?'

'None that were offered to me,' came the absent reply.

'No? Damned poor hospitality.'

'Oh, for God's sake!' muttered Anthony. 'All right, Ben. We'll stick to the script. But do you think people will believe it?'

'Some will, some won't,' shrugged Benedict. 'But gradually, when no other version of the story is forthcoming, they'll either begin to accept it or make of it what they will – as is always the case.'

'And Kit didn't write telling us where he was because ...?' prompted Anthony.

Had he not been looking at Christian just at that moment, Benedict would have missed the odd quiver that crossed his face. What had caused that, he wondered? Presumably one of the many things he suspected Kit hadn't told them.

He said, 'He *did* write. It wasn't until you and Dan turned up that he realised his letters had never arrived – or, more significantly, had never been sent.'

'That could work, I suppose,' shrugged Daniel. And to Christian, 'Also, I'd guess that at least half of the polite world's attention will be as much on developments between you and Miss Kelsall as on where you've been all this time.'

'Forgive me if I don't find that comforting,' muttered Christian.

'It can't be helped, my friend. The ladies love watching a happy-ever-after romance unfold. And the gentlemen enjoy watching it happening to someone else.'

Benedict and Anthony laughed. Christian scowled, reached for the bottle and then, changing his mind, said abruptly, 'I need to see Gerald before I meet my uncle again. I want to know precisely what's been going on in my absence and what the current position is. Gerald says he's kept records.'

'He has – extensive ones.' Benedict took the bottle from him and refilled his glass. 'Invite him to dine with us at Sinclairs this evening. Then, after we've eaten, I'll go and play a hand or two of basset so that you and he can be private.'

'There's no need for –'

'There is. While you've been away, he's been keeping us informed in general terms. With you, he'll want to be extremely specific and without additional company.'

* * *

Over dinner, Mr Sandhurst described the thunderous mood at Hazelmere House.

'Eustace has spent a lot of time locked in the library with the account ledgers, though I've no idea what he expects to achieve by it. The rest of the time, he stalks about scowling. Basil began by whining about his non-betrothal, then moved on to his conviction that you can't *really* evict them. Finally, Eustace rounded on him and told him to either shut up or take his idiocy elsewhere ... since which time, Basil's been lying low.'

'Interesting,' murmured Benedict. 'Have they started packing yet?'

'Not that I'm aware of.'

'Cutting it fine, aren't they? They're supposed to be gone in five days' time.'

'I suspect Eustace is looking for a way around that.'

'Will he find one?' asked Christian.

'No.'

'Anthony thinks we should take an inventory now as well as later.'

'I took one a couple of months ago while they were both away at Newmarket.' He smiled a little sourly. 'They won't steal anything else if I can prevent it.'

After they'd eaten and Benedict had decamped to one of the card rooms, the mood changed. Gerald's tone and expression became briskly business-like and he began laying sheets of figures in front of Christian, detailing amounts of money withdrawn and from which accounts. Next came the bills. Bills from tailors, bootmakers and wine-merchants; bills for a phaeton, a travelling carriage and half a dozen horses; bills for the recent redecoration of parts of Hazelmere House ... and so on.

'Stop,' said Christian weakly, nearly an hour later and only half-way through the sheaf of papers in Gerald's hand. 'I get the general idea. How bad is it?'

'It's not good ... but not disastrous either. Eustace had begun helping himself in small ways during the year of his trusteeship. Consequently, after you reached your majority and were about to embark on the Grand Tour, Henry Lessing and I –'

'Lessing? Who's he?'

'Your new man of law. Old Wharton was retiring, if you recall, and neither of us had much faith in his son, so you asked me to find someone else. Edward Hastings, the manager here, recommended Mr Lessing. You won't be disappointed – he's both capable and efficient.' He scribbled a note for himself. 'I'll make an appointment for you to meet him.'

Christian nodded. 'Good. But you were saying ...?'

'Yes. He and I put safeguards on a number of accounts to place them outside Eustace's reach. We also made sure he couldn't touch the investments – and, fortunately, selling any land was always beyond his scope. But, between them over the last four years, he and Basil have spent some forty thousand pounds and there is currently a further eight-and-a-half thousand owing in unpaid bills. Not to put too fine a point on it, a few more years like these last ones and you might have found yourself in difficulties.' Gerald paused and with a faint but encouraging smile, added, 'As it is, however, the situation is salvageable.'

It was a long time before Christian spoke but eventually he said, 'You haven't mentioned Hazelmere.'

'That is the one bright spot. They've taken surprisingly little interest in the estate – with the result that everything has gone on as normal. Harrington is still the steward and I've been down twice a year to confer with him. He's made repairs where necessary and kept rents at the same level – though he may want to discuss that now you're back. But as things stand, you've nothing to worry about there.'

'Thank God for that at least,' muttered Christian. 'And thank *you*, Gerald. But for you, I dread to think what kind of mess I'd be coming back to.'

'It's bad enough as it is. The difficulty has been erecting barriers without Eustace being aware of it because if he'd had the least inkling of what I was doing – particularly my involvement with Benedict and the others – I'd have been out on my ear without a character.'

'Well, that last thing wouldn't have mattered. Ben, Dan and Anthony would all have been happy to supply one. However, speaking of dismissals ... have there been any?'

'Only your valet when he refused to work for Basil. But Rollo Trent had been trying to tempt him away from you for months so he wasn't unemployed for long.' He made another note. 'You'll need a replacement.'

'Presently perhaps.' Something shifted unpleasantly in Christian's chest. He didn't want a valet but couldn't see how it might be permanently avoided. Pushing his half-full glass aside, he stood up. 'Is there anything else I need to know?'

'Numerous things. But everything else can wait until Eustace and Basil have quit Hazelmere House and you've taken up residence. Since they're dragging their heels, do I have your permission to push them a bit?'

'Yes. And end the pretence. Point out that you're in my employ, not theirs. And I'll write making it clear that I won't tolerate a delay – perhaps with an underlying hint of sending in the bailiffs if necessary.'

'That should do the trick,' grinned Gerald. 'But would you?'

'Oh yes,' came the cold reply. 'I'd prefer blood. But I'll take what I can get.'

* * *

Sophia prepared carefully for her drive with Christian, choosing a floral gown of blue and rose dimity and a wide-brimmed straw hat with matching ribbons. They weren't new. The only new gown she'd had in the last two years was the blue silk she had worn for the Selwyn ball but she hadn't minded the lack. It was only fair that, since she herself no longer went about in society, what little money there was should be spent on Gwendoline, who *did*. And the dimity gown had always suited her.

She hovered between sadness, excitement and worry ... longing to be with Kit but afraid that he was less eager to be with her. The things he had said yesterday had kept her awake half the night as she tried to understand what he'd meant by them and what they might mean for the future. If, she reminded herself, they *had* a joint future. Given the nature of yesterday's meeting, it was important to remember that they might not. She thought she'd been prepared for the likelihood that, after so long, if and when he came back, he'd be different ... but yesterday had taught her that she hadn't been prepared at all. In her mind, *different* had merely equated to *older*. And the reality was nothing like that.

I couldn't allow myself to think of you, he'd said. *After a time, I stopped thinking about other things, too ... home, friends, the future. There was no place for – for emotions of that sort.*

He wasn't just older. He was damaged in ways she couldn't see. And he knew it.

Lord Benedict's phaeton drew up outside at precisely three o'clock. Watching through the parlour window, Sophia saw the groom jump down to hold the horses while Christian climbed the steps to the door. Her heart gave a sudden dizzying lurch. He was no less handsome than he'd been five years ago; all tawny hair, tall, neatly-muscled elegance and a smile that could stop any woman's breath.

But of course he was so much more than that ...

* * *

Six years ago at that Dorset house-party, she and all the other young ladies had been rendered speechless by his perfection. But the first time Sophia actually spoke to him was when he'd come upon her trying – without success – to stop three older boys tormenting Drusilla's five-year-old niece. They had taken the child's doll and were tossing it between them whilst urging her to jump higher and laughing at her 'carroty curls'. And, at the moment Christian arrived on the scene, they'd been telling Sophia to mind her own business when she told them to stop.

'Allow me,' he said, catching the doll in mid-flight and handing it to a sobbing Lucy. Then, to the boys, 'You three – come with me.' And leading them a little way off, he sat down on a bench with them lined up in front of him and started talking very quietly.

Sophia couldn't hear what he was saying. But some minutes later, the trio made their way back to her, red-faced and sheepish. One by one, they apologised – first to Sophia for their rudeness and then to the little girl for teasing her. And at the end, the oldest of the three added awkwardly, 'We didn't mean to be unkind or r-rude. But it wasn't gentlemanly behaviour and it wasn't sporting. We won't do it again, Lucy – promise. And to make up, I'll come and push the swing for you, if you like.'

Instantly pacified, Lucy wasted no time in dragging him off with her.

Meanwhile, Christian strolled back to Sophie saying, with a shrug, 'Just boys being boys. But next time, perhaps they'll think first.'

'Yes. Thank you for lending a hand.'

'Think nothing of it.' He gestured to the seat next to her. 'May I?'

What little air remained in her lungs promptly leaked away. She nodded.

'I'm Hazelmere,' he said, still standing.

'I know. I – I'm Sophia Kelsall.'

His smile did something peculiar to her nerve-endings.

'I know.' He held out his hand and, when she placed hers in it, bowed over it, saying, 'Forgive me ... but I got tired of waiting for an introduction.'

* * *

Now, summoning the role she must play, she went down to greet him with a bright smile and a curtsy. 'You're very prompt.'

He bowed in response but his answering smile was tense.

'Yes. I owe you that much, don't I?'

Oh dear, she thought. *Not the best of starts.*

'Do you think we might put all that behind us – just for an hour? The sun is shining and I can't remember the last time I went driving in the park.'

'Of course.' He offered his arm and, with a creditable attempt at lightness, said, 'But I should warn you that getting from Dover Street to here is the first time I've handled the ribbons for a while. There was a moment when Benedict's groom feared for his life.'

She laughed. 'I'd better hold on tight then, hadn't I?'

'It would be advisable.'

Once in the carriage, she took time arranging her skirts and said nothing until he had set the horses in motion, thinking that perhaps he needed to concentrate on negotiating the traffic for the short distance to the Stanhope Gate. But he sent her a brief sideways glance and said, 'I am remiss. I ought to have told you how lovely you look.'

'Why? It isn't obligatory, you know.'

A hint of colour warmed his cheek.

'Of course. I didn't mean it to sound as if ... as if ...'

'As if you *had* to compliment me regardless of whether or not I deserved it?' she asked cheerfully. 'Perish the thought!'

Christian realised he'd forgotten her complete disregard for her own beauty, along with her lack of flirtatious wiles. He also recognised something about himself ... that, along with a number of other things, he appeared either to have lost the art of making idle conversation or no longer knew what constituted a suitably safe topic.

Sophia let the silence linger until he turned the carriage into Hyde Park, then she said abruptly, 'I loved the letters you wrote to me during your Grand Tour. I read them over and over until I knew them by heart. You described everything so vividly, it was almost like being there. And I *so* envied you Florence and the chance to see works by great artists like Leonardo da Vinci and Michelangelo.'

'Yes. I was ... fortunate.' He scoured his brain for something more to say. 'I bought some paintings along the way – not genuine masterpieces, of course – but good art of the kind that rarely comes up for sale in London. I bought other things, too. Things that were to be gifts for you.'

'Oh.' She swallowed hard. 'What happened to it all?'

'I had it shipped home.'

He paused, frowning, as he remembered one piece in particular. A small portrait of a lady with the face of a Renaissance Madonna that he'd bought, partly because the skill of the artist was unmistakeable, but mostly because – although the lady in the picture was fair-haired not dark – she had reminded him of Sophia. The dealer had known nothing about it and plainly considered it of little value. But he'd eventually said he supposed it *might* be by the hand of one of many painters patronised by the Medici but whose work had gone out of fashion centuries ago.

'I suppose they're in Berkeley Square,' he added vaguely. 'I hope so, anyway.'

Sophia opened her mouth to continue drawing him out but was forestalled when a voice said, 'Hazelmere? I heard you were back but scarcely believed it. How are you?'

'Very well, thank you.' Christian nodded to the rider keeping pace with the carriage and scoured his brain for the fellow's name. 'And you?'

'Never better. But where on earth have you *been* all this time?'

'Any number of places. I extended my tour, then experienced unexpected difficulties making the return journey.' Then, without pausing, 'Are you acquainted with Miss Kelsall? No? Sophie, allow me to present Lord Sedley.'

She smiled. 'How do you do, my lord?'

Touching the brim of his hat with his riding crop, Lord Sedley said admiringly, 'All the better for seeing *you*, ma'am. Unfortunately, my young brother has managed to out-distance me and I'd better catch up with him before he creates mayhem of some sort. Pleasure to see you, Hazelmere. Perhaps you'll look in at the club for a hand or two of picquet some evening?'

'Perhaps,' agreed Christian. And thought, *Not if I can help it.*

'You'll have to put up with a lot of that,' remarked Sophia thoughtfully as his lordship trotted away. And, lowering her voice so the groom wouldn't hear, 'It's going to become tedious – not to mention awkward, if you're to avoid supplying details.'

Mentally shuddering at the thought of *details* becoming common knowledge, he said merely, 'Quite. Benedict, Anthony and Daniel are hoping to diffuse the worst of it. They're going to the Ellingham ball this evening in order to – '

'Miss Kelsall! We haven't seen you this age!' boomed a voice from the carriage currently approaching them. 'And dear me – can that really be Lord Hazelmere with you?'

Groaning inwardly, Sophia pasted a bright smile on her face.

'Lady Bentworth, Miss Bentworth – how lovely to see you both. And yes, it is indeed Lord Hazelmere. Christian ... you remember her ladyship, don't you?'

'Of course.' He tipped his hat. 'But not *Miss* Bentworth, I believe?'

'How could you?' replied the girl's mother. 'Sarah only made her come-out last year and you were still ... well, nobody knew *where* you were, did they?'

'The postal service abroad is truly shocking, isn't it?' said Sophia without a qualm. 'But we are blocking the way, ma'am, so we should drive on. Christian?'

'Indeed.' He touched his hat again and gave the horses the signal to move on. 'A pleasure, ma'am – Miss Bentworth.' Then, as soon as they were out of earshot, 'Thank you for that – though you *do* realise you insulted every country from here to Asia?'

'They won't know.' The smile had vanished and her eyes had grown suspiciously bright. 'I've just realised that, not only were you held against your will, you weren't even permitted to write letters. What kind of monster *does* that?'

'One used to having his own way and possessing the means to make sure he gets it.' He glanced at her and added tightly, 'Don't be sorry for me, Sophie.'

'I'm not *sorry* for you – I'm *furious*. However ... you were saying that your friends intend to start spreading a prepared story?'

'That is the general idea, yes.'

'Then you'd better tell me what it is so that, if asked, I can say the same thing.'

He nodded and, in as few words as possible, told her, before adding abruptly, 'How is your mother's mood today?'

'Much as it usually is. Oh – and this morning she pointed out that I'm in the unique position of being unofficially betrothed to two gentlemen at the same time. I'd half-expected Basil to call by now but, since he hasn't, I've sent a note telling him that any understanding between us is at an end.' She paused. 'Were you serious about him and his father quitting Hazelmere House within the week?'

'Deadly serious.'

Her hesitation this time was longer. 'Don't tell me if you prefer not to ... but is that because Eustace has been behaving as if the earldom was already his or – or because of something Basil has done?'

'I simply prefer not to share my roof with them.'

She was tempted to point out that this was no answer. Instead, she said, 'On your right – Viscount Wingham is nodding to you.'

'What? I don't know – oh. Sebastian Audley. Yes.' Christian summoned a smile and raised a hand in acknowledgement. 'When did he inherit?'

'A little while ago. He married Cassandra Delahaye and they have a son.' For the first time, it occurred to her that there were many such things he wouldn't know. 'Ask Lord Benedict about your other acquaintances. He'll know what you've missed.'

He nodded, but said, 'Sophie ... your mother is right, in one sense. If you and I raise expectations again and nothing immediately comes of them ...'

'It will be exactly as it was before you went away,' she shrugged. 'And anyone with half a brain ought to realise that, after such a long separation, we wouldn't be racing to the altar even if you *didn't* have a mountain of responsibilities awaiting your attention. On the left ... Lord and Lady Amberley. She's smiling at you.'

He located the marchioness and smiled, inclining his head as he did so but murmured, 'Lady Amberley is blind, isn't she?'

'Not any more. An incident involving a goat, so I'm told.' And returning to her earlier point, said with heroic cheerfulness, 'Please stop worrying, Kit. There truly isn't any need. And we made a decision, you and I – so let's stick to it.'

CHAPTER FIVE

While society's most intriguing couple were driving in the park, events at Hazelmere House moved on apace when Mr Sandhurst handed Christian's note to Eustace Selwyn and watched angry colour flood his cheeks.

'Insolent puppy! How *dare* he address me as if I was some tenant late with the rent.'

Gerald was tempted to point out that living – and living extravagantly – at the earldom's expense for nearly three years was a rather more serious offence. But he didn't. He simply remained silent and waited to hear what Mr Selwyn would say next.

'You may reply to this on my behalf,' snapped Eustace, shoving the letter back at him. 'Inform my nephew that we will remove from here when it is convenient for us to do so – which, at present, it is not. You may further tell him that if he has something to say to me, he can do me the courtesy of saying it in person.'

For a moment, Gerald eyed him consideringly. *End the pretence*, Christian had said … and this, it seemed, was his cue to do so.

'You appear to misunderstand the situation, sir,' he said quietly. 'I have remained in my position throughout his lordship's absence and continued to serve the earldom as best I was able. But I am and always have been Lord Hazelmere's private secretary and, from henceforth, will be acting on his orders and his alone.'

If Eustace's face had been red before, by the end of this speech it was apoplectic. He said, 'Then you'll act on them elsewhere – not in *this* house. You're dismissed.'

'You don't have the power to dismiss me, Mr Selwyn. Neither, since his lordship's return, do you have any authority in this house. He has asked you to leave, as –'

'With an irrational degree of haste and not a word of explanation!'

'As is his right,' said Gerald, ignoring the interruption. 'The house is not yours, sir. It belongs to Lord Hazelmere and –'

'He's my *nephew*, damn it – who has been missing for three years *also* without a word of explanation.' Eustace appeared to take a calming breath. 'If he wishes to live here himself, there is nothing to stop him doing so – God knows the house is big enough.'

'He has every intention of living here. But not while you and your son remain in residence.'

'Why not?'

'It isn't my place to answer that question, sir. If you wish to ask his lordship directly, he is staying with Lord Benedict Hawkridge in Dover Street.'

'I know where he is, blast you! But if he wants my son and I gone, he can –'

The door burst open and Basil – also clutching a letter – stormed through it.

'Do you know what she's done?' he demanded furiously. 'She's withdrawn her acceptance of my proposal and ordered me – *ordered* me, if you please – not to give any indication to the contrary.' He hurled the letter into the fire. 'Well, I'm not having it!'

Or her, thought Gerald, repressing a smile. *Well done, Sophia.*

Deciding that now was as good a time as any to terminate Eustace's determination to argue, he said, 'I have a number of things to attend to and will leave you to be private, gentlemen. Please excuse me.'

'This conversation isn't over,' blustered Eustace.

'Your pardon, sir,' countered Gerald, heading for the door. 'But I'm afraid it is.'

Father and son were left looking at each other. Basil said, 'What was that about?'

'What do you *think* it was about? Christian's high-handed insistence on us removing from here. We are ordered to be gone by noon on Monday, if you please.'

'And go where, for God's sake? Maddox Street is still let to tenants, isn't it?'

'No. There was illness in the family so they left Town early and it was too late in the Season to replace them – which, if we have to leave here, is just as well.'

Basil dropped moodily into a chair. 'He can't *make* us go.'

'As I've repeatedly told you, he *can*. The question is, why is he doing it?'

'Sheer bloody-mindedness? How should I know?'

'Do you not? Are you quite sure there's nothing that could account for his attitude?'

'Aside from the obvious, do you mean? Me about to marry Sophie ... you playing the earl ... and us living here, spending his money? He'll know all about that, of course. Sandhurst will have carried tales to Hawkridge and the rest – he was always fawning about them at Oxford.'

Eustace thought this over.

'It could be that, I suppose. And yet I've a feeling there's more to it.'

'Such as what?'

'If I knew that, I wouldn't be asking.'

'Well, it's no good asking me.' Basil stood up again. 'I'm going to Charles Street. Sophie can't just send me a note and think that's the end of it – she can damned well tell me to my face. And the way Kit was behaving the other night didn't much look as if he was still panting to marry her himself, did it?'

His father subjected him to a long, level stare.

'Are you saying – knowing she'd walk away in a heartbeat if Christian crooked his finger – that you'd still be willing to have her?' asked Eustace.

'Yes.'

'Why?'

'What?'

'Why are you so set on *her?* She's a beautiful girl, I grant you. But so are a good many others – some of them with better connections and sizeable dowries. Sophia Kelsall is twenty-two years old and has neither. It seems to me that she is only unique in one respect; and that is the fact that she was Christian's choice.'

'It's not that,' said Basil quickly. 'It's never been that. It's *her*.'

'Mm.' Eustace contemplated his fingernails. 'Let me make something clear, Basil. While Christian was out of the picture and seemed certain to remain so ... while we could look forward to the earldom and all it entails becoming first mine and then yours ... I was content to let you have your way. But that is no longer the case. And since Miss Kelsall has released you from any obligation, I would prefer you to look for a bride who will bring something to your marriage, rather than coming to it penniless. By all means go and settle matters with her if you feel you must. But do *not* do anything irrevocable until you have given proper thought to what I've said and we've discussed this again. Is that understood?'

'Well, yes. But – '

'Good. And please also consider the fact that there must be *some* reason for Christian's hostility. Did you and he quarrel? Was your parting in Athens acrimonious? Is there something – *anything* – that can have been festering in his mind all this time?'

'No! There's nothing, I tell you! As for Athens – God knows we've been through it often enough. I warned him that travelling to Turkey could be dangerous but he went anyway. He set off over the Aegean and I took a ship to Palermo. I waited five weeks for him to join me When he didn't, I sent men to find him but they couldn't,' recited Basil rapidly. 'That's it. Everything. And now I'm going to see Sophie.'

Eustace let him go but remained staring into the fire. There was a question – or rather the *same* question, phrased differently – that he'd never quite brought himself to ask. He had an uneasy suspicion that he might not like the answer ... and if that *were* to be the case, he would rather remain in ignorance. So he comforted himself with the belief that Basil's confidence remained unshaken and hoped his trust wasn't misplaced.

* * *

Basil's phaeton halted outside Kelsall House at the exact moment that Christian drove up from the other direction. For perhaps a minute, the two men stared at each other in silence. Then, despite the thing howling in his chest and clawing at his gut, Christian drawled, 'Nice carriage, Baz. When did I buy it?'

Basil set his jaw, tossed the reins to his groom and dropped to the ground. Ignoring his cousin and offering his hand to Sophia with a smile, he said, 'What excellent timing.'

'Is it?' She made no move to take his hand. 'Why?'

'A few minutes earlier, I'd have missed you. And we need to talk.'

'Ah. I gather you received my note. Was it not clear enough?'

Beside her, Christian had also climbed down and was strolling around to her side of the vehicle. He said, 'Sophie doesn't appear to want your help, Baz ... and neither does she want to sit there all afternoon. But you're in the way – so step aside, why don't you?'

'For *you*? Not a – '

'Do you see anyone else? Do *you*, Sophie?'

'Only Dunne waiting in the doorway for me to go inside. Oh – and the Misses Haddon across the street.' She waved to a pair of elderly ladies who slowed their steps in order to watch whatever happened next. 'Also, the curtains are twitching at number thirty-six. *Do* move and let Kit hand me down, Basil – before we draw a crowd.'

Finally, Basil let his hand fall to his side and stepped back, his jaw tight. Sophia took Christian's hand and, stepping down between the two of them, said, 'Thank you for taking me driving, Kit – it was most enjoyable. Will you come in for tea?'

Had it not been for his cousin standing there scowling at him, Christian would have simply refused and taken his leave. But, unable to react as everything inside him demanded and knowing that Basil wanted to speak privately to Sophia, he said instead, 'Thank you. I'd love to.' And was fairly sure he heard Basil grinding his teeth. 'Unfortunately, however, I had better return Benedict's carriage in case he needs it. I'm very much looking forward to having access to my own vehicles and cattle, as will soon be the case.' He turned to look again at the phaeton Basil had been driving. 'New horses as well, aren't they? I hope we got them at a good price, Baz.'

'Will you *stop* calling me *Baz!*' exploded Basil. 'And it's no business of yours how much I paid for my horses.'

'It is when you pay for them with my money. But that is an argument for later.' He lifted Sophia's hand to his lips, then released it. 'I must go. But perhaps we might walk in Green Park the day after tomorrow if the weather is fine?'

'I'd like that very much.'

He nodded, touched the brim of his hat and swung himself into the carriage. Then, looking at his cousin, said, 'Has Uncle received my letter?'

'Yes. But we – '

'Good. I advise you to start packing.' And he set the horses in motion.

Sophia repressed a sigh and, since there was no help for it, said, 'Come in, Basil. But if you're only here to dispute the contents of the note I sent you earlier, I can tell you now that there isn't any point.' And she swept up the steps, leaving him to follow. 'Are Mama and my sister back yet, Dunne?'

'No, Miss Sophia.'

'Excellent. You need not bring tea. Mr Selwyn won't be staying long.'

Trailing behind her, Basil muttered, 'There's no need to be like this, Sophie – '

'Sophia,' she corrected, stalking into the drawing-room. 'Or better yet, Miss Kelsall. Now ... what is it you wanted to say to me?'

'That I'd like you to reconsider. Don't you think you're being rather rash?'

'Not at all. I can't be betrothed to two men at the same time and Kit has the prior claim.'

'But you and he were never formally betrothed.'

'Neither were you and I,' she responded, 'but that's not how society looks at it. I'm sorry if I've disappointed you, Basil – truly, I am. But there would never have been any question of my being betrothed to you had Kit been here ... and now he is. Surely you can see that makes a difference?'

'It need not. Has he renewed his addresses?'

'That is none of your business.'

'I don't agree. *Has* he?'

Sophia eyed him coolly. Finally, because – in his usual fashion – Basil wasn't going to let it go, she said, 'Kit and I understand each other perfectly and have an agreement. *You* need to understand that the possibility of any future relationship with me is over. As I said, I'm sorry. But it will be best if you simply accept that my mind is made up.' She hesitated and then, trying for a different tack, added, 'Kit's return has changed many things, hasn't it? And I would guess *one* of them may be that your father would much prefer you to marry elsewhere – for which no one could blame him.'

Taken by surprise, Basil opened his mouth on four unwary words but managed to exchange them for, 'I can't imagine why you'd think so.'

'Yes, you can. My dowry is so pitiful it's hardly worth mentioning. For your father not to want something better for you would be astonishing. But that is beside the point, isn't it? We were never in love with each other and – '

'That's not true! Why do you think I've been courting you for months?'

'I think that is a question best neither asked nor answered,' she replied astringently. And on a sigh, 'I don't believe there's anything more to be said, Basil. In fact, I suggest you leave before Mama and Gwendoline come home and decide to share *their* opinions on the matter. You won't want to hear them – trust me.'

* * *

Christian drove back to Dover Street with a Turkish curse ringing over and over in his head. He'd been taught it by

Murad, youngest of Ibrahim's sons and the only one of them he hadn't found completely obnoxious. In truth, translated into English, the insult didn't seem so very terrible ... but Murad had assured him that it was the worst thing one Turk could say to another and that, when using it, it was advisable to be moving swiftly out of reach. Christian's mouth curled. It was far from the worst thing he could say to Basil. And when the time came, he wouldn't be retreating when he said it.

Seeing his cousin this afternoon had been no easier than it had been two days ago. He'd wanted to kill him just as much as he had then and *not* doing it had left his stomach in turmoil and a monumental headache threatening to split his skull open. He needed to think about something else – *anything* else. Sophie. Surely thoughts of *her* could calm the mess inside him? Couldn't they? No, it seemed they couldn't. Basil had got into his head and he couldn't get him out.

But I will, he promised himself. *And by the time I'm finished with him, he'll think a bullet might have been preferable.*

* * *

While his friends attended the Ellingham ball, Christian spent the evening with a book he didn't read and a glass of brandy which he never finished. By the time Benedict came home with Daniel in tow, he'd been considering going to bed for nearly an hour but hadn't done so because agitation was still roiling in him – which meant that he was unlikely to sleep well.

When the two men walked in, he set the book aside and said, 'How was it?'

'Productive,' said Benedict, heading for the decanter and glasses.

'Exhausting,' said Daniel, collapsing into a chair. 'Everyone asked the same questions. Where has Lord Hazelmere been all this time? Why didn't he write, telling someone where he was? Was there some reason he stayed away so long? What was his relationship with Ibrahim Pasha and his sons? Did they regard him as a part of their family? And so on and so on ... and endlessly, tediously, so on.'

'All perfectly true,' remarked Benedict, handing Daniel a glass. 'But it was useful. The three of us told precisely the same story, albeit in different ways, to any number of people this evening. You might say we've sown the seeds. And though some may have fallen on stony ground, the rest will hopefully take root and spread fast enough.'

'Very Biblical,' grinned Daniel. 'Personally, I started to wonder if we shouldn't have simply sent a written account to *The Whisperer*. It would have been easier.'

'No. It wouldn't. We'd *still* have been asked all those questions – or Kit would. People always think there's more to know. At least this way, they think their information has come from the most reliable source ... so from now on, we can leave the ripples to continue spreading naturally.'

'Oh they'll do that all right,' Daniel agreed caustically. 'And then we'll doubtless be kept busy quashing various theories and embellishments.'

'There's no preventing that.' Christian took a sip of brandy and put the glass down again. 'But you've done everything you could and I'm – '

'Don't,' warned Benedict. 'Do *not* say you're grateful. You'd do as much for any one of us – and have done in the past. You got me out of the mess I was in with Lottie Carpenter in our last year at Eton – *and* helped me keep it from Vere. Then there was the time you rescued Anthony from that terrifying widow in Oxford.'

'Where *is* Anthony, by the way?' asked Christian, embarrassed.

'His Aunt Louisa didn't feel well and he was summoned for escort duty,' replied Daniel. 'Don't change the subject. I was about to remind you about preventing me having my legs broken when I'd been idiotic enough to go the moneylenders *knowing* I'd never be able to pay on time.'

'Those were all relatively *small* things,' Christian muttered.

'Not to us, they weren't,' Daniel retorted. And then, 'However ... putting all that aside, what's our next move, Ben?'

'Choosing the right time for Kit to make his first appearance at a full-scale society event.' And to Christian, 'This evening, several ladies asked if you would soon be accepting invitations and I said that you would – because keeping you largely out of the public eye for too long isn't a good idea. Do you agree?'

'Yes. Reluctantly ... but yes.'

'Good. The same ladies referred to you having been seen in the park this afternoon with Sophia – so it's likely that both you and she will receive invitations to various assemblies and routs by tomorrow's post. And, unless I miss my guess, one of them will almost certainly be for the ball at Amberley House in three days' time. I've already accepted that one and so has Anthony. Daniel?'

'Of course. *No one* refuses an invitation from Lady Amberley.'

'Exactly. So it's the perfect place for ... let's call it your debut, Kit.' Benedict smiled suddenly. 'You may want to warn Sophia so she, in turn, can warn her mother. I'd be surprised if Lady Kelsall is usually on the marchioness's guest list.'

* * *

Christian slept for perhaps two hours before the nightmare came.

It began as it always did. He was face down and helpless; from behind him came the maddening, enervating tapping, accompanied by repetitive, stinging pain. Struggling achieved nothing and his curse-laden shouting was met with jeering laughter. On it went ... and on and on, just as it always did. Frustration with that endless rhythmic tapping had him screaming and –

A hand closed around his wrist and a voice spoke his name. He froze.

Something new. What?

Like a trapped animal, he lay still, panting for breath and waiting for he knew not what. Then he wrenched his hand free

– something which, even in his sleep-drugged state, he was aware shouldn't be possible.

Never mind. Take advantage of it.

He swung his clenched fist and forearm, hard and fast at the unseen presence ... felt it slam into some rigid, angular surface ... heard a sort of strangled grunt ... and was finally jerked fully awake.

'Hell!' gasped Benedict, stepping back and clutching his face. 'It's me, you idiot. Just *me*.'

Sitting up, Christian stared at him wildly. 'What the – what are you doing here?'

'Trying to stop you yelling the house down.'

'Was I?' He pressed the heels of his hands over his eyes. 'Sorry. Did I hit you?'

'Yes. And you'd better hope that I don't wake up with a black eye tomorrow.' Benedict hesitated and then said, 'You were having a nightmare – and by no means for the first time. Care to tell me about it?'

'No.' He shuddered inwardly at the thought. 'No. It's just a ... an unpleasant memory that surfaces occasionally. Nothing to worry about.'

'Really? When *unpleasant* clearly doesn't come close to describing it?' asked Benedict dryly. Then, 'All right. We'll leave it for now. But consider talking to me, will you? And meanwhile, try to get some sleep.'

CHAPTER SIX

During the course of the two days that followed, Christian had a second lengthy meeting with Gerald, largely concerning the various investments made by his father ... and a first, almost equally lengthy one with Mr Henry Lessing, his new man of law. He suspected that more of the same awaited him with his steward at Hazelmere and wondered how soon he would be free to go there.

He also allowed Benedict – who, mercifully, did *not* have a black eye – to persuade him to spend another evening at what, during his absence, had become his friends' favourite club. Sinclairs lacked the prestige of White's but its list of members was almost equally impressive and the excellent dinner served in an elegant and comfortable private dining-room went a long way to explaining the club's success. But though Christian met its proprietor and applied for membership of his own, he didn't visit the gaming floor. Such places were best avoided until after the Amberley ball – to which, exactly as Benedict had predicted, he had received an invitation.

He did, however, walk with Sophia in Green Park – though her sisters joined them, which he could well have done without. Not that he minded Julia's presence, in the least; she was a sweet girl and, despite her deafness, always cheerful. But Gwendoline dropped hints as heavy as lead weights about him introducing her to Benedict and Anthony; and worse than either was the fact that he was denied the welcome peace he found with Sophie.

Peace? The knowledge that the thought brought with it shook him. Peace was a far cry from the wildfire that had existed between them five years ago. *Now*, it had been so long since he'd experienced physical desire he scarcely remembered what it felt like. As yet, like so many other things, it didn't seem to matter very much ... but he was distantly aware that one day it would. Afraid of what that might mean, he refused to contemplate it.

Gwendoline had moved on to peevish complaints that, though Sophia had received an invitation to Amberley House, she had not.

In the end, tired of the incessant whining, Christian said, 'Forgive me ... but have you ever met Lady Amberley?' And when, for the first time in half an hour, she remained silent, said, 'I take it that means you haven't. Sophie has. So perhaps that is why she is invited and you are not.'

That shut the annoying girl up but, unfortunately, not for very long. And by the time he'd suffered through a seemingly interminable session of tea-drinking with all three girls and their mother, Christian could feel his control beginning to fracture. The whole business of behaving as he was expected to behave and saying what he *ought* to say, instead of what was quite often in his head, required a level of concentration that exhausted him. How the hell he was going to manage an entire evening of it at a thrice-blasted ball, he didn't know.

Although she kept it to herself, Sophia also wondered if he was even close to being ready to face society *en masse*. She was beginning to recognise the tell-tale signs of strain. His posture grew rigid, his left hand flexed involuntarily and a pulse throbbed in his jaw. He was controlling something that was almost too strong for him ... and, at times, he appeared to be teetering on the edge – though of what, she didn't know. This had begun to frighten her almost as much as it must terrify him. As for their personal relationship, that hardly seemed to have advanced at all. All this resulted in her committing the cardinal sin of having the only housemaid she trusted to take a note to Lord Benedict Hawkridge, asking him to meet her at Scrivener's bookshop on Sackville Street.

His lordship was there before her, lazily browsing through a book on art. But as soon as she appeared, he said quietly, 'My carriage is outside and I'll have my coachman drive around for a while so we can speak privately. It's grossly improper, of course, but – '

'No more so than my requesting this meeting,' she said abruptly. 'Shall we go?'

He nodded and offered his arm. Once inside the carriage, he said, 'It's about Kit, I imagine?'

Sophia nodded. 'He needs help and I don't know how to give it.'

'None of us do. The best thing would be for him to go to Hazelmere for a time – but doing so without first taking his place in society would have caused *exactly* the kind of talk we're trying to prevent. And then there's the matter of getting the Selwyns out of Berkeley Square – which they are not making easy. All of it is taking its toll.'

'I know. But yesterday, after a couple of hours with Gwendoline and my mother – both of whom I admit are equally difficult – he was so tense I thought he might snap. So how will he cope with Amberley House tomorrow evening?'

'Daniel, Anthony and I will be keeping an eye on him. Has he asked you for the opening set?'

'Yes. And the supper dance. But what about the rest of the evening? If he has to spend all of it *talking* and answering questions he won't last an hour.'

'He'll dance with a few of the debutantes – girls who'll be so overcome at being singled out by a handsome earl that they'll scarcely – '

'How?'

'Pardon me?'

'Who is going to introduce him to these debutantes? *You* can't do it – and I don't know any of them.'

'No.' He thought for a moment. 'Some female relative of Anthony's perhaps – heaven knows he's got enough of them so at least one should be there. Or, failing that, somebody's wife. I'll find someone suitable. And from time to time, one of us will spirit him away for a few minutes peace and quiet. Don't worry, Sophia. He'll manage because he knows he must.'

She stared down at her hands for a few moments. Then, drawing a long breath and meeting his lordship's green eyes, 'What *happened* to him? Do you know?'

'Some of it – though by no means all. I suspect there are things he may never tell us. But here's what we *do* know.

Ibrahim values men of culture and education – particularly foreigners. As governor of the province, he has vast authority outside his palace and complete autonomy within it so, once inside, Kit wasn't permitted to leave or allowed any contact with the outside world. His possessions were taken away from him, as was his name.' A grim smile curled Benedict's mouth. 'Well, they were hardly likely to call him Christian, were they?'

'No. I suppose not.'

'As I imagine he's told you, he was required to perfect Ibrahim's English along with that of his sons and give detailed descriptions about all aspects of Western life. In between, he received lessons in Turkish – which he didn't mind because it exercised his brain and enabled him to speak to the palace servants. He was also educated in the Koran and wouldn't have minded that either had it not been aimed at converting him – which, of course, he would have refused. For the rest, he wasn't ill-treated ... or if he was, he hasn't spoken of it. But for three years he was a prisoner, his every move restricted and dictated by others. I can't imagine what that does to a man's mental state – none of us can; and Kit gives few clues. But he's only been free for three months and hasn't yet come to terms with either that or what went before. All of it will take time.'

She nodded, apparently concentrating on smoothing her gloves. Then she looked up at him and said baldly, 'What did Basil do?'

Taken unawares, he blinked and then shook his head slightly.

'Do? What makes you think he did anything?'

'I saw the way Kit looked at him the night of the ball – and again two days ago when they came face to face in Charles Street. Basil did *something*. And Kit knows what it was.'

Like Christian's admission about his violent urges, Basil's perfidy wasn't a subject for anyone else's ears. Or not yet, anyway. So Benedict said smoothly, 'There are a number of things involving Basil that Kit may be angry about. Not searching diligently enough when he first went missing and would have been easier to find ... or taking possession of his home and his money. And there's also *you*.'

'It could be any of those things,' she admitted. 'But I don't think it is. I think it's something worse – and that it's as responsible for whatever is going on in Kit's head as is his time in captivity.'

Since Benedict knew this and agreed with her, he was grateful that the carriage turned back into Sackville Street before he had to find a suitable reply. Rapping on the roof to signal the coachman to pull up outside the bookshop, he said, 'He doesn't respond well to questions so all we can do is hope he'll talk when he's ready. But don't worry too much about tomorrow evening. As I said, with your help we'll get him through it without incident.' The carriage stopped and he stepped out to help her down. Then, with a particularly charming smile, 'Reserve a set for me, if you please.'

* * *

On the following evening, Sophia put on the blue silk that had been made for the Selwyn ball – at which she'd spent no more than an hour. It was new, it was beautiful and she needed every ounce of confidence she could find. Mama nodded approvingly and told her she looked very well indeed. Sophia hoped Christian thought so too but suspected he would be too on edge to notice.

Like Hazelmere House on that fateful night only a week ago, Amberley House was lit with flambeaux and the square outside it was a press of carriages. Inside, the receiving line wound slowly up the magnificent marble staircase to the place where the marquis and marchioness greeted their guests with warm smiles and words of welcome. Sophia's nerves were in knots by the time she and Mama got there ... and then they were inside the flower-decked ballroom with its high, painted ceiling and wall of mirrors.

'My goodness,' said Lady Kelsall faintly. 'Did not a French king commission something of this sort for one of his palaces? It is quite ... overwhelming.'

Sophia hadn't time to be overwhelmed. She was too busy scanning the room for Christian and his friends. For a moment, she thought that perhaps they hadn't yet arrived – and then she spotted Mr Shelbourne beating a purposeful path towards her just as her mother, gazing in a different direction, said, 'Mrs Barstow is waving at me. She appears quite agitated. You will not mind if I abandon you, Sophia?'

'Not in the least, Mama,' she replied politely. And thought, *In fact, please do.*

'Miss Kelsall.' Reaching her side and smiling warmly, Daniel bowed over her hand. 'I'm told Kit has engaged you for the first set. May I claim the second?'

She smiled back because the glint of laughter in those hazel eyes made it impossible not to. 'Thank you, sir. I shall look forward to it.'

'As will I.' Leaning a little towards her, he murmured, 'Kit is over there with Benedict and his brothers – *both* of them.'

Sophia's eyes widened. 'Belhaven is here?'

'He is. Are you acquainted with him?'

'Not at all.'

'Hardly surprising. He's invited everywhere and goes virtually nowhere.'

'Except tonight apparently.'

'Except tonight,' he agreed. And with a grin, 'I don't know if Benedict called in a favour or, like the rest of us, the duke can't resist Lady Amberley. Either way, Anthony and I made a wager. *He* says Belhaven will dance at least once, probably with the marchioness; *I'm* betting he won't dance at all. What do you think?'

She laughed. 'I couldn't begin to guess. You had best ask Lord Benedict … he and Kit are coming over now.'

Christian's eyes met hers when he was still several steps away. She thought there was a faint smile in them but couldn't be sure. Then he was bowing over her hand and saying what she'd *hoped* he'd say but wasn't sure he really meant. 'Good evening, Sophie. You look particularly lovely tonight.'

'Thank you.' She took in his coat of pale grey watered silk, its edges and cuffs lavishly embroidered with gleaming gun-metal thread. 'You are very fine yourself.'

'French tailoring,' Benedict told her with a bow and a smile of greeting. Then, mournfully, 'The rest of us can only struggle to compete.'

Daniel laughed. 'Oh? Tell us, Ben. *How* much did you pay for that opulent vest?'

'Too much, I daresay.' And aware that couples were beginning to assemble, 'It looks as if they're about to start the dancing. I'm promised to Miss Westwood. You?'

'No one, as yet. But one of the ladies sitting with the chaperones will doubtless take pity on me. Will Belhaven be taking to the floor by any chance?'

'Does he ever?' sighed Benedict. And to Christian, 'If you want to sit out the second set, you'll find me outside the card room.'

Christian nodded and turned to Sophia.

'Since I'm hopelessly out of practice, I apologise in advance for any mistakes.'

She smiled up at him, the epitome of unruffled cheerfulness despite her inner misgivings. 'Since so am I, we can just muddle through together.'

Fortunately, it was a minuet of the less complex variety and Christian was surprised, first by how easily the steps came back to him, and then by a sense of distant enjoyment – the latter, he realised, caused mostly by Sophia's radiant smile. Gradually, he felt himself relax just a little.

When Daniel came to claim her for the second set, she watched Christian stroll away to where Benedict stood in desultory conversation with Lord Sarre and Nicholas Wynstanton. That, she decided, was safe enough. They were both pleasant gentlemen ... and the main point this evening was for Kit to become reacquainted with his old life.

Christian, shaking hands and exchanging greetings with one man he knew and one he'd never met before, felt the familiar knot of anxiety forming – then resolutely pushed it aside, reminding himself that Benedict would have chosen these gentlemen deliberately. To the best of his recollection, when he'd last been in London the Earl of Sarre hadn't yet inherited his title and was still abroad in the wake of some scandal or other. Nick Wynstanton, on the other hand, was only a couple of years older than himself and still the same carelessly cheerful fellow he'd been five years ago.

Nicholas said, 'Welcome back, Hazelmere. I'll resist the temptation to ask where you've been all this time. You must be getting pretty tired of that question.'

'Somewhat,' agreed Christian.

'I was away twice as long,' remarked Sarre. 'If it's any comfort, the worst of the curiosity abated reasonably quickly ... but it takes time to catch up with the changes.'

'Yes. I'm beginning to realise that.' He looked back at Nicholas. 'I understand that you're a married man now.'

Nicholas grinned. 'I am. To the lady in green, dancing with Oscar Hawkridge.'

Christian sought Lord Oscar's partner and found a stunning redhead. Turning back to Nicholas, he said, 'You're a fortunate fellow.'

'Aren't I, though? I'll introduce you later. And speaking of fortunate fellows ... I see Miss Kelsall is back among us. Are you and she – ah.' He stopped abruptly. 'I suppose I shouldn't ask that either.'

'No, Nick,' sighed Benedict. 'You shouldn't.' And turning to Lord Sarre, 'Adrian ... Caroline is here somewhere, isn't she?'

'Over there by the potted palms with Cassie Wingham. Why?'

'Kit would prefer to dance without simultaneously being subjected to an inquisition ... so I thought one or two of this Season's shyer debutantes might be the answer. But he'll need a respectable matron to make some introductions.'

Adrian laughed. 'Well, Caroline and Cassie *are* that – though I suggest you don't put it that way to them, since making them sound middle-aged won't go down well.' And to

Christian, 'But they'll be happy to help, Hazelmere ... so come and meet them.'

'Kit,' corrected Christian. 'And thank you.'

Caroline, Lady Sarre, and Cassandra, Lady Wingham, both greeted Christian with warm smiles, then laughed when Benedict explained what he wanted and why.

Cassie said, 'Well, we can do that, of course – or you could dance with Caroline and me, Lord Hazelmere. Neither of *us* will bombard you with silly questions, I promise.'

'That is ... kind. I would be honoured.'

Caroline consulted her card. 'I have the next set free. Cassie?'

'The first after supper.' She smiled up at Christian. 'Will those suit, my lord?'

'Admirably. Thank you.'

'And between those two,' offered Caroline, 'if you *really* need a shy debutante, I'll present you to Andrea Wickham. The poor girl is afflicted by a dreadful stammer and doesn't speak at all if it can be avoided.'

'Perfect,' remarked Benedict. 'And now, please excuse me – I'm promised to Miss Kelsall for the *allemande*.'

During his dance with Lady Sarre, Christian felt the knot of tension in his chest ease a little more. She was a sunny, unpretentious lady and she made pleasantly undemanding conversation as and when the dance allowed. At the end of it, she said quietly, 'Adrian was in exile for a decade, Lord Hazelmere, and I met him very soon after his return. I doubt your experiences and his are remotely similar – but one thing I *do* know. It took time for him to *find* himself. Do you know what I mean?'

'I do. Very well indeed.'

'I thought so. Be patient ... and accept that, though life may never be *exactly* as it was, it will get better than it is right now.' She smiled, took his arm and added, 'Now come and meet Miss Wickham. As I said, she's painfully shy ... but a sweet girl. The next set but one is a quadrille. Ask her to stand up with you for that.'

Sophia's own tension eased when she saw Christian relaxing in Lady Sarre's easy company. She didn't know her ladyship well but she was aware that, like Lady Wingham, she was universally popular. Smiling at Benedict when he escorted her from the floor, she said, 'Well done, my lord. An inspired choice.'

'I thought so,' he grinned. 'If you're not engaged for the next set, let us find Kit and the champagne – in that order.'

'Isn't it a bit premature to celebrate?'

'No. I like to enjoy my successes as I find them.'

They found Christian and Daniel at the centre of a small knot of gentlemen. Numerous laughing remarks were being tossed at Christian – many of them being deftly fielded and tossed back by Mr Shelbourne. Then, just as Benedict and Sophia reached them, Anthony Wendover strolled over and silenced the group with a single word.

'Look.' He gestured to the dancers.

They looked. The Duke of Belhaven was leading the Marchioness of Amberley on to the floor. Sophia laughed. 'Oh dear. Poor Mr Shelbourne.'

'Thank you,' sighed Daniel. And to Benedict, 'He *would* choose to break the habit of a lifetime tonight, wouldn't he?'

Benedict shrugged. 'Vere is a law unto himself.'

Anthony grinned at Daniel. 'Twenty guineas, wasn't it?'

'Yes. If you're going to gloat, do it somewhere else. I need a drink. Join me, Kit?'

'Why not?' Christian offered Sophia his arm, then stopped. 'Ah. Perhaps you're engaged for the next set?'

'I'm not.' She took his arm and, smiling, walked with him into the refreshment room. 'Lord Benedict thinks he deserves champagne because I congratulated him on introducing you to Lady Sarre and Lady Wingham.'

'Do you know them?'

'Lady Sarre, not very well. But my second Season – the one after you went away – was Lady Wingham's last before she married his lordship, so I know her a little better. She's very kind. As, I believe, is Lady Sarre. Did you like her?'

'Yes.' He took two glasses of champagne from a footman and handed one to her. 'Are you enjoying this evening?'

'Very much. Are you?'

'It's ... better than I expected.' Truth to tell, he was constantly waiting for a question or remark he wouldn't know how to answer ... while the light and press of people in the ballroom, all of it reflected in the mirrors, was beginning to give him a headache. 'But I enjoyed our dance earlier and am looking forward to the one before supper.'

'So am I.' Sophia hesitated and then said, 'Is it tomorrow that Basil and your uncle are supposed to move out of Hazelmere House?'

'Yes – *supposed to* being the operative words.'

'You think they'll refuse?'

'I suspect they're considering it. But hopefully, sense will prevail. I'd sooner not create a scene in Berkeley Square by sending the bailiffs in – but I will if I have to.'

She stared at him, shocked. 'Really?'

'Really. I intend to take back control of my life ... and this is where it begins.'

CHAPTER SEVEN

The following morning was overcast with the promise of rain and the message from Mr Sandhurst which was delivered while Benedict and Christian were taking breakfast did not bring cheering news.

'What does he say?' asked Benedict.

Wordlessly, Christian handed him the note. It was brief and to the point.

They are showing every sign of taking root. What do you want me to do?

Gerald.

Benedict handed it back. 'What *do* you want him to do?'

'Bluff – but be prepared to make it real if necessary.'

Christian walked to the writing desk and scribbled a few lines.

Remind them that they have until noon – but have the bailiffs standing by in the square from eleven where Eustace can't fail to see them. And send for Henry Lessing to spell out the legalities; better him than you and he's aware he may be needed.

Keep me informed. I'll be here in Dover Street all morning.

He folded and sealed it, while telling Benedict what he'd written.

Benedict waited until Syms, his manservant, was on his way to deliver Christian's reply and then said, 'Am I correct in supposing you don't intend to put in an appearance yourself?'

'Not if I can help it. And what good would it do? I've made my position clear.'

Benedict eyed him thoughtfully. He looked pale and underslept and was probably nowhere near as calm as he was managing to sound. Was he dealing with this situation remotely because he didn't trust himself not to give way to the violent impulses he claimed lived just beneath the civilised surface these days? Then again, the previous evening at Amberley House had gone exceptionally well, all things considered ... but it had probably taken a good deal of invisible effort.

Really, he decided, *the sooner he is able to settle into his own home, spend an evening at White's and take his seat in the House, the better. With those milestones behind him, he can escape to Hazelmere for a while.*

He said wryly, 'It's going to be a long morning, isn't it?'

'For me, yes. But you don't need to hold my hand and can do whatever you'd planned.'

'I'd *planned* to persuade you to spend an hour with me at either Angelo's or the new *Salle d'Armes* in Cleveland Row. But something tells me today isn't the best time to be putting a weapon in your hand.'

This produced something resembling a smile.

'You'd be safe enough. I haven't fenced in five years.'

'Then let's mend that tomorrow. Meanwhile, do I need to remind you that after a ball it's customary to – '

'Send flowers,' groaned Christian. 'Of course. But I have to stay here in case there are further developments in Berkeley Square. Can you see to it?'

'Yes. But if I'm to send Sophia flowers on your behalf, you'd better tell me what her favourites are and what to write on the card.' He grinned suddenly. 'Not that I think she'll be short of a bouquet or two this morning. Unless I miss my guess, Oscar will be leading the charge. He's quite taken with her.'

'He is?'

'Yes. But let's stick to the matter in hand. Which flowers am I to send?'

'Cornflowers and lily-of-the-valley.'

Benedict nodded. 'And on the card?'

'Just my name. I never wrote poetic messages before so she won't expect one – and she'll know it's not my writing. Also, please send flowers to Lady Sarre and Lady Wingham, as well – violets, perhaps? – thanking them for their kindness.'

'Anything else? You wouldn't like me to deliver them personally?'

Christian's brows rose. 'I hadn't thought of it. But if you wouldn't mind ...'

In three words, Benedict indicated that he would most *certainly* mind; and, for the first time in the last month, heard his friend give a genuinely amused laugh.

* * *

In Charles Street, Sophia received bouquets from Mr Shelbourne, Lord Oscar Hawkridge and one with a card that bore Christian's name but not his handwriting. For a moment or two, she felt a little hurt that he had clearly not sent them himself. Then she remembered what was happening today ... and understood *why* he hadn't. He'd be sitting in Lord Benedict's lodgings, awaiting developments in Berkeley Square.

In Dover Street, the hour up to eleven o'clock seemed endless. Several times, Christian thought the clock had stopped. Benedict returned from the florist and, a little later, another note arrived from Gerald.

Mr Lessing spent almost an hour explaining to your uncle that, if you want him and your cousin to leave, they have no choice but to do so. As you asked, the bailiffs are kicking their heels in the square and drawing some attention. Eustace is red in the face and close to losing the last shred of his temper; Basil is getting twitchy; but so far they show no signs of leaving. What are your instructions?

Christian swore under his breath.

'Is Eustace *really* going to make me evict them by force?'

'It's beginning to look like it. Will you?'

'What choice do I have? I want my home back – with vacant possession.'

'For which no one can blame you.' Benedict glanced at the clock. 'You've got approximately forty-seven minutes. Send Gerald a note giving him your authority to admit the bailiffs at noon ... and write to your uncle, telling him you've done so. If he still refuses to budge, what happens thereafter is on his head, not yours.'

Christian communed silently with the ceiling for a few moments. Finally, he said, 'You say no one can blame me ... but there are some who will. People who will be shocked that I've treated relatives so harshly.'

'Perhaps. But there will also be ones who'll ask themselves why Eustace let it get that far and others who will wonder what your reasons are for behaving this way.' He paused. 'Sophia is already wondering about it. She asked me point blank what Basil did – and no, of course I didn't tell her. But she won't be the only one asking that question.'

'Lovely. As if there isn't enough speculation surrounding me already.' Shoving to his feet, he went back to the writing desk. 'All right. My last throw.'

* * *

In Berkeley Square, at fifteen minutes before midday, Mr Sandhurst read Christian's note and handed it to Mr Selwyn along with the one addressed to him, saying, 'If you force Lord Hazelmere to do this, then he will. It's entirely up to you whether you want to make yourself a laughing stock or not ... but you had better decide quickly, sir.'

Eustace read both messages, then crumpled them in his hand, saying, 'My nephew's experiences abroad have obviously unhinged him.'

'I disagree. And at this precise moment, his reasons are immaterial. You still have a choice to make. Half the residents of the square are waiting to see what it will be.'

That won him a glare before Eustace strode to look through the window. Outside, maids were polishing door-knockers and footmen were sweeping steps; there were faces at windows and Viscount Fleming's son and his friends were leaning against the railings to the garden, laughing. The four bailiff's men still lounged idly across the street.

Behind him, Basil entered the room and said unevenly, 'He's bluffing, isn't he?' And when Eustace turned from the window, his face white and set, 'Father! *Is* he bluffing?'

'No.' It was Gerald who answered. 'He isn't. His lordship would prefer – as I imagine *you* would – that the gentlemen waiting outside will not be needed. But that is up to you and your father. My instructions are to admit them if you are still here on the stroke of noon – which is now ten minutes away.'

Something shifted in Eustace's expression but before he could speak, Basil said belligerently, 'You're not going to let the bailiffs in. I know you won't.'

'Would you like to put money on it?'

Ignoring this, Basil said, 'Fallon won't have it.'

'Mr Fallon will follow Lord Hazelmere's orders,' returned Gerald, already walking away from him. 'As will I.'

Back in the hall and leaving Basil free to listen through the open doorway, Gerald once again assured the butler that even if the bailiffs entered the house – and there was still hope this might be avoided – they had very definite orders regarding their conduct.

'There will be no damage, Mr Fallon. They are merely to oversee the removal of the Selwyn gentlemen and their personal possessions.'

'I sincerely hope you are right, sir. This is all most unfortunate – *most* unfortunate.'

'I agree. But the earl has a perfect right to reclaim his own home. And it isn't as though Mr Selwyn doesn't have a house of his own, is it?'

'No – no, indeed. And I and the entire staff will be delighted to see his lordship back in residence. But *bailiffs*, sir – in *Berkeley Square*. Never did I think to see the day.'

'Quite. But chin up, Mr Fallon. I recall Lord Hazelmere telling me that he didn't believe there was any situation you could not handle.'

Fallon's chest expanded. 'His lordship said that?'

'He did. So I'm sure that, between us, you and I can keep things relatively civilised.'

Behind them, the longcase clock slowly began to chime the hour.

Gerald sighed. The butler was right. This was indeed *most* unfortunate.

He said, 'Open the door please, Mr Fallon.' And when it stood wide, he walked to stand on the threshold while the clock continued to strike.

Outside, the bailiffs sauntered across the road to wait at the foot of the steps. One of them said, 'I'm Peterson, sir. Are me and my team to proceed?'

'It would seem so – but please come inside and wait for a few moments while I give the gentlemen one last chance to leave voluntarily. Mr Fallon, have Mr Selwyn and Mr Basil's valets begin packing their personal effects. Anything left behind can be – '

'That will not be necessary.' Eustace spoke coldly from behind him. 'We will go – but in our own good time and *not* accompanied by these fellows. Fallon ... instruct our valets, by all means – and send a footman to tell the staff in Maddox Street to be ready to receive us in the next few hours. But we will oversee our own packing.'

Gerald opened his mouth to reply but before he could do so, Peterson stepped forward, saying, 'Excuse me, sir – but I'd have to advise against that.'

'Hold your tongue!' snapped Basil. 'Nobody asked *you*.'

Gerald ignored him and turned to the bailiff. '*I'm* asking. Why is that?'

'Goes contrary to normal practice, sir. If it was to be found later that articles had gone missing, my team and me could be blamed for not taking due precautions.'

'How *dare* you?' fumed Eustace. 'That is a monstrous allegation. My son and I are not thieves. We will go to our rooms, Sandhurst, and we will – '

'My apologies,' interrupted Gerald quietly, 'but no. You will not.'

'I *beg* your pardon?'

'You have had ample time in which to give orders regarding your clothes and other possessions but it expired five minutes ago. So ... you may remain here in the company of myself and Mr Peterson while your valets pack or you can leave and await them and your luggage in Maddox Street. But the rest of the house is now off-limits to both of you – and that is quite final.'

Peterson nodded approvingly; Fallon looked as if he wanted to be elsewhere; and Basil stormed across, fists clenched, to stand toe-to-toe with Gerald.

'Who the *hell* do you think you are? You've no right to stand in our way. You're just a bloody secretary! So step aside before I *make* you.'

Gerald smiled at him and said pleasantly, 'Try it, by all means.'

For a moment or two, he thought Basil was actually going to hit him. Then, disappointingly, Eustace drawled frigidly, 'Do not indulge in a vulgar brawl, Basil. It is beneath you. And I believe we have endured sufficient incivility. We will leave. Have the carriage brought round, Fallon.'

'One moment,' said Gerald. And to Eustace, 'According to the inventory and accounts ledgers, all the vehicles currently in the mews either belonged to the late earl or have been purchased in the last four years and paid for by the earldom. You are welcome to use the phaeton to transport you to Maddox Street – where I assume your own carriages are housed – but then it should be returned here.'

'Now wait a minute!' said Basil hotly. 'The phaeton is mine and – '

'No. It is not. Have it brought to the door, Mr Fallon, and instruct the groom accordingly.' Then, when the butler hovered helplessly, glancing from one set face to another, 'Now, if you please.' And to Eustace as Fallon turned away to despatch a footman, 'I'm sorry, sir. But it is the law – is that not so, Mr Peterson?'

'It is, sir. And just the kind of … misunderstanding … we're warned to look out for.'

'Thank you.'

The next few minutes, while everyone waited for the carriage in toxic silence, seemed endless. But eventually the phaeton was at the door and Eustace and Basil stalked outside without another word. Fallon mopped his brow and Gerald released a long, relieved breath. Peterson murmured, 'Nasty situation that, sir – but you handled it very well, if you don't mind me saying.'

'Thank you. Mr Fallon ... send a footman to inform Lord Hazelmere that his house is his own again. And then go and keep an eye on the valets, if you wouldn't mind. We have no idea what orders they may have been given privately.'

* * *

Listening to the footman's excited and somewhat garbled account of the goings-on in Hazelmere House, Christian felt a weight slide from his shoulders.

He said, 'Just to be absolutely clear, John ... the bailiffs weren't needed and my uncle and cousin left of their own volition?'

'Yes, my lord. They did – though they didn't like it. Not at all, they didn't. There was one minute when we all thought Mr Basil was going to hit Mr Sandhurst – and he *would've* if his father hadn't called him off.'

'That's a shame,' remarked Benedict regretfully. 'I don't suppose Basil knows that Gerald boxed at Oxford.'

'No.' Christian sat down and dashed off yet another brief note. Then, handing it to the footman, he said, 'Tell Fallon I'll move in tomorrow if he can have my rooms ready by then. And give this to Mr Sandhurst, please.'

'Yes, my lord. We'll all be happy to have you back where you belong.'

'Thank you, John. I appreciate that.'

When the footman had gone, Benedict said, 'What have you said to Gerald?'

'Well done and join us at Sinclairs this evening. Recently, he seems to have forgotten that he's my friend as well as my secretary. It's time he was reminded.' He dropped into a chair and shoved a hand through his hair. 'He's done a sterling job. But it can't have been easy.'

Benedict laughed. 'That's an understatement. The residents of Berkeley Square must have been disappointed they didn't get to see Eustace and Basil hauled out by their collars. Come to think of it, it's something I wouldn't have minded seeing myself. However, you'll move in tomorrow ... and then what?'

'Take a few days to settle in, I suppose. Why? What do you think I should be doing?'

'You know the answer to that. First of all, break the good news to Sophia. Accept a few invitations over the next week or so; join us at White's one evening; and take your seat in the House. You needn't make a speech ... but you should show the world that the Earl of Hazelmere is back and intends to assume his responsibilities – *all* of them.' He smiled. 'You got the worst of it over last night, Kit. From this point on, everything will begin to get easier. And we can finally work out how we're going to deal with Basil.'

* * *

On the following morning, Christian wandered through Hazelmere House, noting the changes. The drawing-room and formal dining-room now boasted hand-painted Chinese wallpaper which he didn't particularly like but decided to leave for the present since it had doubtless been extortionately expensive. His bedchamber – occupied until yesterday by his uncle – was another matter. The dark red brocade hangings chosen by Eustace rendered it gloomily oppressive and would have to go.

'And until they do,' Christian informed Fallon, 'I'll sleep elsewhere.'

'Certainly, my lord. The blue suite, perhaps? It has neither been touched nor occupied during your absence.'

'Yes. That will do for the time being.'

'Very good, my lord. And with regard to your own rooms?'

'Find samples of something similar to the pale green that was here before. Nothing too heavy or ornate, please.'

'I will see to it personally.' The butler hesitated. 'And since your lordship does not currently have a valet, shall I – ?'

'No. That can wait.' Christian sought a swift change of subject and, finding one, said, 'I had a crate of items shipped here from Italy – roughly three years ago, it would have been. Did it arrive?'

'It did, sir. It was placed in your private sitting-room. But when Mr Selwyn informed me that he and Mr Basil intended to take up residence, I had it removed to the attic for safe-keeping.'

And to remove it from prying hands, thought Christian.

'Well done, Fallon. Have one of the footmen bring it down to the library, will you? I'd like to look through it.'

Fallon inclined his head. 'Will there be anything else, my lord?'

'Yes. Did my uncle send the phaeton back?'

'He did, my lord.'

'Excellent. I think I'll take a look at what else he's left in the stables.'

* * *

It was late afternoon by the time Christian opened the crate of souvenirs he'd sent home from the Grand Tour and of which he had only the haziest recollection. Now, he discovered ornate carnival masks, embroidered silk fans and small watercolours of Venetian canals; numerous sketches of the ruins of ancient Rome, a faintly ridiculous cartoon of himself wearing a toga and a plethora of other small items acquired along the way. But the bulk of the collection had been bought in Florence and consisted largely of pieces of art.

There were some nice sculptures – original but made in the Classical style – which he was pleased had survived the journey intact. Also, some dozen pictures of various sorts, most of them well-executed copies of details belonging to greater works; amongst them, Leonardo da Vinci's *Adoration of the Magi,* a self-portrait of Filippino Lippi and the *Head of Medusa* by Caravaggio. And finally, carefully wrapped in soft blue cloth, the small portrait that Christian believed was *not* a copy but the work of a lost genius and showing the exquisite face of a Renaissance Madonna which might, but for the flowing golden hair, have been Sophie.

He looked at it for a long time, tracing the line of the lady's delicate jaw with a gentle finger. He wasn't sure he could bring himself to give this away, even to Sophie herself. Not yet, anyway. But the attractively youthful Lippi self-portrait ... yes. He thought she might like that. And the masks and fans had all been purchased as gifts for her – as had the whimsical sculpture of a grinning dog which he'd hoped would make her laugh.

He laid all of these carefully aside until he had tissue in which to wrap them and could identify a good time to give them to her ... preferably when they wouldn't be interrupted by Gwendoline.

CHAPTER EIGHT

The tale of Bailiffs in Berkeley Square swept through gentlemen's clubs of St. James's like wildfire before travelling on to the drawing-rooms and ballrooms of Mayfair. To begin with at least, the story provoked more than a little laughter. Since Eustace Selwyn was known to lack a sense of humour, nothing was said to his face but he sensed the general sniggering. Basil, on the other hand, swiftly became the butt of numerous jokes and sly questions such as what he'd been caught pinching – the silver or the housemaids' bottoms?

Then, amidst the laughter, came the whispers. Why, people wondered, had Lord Hazelmere thrown his uncle and cousin out on their ears in such a cavalier fashion? Of course, it was common knowledge that the Selwyns had taken possession of his house and been spending his money; it was also obvious that they must have refused to move out when Hazelmere asked them to do so. But *bailiffs?* The young earl, it was argued by those who had known him before his lengthy absence, had never been either ruthless or vindictive ... so what had brought about this radical change? Why this bad blood between himself and his relatives? What *else* had they done?

No one asked Eustace or Basil these questions but Eustace was uneasily aware of them being whispered behind his back. Benedict, Daniel and Anthony *were* asked but they merely replied with a shrug and a remark about people letting their imagination run away with them ... or asked the questioner what they would do if somebody moved into *their* home and refused to leave?

Christian was asked only twice. After sitting through a stultifying session in the House about whether or not to grant a licence for an extension to an existing canal in Staffordshire and what, if anything, could be done to reduce the number of turnpikes on the Great North Road, a fellow member strolled out with him saying lightly, 'Bailiffs, Hazelmere? A bit extreme, perhaps, but undeniably effective.'

'A reluctant choice but a necessary one and made on the advice of my lawyer.'

'Ah. Well, I'll remember that when Great-Aunt Maud takes root or my sister brings her tribe of children for a week, then stays for six.'

Christian smiled dutifully and went on his way.

The second time was less easily dispensed with.

'I know they've been living at your expense virtually all the time you were away and that they refused to remove from Berkeley Square when you asked them to,' said Sophia. 'But once upon a time, you'd have found a – a less *public* way to be rid of them.'

'Once upon a time, I was more tolerant.'

'And now you're not? Why? What has changed?'

'I have. I thought we'd established that.'

'We did. But ...' She hesitated. 'I can't help feeling there's more to it. You were never particularly fond of Basil but I don't believe you disliked him. *Now* I think you might actually *hate* him – which is very hard to believe because, five years ago, you weren't capable of hatred. If that has changed, there must be a very good reason for it.'

Christian sighed and looked away. He wished he'd brought the assorted gifts with him as a diversion but, not being sure he'd find Sophia alone, had decided against it.

'Leave it, Sophie.'

'I can't. I'm sorry – but I can't. He did *something*, didn't he? Before you went your separate ways in Athens, perhaps? Maybe even the reason *why* you did?'

Oh God, he thought. *Stop guessing or guess wrong. Otherwise, I'm going to have to lie and make a damned good job of it.* He said repressively, 'I don't know how much more clearly I can put this ... but there are things I cannot talk about. Things I may *never* be able to talk about. This is one of them – and I would appreciate it if you could respect that.'

'I can respect it. But I'm not sure if I can accept it.'

'Since it isn't going to change, I suggest you try.'

Realising that she could either change the subject or watch him leave, she gave a reluctant nod and said, 'Will I see you at the Barrington *musicale* this evening?'

Christian's shoulders relaxed and he managed something approaching a smile.

'Is it likely?'

'Not very – although I believe that, on this occasion, there are to be a couple of professional musicians among the assorted amateurs.'

'Insufficiently tempting, I'm afraid. If someone is planning to murder Mozart tonight, I'd prefer to be far away.'

Sophia reflected that it was comforting that *some* things remained the same. Kit had always loathed badly-played music.

'What about Lady Crewe's ball on Friday?'

'Yes – though Benedict did his best to talk me out of going. Something about stale refreshments and inferior wine, I think he said.'

She laughed. 'Oh dear. When did he become so particular?'

'To be fair, it was more to do with the fact that he doesn't want to attend it himself but feels that he must if I'm going.' Christian paused, not wanting to think about how his stomach churned and his breathing malfunctioned each time he walked into a crowded social event. Then, feeling he ought to share something he *could* share in exchange for the many things he couldn't, 'In truth, these evenings are much easier for me when he or one of the others is present. But I have to start managing on my own at some point.'

'And you have. You've taken your seat in the Lords and been to some of the places gentlemen gather, such as White's and the like. But it's still early days, you know.'

'Yes. I suppose so.' Another pause and then, 'I shall probably go to Hazelmere fairly soon although, this first time, I won't make it a particularly extended visit. That can come after the end of the Season.' He smiled at her. 'So … if it's fine tomorrow, would you care to drive to Richmond Park with me?'

Her answering smile was breath-taking. 'I would love to. Thank you.'

She was so beautiful; so warm and vibrant and utterly lovely that it caused something to tighten in his chest. He thought despairingly, *I loved you so much, Sophie – so much I could scarcely contain it. Head and heart, flesh and bone. I burned for you. All the time.*

I know that. I remember it. I just can't feel it. It's lost somewhere inside me. What if I never find it? What, God help me, if it's not lost, but dead? What if I'm never going to be whole again?

Resolutely shoving the terror aside, he stood up and said, 'Then, weather permitting, I'll bring a picnic and call for you at eleven – if that will suit?'

Sophia also rose. 'It sounds perfect. I'll look forward to it.'

* * *

When he had gone, she sat staring into space for quite a long time. It had quickly become obvious that, regardless of how she felt or what she ached to do, her only viable course at present was continuing to be patient. Pushing Christian, even a little, achieved nothing and might even be harmful. Sophia sighed … and then, straightening her spine, told herself to focus on the positive things rather than the negative. There *were* some, weren't there?

Of course there were – greatest among them being that he was *here*. And little by little, he was becoming marginally less fragile, at least with her. But clearly, it was going to take time for this to extend to the world at large. For perhaps the hundredth time, she wondered what had happened to damage him in this way and whether he would ever again be quite the open, sunny-natured man he'd been five years ago. She hoped, for his sake, that he would; but if he didn't … couldn't … well, that wouldn't change how she felt. She loved him anyway. And if she had to live with his shadows, she'd do it gladly.

* * *

Basil Selwyn wasn't happy.

After two years of living in Berkeley Square, the house in Maddox Street felt cramped and its location was much less convenient. He didn't like being the target of sly jokes, innuendo and speculative gossip; he resented the ease with which society had accepted Christian and the insulting speed with which Sophia had dismissed *him*; and finally, realisation that the increased allowance to which he'd become accustomed during Christian's absence, and courtesy of his money, had ceased before he could settle several pressing debts was causing him to lose sleep. But, more than any of this, the thing that Basil was most unhappy about was the loss of his phaeton ... and when he saw Christian driving it with a radiant Sophia sitting at his side, unhappiness boiled over into the same jealous rage that had prompted his actions in Athens.

Why *should* Christian have it all? Title, position, fortune and property ... a big London house at a prestigious address ... the most beautiful woman in town, prepared to wait three damned years for him? And all, *all* of it, because Christian's father had been born a few minutes before his own? Fuming, he thought, *Hell, if that fool of a dragoman had done as he'd been told, Christian wouldn't even be here. He was supposed to have ended up chained to an oar somewhere – not living in a palace as the pet of some fat Turk.* How had *that* happened? And then, of course, Christian just *had* to have the kind of friends who'd move heaven and earth to find him and bring him back, didn't he?

The only thing that prevented all this toppling into outright disaster was that *no one* – not his father, nor Benedict Hawkridge and the rest of them and *certainly* not Christian – knew what he'd done in Athens. If they'd had any idea, they would have accused him by now; either that or Daniel Shelbourne would have slapped a glove in his face. Since neither had happened, it was safe to assume they weren't going to.

That was a relief, of course. But he wanted more than that. He wanted Christian's life to be substantially less comfortable. And he thought he knew a way to make it happen.

* * *

The sun shone in a cloudless blue sky for the excursion to Richmond. Clad in pale green figured tiffany, Sophia beamed at Christian from beneath a lacy cream parasol. He smiled back. The cornflower eyes sparkled and dusky curls clustered invitingly beneath a beribboned hat of buttermilk straw. She was still and probably always would be the loveliest woman he'd ever seen. But it was her expression ... a look that seemed to say there could be no greater pleasure in life than this one moment that played havoc with his breathing.

Smiling back, he shook his head slightly and said, 'You'll have to stop doing that.'

'Doing what?'

'Smiling that way. It's very ... distracting.'

'Well, I apologise for that but how can I help it? It's a beautiful day ... you're home again ... and I haven't been to Richmond since that time we went in Lady Heston's party. Do you remember?'

'Very well indeed. Daniel threw my hat in Penn Ponds and I ruined a pair of perfectly good boots rescuing it when the sensible thing to do, since I couldn't put it back on my head, was leave it to sink.'

She laughed. 'It was a happy day, wasn't it? And how young we were then.'

'We aren't exactly in our dotage now,' he objected. 'Merely a bit less ... flighty.'

'Speak for yourself, sir. I was *never* flighty.'

The silver gaze teased a little. 'You weren't?'

'Absolutely not.'

'Not even a tiny bit? Not even when you insisted that, if I *truly* loved you, I wouldn't condemn you to dancing an *entire* minuet with Lord Anderton?'

'Oh!' She blushed. 'I'd forgotten that.'

'*I* haven't. You could have simply refused him but – '

'I couldn't. If I had, I couldn't have danced with you.'

'But no,' went on Christian calmly. 'You smiled prettily and said yes, then cast me piteous looks from the dance floor until I risked being thrown out on my ear by cutting in. *Cutting in,* Sophie-Rose. It's not done. Gentlemen have been shot for less.'

And entirely without warning, all the love that had been stored up in her heart since she'd first met him burst over her like a tidal wave.

Sophie-Rose. She swallowed hard, wanting to cry but knowing she mustn't.

Her baptismal name was Sophia Rosalie. Sophie-Rose had been Christian's private name for her. She hadn't heard it since that day, five years ago, when he'd come to say goodbye and she'd clung to him, her face wet with tears, and tried not to make him swear he wouldn't forget her.

Controlling her voice as best she could, she said huskily, 'But you did it marvellously. Every female who saw it was green with envy, wishing she was me.'

'Really? The men just thought I'd temporarily lost my wits.' He slanted a lazy grin at her. 'They were wrong, of course. It wasn't temporary.'

She wondered if that meant what she would like it to mean ... but doubted that it did. Thus far, he hadn't touched her except in greeting or when they danced. He'd certainly shown no sign of wanting to take her in his arms or kiss her. She repressed a sigh and told herself to be grateful that he was gradually becoming increasingly relaxed when they were alone – which they were now, if one discounted the silent presence of his groom perched behind them. Of course, that easy mood could be fractured in a heartbeat if she asked a question he didn't want to answer. But it *was* progress because at balls and parties he still vibrated with tension – so she knew exactly why one or other of his friends was never far away. For possibly the hundredth time, she wondered what had done this to him ... and whether the broken part of him would ever be mended.

'Penny for them,' he said.

'What? Oh ... I was just wondering if there are any honey cakes in the picnic basket.'

Christian knew she hadn't been. He even had a fair idea of what had *really* been in her head. But, on a note of surprise, he said, 'Oh. You still like those, do you?'

'Very much. *Are* there some?'

'I've no idea. I left it up to Cook.'

There were a number of carriages and small groups of people already dotted around the park, so Christian drove until they reached a quiet spot, well away from other visitors and the deer peacefully grazing under the trees. Then, while the groom hefted the basket down, he spread a large tartan blanket on the grass for Sophia to sit upon and unlatched the basket for her.

'All yours,' he said, tossing his hat aside. And to the groom, 'Find a shady spot for yourself and the horses, Jim. Your own picnic should contain a couple of bottles of ale, amongst other things.'

'Thank you, my lord. That'd be very welcome.'

Meanwhile, just as he'd expected, Sophia was taking an inventory.

There were dainty sandwiches with three different sorts of filling, prawn and crab patties in flaky, golden pastry and slices of tender cold chicken. Next came bowls of fruit salad, little iced fancies, generous slices of fruit cake and bottles of wine and lemonade. And finally, hidden at the very bottom of the basket, a box of honey cakes.

She looked up at him and shook her head accusingly.

'That was wicked of you. I actually thought you'd forgotten.'

'Would I dare?' He hesitated briefly and then said, 'Would you mind if I removed my coat?'

'Don't be silly. Of course I wouldn't.'

'Thank you.' Having laid his coat beside his hat, he busied himself opening a bottle of wine and, seeing Sophie take out one of the cakes, 'Are you really going to start with one of those?'

She nodded, took a bite and sighed with pleasure. Then, swallowing, 'You still have the same cook. Hers were always the very best ones and they still are.'

'We aim to please.'

Christian poured two glasses of wine, waited until Sophia finished the last bite of her cake and then handed her one of them. 'Your very good health, Miss Kelsall.'

'And yours, my lord.' She took a sip and grimaced. 'I'd forgotten. Wine and honey cakes don't agree with each other.'

'They don't. But you just couldn't resist, could you?'

'No. And you knew I wouldn't.'

'I did.'

'You could have *reminded* me the wine would taste horrid.'

'Would that have stopped you eating the cake?'

'N-no,' she admitted on a gurgle of laughter.

'No,' he agreed. 'I rest my case.'

Answering laughter warmed his eyes and the sun burnished his hair. He was as sinfully handsome as he'd always been ... and, for the first time, they were talking to each other as they used to do. Without warning, tears clogged her throat and spilled over her lashes and, before she could stop herself, all the words she'd forbidden herself to say came tumbling out.

'I missed you – and missed you and *m-missed* you! Every day, every hour – all the time and so *much*. It was bearable while you were making the Tour because I had your letters. But afterwards ... afterwards, I had *nothing*. There was a great black space inside me and all around me that grew and grew and never went away. Nothing had any meaning or any p-point. Some days I just didn't want to get out of bed. When I began to think I might never see you again, I wanted ... I wanted – ' She stopped abruptly and, instead of finishing the sentence, hauled in a shuddering breath. 'And then, without any warning – just when I'd finally given up hope – you appeared from nowhere, smiled politely and said *Sorry I'm late.* And I w-wanted to *hit* you.'

'You should have done. No one would have blamed you. Certainly not I.'

But she shook her head, stemmed the flow with her hands and through them, mumbled, 'I'm sorry. I ought not to have said any of that – it was foolish of me. I know it was w-worse for you.'

Throughout her brief outburst, Christian sat like a stone feeling something carving a hole in his chest. He knew what he should do but wasn't sure he could do it. Then, telling himself not to be so feeble, he crossed the blanket and took her in his arms. As soon as he touched her, she turned and burrowed into his chest, one hand clutching his upper arm through his shirt-sleeve. He said simply, 'Don't apologise to me, Sophie. I'm the one who should be sorry – and I am, believe me. This whole debacle would have been avoided if I'd just turned back after Athens. But I didn't ... and we've both had to live with the consequences.'

Her voice muffled against his throat, she said, 'You couldn't have known.'

'No. I couldn't. But that doesn't make it better. You've every right to be angry – and you should be.'

'There were times when I was,' she confessed. 'Times when I wanted to smash something – *anything* – just to let the anger out. I even tried it once. It didn't help.'

'It never does.' She stirred in his arms as if about to look up at him. Knowing his current expression wouldn't do anything to comfort her, he rested his chin on her hair and said, 'I'd guess there were also days when you hated me.'

'Hated you? No. How could I when I knew something very wrong must have happened to stop you coming home? I never hated *you*. I saved that for those who wouldn't let us be together and separated us so completely. My parents, your uncle – '

'Eustace?' he said sharply. 'What had he to do with it?'

'It was all his idea – you making the Grand Tour, Papa allowing an informal betrothal if you went. All of it. You didn't know?'

'No. No, I didn't.' His arms fell away from her and he thought, *God damn him for interfering.* 'I should have guessed, though.'

She moved away a little and turned, flushed, tear-stained and apparently searching for a handkerchief. 'Why?'

Handing her his own, he said, 'I'd decided against making the Tour. Eustace was pressing me to change my mind because it would mean that Basil could make it with me at little or no cost to them. Had your father not made it a condition of matters between us, I'll *still* have refused to go and Eustace knew it – which accounts for him approaching your parents. If I'd known about that ... but I didn't. I didn't and I just clung to the thought that, if doing what they wanted was the price of us being allowed to marry eventually, it would be worth it.'

Sophia eyed him gravely.

'And it would have been. As perhaps it still *can* be, if we wish it. But that's for the future. There's no hurry to decide.' She picked up the nearest packet of food and offered it to him. 'Have a sandwich. I think these ones are ham.'

He made no move to take it and his mouth twisted wryly.

'Don't think I don't appreciate you making allowances for me – I do. But you'd better stop doing so before I start relying on it and taking advantage.'

She smiled at him and shook her head.

'Have a sandwich. And pour me more wine. I spilled the first glass on your arm.'

'I know.' He held out his sodden shirt cuff. 'I wasn't going to mention it.'

'*Now* who's making allowances?'

'A gentleman is supposed to.' Smiling faintly, he picked up her glass and reached for the bottle. 'And ladies are *permitted* to take advantage.'

'So they say.' She sighed. 'Forgive me for spoiling the afternoon.'

'You haven't spoiled it, Sophie-Rose. Far from it. I suspect that conversation was long overdue ... but that I'd probably have lacked the courage to begin it. So thank you for doing it for me.' He took her hand and lifted it to his lips before handing her the glass. And once again in his former tone, 'Now drink that instead of watering me with it and tell me I may have my usual two dances at the Crewe assembly.'

CHAPTER NINE

The Crewe assembly was little different from any other event of its type. The only thing which distinguished it for Christian was that, for the first time since he'd banished them from Berkeley Square, he came face to face with his uncle and cousin.

He met Eustace first in the doorway to the card room. It was possibly the worst place for the encounter to take place since one of them had to give way to the other and, with so many eyes upon them, some conversation – however awkward – had to be attempted.

Inwardly groaning, Christian bowed slightly. 'Uncle.'

'Christian.' Eustace stood quite still, eyeing him coldly. 'Due to your recent iniquitous treatment of us, it was my impression that you had forgotten we were family. Has your memory – and perhaps also your conscience – returned?'

'Both have always been in perfect working order. There need not have been any unpleasantness had you not made it necessary. I assure you that making our differences public was the last thing I wanted.'

'Prior to this, I was not aware that we *had* differences. Perhaps you'd like to enlighten me as to what they are?'

'Other than your free use of the earldom's resources and your refusal to surrender my house, you mean?' asked Christian. And thought, *Do you know your son tried to get rid of me permanently? Has he told you? Or are you hiding from the truth by not asking him?* Then, 'Isn't that enough? Or am I missing something?'

'Such as what?'

'I have no idea. That's why I asked.'

'This is a singularly foolish conversation – though I am hardly surprised. You re-appear out of the blue after three years and virtually the first thing you say to me is that Basil and I are to remove from Berkeley Square. Why? Why *that?*'

'I suppose because I wanted to have my house to myself – as is my right.' Christian shrugged slightly. 'I believe we've convinced any interested parties that we are still on speaking terms, Uncle. And now you must excuse me. I'm promised to Lizzie Wendover for the next set.' And with another polite nod, he walked away.

Whilst dancing the quadrille with Sophia, Benedict had managed to keep a weather eye on Christian's seemingly civil exchange with Eustace and, seeing him stroll away, decided there was no cause for concern. Then, as the dance brought them together, Sophia hissed, 'Basil's here. He's just come in with those two fatuous friends of his.'

Hell, thought Benedict. But he said rapidly, 'It was bound to happen sooner or later. And he can't make a scene here.'

'No? And what about Kit?'

He shot her a very sharp glance before the figure parted them again and thought, *Why did she say that? Has Kit told her? Or no. Of course he hasn't.*

The dance ended. He bowed, she curtsied and he said, 'Look. Kit's about to take to the floor with Anthony's sister – the youngest of them, I think.'

'You *think*? You don't know?'

'No. There are four of them and I never remember which one is which.' He shrugged. 'Dreadful of me, I know. However, the point I was about to make is that nothing can happen while Kit is dancing. So, if you are not engaged for this set, may I – ' He stopped, seeing his brother bearing down on them. 'Or not. Good evening, Oscar.'

His lordship nodded. 'Ben. Miss Kelsall ... may I beg your hand for the gavotte?'

Resisting the impulse to cast a glance at Benedict, Sophia smiled.

'Thank you, my lord. I'd be delighted.'

'Excellent,' muttered Benedict. And to Sophia, 'Don't worry. I'll take care of it.'

Watching him stalk away, Oscar said, 'He'll take care of what?'

'Nothing of any consequence,' she replied lightly. 'Shall we take our places?'

Since Christian had been sitting beside Anthony's little sister with his back to the entrance to the ballroom, he wasn't aware of his cousin's arrival. And Basil didn't see *him* until the quadrille ended and some people left the floor while others took their places upon it for the next set.

He still might not have immediately noticed Christian had not one of his friends said, 'Oh I say! Ain't that your cousin over there with the latest Wendover chit?'

Basil looked – and froze. 'Yes. So it is.'

'Bit awkward for you to meet him, I daresay,' remarked the other. 'All that bailiff business must've left a nasty taste, what?'

'Very nasty,' agreed Basil. 'But the embarrassment is all on his side. He didn't have any reason to behave the way he did. And *why*, I ask you, is he so set on living alone but for servants?' He shook his head. 'One can't help wondering if there isn't more to what went on while he was in that Turkish palace than he wants anybody to know.'

Both gentlemen nodded wisely. One said, 'Got a theory, Basil?'

'Several, Fred. But I'll keep them to myself for now.'

'I'd go on doing that permanently, if I were you,' said a voice from behind him.

Basil wheeled round to meet a faintly threatening smile. He snapped, 'Didn't anybody teach you it's rude to listen to other people's conversations, Shelbourne?'

'Didn't anyone teach *you* the one about people in glass houses not throwing stones?'

'What the hell is that supposed to mean?'

'It means that tossing distasteful insinuations about with nothing upon which to base them is unwise at the best of times; and downright risky if one has a skeleton or two in one's own closet.' The smile grew. 'Just a thought.' And he strolled away to meet Benedict.

'What was that about?' asked his lordship.

'He was heading towards the implication that Kit did more than perfect Ibrahim's English accent … so I fired a warning shot across his bows. He really is an unpleasant little rodent, isn't he?'

'Yes. And at some point this evening, he and Kit will run into each other. We can't prevent it – but we may need to intervene if it shows signs of getting ugly.'

'They're hardly likely to come to blows, are they? Basil is a coward; and, much though Kit might *like* to beat him to a pulp, he won't do it. Not here, anyway.'

'Not at *all*, I hope. We need a better way – speaking of which, we should get together and formulate a plan before he goes to Hazelmere next week.'

'Fine. Tomorrow at White's?'

'Tomorrow, yes … but somewhere private. Hazelmere House, perhaps – since Kit and Gerald are already there. Tell Anthony, will you? And when the gavotte finishes, I'll arrange it with Kit.'

Christian's dance with Elizabeth Wendover had been surprisingly enjoyable. She was a lively girl and, at every opportunity, she chattered about how much fun her first Season had been thus far. Spared the need to make any conversation of his own, he listened and smiled and nodded … then he restored her to one of Anthony's numerous aunts and was about to go in search of a glass of wine when Benedict emerged at his side, saying bluntly, 'I saw you speaking to Eustace earlier. Basil's here as well now.'

'Lovely,' sighed Christian. 'But I'll avoid him if he'll avoid me.'

'I doubt if he will.'

'So do I, unfortunately.'

'He'll try to provoke you. And – '

'He doesn't have to *try*. The effrontery of looking me in the eye is enough.'

'And he's with Thetford and Bartlett so he'll likely show off in front of them. But that isn't what I wanted to say. Daniel and I are agreed that it's time we planned our strategy. Can we hold a council of war at your house tomorrow?'

'By all means. Come for dinner if you aren't otherwise engaged.'

'I am but it's nothing I can't cancel.' Benedict was aware of Christian's eyes travelling beyond him to the dance floor where Sophia was laughing up at Oscar. He said, 'If you and Sophie intend to make a match of it, is there any chance you could get around to it before my brother is *completely* besotted?'

Something shifted inside Christian's chest. He said, 'Is he?'

'Not yet, perhaps – but heading in the general direction. However, it's *you* I was asking about. Well?'

'I ... don't know. I believe Sophie *thinks* she still feels the same but – '

'Don't be an idiot, Kit. Of course she feels the same. It's written on her face every time she looks at you.'

'But she has no idea how near the edge I am at times and how much effort it takes not to topple over it.'

'I think she sees a lot more than you realise,' said Benedict flatly. 'What she *doesn't* know is how *you* feel about *her*.'

'Neither do I – not really,' Christian muttered. 'When I'm with her, there's calm and peace that's missing the rest of the time. But that's not enough, is it? There ought to be much, much more. And there used to be. But I can't find it.' He stopped, then said abruptly, 'I can't talk about this now – knowing I'm going to have to speak to bloody Basil without putting my hands around his throat. Sort out tomorrow evening with Dan and Anthony. I'm going to get a drink.'

He met Sebastian Wingham on the same errand and managed a few minutes of idle chat until the viscount returned to the ballroom. Then, alone for a few moments, all the reasons he held back from marrying Sophia ... the things he couldn't, *wouldn't* tell his friends ... flowed through his mind. Nightmares, like the one Benedict had unfortunately witnessed and from which he still occasionally awoke, sweating; flashbacks – such as yesterday when the catch on his bedchamber door had somehow stuck and, for a minute or two, he'd been back in Tekirdağ, behind a locked door with guards on the other side of it; and the constant gnawing anxiety along with the so far secret howl that still lived inside him. His friends, he knew, were already thinking in terms of *Before* Tekirdağ and *After* it. But for him there *was* no after and he wasn't sure there ever would be. There was only *before* and *now*. And then there were the things they didn't know about and never would if he could help it. His complete lack of sexual appetite and the question of how on earth he could ever take a wife when he couldn't bring himself to engage a damned valet?

In the ballroom, the gavotte ended and was replaced by something else. The one after that would be the supper dance. Christian drained a second glass of wine and went to look for Sophia. She was on the far side of the room amidst a little group of other ladies and gentlemen, one of whom was Oscar Hawkridge. Christian wondered if Benedict was right about his brother. If he was, it couldn't be denied that Oscar would make Sophia a much better husband than he himself would. He investigated that thought ... and realised it hurt.

'Hatching *more* plans for how best to insult Father and me, are you?'

He turned slowly, knowing who he would see and emptying his face of expression in preparation for it. 'No, Baz. Oddly enough, neither of you are that important to me.' His gaze drifted past his cousin to Messrs Thetford and Bartlett ... two fellows who could usually be relied upon to get drunk and make a spectacle of themselves. 'I see you brought the resident clowns with you. It's nice that someone finds them amusing.'

'Now see here!' burst out Bartlett. 'Who do you think you are?'

'I'm quite certain I'm the Earl of Hazelmere. And unlike Baz here, I *don't* find you amusing. So why don't you go and annoy someone else?'

'Mind your mouth, Kit! These gentlemen are my friends and – '

'Congratulations, Baz ... though our definitions of the word *gentlemen* appear to differ somewhat.'

'I'll not be spoken to like that!' Mr Thetford took a hasty step forward and an even hastier one back when Christian detached himself from the wall. 'Apologise, sir.'

'Or what?' asked Christian lazily. 'On second thoughts, I don't want to know. Baz ... if you've got something to say to me, I suggest you get rid of them ... unless you're uncomfortable facing me on your own? Are you?'

'No, damn you!' White with temper and wishing he hadn't delayed putting his plans to throw Christian's charmed life into disarray when he'd first thought of them, Basil turned to his friends, saying, 'You don't have to put up with this and it need not take long. I'll join you in the card room presently.'

'Sure you don't want us to stay, Basil?' asked Mr Bartlett uneasily.

'Perfectly sure. Just go, will you?' And furiously to Christian, as they walked away, 'Do you *have* to be so damned rude?'

'Yes. You can tolerate them if you choose to – but I don't have to.' He went back to leaning against the wall, arms folded across his chest in an attitude of bored patience. 'So Baz ... what is it you wanted to say to me?'

'I want to know what the *hell* is the matter with you! You're treating Father and me as if we've done something terrible to you when you know perfectly well we haven't.'

'Do I?'

'Oh, for God's sake! Just spit it out, will you?' And when Christian said nothing but continued to regard him with a faintly taunting expression, 'What *is* this injury we've supposedly done you?'

'Have I said there was one?'

'You haven't *said* anything. But you're behaving as if we've committed a mortal sin and we've no idea why.'

'Why don't you take a wild guess?'

'I can't.'

'Nothing springs to mind?'

'*No*, I tell you.' Basil drew an unsteady breath. 'Unless ... are you blaming me for what happened in Turkey? Because if it's *that*, you're completely insane.' He ticked off points on his fingers. 'I *warned* you going to Constantinople could be risky. I urged you *not* to go – but did you listen? No. I sent men to look for you when you didn't turn up in Palermo; and Father sent others as soon as he knew you were missing. So how is any of whatever happened to you *our* fault?'

'I haven't suggested that it was, Baz. *You* are the one who thinks it might be. Why is that, I wonder?'

'You asked me to take a guess. Far-fetched as it is, that's all I can come up with. And stop calling me Baz, will you?'

Christian summoned an annoying smile whilst mentally marvelling at Basil's quite incredible certainty that his treachery remained a secret.

Can he really be so sure of my ignorance? he thought. *Doesn't he ever consider the possibility that I found out somehow... or wake in the middle of the night, wondering?*

He said, 'You are clinging to the assumption that I believe you've wronged me. Some people might think that a sign of a guilty conscience.'

'My conscience is completely clear, thank you.'

'Really? Good for you. There aren't many men who can say that. But as you are so determined to protest your innocence ... let's try this. Since my return, I've obviously learned how you and Uncle have been living in my absence. It has made me wonder just how hard you tried to find me.'

'That's monstrous!' blustered Basil.

'Is it? You can't deny it would have been convenient for you if I was never found.'

'No. We did everything we could, damn it!'

'Did you?' Christian's smile was far from comforting. 'Perhaps I ought to mention that the search party sent by my friends heard no word of any previous searchers.'

'*What?*'

'And when Daniel and Anthony went to the Consulate, no one there recalled other similar enquiries having been made.'

'That can't be true.'

'But it apparently is. Odd, isn't it?' Finally abandoning his lazy stance by the wall, Christian said, 'I think this conversation has reached its natural conclusion ... and the current set is also coming to an end, so you'll have to excuse me. I'm promised to Sophie for the supper dance and am looking forward to it. But this has been fun, Baz. We must do it again some time.'

And he strolled away, aware of his cousin's eyes like knives in his back.

He told himself that, all things considered, he'd handled the conversation tolerably well. He'd feel happier about that if it hadn't left him wanting to go somewhere he could throw up.

Sophia took one look at his expression and asked what Basil had said.

'Exactly what I might have predicted.'

'Which was?'

'That I'm treating him and my uncle unfairly on account of some imagined offence.' He smiled at her. 'Forget him, Sophie – at least for now – and let us enjoy our dance.'

Recognising that he was closing the subject, she nodded and said cheerfully, 'That won't be difficult. I always enjoy dancing with you.'

'That is ... very flattering.'

'No. It's the truth.' She flashed him a wicked sideways glance. 'Don't you know that you're the favourite partner of nearly every lady you've ever danced with?'

'No,' he said slowly. 'I didn't know that ... and find it a touch hard to believe.'

'It's true. Many gentlemen dance well, of course. But few are as graceful as you.'

Christian winced. 'Graceful? You'll forgive me if I say that creates the sort of image that I, in common with most men, would rather not have applied to myself?'

'What do you mean?'

'It makes me sound like a – a mincing fop.'

Sophie gave a gurgle of laughter. 'Don't be absurd. You aren't anything like that. But if you don't like graceful, would elegant be better?'

'Very much so.' The music began and he added, 'Behold my elegant bow.'

'And my infinitely graceful curtsy,' she retorted. 'But if you think there aren't any number of ladies envying me right now, you are utterly mistaken.'

He lifted one eyebrow. 'Having the last word, Sophie-Rose?'

'Every chance I get,' she agreed.

And it was Christian's turn to laugh.

* * *

On the following evening, five gentlemen chatted on numerous topics while they enjoyed a simple but excellent dinner ... and then, when they had settled in the comfort of the library with brandy and port, Benedict said, 'Are you going to tell us what Basil had to say last evening, Kit? And, more to the point, what you said to him?'

'He's very sure of himself. It doesn't seem to ever have occurred to him that I might *know*. So I decided to shake his confidence just a little. I told him that your enquiries hadn't found any trace of the ones he and his father had reputedly made – and no one at the Consulate had previously been asked the questions you did.'

Anthony gave a low whistle. 'That should stir things up a bit.'

'I hope so. If we can knock him off-balance, he may make mistakes.'

'That's all well and good,' remarked Daniel, 'but we can't sit about waiting for him to do that. Last night he was half-way to hinting that you'd been providing Ibrahim with ... let's call them personal services. I nipped it in the bud, of course, but there's no guarantee he won't whisper it elsewhere.'

There was a brief silence. Then, with grim reluctance, Benedict said, 'If he does that and we're *sure* he has, you may have to consider direct action, Kit.'

'Perhaps. But tonight is about devising a scheme to expose him. So let's get on with it, shall we? Remind us of the ideas that were put forward last time, Gerald.'

Mr Sandhurst flipped open his note-book. 'I wasn't there but here's the gist of what I was told. Daniel wants to break a few of Basil's bones until he confesses.'

'The offer still stands,' muttered Daniel.

'We know,' said Christian, 'and have already shelved that idea. Go on, Gerald.'

'Anthony suggested that, since we already know what Basil did and you can testify to it, you could take him to law. But you refused to consider it.'

'And despite the bailiffs, I still won't. What else?'

'Nothing.' Gerald dropped the notebook on the table. 'That's it. Clearly, I didn't miss much.'

'Pitiful,' said Daniel. 'We have to do better than that.'

'Quite,' agreed Anthony. 'But I recall also raising the idea of finding a way to make Basil betray himself.'

Gerald looked sharply across at him.

'Nobody mentioned that. And it's the best notion so far. Difficult, yes – but with the advantage of at least *appearing* to keep our hands clean. There's a lot to be said for that.'

'True.' Benedict glanced around the table. 'So let us explore that and see what we can come up with. Who would like to start?'

Everyone looked at everyone else. No one spoke.

When several minutes had ticked by in silence, Gerald said mildly, 'Shall we try again? Since we have nothing, *any* idea – no matter how wild – is worth considering at this stage. So let's have them.'

They spent the next hour tossing increasingly bizarre ideas around and then shooting them down. Daniel, for example, was in favour of haunting Basil with what he called the Spirit of Retribution.

'We can hire an actor to rant outside his house and follow him about, clanking chains and declaiming that *The End is Nigh* and *All Thy Sins Shall Find Thee Out*. That sort of thing, anyway.'

'And what will that achieve?' Benedict asked. 'Aside from annoying the neighbours?'

'Nothing probably. But it would be fun.'

A handful of other similar scenarios were proposed and also summarily dismissed. Then Anthony suggested writing a short pamphlet, telling the story of Basil's betrayal.

'We change the names and the locations, of course, leaving people to guess what it's really about. Once a few have worked it out, gossip and rumour will – '

'*No!*' snapped Christian. 'That would be as bad as taking Basil to court. It can't be done without mentioning slavers and slavery and all the things I will *not* have made public at any price. How many more times must I say it?'

'None,' sighed Anthony. 'I'm sorry. That was about as sensible as Dan's Spirit of Retribution, wasn't it?'

They all fell silent again.

But finally Gerald said slowly, 'You don't have to *actually* take Basil to court, Christian. You just have to make him *think* you will ... and give the impression you are confident of getting a conviction.'

'And how, exactly, do I do that?'

'Exactly? I don't know. Perhaps by planting the idea that we've acquired a piece of evidence concerning your disappearance? Something featuring his name ... which you might make public?'

'Go on,' invited Benedict. 'And then?'

Gerald shrugged. 'And then we wait to see what he does.'

'If he's got an ounce of sense,' snorted Daniel, 'what he *does* is get as far away as he can, as *fast* as he can.'

'Maybe. Or maybe not.' Benedict considered this. 'I don't see him abandoning everything to flee abroad.'

'What, then?' asked Christian moodily.

'I don't know. I'm not pretending to have all the answers any more than Gerald is. But Basil is a slippery coward ... so he's more likely to look for a way out that leaves him safe with his life and reputation intact, than he is to run.'

'I agree,' said Anthony. 'So ... what other options does he have?'

'Only one that I can see.' Daniel grinned sourly. 'He tries to steal the evidence.'

This produced another abrupt silence which was eventually broken by Anthony saying doubtfully, '*Would* he?'

Gerald nodded. 'He might, I suppose – if he believes it's sufficiently incriminating. He'd almost certainly be pushed into doing *something*.'

Everyone thought about this. Then, 'If he could be lured into showing his hand ...' mused Benedict. 'If, for example, he were to attempt theft and *if* we could catch him in the act ... '

'We'd have him,' finished Daniel with immense satisfaction. 'Good. Now we're getting somewhere. So what is this evidence? And how do we let Basil know we have it without actually *telling* him?'

'One thing at a time.' Gerald thought for a moment, then said, 'Do we have anything from the Consulate, by any chance? I'm talking about something written on their official notepaper.'

Anthony nodded. 'I'm fairly sure I still have a note confirming our appointment with the Consul. Why?'

'As I see it, the 'evidence' can only have come from the Consulate. There's no other source, is there? So we begin with a printer who can run us off a dozen sheets, blank except for the Consulate heading. Once we have that, we can decide what to write on it. Unless anyone already has a suggestion?'

Silence fell again as they all thought about this. Then, 'The dragoman,' said Christian abruptly. 'Somehow or other, the Consulate found him and – '

'And squeezed the truth out of him!' cut in Daniel, triumphantly. '*Yes!*'

'Let Kit finish, will you?' sighed Benedict. And to Christian, 'Go on.'

Frowning down at his hands, Christian said slowly, 'We forge a letter from the Consulate informing me that, shortly after I left Turkey, they found the dragoman and, as Daniel says, squeezed the truth out of him. His confession can be the truth as we know it. What Basil's orders *actually* were – and how the slave-master altered them in pursuit of greater profit. That should do the trick, don't you think?'

'Undoubtedly.' Benedict eyed Christian meditatively. 'And for the sake of a little additional authenticity, two letters. One in Turkish and the other an English translation of it. ... assuming you can write Turkish as well as speak it, Kit?'

Christian grimaced. 'Do you know what you're asking? The Turkish language is written in Persian-Arabic characters. It's an art form in itself.'

'Are you saying you can't do it?'

'No. I can't do it well enough to convince an educated Turk ... but it would be good enough to fool Basil.'

'Then we have the germ of a plan. We can figure out the details while we get the preparations in place.' Benedict rose and walked around re-filling everyone's glass. 'An excellent night's work, gentlemen. Here's to bringing down Basil.'

'Bringing down Basil,' echoed four of them, raising their glasses.

Christian said nothing and stared sightlessly into his brandy.

CHAPTER TEN

Still intending to leave for Hazelmere with Gerald in two days' time, Christian spent the following morning forging a letter from the Consulate, giving precise details of what Mr Basil Selwyn had paid the dragoman to do. He composed it in English, then he set about translating it into formal Turkish, while appreciating the irony of Basil's perfidy resulting in a skill which would hopefully lead to his downfall. And finally, when he was satisfied that both said everything necessary and that the Turkish version was as accurate as he could make it, he had a footman deliver them to Benedict's lodging – which was to be their headquarters while he and Gerald were away.

Daniel, meanwhile, would seek out a printer willing and able to duplicate the Consulate letter-headed paper and once they had that, either Benedict or Anthony could copy out the English letter – which couldn't be in Christian's handwriting because Basil would recognise it. As for the Turkish letter, since Christian was the only one capable of transcribing it, that would have to wait until he was back in London. How they were to leak the information to Basil that new evidence had arisen, Christian had no idea ... but he hoped that the others would have come up with a solution by the time he returned.

This task behind him, he rose, stretched his cramped muscles and asked Fallon to have the phaeton brought round. On the previous evening, he had promised to take Sophia driving in the park as it might be his last chance to see her before he left. He wondered if Oscar Hawkridge would make good use of his absence ... if Sophia would perhaps *like* him to do so. Then he told himself he had no business wondering that – nor would he have unless he either renewed his proposal of marriage or set her free. If he was afraid to face marriage itself ... if he was still humiliatingly doubtful about his ability to be a proper husband ... he *ought* to set her free. He knew that. It was unfair of him not to do so and there was a definite limit to how long they could continue with what looked like a courtship but didn't culminate in an announcement. The trouble was, he didn't *want* to give her up. Losing her would be like losing yet another bit of himself ... and he was sufficiently incomplete already, often still feeling like a mere shadow of himself.

When the butler let him in, he'd hoped to find Sophia waiting. He didn't. Instead, Lady Kelsall looked down on him from the turn of the stair and said, 'Lord Hazelmere. A word with you, if I may.'

Since he didn't appear to have a choice, he said, 'Of course, ma'am.' And followed her into the small, rarely used back parlour, fairly sure he knew what she wanted to say.

As usual, she came straight to the point.

'In the weeks since your return, you have spent a substantial amount of time with Sophia – a good deal of it, alone. I have permitted this because of the unusual circumstances. But it cannot go on indefinitely, my lord.'

'I realise that.'

'I'm delighted to hear it. Now ... I understand that you are about to leave for Oxfordshire. Is that correct?'

'Yes. But this visit will not be a long one. There are matters requiring my attention in London.'

'One of them being your relationship with my daughter, I hope.'

'Naturally.' Despite feeling his muscles growing taut, Christian decided to be both honest and blunt. He said, 'It is not as straightforward a matter as your ladyship may think. In a number of respects, I am not the man I was five years ago and some of the changes are not for the better. Sophie needs to understand and come to terms with that before making a lifetime commitment.'

'Oh *please!*' replied Lady Kelsall derisively. 'Do you think I am simple? It is not *Sophia* who hangs back but *you*, sir. And I am running out of patience.'

'Are you? That is unfortunate, of course ... but of small importance in the general scheme of things.'

She stared at him as if he'd grown a second head.

'I begin to see what you mean about changes that are not an improvement, Lord Hazelmere. You used to have better manners.'

Many things about me used to be better, he thought. But said, 'So I did. However, you have been exceedingly direct, have you not, ma'am? And these days I find myself inclined to respond to that kind of thing in like manner. So now ... if there's nothing else, I will go and await Sophie in the hall.'

And with a slight – a *very* slight – bow, he left her standing mute.

Sophia was already waiting for him. One look at his face told her everything she needed to know and, huffing an irritable breath, she said, 'Don't tell me – I can guess. Shall we go?'

'By all means,' said Christian, offering his arm. 'Hyde Park or St. James's?'

'The latter, please. We'll meet less people there.'

Once settled in the carriage, she said quietly, 'I'm sorry. Recently, she has taken to muttering more than usual but I didn't think she'd go so far as to ambush you.'

'I doubt she'll do it again. I wasn't completely rude ... but not entirely polite either.' He slanted a quick smile at her. 'I left her standing there open-mouthed.'

'*Did* you? Well done!'

'Thank you. But it *wasn't* well done of me, not really. She informed me that I used to have better manners – and she wasn't wrong. But it may have served to convince her that, though I may *look* the same, I'm not.'

'Perhaps.' Sophia thought for a moment. 'Are you still going to Hazelmere on Friday?'

'Yes. And tomorrow, I have meetings with the bank and my lawyer – between which I have to interview three valets, one of whom Fallon is determined to foist upon me.'

She blinked. 'You don't have a valet?'

'No. My previous man was dismissed when he refused to valet Basil and is now happily employed elsewhere. So far, I've managed well enough without ... but Fallon insists that a valet is essential to the dignity and prestige of the household.'

'He can't *really* think that, can he?'

'He says he does. But mostly he feels that my consequence – by which he means that of the earldom – demands a valet and he's impatient with my lack of haste in the matter.'

'You'd prefer to do without one?' she asked, sounding faintly baffled.

Very much so, he thought. And, shrugging, 'I don't mind either way. But Fallon is like water dripping on a stone ... and I've reached the point of thinking it easier to give in than continue to endure the alternative.'

'You're saying you aren't master in your own house?' teased Sophia.

'Yes. And I'm not alone, in that. Benedict's valet rules him with a rod of iron. And Anthony is terrified of his housekeeper.'

She laughed. 'Is there a martinet lying in wait for you at Hazelmere?'

'Not that I recall. However, speaking of that – I don't plan to be away more than a week. I just want to confer with my steward, ride around the estate and satisfy myself that everything is in order in the house and elsewhere. Gerald says that it is, of course. But, after being away for so long, the place deserves my attention and I want to assure the tenants and villagers that, at the end of the Season, they shall have it in full throughout the autumn and winter.'

Sophia looked down at her hands, no longer laughing.

'I'm sure that everyone there will be very pleased to hear that.'

Realising what she must be thinking, Christian said, 'I do understand what it means to us, Sophie. I didn't need your mother to remind me that our personal situation needs to be resolved before Parliament goes into recess. For the moment, however, I'd prefer to continue as we are – if that would be acceptable to you?' He hesitated before adding awkwardly, 'I'll understand if you say it isn't. I'm aware that Oscar Hawkridge is paying you marked attention ... and might go further than that if I were no longer in the picture.'

'I doubt it.' Despite feeling her cheeks grow hot, she said what she knew *had* to be said – although she'd have preferred not to do so quite yet. 'But even if you are right, Lord Oscar need not concern you. Nor any other gentleman, for that matter.'

'Oh.' The words and what they signified caught him unawares. For a moment or two they made him wish he had enough courage and faith in himself to respond to them as she deserved. But he couldn't. And it wasn't just his own self-doubt standing in the way. He was deliberately keeping her ignorant of what his friends regarded as a quest for justice but which, in the privacy of his head, Christian called by its proper name. Vengeance.

Realising he'd been silent for too long, he said awkwardly, 'Right. Well, then ... I'd be grateful if you could be patient with me just a little longer. There's something else that I need to deal with – but as yet, I can't tell you more than that. Later I will, but not yet. *Can* you give me a few more weeks?'

It was Sophia's turn to take her time about answering. Finally, she said quietly, 'No.'

'No?' he echoed, startled. 'Oh.'

'No, I won't give you time to deal with matters you can't or won't share with me but which are plainly more important than us.' She paused, holding his gaze with her own. 'But I'll give you as much time as you need in order to be sure about whether you and I have a future together. Or not. *Completely* sure, Kit. Anything else is unthinkable.'

* * *

Later, alone in her room, Sophie sat staring into space.

Unthinkable, she had said. And it was. No matter how much she wanted to, she couldn't marry Christian while his feelings towards her remained uncertain. If she did, he'd try to keep up a pretence for her sake because the inherent kindness and decency he thought lost still existed deep inside him. But she would know; and bit by bit, day by day, she'd shrivel a little more.

She wished he hadn't said what he had about Lord Oscar. Where had that idea come from? His own observation? Or was it something Benedict had told him; a well-meaning attempt to nudge Christian in what he felt was the right direction? If it *was* that, she wished he hadn't done it because it had left her with no choice but to squash it. There was already too much conflict going on inside Christian's head, without the added pressure of thinking he was in competition with the good looking, uncomplicated brother of a duke. Unfortunately, however, telling him in no uncertain terms that he had no rivals had also told him that that her heart was his – and always would be. And that applied pressure of a different sort.

She wondered vaguely what the other issue he'd spoken of was and why he didn't want her to know about it, then pushed the thought aside as irrelevant because she doubted it was the real reason Christian was still unable to commit himself to her. Perhaps the week at Hazelmere would do him good; perhaps is would clear his head and he'd come back feeling more positive. She hoped so. Keeping her vast ocean of love safely behind the mental dam she'd erected ... denying herself physical expression of it and never asking him for any was becoming increasingly difficult. She forbade herself to dwell on how badly she wanted him to kiss her and how much it hurt that he hadn't. And she tried not to wonder if she was hoping for the impossible; that all he felt for her now was mere fondness ... that he no longer *wanted* her at all.

* * *

Back at his desk in the library, Christian gave up trying to concentrate on the small pile of correspondence Gerald had left for him to deal with. He pushed it aside, accepting that his mind was elsewhere.

Lord Oscar need not concern you. Nor any other gentleman, for that matter.

There wasn't a shred of ambiguity in that statement ... and therefore no mistaking what Sophie meant by it. She loved him; truly and deeply, just as she always had. He investigated the knowledge as if it was new; as if he hadn't known it since that day in Richmond Park but hidden it from himself because it had seemed somehow frightening. Now, he wondered why he'd thought that. It wasn't frightening at all. On the contrary. It warmed something inside him. Something that had been as cold and dead as Arctic tundra for a long time; something a little like the first green shoots of spring.

For a second, he half-wished he wasn't going to Hazelmere just now. Then he dismissed it, knowing that wasn't what he wished at all. He *longed* to go. Hazelmere was home, in a way that London could never be. What he actually wished was that it was possible to take Sophie with him. She had never been there. He found himself imagining her seeing it for the first time ... of himself, showing her the house and all his favourite places in the gardens and park ... and of kissing her beneath the willows fringing the lakeside.

He hadn't kissed her since his return. Why hadn't he? He could have done, couldn't he? Yes, he was sure he could – sure she would welcome it. But he hadn't even tried because he'd feared that the numbness inside would extend even to that. Now he thought about it, that seemed cowardly. If he didn't try, he'd never know, would he? He shied away from contemplating what Sophie might be making of it but a frisson of guilt stirred anyway. When he came back to London, he resolved to do better. She had suffered enough on his account. She didn't deserve to be hurt by his coldness as well.

The next day was a busy one. His meetings with both Henry Lessing and Drummond's Bank were lengthy and between the two, he interviewed the three candidates for the post as his valet. Since, in truth, he didn't want any of them, he didn't think it mattered much which one he chose. But Mr Harris was irritatingly pompous and Mr Rigby had sweaty hands, so he chose Mr Doyle as the lesser of three evils ... and reluctantly told a startled Fallon to have the fellow installed in a chamber half the house away from his own.

* * *

On Friday morning, Christian departed for Oxfordshire.

On Friday evening at Sinclairs, Basil Selwyn heard that he had. For all of five minutes, he debated letting sleeping dogs lie. Then, finding himself beside inveterate gossip, Sir Denys Morton, he said idly, 'If my cousin still intends to marry Miss Kelsall he's taking his time about it. I've just learned that he's left Town to visit his estate.'

'The betting is five to two against at White's,' volunteered Sir Denys. 'It seems to me that, if he was going to do it, they'd have announced it by now.'

'My thoughts exactly.'

'Of course, she nearly married *you*, didn't she?'

'She did.' Basil gritted his teeth and managing to sound airily unconcerned, added with a shrug, 'But then my cousin returned and ... well, he's an earl, isn't he?'

'True. So she wouldn't have turned him down, would she?'

'Turned down a title and after waiting for him all this time? Hardly. No. If I had to guess, I'd say his tastes may have changed while he's been away. Not that one likes to speculate, of course ... but we all know what they say about the Turks.'

'I don't,' said Sir Denys, more helpfully than he realised. 'What *do* they say?'

Basil turned a very surprised gaze on him and murmured, 'Oh dear.' Then, leaning a little closer, he dropped a single word in the other man's ear.

'Good God! *Really?*'

'So I've heard.'

Like most people, Sir Denys did not stop to wonder *where* he'd heard it or from whom. 'I thought it was all harems and exotic dancers.'

'Oh, there's that, too,' agreed Basil. 'But not *solely* that.'

'I say!' For several seconds, Sir Denys appeared incapable of speech. Then he said, 'And you think that Hazelmere has taken to – to – you know.'

'I wouldn't like to imply that he *has*. But after spending three years in a country where it's said to be quite common ... and returning to his beautiful not-quite-*fiancée* but *still* not doing the honourable thing ... well. One has to wonder, don't you think?'

'Yes. One does. One does *indeed*.'

Basil smiled, made an excuse about promising to join Lord Henley for a hand or two of basset and strolled away, well pleased with his progress.

* * *

At Hazelmere, Mr Harrington, the steward, welcomed Christian back as if he'd been gone five months rather than five years and proceeded to deliver a concise report on last year's harvest, recent repairs and renovations to cottages, and a patch of damp in the east wing which had only been noticed a fortnight ago. Finally, he said, 'But you'll want to see for yourself, my lord, I'm sure. Do you wish me to tour the estate with you or would you prefer go on your own to begin with while Mr Sandhurst and I go over the books?'

'The books can wait a day or two,' replied Christian. And to Gerald, 'And I'm sure you'd rather take the opportunity for a ride, wouldn't you?'

Gerald grinned. 'Much rather, thank you.'

'That's what we'll do, then. We'll visit the Home Farm first, then the outlying tenants followed by the village. And the park, of course. Then, when I've had a good look around, you and I can discuss matters more fully, Mr Harrington.'

'Very good, my lord. And allow me to say how good it is to have you back.'

Those same words, accompanied by beaming smiles, were echoed everywhere Christian went ... in the village tavern, at church on Sunday and at every cottage.

After a mere forty-eight hours, he realised he was beginning to feel better. The lurking fear didn't go away entirely but it loosened its grip, making it possible to breathe more easily. And conversing with villagers and tenants was blessedly easy, raising none of the anxieties of London ballrooms. Slowly, he started to relax.

Though one or two near neighbours came to call, most – aware that the earl's visit was to be a short one – contented themselves with leaving their cards. But when, whilst out riding, Christian encountered the same young widow for the third time he told Gerald that he was beginning to feel hunted.

'What did you expect? The likes of Mrs Barlow aren't going to pass up the chance of hooking a good-looking earl, are they?' And then, after a moment's hesitation, 'Or perhaps she isn't looking for a wedding ring. Perhaps she just wants a – '

'Stop. Whatever she wants, she isn't getting it from me.'

'Why not? You're not married yet. And it must have been a while since you last – '

'Enough, Gerald.'

Christian felt his neck growing hot. It hadn't just been a while since he'd last bedded a woman; it had been years. Even in Venice, where the opportunities were limitless, he'd remained celibate – mostly because the only woman he wanted was Sophia but also because he didn't want to risk taking a dose of the French pox home with him. In Turkey, of course, there had been no opportunity at all. And now ... well, he wouldn't think of that.

He said flatly, 'If I wanted a discreet fling with a widow, I'd do it in London – not on my own doorstep. But I don't. And neither am I going to discuss it.'

* * *

For four days, Basil left the seed he'd planted in Denys Morton's ear to germinate and, he hoped, begin to spread. Then he spent an evening at the Cocoa Tree Club looking for a similar opportunity so he could plant a second, quite different one elsewhere. He reasoned that, by only telling one person, he had more chance of denying his part in the ensuing gossip should it become necessary. He hadn't forgotten Daniel Shelbourne's threatening tone. But that one person had to be the *right* one; somebody who could be relied upon to spread the word.

The evening was well advanced by the time he spotted Mr Winterton – a gentleman who not only relished anything of a mildly scandalous nature but also loved feeling that he was the first to discover it. The result was that Mr Winterton shared what he knew with one and all – including his equally gossip-loving wife.

Basil smiled at him and said, 'Good evening, Winterton. My luck has been out for the entire evening. I was thinking of calling it a night ... unless you'd care to join me for a brandy?'

'By all means, sir – by all means.' Beaming, he deposited his substantial posterior in the chair next to Basil's. 'Not seen much of you recently. Been wondering how you've gone on since that nasty business with your cousin.'

Grimly maintaining his smile, Basil beckoned a footman and ordered drinks.

'Oh – well enough, though somewhat annoyed. Kit seems to have come back with some dashed peculiar notions. My father thinks his experiences abroad have left him convinced he's surrounded with dastardly plots. There's just no reasoning with him these days.'

The brandy arrived. Basil sipped his. Mr Winterton didn't even pick up his glass before leaning forward to say, 'And what *were* his experiences abroad?'

'Well, that's rather the crux of the matter. We don't know – or not really. You'll have heard what Kit's said about where he's been, I daresay?'

'Being the guest of some Pasha or other? Yes. But for *three years?*'

'Quite. Hard to credit, isn't it?'

'More like impossible, I'd say. But that's really all you know?'

'It's all my cousin will tell us. But ...' He paused and waited.

Mr Winterton didn't disappoint him. 'But what?'

'Well, the investigators Father sent to look for Kit went to the Consulate in Constantinople,' said Basil slowly, almost reluctantly. 'And when there was apparently no trace of him, the people *there* said ... something quite shocking, actually. But, of course, it was just a theory.'

'A theory about what had happened to him?'

'About what *might* have happened, yes. But there's no evidence to support it so it could be completely wrong. And, so far as we know, Kit doesn't speak of it.'

'At *all?*' And when Basil simply shook his head, 'That *is* peculiar. But surely you must have asked him?'

Basil shrugged. 'He denies us the opportunity. Presumably, the friends who found him know the truth, whatever that is. But all Father and I have is the Consulate's theory – which may merely have been a convenient excuse for their inability to find Kit.'

Mr Winterton couldn't wait any longer. He was agog.

'So how *did* they account for it?'

Draining his glass and casting an uneasy glance around them, Basil lowered his voice still further. 'They said that Kit may not even have *reached* Turkey. They said that when people disappear so completely, there's usually only one explanation. And they said that ... that slavers operate all over the Aegean.'

The other man's eyes nearly leapt from their sockets.

'*Slavers?*'

'Yes. Their conclusion was that if – if Kit *had* been captured by slavers, it was highly unlikely we'd ever see him again because he could have been sold on any of several trade routes and ended up God knew where.' Basil stopped talking and shut his eyes. Then, opening them again, 'But, as I said, the Consulate may merely have been trying to avoid blame for an English nobleman vanishing on Turkish soil. And the fact that Kit's back home and in one piece suggests it can't have been the case, doesn't it? So I really must ask you not to repeat it – and *certainly* not as if it's a fact. It's merely either a theory or an excuse without a shred of proof to back it up.'

'Of course, sir,' replied Mr Winterton. 'Not a word shall pass my lips.'

And presently took his leave, Basil knew, to tell the first person he met.

CHAPTER ELEVEN

On the day before Christian was due back in Town, Benedict received a summons to visit his eldest brother. This was a mercifully rare occurrence because it usually meant that the duke wanted him to do something he'd rather not. So he walked into the library of Belhaven House, saying, 'I hope you don't expect me to go haring off to parts unknown, Vere. It isn't convenient right now.'

'No. These days, you're fully occupied guarding Hazelmere's back, aren't you?'

Benedict's brows rose. 'How would you know?'

'I told him.'

Oscar's voice drifted from behind a newspaper on the far side of the room.

'Did you, indeed? Why?'

The newspaper lowered an inch or two and his brother's eyes appeared over the top of it. 'No particular reason. It just came up in conversation.'

'Between the Battle of Actium and Heraclitus?' asked Benedict aridly.

Oscar and Vere shared a passion for the same Greeks and Romans that Benedict had been happy to leave behind at Oxford. Vere wallowed in literature and philosophy; Oscar's love was history and he'd continued to live at home purely because it gave him access to one of the most extensive Classics libraries in England.

Since Oscar had vanished behind his newspaper again and didn't reply, Benedict sighed and asked Vere what he wanted.

'I wondered,' said the duke, 'if you were aware of certain rumours that are going about concerning Lord Hazelmere.'

Benedict blinked. 'How do *you* know anything of current gossip? You barely leave the house.'

Much as Oscar had done, Vere let this pass.

'I spent last evening at White's – where I was sought out by Rockliffe.'

Oh, thought Benedict, his nerves twitching. *So whatever it is will be accurate – and if Rockliffe troubled to pass it on, probably not good.* But he said, 'That must have been cosy. All dukes together. However ... what did he say?'

'He said there are two unsavoury and quite different rumours in circulation. One is that Hazelmere fell into the hands of slavers and spent the three missing years, not as a Turkish gentleman's valued house-guest, but as his property.' And, when Benedict swore under his breath, 'Is any of that true?'

'I'm not at liberty to discuss it,' came the curt reply. 'And the other?'

'Is no better, I'm afraid.' Vere paused and then went on with a careful lack of expression. 'It is being said that, during his captivity, Hazelmere's position was that of ... of what might be called a male concubine. It is *further* suggested that this may have brought about a shift in Hazelmere's sexual preferences – this being the reason for his seeming disinclination to marry Miss Kelsall.'

'Utter rubbish!' snapped Benedict, furiously. 'Did people *really* expect Kit and Sophie to plunge into matrimony after five years apart? This is the work of Basil Selwyn – and there's not a word of truth in it.'

'Are you sure?' asked Oscar, finally setting the newspaper aside.

'Of course I'm sure! I know Kit as well as I know you – better, perhaps. As do Shelbourne and Wendover. Do you think he could deceive us over something like this?'

'I meant,' said Oscar gently, 'are you sure it's Selwyn?'

'Oh. Who else would it be? It's got his grubby fingerprints and equally grubby mind all over it.'

'Rockliffe said much the same,' remarked Vere. 'But the real reason he told me is that he has also caught a hint of speculation about the nature of the extremely close friendship which exists between you, Hazelmere and the other two gentlemen you just mentioned.'

'*What?*' snapped Benedict.

'Do I really need to spell it out?'

'No.' Benedict stared at him, turning steadily whiter. 'Are you asking if it's true?'

'No – and neither was Rockliffe. For what it may be worth to you, he will dismiss such talk as folly if it takes place within his hearing. He merely thought – as do I – that you should be made aware of it.' The duke sighed. 'Sit down and listen, Benedict. We all know that there are a number of gentlemen in society who prefer their own sex. As Rockliffe pointed out, a very good friend of his is one of them. And although there *are* people who are as intolerant of this as they are of many, many other things which need not concern them in the least, most of us think nothing of it.'

'What are you saying?' asked Benedict grimly. 'That it will be a nine day wonder?'

'Something like that. As always happens, it will be a popular topic of conversation until something comes along to eclipse it. But in the meantime, I would advise the four of you to treat it with the amused contempt such baseless nonsense deserves. If you don't, the gossip will last longer ... and you may find yourselves keeping dawn appointments in Hyde Park.'

'But if it should come to that,' volunteered Oscar unexpectedly, 'I'll be happy to act for any of you who may need it.'

* * *

Returning to Dover Street in a foul temper, Benedict sent urgent notes to both Daniel and Anthony. Then, when they arrived at his lodgings, he repeated what he'd been told.

For a long speechless moment, they simply stared at him. But finally Anthony breathed, 'Hell and the devil take Selwyn.'

'I hope he does,' growled Daniel, coming to his feet. 'But in the meantime, I'm going to wring his sodding neck.'

'No,' said Benedict. 'You're not. Vere says to treat it as the nonsense it is – and he's right. If we start kicking up a dust, it will look as though it's touched a nerve and – '

'It *has* touched a nerve, damn it!'

'And as though there may be some truth in it,' finished Benedict calmly.

Daniel shoved a hand through his hair, far from convinced.

'*You* can stand by and let him get away with it, if you like – but *I* won't.'

'He isn't going to get away with it – not in the long run. But you can't go knocking seven bells out of him now.' He paused, shrugging. 'On the other hand, there's no harm in letting people know that Basil is the source of both rumours and of giving him the impression that if one of us challenges anybody over this, it will be him.'

Daniel grunted and hurled himself back into his chair.

For a few moments, silence fell. Then Anthony said, 'The sooner Kit gets back so we can proceed with our own plan, the better. And with regard to that ... how do we let Basil know that we've come into possession of new and vital information?'

'I've no idea.' Benedict stood staring out of the window and reflecting that it was difficult enough containing his own anger, without having to rein Daniel in as well. 'I'm rather hoping that Gerald will have come up with something.'

'And if he hasn't?' demanded Daniel.

'I don't *know*.'

Another silence ... once again broken by Anthony, saying tentatively, 'We could start our own rumour?'

'We *could*,' agreed Benedict. 'But wouldn't it look like tit for tat?'

'Probably. Unless ...' He stopped.

'Unless what?'

'Unless someone else – someone unconnected with us – started it for us.'

Daniel gave a crack of grim laughter.

'Brilliant. Who do you suggest? Rockliffe?'

'Ideally ... yes.'

Silence yawned yet again. Then, struck by inspiration, Benedict swung round to face them saying, 'No. Not Rockliffe himself. One of his friends ... thus creating the assumption that it had originated with the duke.'

For the first time since hearing the news, Daniel's expression lightened.

'His brother, perhaps? Or Wingham?'

Benedict nodded. 'Someone like that. I don't think it would be hard to persuade them to lend a hand. However, don't do anything until we've explored all the possible ramifications.'

'But in the meantime I can rattle Basil's cage a bit?'

'Yes ... but carefully, Dan. Not a word about what we're planning – nothing beyond what I suggested earlier.'

'That will do well enough for the time being.' He stood up. 'By the time I've finished with him, he'll be quaking in his boots.'

* * *

Christian and Gerald arrived in Berkeley Square late the following afternoon. A note from Benedict lay on the silver salver near the front door so Christian read it whilst crossing the hall. Then, stopping, he turned to Gerald and said, 'Benedict wants to be notified the instant we return. He's uncommonly emphatic about it – though he doesn't explain why.'

'Odd. Shall I send a note to Dover Street?'

'Please.'

Proceeding directly to his bedchamber, Christian found his new valet hovering there.

'Welcome home, my lord,' said Doyle. 'I hope you had a pleasant journey?'

'It was tolerable, thank you.' And realising something more was required of him, 'Have you settled in all right?'

'Very much so, my lord. During your absence, I have familiarised myself with your wardrobe and reorganised the dressing-closet into a more orderly fashion. I also took the liberty of ordering a bath to be prepared as soon as you arrived. I trust that is acceptable?'

'It is. But may I remind you that I don't require you to help me dress or shave me or indeed do *anything* of a personal nature?'

Doyle had spent the earl's absence coming to terms with this peculiar order.

'Of course, my lord. I haven't forgotten.'

'Excellent,' nodded Christian. 'I shall be perfectly satisfied if you confine your activities to caring for my clothes and – and such-like.'

'Very good, my lord. What should I lay out for after your bath?'

'The blue suit will do. It's possible I'll be going out later.'

'Certainly, my lord.' Doyle bowed and went out.

Christian drew a long breath and prayed that the fellow wasn't going to be constantly underfoot. At least he had been lodged far enough away from his own rooms to remain ignorant of the nightmares that still sometimes plagued him – or things would get tricky.

While the valet laid out the clothes he'd asked for and the footmen set the bathtub in the dressing-room and filled it with pail after pail of hot water, he idled away the time flicking through the neat pile of letters and invitations on the escritoire. None of them was of any particular interest or urgency, so he put them aside for consideration later.

When he was finally alone, he stripped and sank gratefully into hot water, leaning his head back against the rim of the tub and shutting his eyes. He wondered what ailed Benedict ... then pushed the thought aside. That, too, could wait until later. It would be pleasant, just for a little while, not to have to think. He sank down beneath the water and then, surfacing again, sat up and reached for the soap.

Without warning, the door from his bedchamber opened.

Christian swung round, sending a tide of water over the side of the tub and, seeing Doyle on the threshold, clutching an armful of towels, bellowed, '*Out!* Get *out*, damn you – *now!*'

'I – I'm sorry, my lord. The towels – I f-forgot them.'

'Drop the bloody towels and *get out!*' yelled Christian, hurling the soap at him. '*Go!*'

The soap whistled by Doyle's ear and hit the door with a slap. But it was the wild look on the earl's face that made the valet toss the towels at the nearest chair and flee, slamming the door behind him.

Christian remained where he was, staring at the closed door and breathing hard, his pulse racing. This ... *this* was exactly why he hadn't wanted a valet.

Oh God, he thought wearily, subsiding back into the water. *Did I react quickly enough? Perhaps he didn't have time to ... and even if he did, it can't have been more than a glimpse, can it?* His heart was thudding in his chest and he dragged in several slow breaths to steady it. Then he thought, *But the devil of it is that I'm going to have to* speak *to him about it – and make some excuse for flying into a rage. Unless I'm very lucky and he's decided I'm a lunatic and is already packing his bags.*

He dropped his head forward and pressed the heels of his hands over his eyes for a long moment. Then he contemplated the knowledge that both soap and towels were on the far side of the room. Muttering a curse, he hauled himself out of the bath and dripped across the carpet to fetch them.

* * *

An hour later, dry and fully dressed but for his coat, a tap at the door heralded Gerald who said, 'Although he hasn't explained why, Benedict wants to see us as soon as possible. Shall I tell him we'll go to Dover Street this evening?'

'Yes. Let's hope it's good news rather than the other sort.'

Absorbing the flat tone, Gerald said cautiously, 'Is something wrong?'

'Possibly. Probably.' Christian sighed. 'Is my valet still in the house?'

'Doyle? Yes, I imagine so. Why wouldn't he be?'

'I ... shouted. And threw the soap at him.'

'Ah.' Gerald suppressed an impulse to laugh. 'Any particular reason for that?'

There was, of course. But it wasn't one Christian intended to share.

'I was in the bath. He ... took me by surprise.'

'I see,' he said. And thought, *Actually, I don't. You never used to be shy.* 'Well, I daresay he won't do it again.'

'He'd better not. But I suppose I'd better speak to him.'

'That might be a good idea. And while you do, I'll write to Benedict. Again.'

Christian pulled the bell. 'Tell him we'll be with him around eight, if that suits.'

Gerald nodded and left, inwardly frowning. Then, passing a very nervous-looking Doyle in the hall, said brusquely, 'Don't worry. He won't bite.' And went on his way.

The valet hesitated before finally summoning sufficient courage to knock. He might have felt better had he known that, on the other side of the door, the earl was forcing himself into at least the *appearance* of calm before bidding him enter.

Two steps into the room, Doyle halted, saying, 'You rang, my lord?'

'Yes. Close the door, please.' And, when the valet had done so, 'I think I owe you an apology for my over-reaction earlier. I can assure you that I don't make a habit of it. But I ... you must understand that I value my privacy.'

'Of course, my lord. And your lordship has no cause to apologise – greatly though I appreciate you doing so. The fault was mine. It won't happen again.'

'I hope not.' Christian hesitated, unable to find a way of asking the question in his head without simply *asking* it. In the end, he said jerkily, 'If you have ... concerns ... or there's something you want to ask me ... do it now.'

Doyle stared at him.

'*Question* you, my lord? *I?*' He both looked and sounded horrified. 'No. Indeed not.'

'Are you sure?'

'Perfectly, sir. It would be the height of presumption to expect your lordship to explain yourself to me. I would *never* do so. I am merely grateful for your lordship's forbearance in overlooking my intrusion. I shall know better in future.'

Christian suspected that all the my-lording was going to become tiresome. On the other hand, he couldn't fault the man's discretion ... unless it *wasn't* discretion. Could that be it? God, he hoped so.

But it wouldn't do to make too big an issue of the incident so, with a weak attempt at humour, he murmured, 'Sorry about the soap.'

'Unnecessary, sir,' said Doyle. And, so softly that Christian almost missed it, 'Being as how you missed.'

* * *

Christian and Gerald arrived at Benedict's lodgings to find Anthony and Daniel already there. None of them were smiling.

'Oh dear,' sighed Gerald. '*Not* good news, then.'

'No,' agreed Benedict. And, as briefly as possible, explained.

Christian listened, slumping further into his chair. Deep down, he'd always feared that keeping every part of the truth secret was going to be next to impossible. And if one bit of it came out, speculation would soon supply the rest ... though he could never have bargained for his friends being dragged into the mire with him. Fleetingly, he recalled the small flicker of optimism that had been alive inside him when he and Gerald had left Hazelmere. It was gone now; killed by the fracas with his valet and the never-ending spite of his cousin.

When Benedict stopped speaking, Gerald said, 'Does Basil have a death wish?'

'If he does, I'd be happy to grant it,' replied Daniel bitterly. 'But the general consensus is that we're supposed to laugh it off. Personally, I don't find it funny.'

'None of us do.' Benedict rose to pour more wine. 'But, for now at least, dismissive contempt will serve us better than slapping a glove in Basil's face. And we're not doing *nothing*, Kit. We've let it be known that Basil is the source of the rumours and – '

'Since which time, the cowardly bastard has gone to ground,' growled Daniel.

'And we've worked out how to let him learn about our new evidence,' finished Benedict. 'Though it may not sound like it, the two things are related.'

'Good,' said Gerald. 'But first ... how far has the gossip spread?'

'We believe it's in most of the clubs,' Anthony told him reluctantly, 'but nothing suggests it's reached the drawing-rooms. Nor has anything been said of it to any of us directly.'

'Yet,' said Christian.

'It hasn't appeared in the scandal sheets either.'

'Yet,' said Christian again.

Since this was undeniable, silence fell for a few moments until finally Benedict said, 'My suggestion is that we continue pouring scorn on Basil's spite – which is clearly his retaliation for being evicted from Berkeley Square – and allow a week or two for whatever talk there may be to die down. Then we put our original plan into action. Anthony has written out the English statement on the Consulate headed paper so now we need you to do the same with the Turkish one, Kit, and we'll be ready to proceed.'

'I'll do it tomorrow,' he said absently, his mind occupied with the unpalatable realisation that he needed to warn Sophia that there was going to be unpleasant gossip surrounding him before she heard it elsewhere; though how he could tell her there might be speculation about the precise nature of his relationship with Benedict, Daniel and Anthony, he couldn't begin to imagine. 'And then?'

'And then we progress to the second phase.'

'Which is?'

'Mentioning the arrival of new evidence to a couple of Rockliffe's friends ... and letting them know – with the utmost subtlety, of course – that we won't mind if they pass it on.' Benedict smiled innocently. 'To Nicholas Wynstanton, for example.'

Christian looked up, something flaring in the silvery gaze. He said, 'You want to involve Rockliffe in this?'

'That is the general idea, yes. Who better? No one will be surprised because he always knows everything. And no one will question his word because he's never wrong.' The smile grew but turned cold. 'He's apparently already inclined to be helpful – so it would be stupid not to take advantage of that.'

CHAPTER TWELVE

Christian awoke on the following morning to the sound of rain and took his breakfast staring at the deluge outside the window which accorded well with his mood. The sound of it accompanied the scratching of his quill as he copied out the Turkish translation of the fake letter on to the Consulate headed notepaper. And when, by late morning, it still showed no sign of stopping, he finally abandoned the notion of taking Sophia driving and instead, sent a note asking if there would be any time during the day when her mother and sisters might be conveniently from home. Then, whilst awaiting her reply, he put the gifts he'd bought for her during the Grand Tour and *still* not found the opportunity to give her into a striped bandbox; a sugarplum to take away the sour taste of what he had to tell her.

Sophia's response came within the hour.

Mama and my sisters are attending the Ladies Benevolent Society's monthly meeting at Lady Easton's house in Clarges Street at four this afternoon. I am supposed to be going with them. Sadly, I already feel a headache coming on.

Christian told himself that this was good. The sooner it was done, the better. The mere thought of Basil's insinuations made him feel sick.

He arrived at Charles Street at a little after four and, bandbox in hand, was shown up to the drawing-room where Sophia waited, smiling.

'I was hoping I might see you today,' she said, eyeing the box but not asking the obvious question. 'How were things at Hazelmere?'

'In good order,' he replied. 'Better than the news awaiting me here, I regret to say.'

Her smile faded and she sank on to a sofa. 'Sit down and tell me.'

Setting the box aside for later, Christian chose a chair facing her. He said expressionlessly, 'Basil has been busy. The result, inevitably, is some unsavoury talk.'

'About you?'

'Yes – and this time, not *just* me.' He hesitated briefly and then forced himself to go on. 'Sophie ... the part involving others isn't something I want to have to explain to you, so I won't. But it's possible that a few of the older married ladies might get wind of it – which means it may reach your mother.'

'Thank you for warning me. But I wouldn't trust a word that comes out of Basil's mouth regarding you or anything else for that matter. You do *know* that, don't you?'

'Let's say that I ... hoped you wouldn't.'

'Well, then. What is the rest of it? The part you *can* repeat?'

'A theory about how I ended up in Ibrahim's palace.' Christian swallowed hard. 'Putting it briefly, Basil's rumour has me captured by slavers and sold to him.'

For a long moment, Sophia said nothing. He didn't need to know that this was a possibility that had already occurred to her and she certainly wasn't going to ask him if there was any truth in it. Finally she said, 'How very like Basil. I don't think I ever realised how truly *poisonous* he is.'

Reflecting that she didn't know the worst of it, he murmured, 'Neither did I.'

'However ... even if it was true, it's not so very damaging, is it?'

Shrugging wearily, he said, 'It's an image I'd sooner not have clinging to me.'

'I understand that. But you can't be blamed for something that wasn't your fault.'

'You're being too logical, Sophie. That's not the way the gossip mill works. The word slavery immediately casts doubt on what my role in Ibrahim's household actually was. And people enjoy exercising their imaginations. As Basil is perfectly well aware, his insinuations will breed whole new scenarios.'

'Perhaps.' A frown touched Sophia's eyes. 'Please tell me you aren't considering challenging him over it.'

'No. That would do more harm than good.' He paused briefly. 'Benedict thinks this is Basil's revenge for tossing him and his father out of Berkeley Square.'

Her brow cleared. 'Almost certainly, I would think. And with a little luck, others will reach the same conclusion.'

'Some may, some will choose not to. But Ben and the others will be circulating that thought whilst simultaneously identifying Basil as the source of the rumours.'

She nodded and then said slowly, 'Speaking of your friends ... is it they who are being slandered along with you in this tale I'm too delicate to know about?'

Christian flushed. 'Yes.'

Sophia was at a loss to think of anything Basil could say about those gentlemen that was so bad she couldn't be told of it. Surely the worst that might be said with any degree of truth was that the ring of protection they'd thrown around Kit must inevitably involve some orchestrated lying – but clearly, it wasn't that. One thing, however, *did* occur to her. She said dryly, 'If Basil is throwing mud at the Duke of Belhaven's brother, he's walking a very fine – not to say stupid – line.'

'Quite. But he'd be in more immediate physical danger from Dan Shelbourne if Benedict wasn't reining him in.' Aware that the conversation was heading in a direction which, if it continued, might lead him to reveal more than he wanted to, Christian decided it was time to call a halt. 'That's all I can tell you, Sophie – aside from offering my thanks for taking it so calmly. I'm sorry.'

To his surprise and great relief, she simply nodded, took the hint and smiled at him.

'In that case ... before I die of curiosity, will you *please* tell me what is in that box?'

He managed a small, fairly convincing laugh and, rising, fetched the box and set it in front of her. 'See for yourself. Telling you about Basil's perfidy wasn't the *only* reason I wanted us to be private today.'

'It wasn't?'

'No. You asked about the souvenirs from my Grand Tour and I told you that many of the things I'd bought were for you. Here are some of them.'

Her face lit up and he felt the tension inside him ease a little.

She said, 'Really? When you said nothing more about them, I supposed that the things you sent home never arrived – or that Basil had helped himself to them.'

'As he might have done, had he been given the chance.' He smiled at her. 'Aren't you going to open it?'

'Of course! I was just savouring a moment of anticipation.' She reached over and lifted the lid to look down on items of various shapes and sizes neatly wrapped in pale blue tissue. 'Oh! Now I can't decide whether to take everything out first and *then* begin unwrapping ... or if a lucky dip might be more fun.'

He took the seat beside her. 'The choice is yours. But please make it before your mother and sisters come back and interrupt us.'

Sophia laughed and took out the first thing that came to hand. Moments later, she was exclaiming over a beautiful silk fan, heavily embroidered in gold thread and mounted on carved ivory sticks. Next came an ornate carnival mask trimmed with paste sapphires and topped with an ostrich plume. This had her insisting he tie it on for her so she could run to the mirror and see how it looked.

'Very mysterious,' remarked Christian lazily. 'No one would ever know you.'

'It's wonderful! There's nothing *nearly* as fine as this to be found in London. I wonder if anyone is holding a masquerade ball?'

'Not that I know of. But there used to be one at Bedford House before the end of the Season, didn't there? However ... sorry as I am to rush you ...'

'I know, I know. You want to escape before Mama comes back.'

'Call me a coward if you will – but, ideally, yes.'

Much swifter than she'd have liked, Sophia unwrapped a framed watercolour of the Grand Canal, a second fan – this one of peacock feathers – a sketch of the Forum in Rome and a lacquered casket containing a necklace of Murano glass. When she came to the small portrait, she gazed at it for a long moment before saying, 'Who is this?'

'Filippino Lippi. It's a self-portrait – only a copy, I'm afraid, but I thought you might like him.'

'I do. He's very young, isn't he? And soulful-looking. Perhaps he was thinking of the girl he loves.'

Christian grinned. 'He was more likely to have been wishing he could afford to pay a model instead of painting himself.'

Sophia pulled a face. 'No, no – he's more romantic than that.' Then, gesturing to the array of gifts on the table in front of her, she added shyly, 'It's all lovely, Kit. Thank you. I never dreamed you'd go to such a lot of trouble on – '

'It was no trouble, Sophie-Rose. You were never far from my thoughts – not ever. So hunting for things to bring home to you was a pleasure.' He smiled at her. 'This isn't everything. There are other things at home – one in particular that I'd like to show you. But I thought this was enough for now – not that you've quite finished. There's just one left. Open it. I think it's my favourite.'

Obediently, Sophia reached into the box and lifted out the last parcel. It was heavier than she'd expected so she had to use both hands to steady it and then couldn't resist feeling the lumpy thing inside the tissue in order to try to guess what it was.

'Is it an animal?' she hazarded, detecting what felt like legs.

'Perhaps. Why not unwrap it and find out?'

So she did – and dissolved into laughter when she encountered the dog's lopsided grin. 'Oh! What a foolish-looking fellow. I love him! Where did you find him?'

'In a backstreet of Naples,' he replied. 'I was reliably informed afterwards that it was an area of the city best avoided by anyone wishing to keep their limbs intact. But by then, Jingo and I had made it safely back to our inn.'

'Jingo?' echoed Sophia. '*Really?*'

'You have a better idea?'

She thought for a moment, running her fingers over the dog's head. Then, giving in, 'I'm sure I *would* have done if you hadn't called him that. But *now* it's all I can think of – so Jingo he's doomed to remain.'

'Excellent. I knew you'd bow to my superior judgement.'

Sophia's choke of laughter turned abruptly into something very different. Tears misted her eyes and Jingo slipped from her fingers on to her lap. Then, without stopping to think about it, she leaned into Christian and, reaching up to kiss his cheek, whispered, 'Thank you ... for all of it. But most especially f-for thinking of me.'

Nothing prepared him for the storm of feeling that kiss released. It was scarcely more than the touch of a butterfly's wing ... just the merest brush of her lips and an instant of warm breath against his skin. But, as if a dam had burst, he was suddenly racked with wanting; raw hunger and searing heat, all the more fierce for the months it had lain dormant. Even as shock hit him, his body reacted with alarming speed. Every nerve and cell in his body howled for him to haul her into his arms, to devour her mouth and fill his hands with her body. The urge was so strong he didn't know how to resist it. And yet, with the tiny fragment of his brain that was still functioning, he knew that he must. He *must* because, if he didn't, there was no predicting how far he might go.

He was distantly aware that the earth had just shifted in wholly unexpected ways. As his mind slowly cleared, he started to recognise the significance of what had happened. He hadn't experienced physical desire for so long he'd thought it lost to him. But it wasn't, was it? Right now, his body was enthusiastically demanding something which it wasn't going to get. And yet, uncomfortable as that was, he was glad of it. Glad that at least some part of the numb detachment which had been holding him in its grip for so long had fractured.

But now wasn't the time to think of that. *Now* was for being sensible. And the first thing he needed to do was to put a little distance between himself and Sophia. He did so and knew instinctively that he'd disappointed her. Summoning something he hoped was a smile, he tried to mend it.

'Don't thank me – and especially not for that. As for the assortment of trifles … at the time I bought them, I was conscious that your parents would have condemned more extravagant gifts as improper.'

She nodded. Then, deciding it was time to grasp the nettle, she said baldly, 'Kit … since your return, you haven't kissed me. Not even once. Don't you want to?'

The breath left his lungs. He'd grown accustomed to her letting him off easily and he hadn't expected her to challenge him – particularly not over this. But she was entitled to an answer and he wasn't going to lie, so he said, 'Yes. Just now, very much indeed. *Too* much, in fact … which is why I didn't.'

'Is that supposed to make sense?'

'Yes.' Christian hesitated and then, on a bracing breath, said, 'There are times when I can't trust myself. Times when I can feel my self-control slipping away. I dare not let it.'

She stared at him, baffled. 'I don't understand.'

'Neither do I, in truth. But it's part of me now. Violent feelings I have to restrain because I don't know what may happen if I don't.' He hesitated and then added abruptly, 'If I'd kissed you just now, I was afraid I wouldn't stop when I should.'

'Oh.' Sophie thought that sounded promising. She also thought it offered a simple solution. She said, 'Not even if I told you to?'

He opened his mouth to say he didn't know … and then realised the full importance of what that meant. Put simply, if a lady said no, honour demanded a gentleman respect it. If he didn't – couldn't – what did that make him? So he said slowly, 'I would certainly hope so.'

'Then perhaps next time you'll trust me to do it.'

He gave a tiny huff of wry laughter. 'We could try that, I suppose ... though not right now, if you don't mind. Also, you might need to give me a hefty shove.'

'I can do that.' She smiled at him, gauging his expression. 'So aside from your self-control and Basil's spiteful rumours ... what else is worrying you?'

Christian sighed and took his time about answering. Finally, he said, 'Not *worrying* exactly ... but the other matter I told you about is still unresolved.'

'Don't you mean the other matter you *didn't* tell me about?'

'Yes. I'm sorry, Sophie. I'm a hopeless case.' Oddly, considering what else was going on inside him, he realised he felt better than he had in a long time. More himself; less ephemeral. 'You couldn't be blamed for losing patience with me. I deserve it, don't I?'

She reached out and curled her fingers about his hand. 'Without all the facts, how can I answer that?'

'Ah. You can't, of course. How clever of me to keep you ignorant of the details.'

'Very cunning,' she agreed. 'Or would be, if that's why you did it. But promise me something. Whatever it is you're doing, promise you aren't doing it alone.'

'I'm not. Far from it. Without Ben and the others, it couldn't be done at all.'

'Then I'm satisfied.' She restored Jingo to the bandbox and stood up. 'If you don't want to bump into Mama on the doorstep, you should go. It's the Tyndale assembly this evening. Will I see you there?'

'I can't say I'm looking forward to facing the gossips – but yes.' He rose to face her and took her hands, saying gravely, 'Thank you, Sophie.'

'For what?'

'For being the remarkable person you are. And far kinder than I have any right to expect.'

Then, bringing her closer, he dropped a fleeting kiss on her lips ... and left.

*   *   *

Christian drove home, his mind simultaneously reeling and rejoicing at the extraordinary discovery of the last hour. From very soon after his return to England until this afternoon, he had truly despaired of ever being whole again; of being able to give and receive the pleasure of making love to a woman; to Sophie.

Among the reasons that had prevented him committing himself to her, this had gradually become the most important – and not only because of the humiliation of having to admit it. The mere thought of doing that turned his skin cold and sent nausea roiling through his insides. And that hadn't merely been about him. How could he allow Sophie to tie herself to a man who wasn't capable of being a proper husband to her? How could she ever be made to understand that the problem wasn't with her but with him? She'd always doubt, wouldn't she? And that doubt, along with the absence of the children she'd always wanted, would eat away at her until she was slowly dying inside ... as would he, watching it happen.

But today had proved him wrong. It seemed that time – or more probably Sophie herself – had mended whatever had been broken. That wild surge of arousal had been unmistakable and very nearly overwhelming. Hope flooded him and he found himself grinning. If *that* could come right, there was a possibility that so, too, could all the other things; the nightmares, the anxiety attacks, the unreasoning sense of dread and the impulse to smash his fist into something or someone. Perhaps none of those were permanent either. Perhaps, just perhaps, he wasn't as irrevocably damaged as he'd believed.

*   *   *

Whilst admiring her gifts prior to putting them neatly away, Sophia also considered what had happened between them. She had been disappointed and a little hurt when he'd immediately moved away after that mere ghost of a kiss. But when she'd blurted out a question she had never intended to ask, his reply had been unexpected.

He'd not only said that he *did* want to kiss her – he'd implied that he wanted to do a great deal more than that. Even now, recollection of his words brought heat to Sophia's cheeks and secret places in her body; heat and sensations she recalled him kindling in her five years ago, sometimes with little more than a look. It was the first time since his return that anything of the sort had occurred between them and she'd begun to wonder if it ever would or whether the magic spark that had existed between them from the very beginning had been extinguished forever. That it hadn't ... that Kit still wanted her as much as she wanted him ... was a gift greater than any other he could have given her.

Her thoughts were interrupted by a tap at the door, followed by Julia's head – her expression unusually stormy – peering around it. Sighing and beckoning her inside, Sophia signed, 'I'm sorry. Have you had a horrid afternoon?'

'It was *awful*. They all either ignored me or looked embarrassed.' And taking in the evidence lying on the bed, 'I came to ask if your headache was better. But you didn't *have* one, did you? His lordship came.'

'Yes. I'm sorry – really I am. But he wanted to see me privately and – well, I couldn't think what else to do. And he didn't come *just* to bring me those,' she said, gesturing to the gifts. 'There was something important he needed to explain to me. And no, I can't tell you what it was any more than I could think of a way for *you* to get out of this afternoon as well as me.' Sophia picked up both of the fans and laid them on the table in front of her sister. 'Choose one – whichever you like best. Kit bought them in Venice.'

Julia's eyes widened and her expression softened. 'Really? Are you sure?'

'Quite sure. I'd have given you one of them anyway even without a need to apologise. Just don't tell Gwendoline.'

'As if I would!' And stroking the peacock feather fan, 'May I have this one?'

'It's yours. Now go and hide it somewhere and leave me to put the rest of this away before Gwen comes up and catches the pair of us red-handed.'

Julia laughed again, brushed Sophia's cheek with the feathers and went.

Rewrapping the remaining fan in tissue and laying it in a drawer, Sophia resumed her earlier musings – in particular her offer to prevent Christian becoming carried away and taking things too far. Smiling a little guiltily, she decided there was some leeway in that. She *would* stop him, of course – if it became necessary. But she didn't have to call a halt the exact *instant* he went beyond what Mama would consider proper, did she? Also, Kit couldn't expect her notion of 'too far' to mirror his. The matter was subjective, surely?

Placing Jingo on her bedside table, she reminded herself that she was twenty-two years old and, had life not gone unexpectedly awry, would have been married for three years by now. Consequently, she told herself that finding subtle ways of luring Kit into being just the *tiniest* bit wicked couldn't do any harm and, given the circumstances, wasn't even unreasonable.

She patted the dog's head and whispered, 'So that's what I'll do, Jingo ... just as soon as I've worked out how.'

CHAPTER THIRTEEN

The Tyndale assembly was less of a trial than Christian had anticipated. Whilst dancing the first set with Sophia, he encountered a few speculative glances from a handful of gentlemen and some oddly sympathetic ones from the ladies. But in the half hour or so after it, no one cut him, refused to meet his eyes or asked any awkward questions. Then Sebastian Wingham materialised at his side, his expression unaccustomedly irritable, and said, 'You'll have heard the latest, I daresay?'

There was no need to ask what he meant. 'Yes.'

'Well, don't let it concern you. It's doing Selwyn more harm than it will you.'

Christian blinked. 'Is it? How come?'

'His dubious insinuations about your close male friendships haven't been well received. After all, it's a sad fellow who doesn't have at least *one* such. Someone you've known since childhood or formed a bond with at university. A friendship made of mutual liking and trust.'

'Quite. But how is that harming Basil?'

'There's a growing view among the older and highly respected members of White's that Selwyn's tasteless innuendos have crossed a line. The general feeling is that when Selwyn hinted that there is more between you and Hawkridge and Shelbourne than meets the eye, he indirectly implied that the same is true of other, similar friendships.'

'Oh.'

'Exactly. Take Rockliffe, for example. He and Charles Fox — whose preferences are no secret — have been close friends for the best part of two decades. And has anyone ever wondered about the nature of that?'

Not entirely sure where this was going, Christian said cautiously, 'Probably not. *I* certainly haven't. Is he offended?'

'Rockliffe? No,' replied Sebastian. And with a grin, 'It's *Fox* who's offended. He says the implication that one's sexual preferences stand in the way of platonic friendships is as cretinous as saying that a partiality for meat means one can't eat fish.' He glanced around the room. 'Neither he nor Rock are here tonight, more's the pity ... but if your cousin puts in an appearance, the betting is in favour of more than one gentleman cutting him. But enough of that. Can I tempt you to join Adrian, Nicholas and me for a hand of cards?'

* * *

Unlike his cousin, Basil Selwyn *had* looked forward to Lady Tyndale's party. The rumours he'd started had gathered pace while Christian had been away – particularly that about him being taken by slavers. It was a little disappointing that the tale hadn't been picked up by *The Whisperer* but he supposed there was still time for this to happen. Now, aware that Christian was back in Town and would almost certainly attend tonight's assembly, Basil had been eager to see how society behaved towards him. He also wondered whether any of the talk had reached Sophia and, if so, what she made of it.

All in all, Basil was feeling rather pleased with himself. Recently, the only fly in his ointment had been the nasty glint in the Honourable Mr Shelbourne's eyes ... but if the fellow was going to challenge him, he'd have done it by now so Basil didn't let it worry him unduly. Consequently, he set off for Tyndale House with a sense of pleasant anticipation.

Unfortunately, it rapidly became clear that the evening wasn't going to live up to his expectations. Christian hadn't suddenly become a pariah. No one appeared to be treating him any differently. As for Sophia, she was positively glowing and she looked at him as if the sun shone out of him.

Why? Basil asked himself. *Where are the cold shoulders and whispers and sideways glances? What has gone wrong?*

And then, as he offered Lady Rainham a smiling bow, the unthinkable happened. She eyed him very briefly but with frigid distaste ... and turned her back on him. Then, addressing the lady beside her, she said, 'It's sometimes a pity that one can't choose one's relatives as well as one's friends, don't you think?'

It was the first snub of the evening but not the last. Two other gentlemen also cut him and a number of others sauntered away before he could join them.

Next, Basil became aware that the look on Daniel Shelbourne's face had changed from *Give me an excuse to hit you. Please. Any little thing will do*, to a sardonic, mocking smile which was actually a lot more alarming.

Angry and frustrated, Basil left the assembly early, set off in the direction of Sinclairs and then, changing his mind about risking further rebuffs, headed home, to brood over what had gone wrong.

Until this evening, everything had seemed to be working well. A number of gentlemen had been chewing over the question of how Lord Hazelmere had ended up in a Turkish palace and what he'd *really* been up to during those three missing years. And one or two – fellows like Thetford and Bartlett, for example – had openly debated the precise nature of the relationship between Hazelmere and Benedict Hawkridge. But Thetford and Bartlett weren't the men who counted. The ones who *did* were those who'd befriended Christian since his return and who Basil had hoped might now distance themselves; the likes of Wingham and Sarre and Rockliffe's brother ... all of whom he'd seen laughing with Christian in the card room – thus suggesting that the opposite was happening.

Somehow, the plan had backfired and it was Basil himself who was the target of cold looks and even colder shoulders. But *why?* He couldn't understand what could have caused it.

The entire evening had been a disaster ... on top of which he had a nasty suspicion that Shelbourne knew something he didn't which, if true, was seriously unnerving. It could even mean that it was Shelbourne he had to thank for the coolness of his reception tonight.

His valet helped him out of his coat, poured him a large glass of brandy and listened sympathetically to his diatribe about Mr Shelbourne. Then he said quietly, 'If I may offer an opinion, sir ...?'

'What?'

'It sounds as if the gentleman might benefit from a small lesson.'

Basil looked at him. Brinklow was a useful fellow in a number of unusual ways – spying and obtaining information, for example. Perhaps his talents didn't end there.

'What are you suggesting?'

'The details need not concern you, sir,' the valet replied, brushing the coat prior to returning it to the wardrobe. 'But if you wish it, something could be ... arranged.'

Basil decided it would be better not to ask what that might mean. Instead, gazing into his glass, he said, 'You could do that?'

'I know people who can. A few guineas, the right information and the thing is as good as done.'

Basil hesitated. He ought to say no – he knew that. He ought not to contemplate it even for a second. But there was that smug, taunting smile; the many occasions when Shelbourne had threatened him, albeit obliquely; and worse than any of that, what had happened tonight. So he downed the rest of the brandy in one swallow and said, 'Let me think on it.'

* * *

Half an hour later, when he was enjoying a second brandy in the drawing-room, his father stalked in with a face like thunder. In a tone of barely controlled fury, he said, 'Have you *completely* lost your mind?'

Basil blinked. 'What?'

'These rumours about Christian. Your work, are they?' And without waiting for an answer, 'Of course they are. And everyone knows it – which is why it's taken a week to come to my ears. And you didn't stop at Christian, did you? *You* were stupid enough to drag his friends into it. What the hell were you *thinking?* Didn't you realise where that would lead?'

Flushing, Basil shifted uncomfortably and, ignoring the question, summoned what he hoped was a baffled expression. 'Who told you this?'

'Who do you think? I was at White's. Belhaven made one of his infrequent appearances and sought me out for a private word.' Eustace stared down on him over folded arms, his expression grim. 'Our conversation was far from pleasant. The duke told me what you've been saying. And he suggested, with a courtesy which very clearly meant nothing, that I should warn you to cease saying it – or, in fact, anything else in a similar vein. Consider yourself warned. I do not want Belhaven as an enemy thanks to your idiocy. Is that clear?'

'Yes. But – '

'There are no buts, Basil. He has already muzzled *The Whisperer* – and he says that if you ever drag his brother's name into what he describes as "*your unfortunate passion for scandal-mongering*" again, he will sue. If he does that –'

'He can't. He'll never *prove* anything! I only – '

'I don't care what you *only* did. You did enough, it seems. Belhaven is a powerful man with a great deal of influence. If he brings a case against you, he will win – and we will be ruined, both socially and financially. Did that possibility not enter what passes for your brain when you embarked on your sly little game?' And not waiting for an answer, 'No. Of course it didn't. You just plunged in without a thought for the consequences – as usual.'

'I didn't say anything about Hawkridge. His name never came into – '

'It has now. So you obviously said *something* to cause it.' Eustace's expression darkened still further. 'And there's more. Belhaven is also questioning your attitude towards Christian – not just since his return, but also in the past. He feels your behaviour suggests a deep and long-standing resentment – if not actual hatred. So much so, he said, that it raises concerns about what *really* happened when you and Christian parted company in Athens.'

This time Basil said nothing and looked anywhere but at his father.

There was a long silence. Finally Eustace said, 'You did something, didn't you? No – don't tell me. I've always half-suspected the circumstances weren't what you said they were ... that you know more about Christian's disappearance than you want to admit. But I suspect I'll be happier not knowing what it was. Just tell me one thing. Is there *any* possibility that Christian knows?'

'No. There's – '

'None at all? Or any of his friends?'

'No – because there's nothing to know!'

'Are you quite, quite *sure* about that?'

Basil realised that he couldn't be – not completely – but every probability was against Christian knowing anything, so he muttered, 'As I said, I didn't do anything so there's nothing to know. So, yes. I'm sure.'

'You'd better be. You had better be – or it may well be *you* who finds yourself on the wrong side of society, not Christian. Am I making myself clear?'

Basil swallowed, thinking uneasily of what had happened at Tyndale House. His father might not know about that yet but, if it continued, he soon would.

'Yes. Quite clear.'

'I hope so. There is to be no more gossip, Basil. No more sly innuendos – none. There is already enough bad feeling between Christian and us. I do not want it made any worse – so you will leave him and his friends alone from now on. I want your word on that.'

'Of course, Father.' He stood up, thanking God he hadn't said yes to Brinklow's suggestion and intent on escape. 'If you'll excuse me, I – '

'Your *word*, I said,' snapped Eustace. 'Do I have it?'

'*Yes*, damn it! But you can't blame me if people talk. They were doing it anyway and still will. Nobody really believes Kit spent three years giving some fellow and his sons English lessons – and without a word to anyone about where he was. It's ridiculous!'

'That may be so. But you will do nothing to stir the pot. Thanks to what you've already done, anything further will be laid at your door – regardless of whether or not you are responsible for it. And I'd prefer not to have this conversation with you again – as, I'm sure, would you. On which note, I'll bid you good night.'

* * *

Watching his son make a hasty exit, Eustace wondered if he dared trust him to do as he'd been told. He hoped so, he really did. Everything he'd said about Belhaven's attitude and the likely consequences of Basil continuing to stir up trouble of any kind was perfectly true. So far, Christian hadn't fought back ... but there was no guarantee that he wouldn't. Worse still, Belhaven had been alerted to Basil's ill-judged rumours by a fellow duke; Rockliffe, for heaven's sake! The last thing Eustace needed was *that* gentleman taking an interest in what was starting to look like a family feud of Shakespearean proportions.

Although he didn't want to know, beyond any shadow of doubt, what Basil had done in Athens, he couldn't help wondering what it had been. On the night of Christian's out-of-the-blue reappearance, Eustace had experienced a moment of overwhelming certainty that Basil had never expected to see his cousin again – and not only because, after an absence of three years, it had become a possibility. Just for an instant, Basil had looked at Christian as if he was a ghost ... his face a picture of horrified disbelief. At the time, Eustace had merely hoped no one else had noticed; later, he'd grappled with the uneasy suspicion that, if Basil thought was Christian dead, he must have reason to do so; and later still that, regardless of anything he might have done being dragged into the light of day, here he was busily inciting further hostility and attracting the unfavourable notice of not one but two dukes. Eustace began to fear that, thanks to his idiot son, they were hovering dangerously near the brink of disaster.

* * *

On the following evening, Anthony Wendover agreed to join Lord Oscar and a couple of his friends at the Cocoa Tree Club. Christian and Benedict declined the invitation in favour of a quiet dinner at Sinclairs; but Daniel who, though he rarely gambled himself, was content to watch others hazarding their money, agreed to join the party.

Since cards, dice and wagering were the main activities at the Cocoa Tree, the company was frequently what might politely be described as robust. As Anthony and Daniel entered the club, something that the uninitiated might have mistaken for a small riot was taking place around the Hazard table – and drawing irritable protests from those gentlemen attempting to enjoy a sedate game of cards.

Daniel looked around, grinned and remarked that he'd seen less rowdy taverns.

'What?' shouted Anthony. And then, 'Never mind. I can't see Oscar, so let's try the other room, shall we?'

The next room was quieter, though not by much, with the noise from beyond drifting through the open doorway. But they spotted Lord Oscar, together with Viscount Rainham and a fellow neither of them knew, at a table in the far corner and made their way over to them.

Smiling, Oscar rose to greet them. His companions remained seated; Rainham, managing to look both affable and sleepily dangerous ... the other fellow, alert and somehow measuring.

'Welcome,' said Oscar. 'I'm presuming Rainham needs no introduction to either of you ... but I don't believe you know Adam Brandon. Adam – meet Anthony, Lord Wendover and Daniel Shelbourne.'

Everyone shook hands and, with the civilities behind them, Daniel took the seat beside Mr Brandon, saying, 'You're the gentleman who owns the *Salle d'Armes* in Cleveland Row, aren't you?'

'I *co*-own it,' corrected Adam easily. 'Thinking of giving us a try?'

'Eager to do so.' Daniel grinned. 'Sebastian Wingham's been singing your praises.'

'Ah. Doubtless he'll be asking me for a discount.' He looked across at Anthony who had taken the chair opposite.

'And what of you, my lord? Have you any interest in swordplay?'

Anthony laughed. 'None at all. I'm a peaceful mortal. Also, if Rainham is one of your pupils – '

'I'm not,' said the viscount.

'He isn't,' confirmed Adam with a lurking smile. '*He* likes pistols.'

'And he *doesn't*,' added Rainham, purely to have the last word.

Having ordered more wine, glasses and decks of cards, Oscar resumed his seat and, breaking the seal on one of the packs, said, 'Very well, gentlemen. What shall it be? Basset, perhaps? Or whist?'

Rainham shrugged. 'Either suits me.'

'Count me out,' said Daniel firmly. 'I won't play – but am happy to watch.'

'You disapprove of gaming?' asked Rainham lazily.

'Not at all. But the most useful lesson I learned at Oxford was that of not getting drawn in beyond my means,' came the rueful reply. 'And fortunately, I'm not particularly fond of cards. But please don't let me stop the rest of you.'

Adam opened his mouth to speak, then changed his mind. The others agreed on basset and the game began with Anthony winning the privilege of the first bank. In a lull between hands, Adam said, 'I imagine that you fence, Mr Shelbourne?'

'Daniel, please – and yes. Tolerably well, I believe. But I've no experience at all with swords.' He gestured to the one at Adam's hip. 'That one looks very … intimidating.'

'It's supposed to. Sebastian will presumably have told you that the biggest difference – and the most immediate difficulty – is getting used to the extra weight?'

'He mentioned that after each of the first few sessions his arm and shoulder ached like the devil,' grinned Daniel. 'But he also admitted it gets better.'

'Adam – are you in or not?' prompted Oscar. 'It's your play.'

'My apologies.' Adam pulled a card from his hand more or less at random.

'Thank you,' said Anthony mildly, when Adam lost again. 'Might I suggest that you consider at least *glancing* at the bank's card and then at your hand before you play? You'll find the game goes better for you that way.'

'Yes,' agreed Adam with a wry grin. 'I imagine that it might.'

During another pause when the bank passed from Anthony to Rainham, Adam said quietly to Daniel, 'I'm not much of a gamester either. But for the fact that they needed at least four players for basset, I'd have challenged you to a round or two of cribbage for shilling points instead.'

Daniel laughed. 'I'd have accepted.' Then, rising from his seat, he added, 'If you'll all excuse me, I think I'll stretch my legs and watch good money being thrown after bad at the Hazard table for a little while.'

'I'll accompany you, if I may,' said Adam. And politely to the others, 'And if the game can spare me for a few minutes?'

'I daresay we'll manage,' retorted Oscar. 'I wanted a word with Anthony anyway ... and wouldn't mind hearing any thoughts *you* may have on the matter, Rainham.'

His lordship's brows lifted and he shrugged. 'They're yours if you want them.'

As Adam and Daniel left the table, they heard Oscar say, 'These rumours of Selwyn's, Anthony ... are you and my brother doing anything about them?'

'Why are you asking me rather than Benedict?'

'Why do you think?'

'Oh dear,' murmured Daniel as he and Adam moved away, 'Doesn't Oscar know that, if Ben isn't talking, Anthony won't either?'

'Or you, presumably?' asked Adam.

'Or me.' Daniel glanced at him. 'You've doubtless heard the said rumours?'

'Yes. Selwyn appears to have run out of viable gossip that would be sufficiently damaging and is now reduced to scraping the barrel.'

'Thank you.'

'No thanks needed. A few months ago, my younger brother was the target of something similar – though in his case the eventual outcome was a happy one.'

The crowd around the Hazard table had lessened but was no less boisterous. Daniel sent a grin in Adam's direction and, in doing so, noticed the three men sitting at a table to his left. As though mention of his name had summoned him, Basil Selwyn sat there with his usual friends. None of them had seen Daniel yet; Basil, because he had his back to him, Thetford and Bartlett because they were intent on their cards.

Daniel took in all this at a glance ... and one thing more. A footman was about to set down a steaming bowl of rum punch. Opportunity and temptation coincided. In one smooth and very slight movement, Daniel pivoted as if about to say something over his shoulder to Adam ... and the unfortunate waiter tripped, lurched and fumbled with the bowl. Just for a second, he seemed to right himself and it looked as if catastrophe might be averted. Then, for no apparent reason, he stumbled again ... and a couple of pints of hot punch cascaded over Mr Selwyn, soaking his back, right arm and splashing into his hair.

'*What the – ?*' Basil leapt from his seat, sending a sticky shower flying across the table. Whirling on the footman and about to deliver a blistering tirade, his eyes met Daniel's ... and he froze.

Then, '*You!*' he spat. '*You* did that, you bastard. And on purpose.'

Several gentlemen at the Hazard table stopped playing and looked around.

'What?' asked Daniel, looking baffled. Then, irritably, 'Don't be ridiculous. It was an accident. The poor fellow tripped, that's all.'

'Oh he did that, all right – but not without help,' raged Basil, dripping and trying to drag off his ruined coat. 'You tripped him. Deliberately.'

'And risk the stuff being spilled over me? I'm not *that* stupid. Er ... dare I mention that you have a slice of lemon in your hair?'

Finally getting out of the coat, Basil hurled it down, furiously aware that the punch had already soaked through both vest and shirt. Then, groping blindly for the lemon, he glared at the footman who was still rooted to the spot, unsure what to do for the best. 'You. Tell me the truth. He tripped you, didn't he?'

Hesitating, the footman threw a hopeful glance in Adam's direction but didn't find the sight of a cool-eyed stranger with one hand resting on the hilt of a nasty-looking sword reassuring. He swallowed uncomfortably and, looking back at Basil, stammered, 'I'm sorry, sir. It – it was an accident. I don't rightly know how it happened. I'll take your coat, sir, shall I? And bring you a – '

'You can fetch the manager,' snarled Basil. 'Either I get the truth or I'll have you turned off without a character.'

'Calm down, Selwyn,' advised Daniel as the footman fled. And with an annoyingly indulgent smile, 'You're overwrought. What you need is a brandy to settle your nerves and a hackney so you can go home and take a bath.'

More heads turned, somebody sniggered and play at the Hazard table ceased.

Seemingly oblivious to this, Basil shouted, 'Don't tell me what I need! *You* did this. I *know* you did.'

'You don't because I didn't.' Brushing an invisible bit of fluff from his sleeve, he added sympathetically, 'Your imagination is running away with you. It's been doing that a lot recently, hasn't it? You should try *Mrs Baxter's Elixir*. My great-aunt swears by it when her nerves are – '

'There's nothing wrong with my nerves, damn you! You tripped the footman deliberately. Admit it!' And when Daniel merely shook his head, 'Then you're a bloody liar!'

The gasp of shock that rippled through his audience was lost on Basil, as was a voice saying, 'Take that back while you still can, Selwyn.'

But Thetford and Bartlett, who had been keeping wary eyes on Adam, and choosing not to get involved, heard both. They glanced at each other and pushed back their chairs but before they could rise, Basil snapped, 'Where do you think you're going? You saw what happened. *Tell* him.'

'I didn't see anything,' mumbled Thetford.

'Nor I,' added Bartlett quickly. 'Was concentrating on the game.'

'And you can't leave now,' said Daniel, folding his arms and his eyes never leaving Basil. 'Things are just getting interesting. You called me a liar, Baz. That's a bit rich coming from you – a fellow who wouldn't know the truth if it sat up and bit him. However ... now everybody is listening and waiting for one of two things; your apology or my cartel.' He smiled again. 'Your move.'

He stopped as, arriving belatedly at his side, Anthony's hand closed hard on his arm.

'Leave it, Dan. This isn't helpful. Just walk away.'

'In a minute.' And shaking off the restraining hand, 'Well, Basil – *are* you going to apologise?'

Finally aware just how many eyes were on him, Basil snapped, 'To you? No. Damned if I will.'

'I see. Then count yourself fortunate that *I'll* be damned before I lower myself to fight a sneaking, cowardly little weasel like you,' enunciated Daniel clearly and with calm contempt. 'So run along home, why don't you? No one here will be surprised – or miss you.'

There was a faint murmur of what might have been agreement and it caused Basil to lose what little was left of his temper. Sweeping up his glass, he dashed its contents in Mr Shelbourne's face and said, 'Maybe this will change your mind!'

The audience and Anthony emitted a collective groan.

Quite without haste, Daniel reached for his handkerchief, mopped his face and said, 'Indeed. Viscount Rainham and Lord Oscar Hawkridge will act for me. They're in the next room – though I suggest you take time to consider before you send your buffoons to set matters in motion. Goodnight, Selwyn.' And to the room at large, 'And gentlemen ... my apologies for the disturbance.'

The room erupted into a buzz of chatter.

Anthony stalked irritably away without a word.

Adam, strolling at Daniel's side, said softly, 'That was the result you wanted?'

'Yes.'

'Right from the moment you tripped the footman?'

Daniel grinned. 'You saw that?'

'No. But it's the only logical explanation. May I ask *why* you were so determined to force Selwyn to challenge you?'

'Because I'm under orders not to challenge *him*,' came the regretful reply. Then, more cheerfully, 'Also, it gives me the choice of weapons. I intend to be ... creative.'

Upon learning that they were to have the honour of seconding Mr Shelbourne, Oscar said, 'My pleasure.'

Rainham, on the other hand, said, 'Why me?'

Daniel shrugged. 'Anthony and Benedict would probably refuse and I thought it best not to involve Kit ...or any of the four of us, for that matter. But I shouldn't have presumed.'

'Perish the thought.' Smiling, Rainham rose and stretched. 'Life has been tedious recently. The only thing you need apologise for is that Selwyn's seconds will almost certainly be Thetford and Bartlett ... neither of whom has either a brain or any manners worth mentioning. But into each life a little rain must fall, as they say.'

CHAPTER FOURTEEN

On the following morning, Sophia was, by turns, both excited and nervous thanks to the plans that she and her friend, Drusilla Colwich, had hatched on the previous evening. These had come about because she hadn't had more than five minutes alone with Christian since he'd admitted that he *did* want to kiss her. Consequently, she had been unable to try out her own scheme of luring him to do a little *more* than that and couldn't see the next few days changing it unless she *did* something. So she had ... only now she was being plagued by second thoughts.

It was annoying. More annoying still, was Gwendoline.

'How much longer is it going to take you and Hazelmere to stop dithering?' she demanded petulantly. 'This 'getting to know each other again' business is taking forever.'

'It's only been a few weeks. And he was away for – '

'For five years. Yes. We know. But he takes you driving nearly every other day and Lucy Bentall says he dances with you twice at every ball. If the two of you don't know your own minds by now, you never will. So ... what are you waiting for?'

There being no easy answer to this, Sophia hesitated, thus giving Gwendoline the chance to add, 'As if I don't know. You're waiting for him to ask again.' And impaling Sophia with a gimlet stare, 'Because he hasn't, has he?'

Sophia sighed. 'Not yet, no.'

'So the real question is what *he's* waiting for. Or whether he's going to ask at *all*.'

Silence fell as both of them contemplated the possibility that he might not.

Finally, Gwendoline said bitterly, 'Well, you'd better find out what his intentions are, Sophie, because I need to know where I stand. Edwin is getting closer and closer to making me an offer. He almost scraped up the courage to do it yesterday after he'd examined Papa. But if you're going to marry Hazelmere – '

'Wait a minute,' interrupted Sophia. 'What have Kit and I to do with whether or not you marry Doctor Freeman? And I thought you liked him?'

'I *do* like him and I'm aware that I could do worse. He may be a younger son but he's from a good family with money. But, given the opportunity, I could do better – and that depends on you. If you marry Hazelmere, I can refuse Edwin. If you don't, I'll have to accept. And I'd like to know which it's going to be.'

Sophia considered asking her sister if she realised just how unpleasant this attitude made her sound. But knowing that saying so would do little good, she settled for, 'You don't *have* to marry him, regardless of what *I* do.'

'Of course I do! I was to have a second Season once you were safely betrothed to Basil but that didn't happen and I've been left in limbo. So Mama isn't going to let me turn Edwin down unless there's a better prospect – which there *won't* be unless you're in a position to help me to find one. And it isn't as if you don't want to marry Lord Hazelmere. Goodness knows you've been pining for him – and waiting for him – long enough. Delaying yet again now he's finally back in England isn't at all fair of him.'

'This has nothing to do with fairness,' murmured Sophia. 'After what he's been through, Kit needs time to – '

'And he's had it,' said Gwendoline flatly. 'Have you even *tried* to bring him to the point?' And when Sophia said nothing, 'I see. Then it's time you did.'

'It's not that simple.'

'Yes, it is. According to Mama, the whole of society is speculating about whether his lordship is going to come up to scratch or not. In case he hasn't realised how humiliating that is for you, it's time you told him. Or if you can't, *I'll* do it.'

'No!' Sophia stood up, her patience finally snapping. 'Kit and I have an understanding. If and when he's ready to ask me to marry him, he will. What he most assuredly does *not* need is you and Mama badgering him about it for no better reason than that it would be convenient to *you* if he and I married. So you will not say a word about any of this to Kit. And you can stop nagging me as well.' Then she walked out.

Alone in her bedchamber, she scowled at Jingo and said, 'It's all very well for you to grin. *You* don't have people trying to make you do things that are solely for their benefit but the very worst you could do regarding your own. Of *course* I want to marry Kit. But first, I want him to hold me and kiss me and tell me he loves me ... and if only it will go on raining this afternoon, there may actually be some chance of that happening.'

* * *

In Dover Street, meanwhile, Benedict glared balefully at Daniel and said, 'What part of "ignore Basil for now and save retribution until we're ready" didn't you understand?'

'I understood all of it. But the opportunity was there and –'

'And you didn't even *try* to resist it.'

'No. And if you'd seen Baz Selwyn, drenched in rum punch and decorated with bits of lemon and the odd clove, you'd understand why.'

'I already know why. For weeks, you've been wanting an excuse to – if not fight him, then at least do *something*. And now you've got your wish; a damned *duel*, for God's sake!'

'His challenge, not mine.'

'That makes scant difference. And according to Anthony, you goaded him into it.'

'Tattle-tale,' muttered Daniel with a sour glance in Anthony's direction.

'If I hadn't told him, somebody else would have,' came the calm reply. 'There were plenty of witnesses – and nobody was in any doubt about the real reason you were baiting him. I suppose you *did* trip the footman?'

'He's already admitted as much, hasn't he?' observed Christian dryly. And to Daniel, 'Who else knows that for certain, by the way?'

'Only the footman, but he won't talk. I squared it with him last night and spoke to the club manager so he won't lose his position. Oh – and Brandon guessed, but he won't say anything either.'

'Sure about that, are you?' demanded Benedict.

'Yes.'

'Even though last night was the first time you'd met the fellow?'

'Yes. Spare me the lecture, Ben. What's done is done. So why not ask me whether it's to be swords or pistols.'

Since Benedict simply scowled, it was left to Christian to say, 'Well? Which is it?'

'Neither, as it happens.' Daniel's expression lightened and he laughed. 'After all, there's no law that says it has to be one or the other, is there?'

'So?'

'So we'll duel on the bridge over the Serpentine in Hyde Park, each of us armed with a paddle. Whoever hits the water first, loses.'

Benedict, Anthony and Christian stared at him in silence for a moment. Finally, Christian said, 'Will that even work? Won't the railings be in the way?'

'No. We'll be doing it *above* the railings from a temporary platform. Rainham and Oscar are finding a carpenter who'll knock something up for us.' Daniel grinned. 'When everything is in hand, they'll tell Thetford and Bartlett. I'd give a lot to see their faces.'

'Oh my God,' groaned Benedict. 'Didn't my fool of a brother even *try* to talk you out of this?'

'Out of what? The duel or the manner of it?'

'Both.'

'Why would he? In fact, it was Oscar who suggested setting the meeting up for the day after tomorrow to allow word to get around.'

'Wonderful! Why don't you just sell tickets?' asked Benedict. And then, 'Vere is going to have a fit.'

Silence fell again. Then Anthony said doubtfully, 'Basil won't do it.'

'He will,' insisted Daniel. 'He'll have to – because the only way he can refuse with a shred of honour is to withdraw his challenge and apologise to me. And he won't do that – partly out of bloody-mindedness and partly because the fool won't be sure I'll accept his apology. Then again, even if he didn't already know, by now someone will have told him that I've been out twice before and what happened on those occasions.'

'What *did* happen?' asked Christian.

'Both of my opponents left the field with a nice, tidy sword-thrust to their left arm … after which we all enjoyed a hearty and very merry breakfast.' Daniel shrugged and added simply, 'The chances of my encounter with Basil ending that way are somewhere below zero.'

* * *

By the time Christian arrived in Charles Street that afternoon, the light drizzle that had been falling on and off all morning made driving in the park a poor choice. He said, 'Montagu House, do you think?'

And Sophia, in the wake of some hasty correspondence exchanged with Drusilla during the last couple of hours, said brightly, 'That's a lovely idea – but another day, perhaps? Lady Colwich sent a note inviting us to call on her if the rain persisted. So might we do that instead?'

'Of course, if you wish. Where does she live?'

'Hill Street. It's no distance so we could walk.'

'It's no distance from Berkeley Square either – and if I'm to leave the horses standing, I'd sooner do so at home.' He smiled at her and offered his arm. 'I'll also get an umbrella. So … shall we?'

Pulse racing, she nodded enthusiastically. He didn't need to know what she and Drusilla had agreed until the time came.

In Hill Street, they handed the wet umbrella to the Colwich's butler and received a warm welcome from her ladyship. Christian didn't know Anthony's Cousin Drusilla particularly well but was aware of her close and long-standing friendship with Sophia so he prepared himself for an hour of drinking tea while the ladies gossiped. In fact, that didn't happen. They *did* drink tea, of course ... but, while they did so, Drusilla asked him non-intrusive questions such as how it felt to be back in his own home and whether the alterations made by his uncle were to his taste.

Then, to his absolute astonishment, she rose and, smiling, said, 'I haven't forgotten how, when Jonathan and I were in your situation, holding a truly private conversation was virtually impossible. So I don't suppose you will mind in the least if I leave you in order to attend to matters elsewhere.' And she walked out.

Christian eyed Sophia with an expression that defied interpretation. Then he said, 'You planned this.'

'Yes.' She swallowed, suddenly uncertain. 'Do you mind?'

'No. I'm merely somewhat taken aback. Why didn't you warn me?'

'You might have felt that it wasn't a good idea.'

'Really?' Amusement touched his gaze. 'On a scale of one to ten, how likely do you suppose that was?'

She tilted her head, considering it. 'Five?'

He laughed. 'Not even close. It's a good thing you didn't have money riding on it. On the other hand, it shows how little confidence you have in me. My fault, of course.'

'Don't say that. Blame has no part in this, Kit. We made an agreement.'

'More than one, as I recall.'

Sophia felt her colour rise but she refused to look away. 'Yes.'

Christian wondered if she had arranged this afternoon in the anticipation of something more than conversation ... and discovered that he hoped she had because he wanted the same thing. He'd made a mess of it last time. Today, he felt remarkably clear-headed and confident that he could do better. So he rose, crossed to sit beside her and slid an arm about her, saying, 'One.'

She blinked. 'One what?'

'One out of ten that I'd have refused to come.'

And gathering her against him, he found her mouth with his. Sophia made a tiny, inarticulate sound and her hand rose to touch his cheek. It was all the encouragement he needed. He folded her closer and sank into the heat and sweetness she offered. As it had before, though mercifully less overwhelmingly, desire stirred and this time he found he was able to welcome it. He kissed her jaw, her cheekbones, her eyelids, then her lips again. She sighed into his mouth and her hands tangled in his hair. Christian stopped thinking and set his hands free to go where they would.

Sophia wasn't thinking either. This ... *this* was what she'd wanted but hardly dared hope for; Kit as he'd been five long years ago. Holding her, touching her, kissing her as if she was the entire world to him ... his mouth and hands lighting little fires which blazed and merged and sent sparks exploding through her body. His palm grazed her breast and she gave a tiny, involuntary sob of pleasure as she traced his jaw with kisses.

And without warning, for Christian everything suddenly seemed *right*. All the bits of him that had felt jumbled or broken or missing suddenly fused into wholeness and a sense of self he hadn't known in three years. This was Sophie-Rose ... and he *loved* her. He'd *always* loved her. Distantly, very distantly as yet, he wondered why it had taken him so long, not to remember – but to *feel* it in every fibre of his being. The knowledge brought increased arousal with it. He acknowledged it and, for a moment or two, allowed himself to enjoy it fully. Then, with reluctance, he eased Sophia away just a little and, taking her hands from around his neck, held them in his on her lap.

He read several things in her face. Love, wonderment and sexual languor, slowly fading into rueful disappointment. She opened her mouth to speak but, as rueful as she, he said quickly, 'Don't, Sophie. It wouldn't take much to tempt me, love. But it's my job to call a halt, not yours. I don't know what I was thinking when I said I'd trust you to tell me to stop.

Actually, I don't know what I've been thinking about a lot of things these last weeks. Can you forgive me?'

She smiled a little and shook her head. 'There's nothing to — '

'Stop. Stop letting me off lightly. There are matters for which I ought to ask forgiveness. And I want to set some of those transgressions right – now, while we have a few minutes of privacy.' He hesitated briefly and then said, 'As you're aware, I've been keeping things from you. I don't know *why* I did but I do know I didn't need to. I never did so before, did I?'

'No. I don't believe so.'

Christian nodded. 'And there's no need to do it now – so let me put that right. I won't bother with the mess that's been going on inside my head. You're all too familiar with that. But that other matter I spoke of ... the one I was convinced needed to be resolved before things could be settled between you and I ... well, I doubt you'll be surprised to learn that it concerns Basil.'

'No. I suspected as much.' She smiled at him. 'You don't have to tell me about it if you'd rather not.'

'When it comes to the results of his actions, I'd *much* rather not. But it's necessary. I can't leave that secret lying between us. Firstly, if you and I are to – to move forward, you have a right to know; and it would come out eventually anyway.' He drew a deep breath. 'You once asked me what Basil did, so here it is. His rumour about me being taken by slavers is true. But it wasn't an unfortunate accident. It happened because he paid a man to arrange it.'

'*What?*'

'Yes. Incredible as it sounds, it's true. Basil paid my guide to hand me over to the slavers and to instruct the slave-master to sell me to the galleys. Had that happened, I'd almost certainly be dead by now. Fortunately, the slave-master decided I'd be worth more elsewhere ... and elsewhere turned out to be Ibrahim's palace.'

When he stopped speaking, Sophia's hands tightened on his and she stared at him. Her face was pale and her eyes furious. 'That is – no. I don't know *what* that is. There aren't words. How could Basil be so *evil?* How could *anyone?*'

'He saw a way to get rid of me and he used it,' came the grim reply. 'And the longer I was missing, the longer I seemed to have vanished without a trace, the more certain he'd have become that I was gone for good. My reappearance would have been a nasty shock – yet he brazened it out and remains confident that he got away with attempted murder.' A slow, unpleasant smile ... one Sophia didn't recognise ... touched his face. Finally, he added simply, 'He thinks I don't know what he did. He thinks nobody knows. He thinks he's safe.'

She expelled a long, slow breath. 'But he isn't.'

'No. For the moment, we're letting him continue to think it but very soon we'll set about exposing him. We believe we have a way to do it.' He paused and then, almost as an afterthought said, 'Benedict and the others call what we're planning justice. *I* call it what it is. Revenge. I tell myself that, when I have it, I'll be able to put those three stolen years and their after-effects behind me. That I'll stop feeling incomplete ... almost insubstantial ... as if I'm only a shadow of the man I was before.'

'*Is* that how you feel?'

'Some of the time – and less often now than I used to. But not today, here with you.' The silver eyes looked deeply into hers, their expression intense. 'I love you, Sophie-Rose – even more, perhaps, than I ever did. I'm only sorry it's taken me so long to say it.'

A starburst of joy exploded within Sophia and she threw herself back into his arms. 'Oh *Kit!* It doesn't matter how long it took. It only matters that you've said it now. And I love you, too. I always have and always will. But I think you know that.'

'Yes. I think I do, too.' Because it felt so good to hold her, he went on doing it but said, 'Bear with me a little longer because I'm not finished yet. Although I've so far avoided asking that all-important question, I want you to know that I *will* ask it ... when I'm no longer planning vengeance and can come to you with clean hands.'

Her reply was a smile so incandescent it dazzled him.

'Then I'll wait. But you must know there isn't anything you can do that will change the answer I gave you the first time.'

'There you go again,' he reproved. 'Don't you want to punish me even a little?'

'I might ... except that I think you've already suffered enough.'

'Perhaps. But not at your hands.' Unsure how much longer Lady Colwich would leave them alone, he kept his kiss brief before creating a little space between them. Then, electing to lighten the mood, he whispered, 'Shall I tell you something I really shouldn't? Something we gentlemen try very hard to keep from you ladies?'

She nodded. 'Please.'

'Last night, Basil challenged Daniel to a duel.'

'*Basil* did? Why?'

'Daniel caused a footman to tip a bowl of punch over Basil's head and then taunted him until he completely lost his temper.' Taking out his watch and glancing at it, he said, 'Round about now, I imagine Basil is regretting that. On the other hand, at least he knows nobody will die.' Christian grinned suddenly. 'They're going to settle it by trying to knock each other off the bridge over the Serpentine. And Oscar Hawkridge will be inviting spectators.'

Sophia laughed but said, 'I doubt if this is part of your plan to expose Basil's villainy?'

'Far from it. And Benedict is less than happy about it. But hopefully it will cause more laughter than speculation about anything more sinister.' Then, his expression growing serious again, he lowered his voice to say, 'I meant what I said earlier, Sophie. You do know that, don't you?'

'Yes. Deep down, I think I always knew it.'

'If so, that's more than I deserve.' He brushed his lips lightly over hers. 'But ... thank you. And forgive me for taking so long to say it.'

'Stop that, Kit. Even before you told me about Basil, I realised that those three years had left their mark – and I'm aware that you haven't told me even *half* of what they were really like. Perhaps you never will. But at least now I understand it a little better. And though you can never forget what happened, you will gradually leave it further and further behind you.' She hesitated and then added, 'I'd like to help you do that, if you'll let me.'

'Sweetheart, you already help. More,' he said quickly, rising in response to the sound of a hand on the door latch, 'than I can tell you.'

CHAPTER FIFTEEN

As Christian and Anthony had predicted, Basil did not take the manner in which the duel was to be fought well.

'Why the hell didn't you say I wouldn't agree to anything so damned ridiculous?' he demanded of a very hangdog Thetford and Bartlett – neither of whom, truth be told, wanted anything to do with either the duel or Mr Shelbourne's intimidating seconds. 'It's an affair of honour – not a circus act!'

'We tried,' mumbled Mr Thetford miserably. 'We told them you wouldn't do it and nobody could blame you for that. But Rainham said Shelbourne has the choice of weapons so you must either accept it or withdraw your challenge and apologise unless …'

'Unless what?'

Thetford cast a glance of appeal at Bartlett but got no help.

'Unless you don't mind sacrificing your – your honour as a gentleman.'

Basil swore, long and hard.

'Those are the rules, Basil, old boy.' Bartlett finally shouldered his share of the disagreeable task. 'No denying that.'

There was a long, smouldering silence into which Thetford forced himself to whisper, 'And Hawkridge said that since the offence was a public one, so should the apology be.'

Hot colour burned in Basil's cheeks. He snapped, 'I am not damned well apologising at *all*. And I'm not making a spectacle of myself in Hyde Park, either.'

'Shelbourne will be making a spectacle of himself as well,' offered Thetford hopefully.

'*Shelbourne* will make sure word gets out so there'll be an audience – mostly of his friends. No. I won't do it. Go back to Rainham and Hawkridge and tell them I demand the affair be conducted in a proper manner. Swords or pistols – not this bloody fiasco.'

'Not disagreeing with you, Basil ... but at least this way, nobody really gets hurt. Pistols are risky – good chance of getting killed by accident with pistols.'

Bartlett shook his head. 'Shelbourne won't choose pistols, Fred. He's been out twice, chose swords both times – and won, as well.'

'He did?' Basil's expression shifted, suggesting he hadn't known this.

'Yes. The other fellows went about with an arm in a sling for a week or so afterwards.' Bartlett decided to press what he hoped was an advantage. 'I reckon this mad start gives you as good a chance of winning as it does him. And really, if you won't apologise, what choice have you got? Because I can tell you now, there'll be no budging Rainham.'

Basil encompassed his friends in a filthy look. Then, because he knew they were right – he really *didn't* have any choice – he said curtly, 'When?'

Thetford heaved a sigh of relief. 'The day after tomorrow at eight in the morning. Shall we tell Rainham and Hawkridge you've agreed?'

'What do *you* think?' growled Basil.

* * *

That evening and throughout the following day, word of the duel spread to every gentleman's club, gaming house and sporting venue. Gentlemen who rarely rose before noon decided that this was something it might be worth getting out of bed early for. Everywhere Mr Shelbourne went, he was greeted with teasing laughter ... and the fact that Mr Selwyn hadn't stirred from his house since issuing his challenge caused a similar reaction.

Predictably, Mr Eustace Selwyn had opinions on the matter.

'I despair, Basil – I really do. Were you drunk?'

'No.'

'Then could you not have *pretended* the incident with the punch was an accident? Or, at the very least, refrained from accusing Shelbourne? And why, when – mystifyingly, in my opinion – he held back from challenging you, did you *have* to force a challenge on him?'

'He was sneering at me,' came the surly reply.

'Since you made it so easy for him, I'm not surprised. Neither am I surprised those whispers of yours have provoked some reprisal. It might have been worse, I suppose. As for the nature of the duel itself ... well. What can I say?'

'I tried to get it changed. Do you think I *want* to prance about like an idiot?'

'Probably not. But prancing about like idiots may be the one saving grace.' Eustace rose and prepared to quit the room. 'While people are laughing, they aren't coming to less savoury conclusions.'

* * *

On the night before the duel, at Lady Elliott's supper party-cum-informal ball, Christian partnered Sophia for the quadrille and then strolled with her to the neighbouring room where refreshments were laid out for a glass of wine.

She said, 'There's no sign of Basil. But perhaps he wasn't invited. Drusilla told me he's been receiving a few cold shoulders recently.'

'So I believe. *My* spies say he hasn't been seen since that night at the Cocoa Tree.'

'Well, he'll have to leave the house tomorrow. Will you go?'

'To watch the duel? Yes. Benedict thinks it will draw quite a crowd.' He leaned a little closer. 'Apparently, a lot of gentlemen are wagering on the outcome – most of them putting their money on Daniel. And speaking of Daniel, here he comes with Oscar.'

Sophia smiled at both gentlemen but said severely, 'You're rather late, aren't you?'

'A little, perhaps,' shrugged Oscar. 'But her ladyship has graciously forgiven us.'

'Of course she has. Dukes' brothers are *always* welcome.'

He winced. 'Ouch. That was unkind.'

'To me, as well,' complained Daniel. 'The implication being that *I'm* merely welcomed for the company I keep.'

Her brows rose. 'Did I say that?'

'You may as well have done.'

'Peace, children,' said Christian on a note of laughter. And then, 'Ready for the morrow, Daniel?'

'As much as one can be. It's not the sort of thing you can actually practise.'

'I suppose not. And how is Belhaven taking *your* involvement in the affair, Oscar? Benedict says he won't be happy about it.'

'Benedict's wrong,' came the calm reply. 'Vere is amused. He even said that if the meeting was being held at a more civilised hour, he'd consider attending.'

'Did he?' asked Sophia. 'That *would* turn a few heads.'

'And raise a few eyebrows as well, no doubt. But he won't come. He generally stays up reading until all hours, then sleeps most of the morning. A bad habit, of course ... but I daresay we all have one of those.' Oscar looked at Daniel. 'And speaking of sleep, I assume you intend to go to bed betimes and sober tonight?'

'Sober, yes . Early ... we'll see. Why do you ask? Still deciding on whom to place your money?'

'No. I did that yesterday – as did Benedict and Vere. The book at White's had odds in your favour of eight-to-one, though that may have increased by now.'

It was Daniel's turn to wince.

'Do you know,' he said, 'I'd really much rather you hadn't told me that.'

* * *

The morning of the duel dawned dry and bright. Lord Oscar and Viscount Rainham called for Daniel promptly at twenty minutes past seven to conduct him to his engagement. They arrived at the Serpentine to discover a crowd of some two dozen gentlemen already there and others still making their way through the park.

Watching Daniel survey the sturdy, if temporary, structure that the carpenters had erected across the railings at the top of the bridge, Rainham asked, 'Do you still think this was a good idea?'

'Yes.' In one lithe movement, Daniel swung himself up on to the platform and tested its solidity with a bounce or two. A handful of onlookers applauded and he bowed. 'Save it for later, gentlemen. I haven't won yet,' he called. And more quietly, 'This is perfect, Rainham. Thank you for getting it done.'

'It was scarcely arduous.'

'Even so.' Stooping, he rested one hand on the boards in order to drop back down. Then, pulling off his coat, he asked what the time was.

'Five to eight,' supplied Oscar. 'No sign of Basil as yet.'

'Well, I hope he turns up.' The vest followed the coat and Daniel sat down to pull off his boots. 'If he doesn't, I'll need a volunteer to take his place rather than deprive our friends of their entertainment.'

Oscar laughed but said, 'Well, don't look at me.' And as he turned away to rejoin Rainham, 'Here's Kit.'

Glancing at Christian whilst yanking off his other boot, Daniel said, 'I wasn't sure you'd come. Benedict and Anthony won't.'

'Showing their disapproval.' Christian leaned against the railing, gauging the height of the platform before looking down into the water. 'Is it deep enough here to be safe?'

'Rainham says so.'

'Then let's hope he's right. Who is that fair-haired fellow with him?'

Daniel finished removing his stockings and stood up, clad only in shirt and breeches.

'Adam Brandon. I'm surprised he's here ... but perhaps I shouldn't be. I've an idea that he and Rainham know each other much better than one would expect. By the way, I'm going to book a session at his *Salle d'Armes*. If you're interested in joining me, I'll introduce you. But for now, would you mind putting my clothes out of harm's way — and somewhere nobody will think it hilarious to make off with them?'

'Certainly.' Grinning, Christian gathered up the discarded clothing. 'I'm sure we're all relieved you didn't remove quite *everything*. Ah … here's Basil now, along with the attendant clowns. None of them look happy.'

They weren't. The crowd had continued to swell and was now between thirty and forty strong, with knots of gentlemen spread along either bank. Scowling at Rainham, Basil said, 'This isn't appropriate. I suppose I don't need to ask who is responsible for it.'

'No. You know how it is,' replied his lordship lazily. 'Word gets around. But we should make a start. I suggest you and your seconds make whatever preparations you think necessary on this bank, while Hawkridge and I take the other. Before the duel commences, I shall announce the rules — such as they are. If you have any questions, ask them then.' And he strolled on to the bridge, followed by Oscar.

Basil glared at Daniel, lounging against the railing on the far side.

'Look at him! Half-naked and already making an exhibition of himself. Well, I shall *not* be doing the same.'

Bartlett eyed the pair of paddles leaning against the platform. They'd been shortened a bit but still looked awkward things to wield. He said uneasily, 'Only a suggestion … but it'd be easier without your coat.'

'What the hell would you know about it?' snarled Basil.

And Thetford — who'd been about to recommend removing his boots as well, in the event of a ducking — promptly shut his mouth.

Basil stamped on to the bridge. 'Let's just get this over, shall we?'

On the far side, Oscar shook hands with Daniel and departed, laughing. Rainham took up centre stage, caused the onlookers to fall silent with a mere glance, and said,

'Gentlemen ... please take your positions on your end of the platform.'

As before, Daniel hoisted himself up easily. Basil stared at the structure as if he didn't know where to start. Somebody shouted, 'Better fetch him a ladder, Rainham.' The crowd laughed. Basil grabbed hold of the platform with one hand, the railings with the other and heaved himself up part of the way to the sound of tearing stitches. It took several more ungainly movements before he managed to clamber to the top.

Rainham waited patiently, watching with a critical eye. Then, when both parties seemed ready to begin, he said, 'You each have a paddle, gentlemen. The point of them is *not* to inflict the greatest bodily harm – and blows above shoulder height are fouls. One of these will be considered an error; two, and you will immediately be declared the loser. But you may avoid your opponent's blows however you choose ... and whichever of you sends the other into the water has won. Any questions?'

'No,' said Daniel.

Silence. Then, 'No,' echoed Basil.

'Very well.' Rainham left the bridge and joined Oscar on the bank. 'Take up your weapons ... and *begin!*'

Daniel tested the weight and heft of the paddle in a downward swing; Basil took a wild swipe, lost his balance and very nearly went overboard. Laughter swelled.

'If Selwyn falls in by accident, does Shelbourne still win?' shouted someone.

'Save your energy, Dan,' advised another. 'If you're patient, he'll do the job for you.'

Basil ground his teeth and aimed a blow at Daniel's knees ... clumsily, due to the tightness of his coat. Seeing it coming, Daniel blocked it with his paddle and, with a grin, said conversationally, 'I stripped for a reason, Baz. Wishing you'd done the same?'

The reply was a furious swing at chest-height. Daniel dropped into a crouch to let it sail over his head ... and then, before Basil had time to react, made a quick jab at his midriff.

This very nearly ended the affair. Basil tottered on the edge of the platform, arms flailing like windmills; then in a movement that looked scarcely possible, he somehow twisted to the side and dropped to his knees. The onlookers whistled and there was some desultory applause. Heart beating erratically and far too fast, Basil clung to his paddle with sweating palms and sat back on his heels, trying to catch his breath. Several voices told him to get up.

'Are you conceding, Mr Selwyn?' asked Rainham presently.

'No,' panted Basil, 'No, I'm not.'

'Then I suggest you stand up. Mr Shelbourne is within his rights to continue whether you do or not.'

'I don't mind waiting,' said Daniel, 'though not indefinitely, of course. I want my breakfast. Come on, Baz. We've barely begun. You can't be done for already.'

'If you ask me, he was *done for* before you started,' called out Nicholas Wynstanton. Then, 'Get on with it, Dan. You're not the only one who's looking forward to breakfast.'

Daniel shrugged. 'On your feet, Baz. I'll give you to a count to ten. One …'

Obligingly, the crowd took up the count on his behalf. Basil started struggling to his feet when it reached six. At ten, he was upright but unprepared for Daniel's quick, playful poke at his stomach. He tottered again and took a step back, ending up perilously close to the edge.

'Whoa!' shouted half the crowd while the rest roared for Daniel to finish it.

Yet again, Basil somehow managed to regain his balance. Across the width of the bridge, Daniel grinned provocatively at him, saying, 'Your turn, Baz. I'm right here. Take a swing at me, why don't you? Otherwise the gentlemen who've put their money on you – and I believe there *are* a few of them – may be a bit annoyed that you didn't make more of an effort.' And over his shoulder, 'Anyone know what the current odds are at White's?'

'They were twelve-to-one on you when I left at midnight,' supplied Sebastian Wingham.

'And fifteen-to-one by three this morning,' shouted somebody at the back.

'Oh dear. Not exactly a tribute to your abilities, is it? Or, dare I say it, your popularity.' Daniel's smile grew sympathetic. 'Are you going to try proving them wrong by managing to hit me at least once ... or are you going to let me have it all my own way?'

Throughout all this, Basil had been growing steadily white with temper. He growled, 'Why you arrogant bastard, I'll bloody kill you!' And, putting every ounce of his strength behind it, swung the paddle. If it had connected, it would have hit Daniel's head, causing the crowd to roar, 'Foul!' But the cry was unnecessary.

Daniel ducked. Basil, borne by his own momentum, spun on sideways and, not even having the presence of mind to drop the paddle, was carried over the edge of the platform with something between a shriek and a grunt, to land in the Serpentine with an enormous splash. A cheer went up.

Looking critically down to where his erstwhile opponent was losing a floundering battle to keep afloat, Daniel called, 'Somebody ought to fish him out. The idiot's still wearing his coat and boots.'

'You two,' snapped Rainham, to Thetford and Bartlett. And when they didn't move, 'He's *your* principal. Are you going to let him drown?'

They looked at each other, then at the head once again disappearing beneath the water and finally took a couple of plainly reluctant steps towards the edge of the lake.

'Oh for God's sake,' muttered Daniel, sitting down on the edge of the platform.

Then, with a muttered curse, he jumped in after Basil.

* * *

Weighed down by his clothes, unable to clear the surface and already taking in water instead of air, Basil was panicking. It took Daniel three attempts to get a firm hold on his collar –

by which time Basil had hit him in the face twice, almost wrenched out a handful of his hair and nearly drowned them both. Daniel didn't waste what little breath he had telling the fool to calm down and stop fighting; he concentrated on replacing his grip on Basil's collar with a stranglehold around his neck. Then he set about trying to reach the bank.

Hands reached out when he got there. Someone – Rainham, he thought muzzily – hauled Basil out to drop him face down on the bank and bellowed an expletive-laden order for Thetford and Bartlet to make themselves useful. Then two other men knelt down to grasp his own arms and heaved him out.

For a few moments, he remained on his hands and knees, coughing up the Serpentine and trying to shake the water from his ears … and was distantly aware of somebody saying coolly, 'Well done. You can't have wanted to do that.' It was Adam Brandon.

'I didn't,' Daniel croaked. 'But somebody had to.'

A blanket settled around his shoulders and a silver hip-flask was put in his hand. Christian said, 'Brandy, courtesy of Rainham. Drink it. Oscar's taking your clothes to my carriage but you won't want to put them on – so as soon as you're ready, I'll drive you home. There are a lot of fellows eager to clap you on the back but they'll have to wait. Mr Brandon … do you think you could clear a path?'

'I'll certainly help,' replied Adam. And with a hint of amusement, 'But I think you'll find Rainham's already shooing everyone away – and sensible men don't argue with him.'

Shivering a little, Daniel took a second swallow from Rainham's flask, then struggled to his feet. 'Where's Basil?'

'The clowns have him,' said Christian, his tone suggesting he couldn't care less. 'You probably saved his miserable life just now – for all the thanks you're likely to get.'

'At least nobody can say I was responsible for killing him.'

'They couldn't have said that anyway,' observed Adam.

'Somebody would have. This whole thing was my idea. But I didn't bargain for him being stupid enough to do it fully dressed.'

'Then you should have,' said Christian. 'He doesn't *think*. He *never* thinks. He just acts on the first thing that comes to mind. But never mind that. Let's just get you home and into a hot bath.' He held out his hand to Adam. 'It was a pleasure to meet you, sir – and thank you for your help.'

'No thanks needed.' Adam gripped the offered hand and smiled. 'It's been an interesting morning. If you want another – but rather different one – drop in at Cleveland Row some time. You can watch one of my sessions or, if I'm free, try what we offer for yourselves. And no. I am not touting for business. My partner and I don't need to. Trial sessions are given free of charge because we prefer not to take on paying clients who only come out of idle curiosity, haven't the necessary stamina or demonstrate little or no aptitude.'

CHAPTER SIXTEEN

Leaving Daniel soaking in a hot bath, attended by his valet, Christian went home intending to devote the rest of the day to dealing with sundry business matters. A letter in Sophia's hand waited for him on the salver in the hall so he picked it up and took it with him to the library. Sitting behind the large, carved desk with various ledgers already open before him, Gerald looked up and said, 'How did it go?'

'Not entirely as planned,' replied Christian. And, in as few words as possible, recounted the events of the morning. 'By this evening – if not sooner – there will be rousing choruses of *See the Conquering Hero Comes* every time Daniel shows his face.'

Gerald grinned. 'And what will they sing for Basil?'

'Nothing he'll like or want to hear.' Sitting down on the other side of the desk, Christian broke the seal of the letter and started to skim the contents. Then he sat up, frowning, and began again.

Kit, she had written.

Please come as soon as you can. Papa had a second apoplexy during the night and remains unconscious. Doctor Freeman says we should be prepared for the worst. Everything is in turmoil and Mama is distraught. She is convinced that we will be evicted from the house the very instant Papa breathes his last. She will not listen to reason, so I cannot convince her otherwise – and Gwen is no help. I know you can't do anything about any of this. But it will be such a relief for me to discuss the situation with someone sane, so I ask again. Please, please come.

Yours, with love,
Sophie

By the time he reached the end, Christian was already on his feet.

'My apologies, Gerald. Our business will have to wait for another day. I have to go out.' He tossed the letter towards him. 'Read it for yourself.'

And was gone.

* * *

In Charles Street, there was no sign of the butler and the footman who answered the door bore all the appearance of somebody who had been attempting to do three things at once. Christian said, 'Where are the ladies?'

'Her ladyship is upstairs with – with his lordship and the doctor, sir. The young ladies are in the drawing room.'

'Thank you. There's no need to show me up – I know the way and am sure you've got your hands full.'

He tapped on the drawing-room door before opening it. Sophia was on her feet in an instant and half way across the room, hands outstretched.

'Kit – thank goodness!'

He accepted her hands and continued to hold them.

'How is your father?'

'The same as he was when I wrote to you.'

'And the doctor's opinion?'

'Also unchanged. I'm sorry to drag you here when I know there's nothing you can do but I hoped – '

'Of course there's something he can do,' cut in Gwendoline. 'If he chooses to, that is.'

'Not another *word!*' snapped Sophia, dragging her hands free and whirling furiously on her sister. 'You will not interfere in this. And if you persist in attempting to do so, you can forget getting help of any kind from me in the future. In fact, it's unlikely that I will ever *speak* to you again. Do you understand me?'

Gwendoline shrugged, looking mulish, but remained silent.

'Ignore her, Kit. As usual, she's only thinking of herself. Come to the library where we can be private. I'll ask one of the servants to let Mama know you are here and ask her to join us when she comes down.'

Once inside the library with the door closed behind them, Christian took her in his arms and said, 'Your mother is being irrational ... but that is understandable under the circumstances. I'll talk to her. She may be more inclined to listen to a man – *any* man – than she is to her daughter.'

'Yes. That's what I hoped when I wrote to you.' She sighed, leaning against him. 'Cousin George won't *really* throw us out on the street before Papa is even cold, will he?'

'I'm not acquainted with him but I'd have thought it unlikely ... unless there's bad blood between him and your father. Is there?'

'None that I'm aware of. Papa hasn't seen him in years and the rest of us scarcely know him.'

'Then there would seem to be no reason for him to act callously – and, in any case, doing so will be beyond his power until the Will has been read and all the other formalities taken care of.' He held her close and stroked her hair. 'He has an estate of his own, doesn't he?'

Sophia nodded against his shoulder.

'In Cheshire – a more profitable one than ours, if Mama is to be believed. But no London house. And the entail covers nearly everything.'

'I know.' Christian chased various thoughts around his head. 'Wait and see what the lawyers say. It's possible that all these anxieties are needless. But if it turns out that they're not and if your mother will allow me to help – '

'*If?*' She gave a choke of sardonic laughter. 'She'll *demand* that you do before you have a chance to offer.'

'Very likely. But that's of no consequence. Do you honestly think I'd stand idly by while your family is made homeless?'

'No. But – '

'Good. Because I won't.'

Partly to distract her and partly because he wanted to, he tilted her face up to his and kissed her. Fortunately, the tap of heeled shoes approaching the door gave him sufficient warning to release her and create some distance between them, just before Lady Kelsall whirled in, wild-eyed and already talking.

'Hazelmere! Thank goodness! Sophia has told you, of course? Joseph hasn't woken up and the doctor says he may never do so. This is so cruel. How are we to say goodbye to him? And I don't know *what* is to become of the girls and me if he dies. You are aware how things stand with us.'

'I am, yes.' Keeping his voice level and utterly calm, Christian led her to a sofa and sat down beside her. Then, in as few words as possible – despite her ladyship's continual interruptions – he repeated everything he'd said to Sophia, finishing with, 'At present, all we can do is hope that Sir Joseph recovers. If he does, the situation is no worse than it was yesterday. If, sadly, he does not –'

'If he does *not* we are at George Kelsall's mercy. And he has four sons. *Four!*'

Refraining from asking what difference that made, Christian said, 'Be that as it may, there is no point worrying until you know precisely how matters stand. At present, you are making assumptions without having a clear picture of the facts.'

'I know *one* thing,' she said, rending her handkerchief into tiny pieces. 'If you and Sophia had not delayed and delayed and delayed, you might be married by now and I would be spared all this worry. But if –'

'Mama, please *stop!*' begged Sophia. 'That is neither true nor fair.'

'If your father dies *now*,' continued Lady Kelsall inexorably, 'even if the two of you reach an agreement today, you won't be able to marry for a year. A *year*, do you hear me?'

Aware that all this was getting them nowhere, Christian said firmly, 'You are back to speculation and baleful prophecy again, my lady. Who are Sir Joseph's lawyers?'

'What? Oh. Harding, Gillow & Son. Why do you ask?'

'In the event of Sir Joseph's death, should anything require clarification, I'd like my own man of law, Henry Lessing, to confer with them. Would that be acceptable to you?'

'I – yes, I suppose it would. But I don't see what you expect that to achieve. There would still be the wretched entail.'

'Quite. There's no escaping that, I'm afraid. But you really must stop dwelling on the worst case, my lady. You will make yourself ill – which won't help anyone.'

'And telling me that everything will be all right *will*?'

'That isn't what I'm doing. But as yet, for all you know to the contrary, it might be. Mr George Kelsall may have little interest in this house for the immediate future. He may equally be content for you to continue to live in Kelsall Grange for the time being – or, if not, put the Dower House at your disposal as, indeed, one would expect.' He rose, preparing to take his leave. 'You are not staring into the abyss – not yet, at least. And although we can consider what may be done about it if and when you are, we can do nothing at all yet. Sophie ... a word, if I may, before I go?'

'Yes, of course.'

She stood up. 'Allow us a few moments if you will, Mama.'

'I've allowed you a good many moments,' returned her mother bitterly, 'for all the good it's done.' And she swept from the room.

Sophia gave a sigh of relief but said uncomfortably, 'I'm sorry, Kit. She behaves as if helping us is no more than you ought to do and it's quite wrong of her.'

'As I said earlier, that is of no consequence because I want to help and I will,' he replied rapidly. 'But I want to talk about us. Your father's sudden decline alters several things – not least the priorities I spoke of a few days ago. Dealing with Basil can wait. *You* are what matters. But I won't risk you thinking I'm only offering marriage because your mother and sister think I should. And when I go down on one knee and tell you what is in my heart, I'd like it to be at a less fraught moment than this – though how we're to find one while your father's life hangs in the balance, I have no idea.' He paused and drew a long breath. 'I believe there may be *one* possible solution. Admittedly it's one that your mother won't like ... but it will achieve the desired result. Can you give me a few hours to try and work it out?'

'Of course. You know you need not ask.'

'Thank you.' He pulled her into his arms for a long, sweet kiss. Minutes later and continuing to hold her, he said, 'Our secret for now, then?'

'Yes.' She smiled although tears trembled on her lashes. 'Our secret.'

* * *

Back in Berkeley Square, Gerald was working on the quarterly accounts from Hazelmere but as soon as Christian walked in, he laid down his pen and said, 'Well?'

Christian dropped into a chair and passed a weary hand over his face.

'Sir Joseph is still breathing ... but that's about all he's doing. His wife, predictably, is the Voice of Doom. And naturally, when disaster strikes, it will be my fault.'

'How so?'

'For not marrying Sophie before they're made homeless due to the entail.'

'Nonsense.'

'I know.' He fell silent for a moment and then said, 'I want to marry Sophie and I will. The only reason I haven't already proposed for a second time is that I'd hoped to put the Basil situation behind me before I did so. That will not be possible now. Furthermore, Lady Kelsall cheerily pointed out that, if Sir Joseph dies, the family's year of mourning will make a wedding out of the question.'

'Ah. Yes. There is that.'

'There is. But surely it's *only* true in the case of a lavish affair at St George's, Hanover Square, followed by an extravagant wedding breakfast with the whole of the *ton* in attendance. Surely a small, private ceremony must be allowable?'

'One would certainly hope so. Is that what you're thinking of?'

'Yes. But I want to go a step beyond it. I want to be able to marry Sophie at the drop of a hat if circumstances make it either desirable or necessary – and for that I'm going to need to have a special licence already in my pocket. The question is … how do I go about getting one?'

Gerald rubbed the bridge of his nose.

'I *think* you get them from the Archbishop of Canterbury. But there must be a process that means you don't have to approach His Grace directly.' He thought for a moment. 'The place for ecclesiastical law is Doctors' Commons. Presumably, someone there will be able to point me in the right direction. But I imagine that you'll have to make the actual application in person … and doubtless there's a fee. I'll look into it.'

'Make it a priority, please.' Christian let his head fall back against the chair and communed silently with the ceiling for a moment. Then, 'One way and another, this has turned into a hell of a day. I'm half inclined not to step out of the house again in case of further dramas.'

'In that case, since there are several hours left of this afternoon, can I persuade you to look through the Hazelmere accounts?'

Christian groaned. '*Must* I?' And before Gerald could answer, 'Yes, I suppose I must. But can we *please* do it over a glass of wine and some food? Thanks to the duel and Sophie's note, I've had nothing to eat today.'

'Fine.' Gerald pulled the bell for Fallon. 'We'll eat. And later, while you study the accounts, I'll go to Doctors' Commons.'

* * *

In Charles Street, Doctor Freeman left for a short while to fulfil commitments to some of his other patients. During his absence, Sir Joseph's care fell to his faithful valet of thirty years while Lady Kelsall paced back and forth in the hallway outside, insisting that she be immediately informed of any change. And downstairs, Sophia and Julia held a silent conversation that Gwendoline couldn't follow.

'What are you talking about?' she demanded at length. 'It's rude to do that when someone else is in the room.'

'It's also rude to talk non-stop when one person can't hear you,' retorted Sophia. 'And you could have learned to sign but you couldn't be bothered. However ... Julia asked what things must be done if – if Papa passes away. So I was explaining about mourning clothes and arrangements for the funeral and black-edged stationery and – and so on.'

'Black,' muttered Gwendoline. 'I *hate* black and we'll be wearing it for *months*.'

Letting her hands join her voice for Julia's benefit, Sophia said aridly, 'What we'll be wearing is the least of our worries since we won't be going anywhere.'

'*I* wasn't going anywhere anyway unless you count walks in the park and tea with Mama's friends. *You're* the one who's been going to balls and parties and drives to Richmond.'

'And for the foreseeable future, I won't be. Happy now?'

Julia grinned and signed something which made Sophia smile.

'What did she say?' asked Gwendoline suspiciously.

'Nothing you'll want to hear.' She rose, hearing sounds betokening an arrival. 'That's probably Doctor Freeman coming back. Thanks to all the letters I wrote cancelling Mama's engagements as well as my own, no one will call today.'

A tap at the door was followed by the butler, saying, 'Lady Colwich is here to see you, Miss Kelsall. But she says she will understand if it is inconvenient.'

'It isn't. I'll receive her in the library, Dunne.'

He bowed and withdrew. As Sophia made to follow him, Gwendoline said, 'Secrets, Sophie? Otherwise, why can't she come up here?'

'No secrets, Gwen. But a conversation that isn't punctuated by your constant complaints would be extremely pleasant,' replied Sophia. And sailed out.

Drusilla greeted her with outstretched hands.

'Sophie – I'm so sorry. How is he?'

'The same.' She gripped her friend's fingers and swallowed hard. 'I think ... I think this may be the end, Silla.'

For a moment, Drusilla regarded her in sympathetic silence. Then she said carefully, 'One isn't supposed to say these things ... but your father has had no real life in – what, two years?'

'I know. And it ought to make it easier.' Sophia gestured to a sofa and when they were seated, 'But somehow it doesn't.'

'And your mama?'

'*Definitely* doesn't.'

'Yes. I can imagine.' And Drusilla could – well enough not to pursue this line of conversation. 'Have you had any word from Lord Hazelmere yet?'

Sophia nodded. 'He was here earlier. I – '

'He was? Good heavens! Jonathan came home directly afterwards. But he said his lordship would probably join the rest of them for a long, boisterous breakfast.' She stopped. 'Oh. Perhaps you didn't know about the duel?'

'I did,' groaned Sophia. 'I'd just forgotten about it. And, for obvious reasons, Kit didn't mention it. Do you know what happened?'

Drusilla nodded, her eyes dancing.

'Apparently it was a complete farce until Mr Selwyn fell into the water by accident – fully dressed, including his boots. Jon said it stopped being *quite* so funny when, nobody seemingly being in a hurry to help him out, he went down for the third time.'

'Judging by your expression, I'm guessing he didn't drown?'

'No, he didn't. And guess who rescued him.'

'I can't. Not Kit, I imagine.'

'No. Not him. But the *next* most unlikely person.' And when Sophia continued to look blank, 'Mr Shelbourne, of course! Apparently, he'd stripped down to shirt and breeches before the duel began so, when Selwyn sank, he just jumped off the bridge into the Serpentine and pulled him out.' She sighed. 'I'd like to have seen that. Just think of wet clothes clinging to those muscles and *excellent* shoulders.'

Sophia couldn't help laughing. 'Silla, you're a married woman.'

'Yes. And I adore Jon. But I'm not blind. And Daniel Shelbourne is a particularly fine specimen of masculinity. Admit it.'

'I'm saying nothing ... except thank you.'

'For what?'

'Distracting me from everything here for a few minutes. That is what you were doing, isn't it?'

'Perhaps. And what are friends for? Speaking of which ... what did Hazelmere say?'

'That he'll help, of course. But we had very little time to ourselves. Most of his visit was spent trying to stop Mama's hysterical conviction that we'll all be homeless in a week.' Sophia paused, then added, 'He also said that he and I need to speak privately but doing so for more than a few minutes at a time just now is going to be virtually impossible. Without a very, very good excuse, I can't go out; and, if he comes here, somebody will interrupt – probably at the worst possible moment.'

'My house?' suggested Drusilla.

'Yes. But how can I justify it to Mama?'

'I don't know – yet. However, I'm bound to think of something. Meanwhile, if you want to send a message to his lordship without anyone being the wiser, do it through me. I'll pass it on and bring you any reply.' She rose and shook out her skirts. 'I should go. I promised myself I wouldn't intrude for more than a few minutes ... and all I really wanted to do was assure you that I'm not far away if you need anything. And that offer extends to Lord Hazelmere as well.'

* * *

Sir Joseph Kelsall relinquished his hold on life at eighteen minutes past four the following morning. Lady Kelsall promptly retired to her rooms with a bottle of her special nerve tonic and refused to see anyone but her maid.

By a little after eight, the hatchment was on the door, an order had been placed for mourning stationery and the undertaker summoned to lay out Sir Joseph's body. This done, Sophia took a moment to send hurried notes to Christian and

Lady Colwich. By ten, Lady Kelsall's maid had relayed orders that her ladyship's modiste should be sent for and that her daughters were to have some of their own gowns taken to the kitchen to be dyed black. And, at half past eleven, in answer to Sophia's request, the Earl of Hazelmere arrived ... accompanied by a complete stranger.

Taking her hands in a warm, comforting clasp, Christian said, 'I'm so sorry, Sophie. And presently, you must tell me what else I can do to help. But for now, please allow me to introduce Mr Henry Lessing – the lawyer I told you about yesterday.'

CHAPTER SEVENTEEN

'Oh.' Sophia stared at Mr Lessing. 'I didn't expect ...' And stopped.

'I know. But I asked him to come with me because I thought hearing the likely legal realities from someone well versed in them might help to ease your mother's mind. Will she see him, do you think?'

'I don't know.' Had they been alone, she might have told him that it all depended on how much 'nerve tonic' Mama had consumed. Since they weren't, she said, 'I'll have Dunne bring tea while I find out.' And to Mr Lessing, 'This is very good of you, sir. But, as I'm sure you appreciate, everything is a trifle ... fraught ... at present.'

'Perfectly understandable, Miss Kelsall,' he replied calmly. 'It is always the way when there is a death in the house. And I am sure you are managing admirably.'

'No. Not really. But please excuse me for a few minutes.'

When she had left the room, Christian said grimly, 'If Lady Kelsall deigns to come down and listen to you, that is the most we can expect. Otherwise, she is likely to be more hindrance than help.

'Ah. It appears that Miss Kelsall's only support are her servants. Is that correct?'

'Until now, yes.'

'You will be staying yourself, then?'

Christian nodded. 'I'll be here as much as is possible until all the most immediate arrangements are in place. And, if Miss Kelsall hasn't done it already, I'll send word to her friend, Lady Colwich, in the hope that she can spare a few hours today to provide some female companionship.'

'Of course. But will not Miss Kelsall's sisters –?'

'No. The one nearest to her in age is unintelligent, selfish and will do nothing but whine. The other is seventeen years old and deaf.'

'Oh dear. That is ... unfortunate.'

'Isn't it?' He fell silent as the butler ushered in a footman bearing the tea tray. Then he said, 'A moment, if you can spare it, Dunne.'

'Certainly, my lord.' And when the footman had left, 'How can I help?'

'I'm sure you've been doing your best in that regard already. But can you tell me what is already in hand – and what is not?'

Dunne nodded and did so. When he stopped speaking, Christian said, 'As yet, Sir Joseph's lawyers haven't been informed of his passing?'

'Not to my knowledge, sir. With there being no male relative and her ladyship overset by grief ...'

'Quite. If necessary, I'll attend to it on the family's behalf – but probably not until tomorrow. In the meantime, is there anything you and the staff need?'

'If I may be so bold, my lord, the knowledge that you are here will be sufficient.'

'I doubt that – but appreciate the sentiment. Thank you, Dunne.'

'My lord.' The butler bowed and withdrew.

'Harding, Gillow & Son can wait for twenty-four hours, can't they?' Christian asked Mr Lessing bluntly. 'I'd like the family to have a small breathing space before being confronted with the formalities.'

'Tomorrow will do,' responded the lawyer. 'In truth, legally there's little to be done until after the funeral. One of the partners should pay a condolence call, of course – but he will take care not to intrude further on the family at this time.'

Christian opened his mouth to ask something else but changed his mind as the door opened on Sophia and her mother.

Lady Kelsall acknowledged her visitors with a listless nod and took a seat, keeping Sophia beside her. She said, 'I daresay you mean well, Hazelmere ... but with my husband barely cold, could not whatever this is have waited?'

'Of course, my lady. And it still can, if you wish it. But please allow me to express my most sincere condolences.' And when she merely sniffed into her handkerchief, 'As for Mr Lessing's presence, it occurred to me that a few words from him might go some way to alleviating the worst of the worries you spoke of yesterday. But the choice is yours.'

When she didn't answer, Sophia said gently, 'It need only take a few minutes, Mama and it may make you feel better.'

'I doubt anything will do that. But very well, sir. Say your piece.'

It was scarcely a gracious invitation but Christian supposed that Mr Lessing had heard worse. Certainly, nothing untoward showed in the lawyer's demeanour as he took a few steps nearer to the widow and began quietly explaining the legal order and time-frame observed by his colleagues when dealing with bereavement .

When he stopped speaking and her mother remained silent again, Sophie said, 'So we have time? We need not worry about the future until after the funeral and perhaps not immediately even then?'

'That is correct, Miss Kelsall.'

'You see, Mama? Kit was right.'

'So it seems,' sighed her ladyship. 'Is that all, Mr Lessing?'

'Not quite. It is perfectly customary for your late husband's lawyers or his executor, assuming he named one, to deal with the funeral furnisher on your behalf and to your instructions. Many widows prefer to be spared that ordeal.'

'As would I,' she admitted grudgingly. And rising, 'If there is nothing further, my modiste will be here shortly so I will leave you. As for you, Lord Hazelmere, 'if you *really* wish to help, you know what will do the most good.' And she drifted from the room.

More to dispel the awkward silence than for any other reason, Sophia said, 'Dunne sent to the undertaker's earlier. I wanted them to send some women to – to lay Papa out. But no one has come as yet.'

'Give me their direction and I'll remind them,' said Christian in a tone which suggested whoever had ignored her request would regret it. He turned back to the lawyer. 'Thank you for sparing time for this, Mr Lessing. I may be a little while longer here – but please make use of my carriage if you wish to return to your office.'

'Thank you, my lord. I would appreciate it.' He bowed to Sophia. 'My sincere condolences, Miss Kelsall. Should you wish to consult me further, Lord Hazelmere knows where to find me.' And, with a slight bow, he was gone.

Alone with Sophia, Christian said bluntly, 'How are you bearing up?'

'I hardly know. There seem to be so many small details to take care of that I've begun to lose track. And when the mourning stationery arrives, Mama will have me writing endless letters on her behalf.'

'Have you sent a notice to the *Morning Chronicle*?' And when she shook her head, 'That should reduce the number of letters somewhat. I have an appointment in the City this afternoon and can call at the newspaper offices while I'm there, if that would help.'

'It would. You merely *being* here helps.'

'I'm glad. Send for me at any time and I'll come. Meanwhile, have you been in touch with Lady Colwich?'

'She visited yesterday a little while after you.' The merest hint of a smile dawned. 'She told me about the duel.'

'God. Was that only yesterday?' Then, sticking to the point, 'But what about today? Have you told her your father has died?'

'I sent her a note at the same time I wrote to you. She'll come if she can.'

'I hope so.' He drew her against him and stroked her hair. 'Now, as I said, I've an appointment I need to keep – but I'll be back later.'

'It's all right, you know. You don't have to devote all your time to me. I'll be fine.'

'I know you will. But I'd feel better if you had someone reliable to lean upon in my absence.' He fell silent, continuing to hold her and recalling something that had occurred to him earlier. 'Your mother is ordering mourning clothes. Aren't you?'

A quiver of something that might have been laughter rippled through her.

'No. The maids are currently dyeing some of my and my sisters' gowns black.' Christian muttered something angry under his breath, causing her to add, 'It doesn't matter, you know. As I pointed out to Gwen yesterday, we won't be going anywhere or even receiving many visitors so clothes are the least important thing right now.'

'Except, apparently, to your mother.'

'If it keeps her quiet, it's worth it.'

'You're too forgiving, sweetheart. But I can't complain about that, can I? If you weren't, you'd have given me my marching orders weeks ago.'

'No.' She shifted so that she could look up at him. 'Kit, no. Not ever.'

Christian took the opportunity to kiss her, letting his mouth linger over hers before gliding to her cheek and jaw. His body stirred but he ignored it, keeping the caress light and sweet. Finally, however, he lifted his head to say reluctantly, 'I'm sorry, love. I have to go.'

'You don't have a carriage. Mr Lessing has taken it.'

'I'll get a hackney.'

'You need not. Take ours.'

'Are you sure? As I said, I'll come back later but – '

'So you'll return it then. And we won't need it, will we?' she pointed out reasonably. 'Tell Dunne to have it brought round.'

He smiled a little and tucked an errant curl behind her ear.

'Are you managing me already?'

'Yes. Do you mind?'

'Not in the least. In fact, I'm looking forward to being managed in other ways, too.'

'I'm not sure I know what you mean.'

'You will,' he assured her, a gleam lighting his eyes. 'One day – quite soon, I hope, you will.'

* * *

It being on his way, Christian visited the offices of the *Morning Chronicle* first and placed the appropriate announcement. Then he drove on to Doctors' Commons and, somewhat to his annoyance since he had an appointment, was kept kicking his heels.

It was while he waited that he realised something about himself and wondered why it had taken him until now to notice it. The nightmares had always been intermittent but he couldn't recall the last time he'd had one; and the churning anxiety that had been his constant companion since his return seemed to have disappeared. He felt … whole, at peace with himself and able to focus his entire mind on the current situation and the problems contained within it.

He tried to pinpoint exactly when the change had occurred and eventually traced it back to that afternoon in Drusilla Colwich's house with Sophie. The day he'd held her and kissed her and told her that he loved her. He'd recognised this sense of *rightness* in himself then, hadn't he? Yes. He remembered feeling it. But, although he hadn't actually considered the matter, he realised that, deep down, he hadn't expected it to last. That it seemed to have done so, surprised him. Was opening himself up to Sophie-Rose really all it had taken to set him free, he wondered?

He was so deep in thought that he didn't hear the clerk summoning him to his appointment until the fellow stood in front of him, saying testily, 'Lord Hazelmere! Mr Forrester is ready for you. Please follow me, sir.'

Nodding, Christian did so. Mr Forrester, a middle-aged fellow in wire-rimmed spectacles, rose from his desk and, holding out his hand, said, 'Good afternoon, my lord – and my apologies for the delay. Please be seated and I will try to expedite the matter. A special marriage licence, wasn't it?'

'Yes.'

'We will begin with the necessary details, then. The full names and addresses of yourself and your prospective bride.'

Christian supplied them and watched the lawyer carefully entering them on what he assumed was the requisite form. Then, this done and peering up at him over the spectacles, Forrester said, 'And the bride's date of birth, sir?'

Christian supplied that, too, adding dryly, 'She's over twenty-one. And, before you ask, there is no problem with parental consent, either.'

'A sworn allegation to that effect is required, my lord. It must also state that there is no other impediment to the marriage.'

'There isn't. A sudden death in Miss Kelsall's family means that, if we are to marry in the near future, it must be done quietly – which is why I'm here.'

'Ah. Yes. Of course. My sympathies. Very well, then. Let us proceed.'

And twenty minutes later, having paid the necessary fee, Christian climbed into the Kelsall carriage with the special licence tucked safely inside his pocket.

* * *

Before going back to Charles Street, he decided to make a brief call on Benedict.

'Anthony and I half expected to see you at White's last night,' said that gentleman. 'However, there were plenty of others eager to describe the comedy in Hyde Park. As you'd expect, there was a lot of laughter – so much that I rather regret missing it. And if Daniel had accepted every drink he was offered, we'd have had to take him home in a wheelbarrow.' He smiled wryly. 'You know, Daniel never ceases to surprise me.'

'I think he surprised himself yesterday – which was just as well for Basil.'

'So I've heard.' He gestured to a chair and, when Christian remained standing, 'Do I gather you're not staying?'

'Not for long, no.' He paused and then said simply, 'Sophie's father passed away early this morning.'

'Oh. I'm sorry to hear it. How is she?'

'Coping.'

'And Lady Kelsall?'

'Being her usual self,' supplied Christian tersely. Then, 'Sir Joseph's death brings complications in its wake – some of which I'm attempting to solve in advance.'

'Such as what?'

'Such as the fact that I was on the brink of proposing to Sophie again. I'd have done it already except for some muddled idea of first putting the business of calling Basil to account behind me. Ah.' He stopped abruptly. 'Sophie knows about that, by the way.'

'She does?' And when Christian nodded, 'Does she also know why?'

'Yes. But everything is changed now. Unfortunately, we've got the obligatory year of mourning stretching ahead of us ... so I've acquired a special licence, enabling us to marry quietly. What do you think?'

'I think it sounds like the best – and probably only – solution,' said Benedict. Then, 'What can I do to help?'

Christian smiled for the first time. 'Stand up with me on the day.'

'My pleasure. Meanwhile, why don't we look in at Sinclairs this evening? If Anthony and Daniel are free – and perhaps Oscar, as well – we can dine and you can break the good news. Drag Gerald along as well, if you can.'

* * *

In Charles Street, during Christian's absence, the undertakers arrived to lay out Sir Joseph's body. Downstairs, Gwendoline continued to complain about sacrificing three of her gowns and Julia, who had originally taken the news of their father's death quite calmly, had dissolved into tears on Sophia's shoulder. Fortunately, Lady Colwich arrived and put a stop to both.

Putting a clean handkerchief in Julia's hand and turning the girl's face to hers so she could lip-read, she said slowly, 'It's very sad for us – of course it is. But your Papa has been ill for a very long time and now he is in a better place. Try to remember that.'

Drawing a shaky breath, Julia nodded, swallowed and tried to smile.

'Good girl.' Drusilla patted her cheek and turned towards her sister. 'And as for you, Gwendoline, you really should try to curb this habit of grumbling over everything. It is *most* unattractive. If you have shown that side of yourself to the gentlemen, it's no wonder your Season didn't result in an offer.'

Gwendoline shot to her feet. 'That's not fair! All I said was – oh, never mind. No one *ever* listens to me!' And she swept out.

Julia touched Sophia's sleeve and signed something. Sophia replied and the younger girl managed a shaky laugh. Drusilla eyed them enquiringly.

'She asked what you said to Gwen and I told her,' said Sophia. And then, 'You wouldn't like to try those tactics on Mama, I suppose?'

'No. I know my limitations.'

'Pity.'

Julia stood up, signing that she would leave them to be private.

'You need not,' Sophia told her.

'I know,' came the reply. 'But I'll do it anyway.' And with a little wave for Lady Colwich, she was gone.

Drusilla sighed. 'She's a sweet girl. She never complains, does she – even though she has good cause? But I'm remiss, Sophie. I ought to have begun by offering my condolences. I'm so sorry you have this to bear.'

'Thank you. But what you said to Julia was the truth. Papa *is* in a better place.'

Silence fell for a moment before Drusilla said, 'You've informed Lord Hazelmere?'

'Yes – he was here earlier. He brought his man of law to try and calm Mama.'

'Did it work?'

'For a little while, I think. And fortunately the arrival of her modiste distracted her. That was what brought on Gwen's fit of sulks. As for Kit, there was an appointment he needed to keep but he said he'll be back later.' Sophia's mouth trembled a little and she said unsteadily, 'Silla, I can't tell you how *good* he's being. It's as if he's trying to take the entire burden on to his own shoulders. No one could be kinder.'

'Well, he always was that way, wasn't he? It was never just the stunning good looks that had all the girls sighing over him.' She hesitated and then said, 'Can I ask a bold question?'

'Of course.'

'Do the two of you have an ... understanding?'

It was several moments before Sophie answered. But finally she said, 'Yes. Since that afternoon at your house. But we're not ready to make it public yet.'

'Even if you were, your father's death would make any announcement tricky. But I'm glad things are on the way to being settled between you. To be honest, I never understood why it was taking so long. Whenever you were seen together it was clear to the world that the two of you were still besotted with each other.' She paused again and then added, 'I suppose it was to do with those three years he was missing?'

'Yes.'

'Has he told you about them?'

'Some of it. Less about his actual captivity than how it affected him.'

'And ... how it came about?'

'That, too.' Sophie's expression darkened. 'I'm not permitted to tell you, Silla. All I can say is that it's truly shocking – and will all come out eventually.'

* * *

Christian arrived at the Kelsall house just as Lady Colwich was leaving it. He bowed, escorted her out to her carriage and, without any preamble, said , 'How is she?'

'She's doing as well as one may expect.' Drusilla eyed him thoughtfully and, lowering her voice, said, 'It's no business of mine but I'm going to say this anyway, Lord Hazelmere. The sooner you marry her, the better.'

'I know.'

'Good. Then you are presumably taking steps to do something about it?'

He handed her into her seat and gave her a devastating smile … full of charm but edged with a hint of inflexibility.

'Perhaps,' he said pleasantly. 'But that would be telling, wouldn't it?'

Then, closing the carriage door and signalling to the coachman, he turned back to the house and Sophia … and a decision that had been put off for far too long.

CHAPTER EIGHTEEN

He found her staring gloomily at a stack of black-bordered writing paper and said abruptly, 'Please tell me your mother is going to help with that.'

'At present, it doesn't look like it,' she sighed. Then, 'You just missed Drusilla.'

'We met as she was leaving.' A rueful smile touched his mouth. 'She's extremely ... direct ... isn't she?'

'Extremely. You should have heard the dressing-down she gave Gwen. It was brief but masterly.'

'And well-deserved, I'm sure. But about the letters and so on. I've put the notice in the *Morning Chronicle* and it will be in the newspaper tomorrow. As to the rest, you can't be left to do everything on your own. It's ridiculous. Shall I lend you Gerald tomorrow?'

'Gerald? Oh – your secretary?'

'And also my friend. So ... shall I?'

'I don't know. Would it be appropriate?'

'I don't see why not. He could help you construct what needs to be said and start making copies. Then all *you* need do is add the name of the recipient at the top and your signature at the bottom. What do you think?'

She crossed the room to wrap her arms about him.

'I think you must be the most thoughtful man in the entire universe.'

'That may be an exaggeration. Perhaps the second most thoughtful?' He held her close for a moment and then said, 'Is your mother still in her rooms?' And when she nodded, 'What about your sisters?'

'Gwen is still sulking and is unlikely to show her face before dinner so no one can ask her to *do* anything. And I think Julia is probably working on her tapestry. She suddenly got upset about Papa and needlework soothes her.'

'Good. Then perhaps you and I could stroll in the garden? It's still warm outside and, from what you say, it sounds as if we'll have it to ourselves.'

'Yes. I'd like that.' She picked up a shawl that Julia had left lying on the arm of a chair. 'Let's escape while we have the chance.'

The garden wasn't large but, in the late afternoon, it was a pleasant place with sun in some areas and dappled shade in others. Remembering it from former days, Christian led Sophia to a bench set well away from the house and hidden from it by a vine-covered trellis. Then, when she was seated, he sank to one knee in front of her and coming straight to the point, said, 'Sophie-Rose Kelsall ... love of my life, heart of my heart and true centre of my world ... will you marry me? Not because it's what your mother and sister want or even because it will make whatever your father's cousin does or does not do irrelevant. Will you marry me because I love you and want you and can't imagine a future without you in it? And perhaps, just a little bit, because you feel the same way?'

'Kit,' she whispered, tears trembling on her lashes. 'Oh *Kit*. You have my whole heart. You always did – ever since that moment when you introduced yourself because you were tired of waiting for someone else to do it. But you wanted to deal with Basil first ... so are you quite, quite sure?'

'Utterly, one hundred percent, not a shadow of a doubt sure – and Basil is no longer a priority. So will you?'

'Oh. Then, yes. Yes, please. Of *course* I'll marry you.'

'Thank you.' He rose and pulled her into his arms for a long and increasingly hungry kiss. Minutes later and continuing to hold her, he murmured, 'Before I get completely carried away, we'd better sit down and discuss how to proceed.'

Settling back on to the bench within the curve of his arm, Sophia said, 'Yes. We can announce our betrothal ... but we can't celebrate it, can we? As for the wedding, we've waited so long already. Must we *really* wait for a year as Mama says?'

'No. Or not unless you have your heart set on a big wedding with all the usual trimmings. Have you?'

'No. Not at all. What are you saying?'

'First – just to be clear – I'd like you to have the wedding of your dreams. But your father's death makes it impossible in the near future. We can, however, marry quietly. A private ceremony with only family and very close friends. Would you mind that?'

'No! Of course I wouldn't! But can we? Really?'

'Yes.' He smiled at her. 'My appointment this afternoon was at Doctors' Commons to get a special licence. We can be married anywhere and at any time of our choosing. But the real benefit is that we can do it soon. If you agree, I suggest settling on a day a week or so after your father's funeral. How does that sound?'

She gazed at him, pink and slightly breathless with excitement.

'As soon as that?'

'Yes. If you want to be married in church, we can find one in a less fashionable area. Alternatively, we can be married here at your home or at mine. All you need do is tell me what you want and I'll arrange it.'

'As easy as that?' she teased.

'Yes. So ... what is your preference?'

She thought for a moment. Then, slowly, 'Church or Berkeley Square, I think. After Papa's funeral, this house will still be swathed in black; all the mirrors and some of the windows, Dunne says.'

Christian shuddered. 'It was the same when my father died. Ghastly custom. All right. I'll look for a church and, if I find one I think will do, I'll take you to see it. Then you can decide between that and Hazelmere House.'

Sophie reached up to plant a kiss on his jaw. 'Thank you.'

'Don't thank me, sweetheart. We could have married in St. George's, Hanover Square with half the *ton* in attendance if I hadn't put giving Basil his comeuppance first. But there's one thing I'm determined you *will* have – and that is the perfect wedding gown, which will *not* be black. Don't rely on your damn – I beg your pardon – on your *dear* Mama for this. Go to the best modiste in London – tomorrow, if you can, since there won't be much time. Order exactly what you want and tell them to send the bill to me. Will you do that?'

'Yes. But –'

'No buts, Sophie-Rose. By the time I pay it, you'll be my wife. And if your mother has anything to say on the subject, either tell her to say it to me – or remind her that we're doing what she wants but that *how* we do it is our decision, not hers.'

She looked up at him, laughing a little.

'You're becoming very masterful all of a sudden.'

'And about time, don't you think?' Then, dropping a light kiss on her brow, 'But don't worry. It's unlikely to last long.' He grinned. 'You'll be back to twisting me around your little finger before you know it.'

'Only because you allow it. Do you imagine I don't know that?'

He shook his head. 'That's just what I want you to think. After all, it wouldn't do for you to realise that I'm mere wax in your hands. Other people might start to suspect it, too – and where would that lead? Also, a fellow has his pride, you know.'

'Quite. But I don't think you have anything to worry about there.' She gave a little gurgle. 'Unlike Basil, after yesterday. Have you heard what people are saying?'

'Not as such. But I spoke with Benedict earlier and, according to him, it was the most popular and amusing topic at White's last night. Basil is probably staying out of sight until the worst of it blows over.'

'Hiding, you mean?'

'Hiding,' agreed Christian. Her head was against his shoulder and the garden was an oasis of tranquillity about them. It would be pleasant, he thought, to spend a further hour like this. But the outside world awaited … as, more to the point, did Lady Kelsall. So he said, 'Are you ready for us to go and make your mother's day?'

'Must we?'

'I fear so. Do you think she'll fall on my neck?'

'No,' said Sophia, rising reluctantly. 'I think she'll say *"About time."* Or something very like it.'

* * *

If Lady Kelsall did not fall on his neck, neither did she say anything utterly tactless. She merely conveyed, in fading accents, the impression that her daughter and future son-in-law were finally doing what was expected of them – though it was a great pity that the wedding had to be such a hole-and-corner affair. But at least she deigned to quit her rooms long enough to come downstairs and say it which, as Sophia pointed out to Christian when he was leaving, was a step in the right direction.

By the time she returned to the drawing-room, the glad tidings had been shared with Gwendoline and, less successfully, with Julia who immediately caught her hand and signed, 'What are they saying about his lordship and you?'

'We are going to marry – as soon as possible after Papa's funeral. But because of Papa's death, it will have to be a very small wedding.'

'Does Mama know that?' asked Julia naughtily.

'She knows and is still getting used to the idea,' returned Sophia. Then, in answer to the impatient question that Gwendoline had already asked twice, but continuing to sign for Julia's benefit, 'No, Gwen. The wedding will *not* be a grand affair in St. George's. And if you're about to demand that, as soon as Kit and I are married, I'll start taking you husband-hunting in society, don't. That isn't going to happen either.'

'Well, no. Not *immediately*, perhaps. But after a month or two, you could – '

'No. I couldn't.'

'Enough, Gwendoline,' said Lady Kelsall, irritably. 'We shall show your Papa all the proper respect that is his due.'

'But – '

'*No*. There is a strict etiquette to be observed and if we flouted it, people would be shocked. So we will not. And I wish to hear no more about it. Sophia ... I see that the mourning stationery has arrived. Perhaps tomorrow we can begin informing people?'

'We?' queried Sophia with interest.

'Well, I shall go through the list with you, sorting out those who must be informed and those who need not be. I suppose a notice should also be sent to the newspaper.'

'Kit has already done that. And since it appears that the sole task of letter-writing is going to fall to me, he is also sending his private secretary here to help with it.'

'Is he? How very efficient of him. And how useful it is having a gentleman to take care of these things.'

'Isn't it?'

'I suppose – though, given the nature of it, there will be little enough to do – Hazelmere's secretary can also make the arrangements for your wedding. I forgot to ask. Have you settled upon when and where?'

'Not precisely.' Tired of constantly needing to grit her teeth, Sophia stood up. 'Kit suggests holding it a week after Papa's funeral. As for where ... either a small, discreetly situated church or Hazelmere House.'

'Why not here?' asked Gwendoline.

'Ask me that again tomorrow after the servants have finished readying the house for Papa's funeral,' replied Sophia, already on her way out of the room. 'If you need to.'

* * *

Since both Anthony Wendover and Mr Sandhurst were engaged elsewhere that evening, the gathering at Sinclairs comprised only four gentlemen; Lords Benedict and Oscar, Daniel and Christian. Naturally enough, conversation over dinner initially revolved around the duel.

'No one has seen Selwyn since,' grinned Oscar. 'Thetford and Bartlett have been putting it about that he took a chill from his ducking. I suppose he may have done. But my money is on him being reluctant to show his face in public – and never wanting to lay eyes on Daniel again.'

Shrugging, Mr Shelbourne helped himself to more turbot.

'That would suit me. But he's bound to surface at some point.'

A collective groan greeted his choice of expression, then Benedict said, 'He won't live this down in a hurry. Losing the duel would have been bad enough. But having to be hauled out of the Serpentine by his opponent? He'll be twitted about it for weeks.'

'Probably,' agreed Daniel, 'though perhaps he'll find the sniggers preferable to the cold shoulders he's been receiving recently. However, it wouldn't surprise me if he left Town for a while. And if he does ... well, we know what that means.'

'*I* don't,' objected Oscar. And when no one replied, 'It's glaringly obvious that the three of you, together with Anthony, are planning something which you're all intent on keeping to yourselves but – '

'It's not just the plan,' said Christian. 'It's the reason for it.' He glanced around the table. 'I've nothing against including Oscar. He may see possibilities that we haven't. And I've already broken the bond of silence by telling Sophie.'

Daniel stopped eating. '*All* of it?'

'She knows that we intend to bring Basil down and why. Everything but the actual means we'll be employing to do it – and I'll be sharing that with her, too, when there's an opportunity to do so. It's necessary.' He hesitated and then said, 'Sir Joseph Kelsall died early this morning. The notice will be in the *Morning Chronicle* tomorrow.'

'Ah.' Oscar frowned. 'I'm sorry to hear that. He's been bed-ridden for a long time, of course ... but this will be a difficult time for the family.'

'I second that sentiment,' said Daniel to Christian. 'But how is her father's death responsible for you suddenly telling Sophia everything?'

'Because the day after tomorrow, there will be another announcement in the newspaper; that of our betrothal.'

Benedict, since he was already aware of this, watched his brother's face and saw the slight, wry twist that briefly touched his lips. Then, smiling, Oscar stretched out his hand to Christian, saying, 'My sincere felicitations. I'm sure you'll both be very happy.'

Daniel grinned, slapped Christian on the back and said, 'Well done – and about time, too. But you're surely not going to suffer through a year of mourning before tying the knot?'

'No. We're going to marry quietly by special licence soon after Sir Joseph is laid to rest. And to answer your earlier question, I told Sophie everything because I refuse to begin our life together by keeping secrets.'

'Quite right,' remarked Benedict, replenishing everyone's glass. 'And may I propose a toast to the happy couple. I'm sure I speak for us all – and Anthony as well if he were here – when I say that, though this day has been long in coming, I don't think any of us ever doubted that it *would* come.'

Glasses were raised and the toast drunk. Oscar asked Christian if he and Sophia had decided where to hold the wedding; and Daniel expressed the hope that, small though the occasion would be, the bridegroom's oldest friends would all receive an invitation.

'Count on it,' responded Christian. 'Who else would I want there? And Benedict has agreed to stand up with me.'

'In that case, I'll arrange your bachelor party. It will be a night to remember.'

'As long as I *do* remember it, Dan. The last time we let you organise an evening on the town, we spent the latter part of it in the lock-up.'

'That was years ago in Oxford,' retorted Daniel dismissively. 'And we were twenty, for God's sake!'

'*You* just insisted on fighting a duel with paddles on a bridge over the Serpentine,' countered Benedict. 'At times – mentally, at least – you're *still* twenty.'

'Would anyone mind if we got back to where this conversation started?' asked Oscar, sounding resigned rather than hopeful. 'I asked what you're up to with regard to Basil and Kit said he didn't mind me knowing because I might be able to help. Well?'

Daniel and Benedict exchanged glances.

'Fine with me,' said Daniel, reaching for the wine bottle.

And, 'Very well,' sighed Benedict. 'Just don't go running to Vere with it, will you?'

'No. Is my word good enough or do you want a blood oath?'

Benedict ignored this. 'Kit?'

Christian nodded then, without expression and in as few words as possible, told Oscar what Basil had done in Athens.

His lordship let fly a shocked oath and then said, 'Is that true?'

'Yes.'

'Completely and unequivocally?'

'Again, yes.'

'Then I'm amazed you haven't put a bullet into him.'

'That wouldn't have achieved the result I want,' said Christian. '

'Exposure?' Oscar guessed. And when Christian nodded, 'Can you prove it?'

'Only with my sworn word – which, unfortunately, may not be sufficient.'

'It damned well *should* be,' muttered Daniel.

'I agree. But I can understand why you prefer not to take the risk. And so?'

'And so,' said Christian, 'we are hoping to lure him into betraying himself ... and confessing what he did within earshot of unseen witnesses.' He paused and then added, 'Actually, that is where Belhaven could be extremely useful.'

'He'd do it, too,' admitted Benedict. 'He'd even enjoy it.'

Oscar nodded. 'True. But how are you going to bring this about?'

'By taking a leaf out of Basil's book and employing dirty tactics,' replied Christian grimly. 'In short, we'll be drawing him out by means of forgery and lies.'

And proceeded to explain their plan.

When he stopped speaking, Oscar stared at him silently for a moment before saying dubiously, 'Well ... I suppose that *might* work if you can plug the two gaping holes in it. I'm presuming you know what they are?'

'We do, thank you,' said Benedict repressively. 'Namely, whether Basil will do what we think he'll do ... and, if so, how to predict when he'll do it.'

'Quite. And even if you figure that out, it will still be a long shot.'

'We know that, too,' agreed Christian. 'Unfortunately, implementation of it has had to be postponed, first by Basil's recent crop of scurrilous rumours and more recently by Daniel's duel. If it looks as if we're merely playing a game of tit-for-tat with Basil, it will weaken our credibility. And now there's Sir Joseph's death and my forthcoming wedding ... neither of which I want shadowed with this. So we're going to have to proceed very carefully.'

* * *

Eustace Selwyn saw the notice of Sir Joseph's death on the following morning at breakfast. He was still considering the likely implications of this when Basil sauntered in looking sulkily mulish. It was the first time Eustace had seen him since before the fiasco in Hyde Park ... and, handkerchief in hand, he was still maintaining the fiction of having caught a severe chill.

Eustace said, 'Good morning. Finally ready to face the outside world, are you?'

'Doh,' came the reply, followed by something that sounded like, 'I'b bost udwell.'

'Oh, for God's sake! Don't play the invalid for my benefit. I know what the problem is – and cowering here won't solve it.'

'I'm not cowering.'

'No? What would you call it, then? Not that it matters. The duel was a bad idea – and it's turned out even worse than I expected. The clubs are toasting Shelbourne as a hero. Did you know that?'

Dull colour stained Basil's cheeks but he said nothing.

Eustace sighed. 'Do you think you might try *not* to do anything unutterably stupid for at least a week or two?'

'Actually, I thought I might leave Town for a few days.'

'Oh – by all means! Taking to the heather rather than facing the music will make it all go away, won't it?'

'It will die down.' As, he hoped, would the social slights he'd been receiving since the Tyndale party. 'These things always do.'

'Not if you give the wits even more ammunition by hiding. But suit yourself. After all, you must be accustomed to being laughed at by now. And there are more interesting things to discuss.' Eustace pushed the *Morning Chronicle* across the table. 'Sir Joseph Kelsall died yesterday following a second apoplexy. Unless I am much mistaken, the announcement of Miss Kelsall's betrothal to Christian will follow hard on its heels.'

Basil picked up the newspaper but muttered, 'Why would you suppose that?'

Not for the first time, Eustace wondered how stupid his son really was.

'Because,' he said wearily, 'they've been enacting a second courtship in full view of society for several weeks now; because Sir Joseph's estate is entailed to a cousin; and because Lady Kelsall will see Christian as financial security both for herself and for the younger girls.' He rose from his seat, preparing to leave. 'Finally – and most important of all – because, knowing all this, Christian won't hesitate to step in.'

CHAPTER NINETEEN

While his uncle was taking his cousin to task over breakfast, Christian went to Charles Street in order to introduce Gerald to both Sophia and her mother. However, as he might have expected, Lady Kelsall was still in her rooms and Sophia's only companion was Julia. Christian smiled at the younger girl and made the sign that Sophia had taught him meant 'hello'. Julia smiled back and signed something complicated.

'She said she's glad you're going to be her brother,' translated Sophia. And, to Gerald, 'Good morning, Mr Sandhurst. This is very kind of you. Are you quite sure you don't mind?'

'A few hours with two charming ladies instead of a fellow who imagines everything gets done at a mere wave of his hand? No, Miss Kelsall. I don't mind at all.' He watched her passing his words to her sister, fascinated by the speed with which her hands moved. 'That is most impressive. Was it difficult to learn?'

'The early stages were but one eventually gets the knack of it,' she replied, still signing. 'After that, it's a matter of practice. Julia is much better at it than I am. If you'll excuse Kit and me for a minute, she'll show you where the stationery is and also the rough draft of the letter that I did yesterday.' Then, drawing Christian away towards the window, she said, 'There was a letter from Harding, Gillow & Son this morning. I don't know what it says because Mama has it – but I suppose it's probably their condolences.'

'More than likely.'

'And Drusilla replied to *my* note saying I must go to Phanie for my wedding gown and I must go *immediately* or it won't be done in time. So she's taking me there tomorrow morning.'

'Good. Take Julia with you and let her choose something as well.'

Sophia shook her head regretfully. 'That's kind of you – but I can't possibly.'

'Why not? You heard her – if heard is the right word. I'm going to be her brother.'

'You're going to be Gwen's brother as well. If I take Julia but not her, she'll never let either of us – or *you*, for that matter – hear the last of it.'

He groaned. 'No. All right. Take Gwendoline as well, then.'

'No! I am *not* going to choose styles and fabrics with Gwen at my elbow giving endless opinions I neither want nor need. I want to *enjoy* myself.'

'Oh. When you put it like that ...' he said. 'Very well. But here's another task for you. If at all possible today, try to persuade your mother to settle on a date for the funeral so you and I can do the same for our wedding. Meanwhile, I'll take the announcement of our betrothal to the *Morning Chronicle* and begin looking for churches that I think you might like but which are outside Mayfair.' He took the opportunity to steal a brief kiss. 'I'll report back if and when I find something suitable.' And with a grin, 'Don't work Gerald too hard.'

* * *

Christian had visited six churches before he stumbled upon St. Bride's in Fleet Street and thought he might have found the perfect place. Although the 'wedding-cake spire' had lost a couple of yards in height due to a fairly recent lightning strike, the inside was still as Sir Christopher Wren had built it a century ago. Christian admired the glossy black and white floor, the rich woodwork and the graceful arches of the ceiling ... and decided that St. Bride's would do very well indeed – much better than the drawing-room at home; and his house could host a modest wedding breakfast afterwards. Pleased with himself, he set off back to break the news to Sophia.

In Charles Street, Mr Sandhurst was making Julia laugh with enthusiastic but apparently ridiculous attempts at sign language. When Christian walked in, she was shaking her head and signing back so fast that apparently even Sophia had stopped trying to keep up and was sitting on the side-lines, laughing as much as the other two.

Christian watched from the doorway for a moment or two, then strolled onwards saying mildly, 'I can see you're all still hard at it, so don't let me interrupt.'

Alerted to his presence by the change in Mr Sandhurst's expression, Julia swung around to face him, signing something brief and, Christian suspected, possibly pungent. Then, grasping his hand, she dragged him over to the neat pile of completed letters and indicated them rather like a conjurer producing a rabbit.

'In case you're in any doubt,' remarked Gerald helpfully, 'Miss Julia is pointing out that we have, in fact, been working.'

'I never supposed that you hadn't,' retorted Christian. And, with a grin, 'I'm just glad you're also managing to enjoy yourselves – so please, do carry on and don't mind me. Sophie ... a word, if I may?'

'By all means,' she said, crossing to wrap her fingers about his arm and drawing him to the far side of the room. Then, softly, 'It's remarkable. I don't quite know how your Mr Sandhurst has done it because communication between him and Julia is very limited without me translating. But they seem to manage and I've never, ever seen Julia so animated.'

'It may interest you to know that I haven't heard Gerald laugh like that since Oxford. I didn't realise how serious he'd become until I walked in just now – and I should have done. He's a good friend. As good as Benedict and the others.'

'Well, having him today has been a godsend. Thank you.'

Christian shook his head. 'Don't thank me. He can come again tomorrow if you'd like. I don't think he'd mind. However ... what is the situation with your mother?'

'She had me send a note to the lawyers, asking them to wait on her tomorrow. And she's agreed to holding Papa's funeral a week tomorrow if it can be done. The service will be here in London but Papa's body must be taken to Kelsall Grange for burial in the family cemetery and I don't know how that is to be managed. I explained all that to Mr Sandhurst and he immediately wrote on Mama's behalf to Collingwood &

Sons in Beak Street. He said that they handled your father's interment.'

'If he says so, then they did. We were still at Oxford and it's all a bit of a blur ... but Gerald probably looked the information up in the ledgers before he came here in case it was needed.'

'He's a marvel.'

'He is – so don't make me want to kill him.'

Sophia lifted one eyebrow. 'Jealous, Lord Hazelmere?'

'Have I cause, Miss Kelsall?'

She laughed. 'Absurd man!' Then, 'Did you find a church?'

'As it happens, I did.' He pulled out his watch and glanced at it. 'Since you're going to the dressmaker tomorrow morning and the phaeton is outside the door, I could take you to see it now if you would like.'

'*Now?*' Excitement lit her face. 'Yes! I'll get my hat and cloak.'

Smiling, Christian watched her all but run from the room. Then, strolling over to where Gerald was sorting papers into various piles before handing them to Julia and indicating where they should go, he said, 'I'm taking Sophie to look at St. Bride's in Fleet Street. It shouldn't take much more than an hour.'

Mr Sandhurst nodded and, without looking up, said, 'There are still one or two things to finish off here ... so I'll stay until you get back.'

'Things such as keeping Miss Julia company?' asked Christian slyly.

'Don't be an idiot,' muttered Gerald. 'What is she? Fifteen? Sixteen?'

'Seventeen. But her deafness has left her more sheltered than most girls.'

'*Too* sheltered. From what I've gathered, the only person in this house with whom she can hold a conversation is Miss Kelsall.' Gerald looked up, his expression hard. 'What is the *matter* with her mother and the other sister?'

'Monumental selfishness,' returned Christian quietly. And as Sophia appeared in the doorway, 'Ready?'

'One minute.' She gathered her sister's attention and signed something to which Julia replied with rapid enthusiasm. Then, to Christian, '*Now* I am.'

* * *

Sophia thought St. Bride's as perfect as Christian did; so they sought out the Reverend Highsmith and set a tentative date for their wedding in two weeks' time.

And on the following morning, while Christian braved Theed & Pickett to solve the tricky question of which betrothal ring his love would like best, Sophia set off for Maison Phanie with Drusilla Colwich without telling anyone but Julia where she was going.

On learning what was required, the modiste threw up her hands in horror.

'A bridal gown? In *two weeks? Mais non!* It cannot be done.'

Sophia's face fell.

Refusing to be daunted, Drusilla took the modiste to one side and said softly, 'You *do* realise who Miss Kelsall is and, more to the point, who her husband-to-be is? No? He is Lord Hazelmere – the gentleman frequently referred to as the Lost Earl. And she is the *fiancée* who, for five years, clung to the belief that he would return.'

'Ah.' Phanie's expression changed. '*Vraiment?*'

'Indeed. Unfortunately, the recent death of Miss Kelsall's father means that, unless it is postponed for yet another year – which the couple cannot bear to do – the ceremony must be a private one. So the bridal gown is *crucial* because, after it, the new countess will be condemned to wear black for at least six months – for which she will need a complete wardrobe. Then later ... well, I'm sure you appreciate the situation, *Madame*.'

'Of course.' Phanie took a long look at Sophia and then, drawing a deep breath, said, 'It will be a challenge, *mademoiselle*. But we shall rise to the occasion.' And, clapping her hands, she summoned her assistants and emitted a *feu de joie* of orders.

Collapsing exhausted into the carriage beside Drusilla some four hours later, Sophia said, 'How do you suggest I break it to Kit that, in addition to the wedding dress, Phanie will be furnishing me with two complete wardrobes – one now and one later?'

'Leave mentioning the later one until ... well, later. As for the mourning clothes, if he knows the gown you're wearing used to be blue he'll know why you need them.' Her ladyship smiled. 'I had to do *something*, didn't I? And your wedding gown is going to be *gorgeous*.'

* * *

On Ludgate Hill, it took Christian nearly two hours to narrow down the bewildering array of rings young Mr Rundell laid before him to just six; then the best part of a further hour to reduce the choice to a fine solitaire diamond or a marquise-cut sapphire flanked on each side by moonstones. In the end, he chose the sapphire, allowed himself to be tempted by the necklace and bracelet that matched it, and told Mr Rundell to put the solitaire aside for him.

After he'd put the ring on her finger, Sophia stared at it in silence for so long that he began to worry that he'd got it wrong. Then she looked up at him, eyes misty with tears, and whispered, 'Oh Kit. It – it's *beautiful*. I love it. Thank you. But ...'

'But what?'

'Wait until you see the bills from Phanie,' she said guiltily. 'It's – it isn't just the wedding gown. Between them, Madame and Drusilla talked me into ordering half a dozen mourning ensembles as well.'

'Good.'

'What?'

'Good. I'm *glad* you're having something new rather than making do with old gowns dyed black. But I hope you've also ordered ... other things.' He hesitated and then, with an openly suggestive smile, 'The sort of garments that I alone might see you wear?'

'Oh.' She smiled back, blushing a little. 'Yes. Now you mention it, I *did* purchase a few things which I – I think you may like.'

'In that case, Sophie-Rose,' growled Christian, pulling her onto his lap, 'it will undoubtedly be money well spent.'

* * *

The days leading up to the funeral passed slowly for Christian. He visited his tailor, had Gerald despatch wedding invitations to his closest friends, to Lord and Lady Colwich and to Lady Kelsall's three bosom-bows. Then, in consultation with Sophie, he agreed a menu with his cook for the wedding breakfast.

For Sophia, kept busy with fittings at Phanie's and replying to a renewed cascade of letters, some of condolence and others felicitating her on her betrothal, the time passed a little quicker. Then, three days before the funeral, Cousin George Kelsall – now *Sir* George – arrived, accompanied by Jasper, his second son.

He began by telling them that he'd neither consulted the lawyers nor, as yet, had any word from them but that he didn't anticipate any surprises. Then he bluffly and unwittingly proceeded to demolish all Lady Kelsall's earlier fears.

There would be no need, he said, for the Kelsall ladies to quit the London house.

'Lucy and I have no interest in Town life – never have had – and we've no daughters to establish. But if you could give one or other of my boys house room here from time to time, they'd appreciate it.'

Neither, he said, were they to be evicted from the Wiltshire estate.

'Matthew, my eldest, will inherit all the Cheshire property when I stick my spoon in the wall, so I'll be settling Kelsall Grange on Jasper, here. He knows how to run an estate and it's time he had something of his own to manage. Give him a month or two and he'll see to it that the Dower House is in good repair and comfortable enough for you and your girls to live in at any time. And when you're staying there, he'll make a carriage available for you.' He paused, frowning. 'Now ... there was something else and for the life of me I can't think what it was.'

'Cousin Joseph's burial,' murmured Jasper.

'Yes. That's it. After the funeral service here, I expect you want Joseph laid to rest in the family graveyard at Kelsall Grange?' And when the Dowager nodded, 'Well then, Jasper and I will accompany the coffin on its journey and see to the interment according to your instructions ... or I'll make the necessary arrangements if you wish to attend the burial yourself. Do you?'

'I do. But, alas, I fear it would be too much for my nerves and so I will not.'

Sir George nodded. 'And what I've said regarding the Dower House and this one ... how does all that sound?'

Lady Kelsall inclined her head and magnanimously agreed that it sounded most suitable. Sophia – the only one of her ladyship's daughters permitted to be present at this interview – gritted her teeth and wondered if even the smallest show of gratitude was completely beyond Mama's ability. Later, escorting Sir George and his son to the door, she did her best to remedy the lack and scarcely knew how to reply when George patted her hand and said, 'Only doing what's right, m'dear – only doing what's right. And it's to be expected that your mama isn't herself at present.'

Sophie smiled weakly and swallowed the observation that Mama was *precisely* herself. Unfortunately.

* * *

As was so often the case on these occasions, the day of the funeral was overcast and damp. The service at the church of St. James was no more than moderately well-attended and the deluge which had been threatening all morning, arrived after it ended and the mourners were outside, waiting for their carriages. This caused a number of them to repeat their condolences and offer their regrets for being unable to accept the Dowager's invitation join the family for refreshments. And, with the exception of Sir George and Jasper, those who *did* go to Charles Street did not stay long. The Dowager's bitter observations on this were briefly suspended during the reading of Sir Joseph's will, then resumed immediately after it.

As for the will itself, there were indeed no surprises. The widow's jointure was not large and the sums settled on her daughters, smaller still. Listening to the figures read out by Mr Gillow, Christian found some sympathy for the Dowager's earlier concerns. Without Sir George's generosity, the ladies would have been struggling to live comfortably ... and even with it, Christian realised that he himself would need to supply additional help. He also realised that if that help wasn't carefully managed, his future mother-in-law could be relied upon to take advantage. He made a mental note to consult Mr Lessing and have him put something in place before the wedding – which was now, thank God, a mere week away.

He managed to steal a few minutes alone with Sophia while Sir George, his son and the Dowager were still closeted with the lawyers. Gwendoline tried to follow them but he dissuaded her with a look that clearly said that her company wasn't wanted. Then, as soon as he and Sophia were alone, he took her in his arms and said simply, 'How do you feel?'

'Better thanks to this,' she mumbled into his cravat. 'And I'll be better still in a week's time.'

'Exactly what I've been thinking myself.'

'Kit, I could strangle Mama. After all the things she said about him, Sir George couldn't have been kinder. And she's never once *thanked* him. It's mortifying.'

'Yes, love. I could see you gritting your teeth.'

'Grinding them, more like.' She groaned. 'And she's going to be just the same with you – worse, probably, because she'll make demands and assumptions and – '

'Stop,' said Christian calmly. 'I'll have Henry Lessing make an adequate quarterly allowance to help support her and your sisters. But I'll be making it crystal clear that these additional funds will be administered by Henry and Gerald, not me. They will make sure she understands that the allowance is finite – not an ever-expanding purse.'

'And you think that will work?'

'Yes. Not the first time, perhaps. But eventually. Of course, whatever gifts *you* choose to bestow on her or your sisters are entirely your own affair – though I'd recommend that you don't tell her that.' He paused to kiss her lightly and nibble her ear-lobe. 'And now, something more pleasant for you to think about. I wondered if, after the wedding, you might like to go to Hazelmere for a few days.'

She looked up at him out of glowing eyes, '*Could* we?'

'Yes. You've never been there and I'm looking forward to showing it to you.' Another kiss, this one more lingering. 'I thought we might perhaps spend our first two nights in Berkeley Square, then leave for Oxfordshire next day. We could have a week there away from everyone. I'd like to take you somewhere more exotic and for longer but ...' He paused. 'Well, you know what the 'but' is. So what do you think?'

'I think Hazelmere sounds perfect. And as for the 'but', I know you are impatient to put that behind you and now I know the reasons for it, I understand its importance. So when the time comes, I'll leave you free to do whatever you must or help in any way I can. The choice will be yours.'

* * *

If Christian had thought the week before the funeral slow, the one leading up to the wedding felt endless. With everything arranged, he was left with little to do and scarcely a glimpse of Sophia who seemed to be all but living at the modiste's these days.

But finally, the night of his bachelor party told him that the end was in sight. Bowing to wiser counsels, namely Lord Benedict, Mr Shelbourne regretfully kept his plans for the occasion simple and restricted them to dinner and a little gaming at Sinclairs two evenings before the wedding. For this, Christian was grateful. As he'd expected, Benedict, Anthony, Gerald and Oscar were all there; but so, too, were Lords Sarre, Wingham and Rainham, Nicholas Wynstanton ... and, surprisingly, Adam Brandon, with whom he'd barely exchanged two words whilst heaving Daniel out of the Serpentine.

As they shook hands and, as if Christian had spoken, Adam said, 'No, *I'm* not sure why I was invited this evening either – unless Mr Shelbourne wants a cribbage partner if and when the rest of you plunge into deep basset?'

'Possibly,' agreed Christian, deciding to withhold what Daniel had said about Mr Brandon on the day of the duel and which he suspected was probably nearer the mark. 'Or it may simply be that he enjoyed his visit to your *Salle* and hopes to tempt me to join him in the future.'

'And will you?'

'Probably. But, being woefully out of practise, I'd better stick with foils to begin with.' And changing the subject, 'Leo Brandon the portraitist is your brother, isn't he?'

'For my sins, yes. You have a commission for him?'

Christian nodded. 'In a few weeks, when life returns to normal, yes. I'd like him to paint my bride-to-be.'

* * *

Meanwhile, on the same evening, Sophia's pre-nuptial party took place at Lady Colwich's house because, as Drusilla had said, 'You can't possibly celebrate your last but one night as a spinster surrounded by all the trappings of mourning. Come to Hill Street. I'll invite some other ladies and send the carriage for you and your sisters and mother. Though with a bit of luck,' she finished under her breath, 'one or two of the latter won't wish to come.'

Sophia knew what she meant but thought it a vain hope. Gwendoline wouldn't refuse an evening out, regardless of what it was and it was unlikely that Mama would either. But just as she was about to ready herself for the evening, her mother appeared and said, 'Please give Drusilla my regrets, Sophia. Mrs Bilston has invited me to a small card party at her house – just the two of us, together with Lady Winslow and Mrs Baxter. That will suit me much better just at present. I'm sure Drusilla will understand.'

Drusilla wouldn't just understand – she'd be delighted that Mama had preferred to spend the evening with her three long-standing bosom-bows. Suddenly, Sophie's own evening looked immeasurably brighter. She wondered if, just for tonight, she could get away with wearing one of the gowns that had escaped the dye-vat and then thought mutinously, *Drat it. I'm going to do it anyway. Why not?*

She and her sisters shared a maid and, as usual, Gwendoline had commandeered the girl's services first. For once, Sophie didn't mind and by the time Betty came to her room, she'd laid out a lavender polonaise trimmed with pale grey ribbons. The girl looked at it and said, 'Oh miss! Are you sure? I mean, won't you get in trouble?'

'Not tonight.' And then, 'Miss Gwendoline is wearing black?'

Betty nodded. 'Not that she wanted to.'

'I'm sure,' said Sophia, hiding a smile. 'Help me into the gown, pop along to Miss Julia and lay out her blue dimity, then come back and do my hair, please.'

Consequently, it wasn't until all three of them were in the hall with Lady Colwich's carriage at the door that Gwendoline realised neither of her sisters were wearing black. She said furiously, 'You've done this on purpose! If you hadn't, you'd have *told* me.'

'I didn't decide until the last minute,' shrugged Sophia, 'and by that time you were already dressed.'

'I could have changed. I still can.' And she turned back towards the stairs.

'In which case, Julia and I will leave without you.'

'You can't!'

'We can. So are you coming or not?'

Gwendoline muttered something under her breath, then stalked to the door.

Julia looked enquiringly at Sophia, who signed, 'After my wedding gown was delivered, I asked you both to stay out of my room. You listened. Gwen didn't. This is the result.'

Julia laughed. 'That's evil, Sophie!'

'Isn't it?'

In Hill Street, they found Lizzie Wendover and a select group of young matrons; Caroline Sarre, Cassie Wingham and

Madeleine Wynstanton, all of whom Sophia knew. And two ladies she only knew by sight ... Mrs Adam Brandon and Viscountess Rainham. Having presented Sophia to these two and waited while she, in turn, introduced Julia, Drusilla said, 'Mr Brandon and Lord Rainham are celebrating with the groom's party tonight – so it seemed only fair that their wives should join our festivities. Now ... where is Mason with the refreshments?'

Amidst talk and laughter, they drank wine and ate small sweet and savoury tartlets. Lizzie sat with Julia and tried, much to everyone else's amusement, to master basic sign language. At some point later in the evening, Cassie Wingham asked Sophie to describe her wedding gown, 'Because only Drusilla and your sisters will see it on the actual day.'

So Sophie obliged and everyone agreed that it sounded exquisite. Then, Lady Rainham asked if she minded the constraints mourning placed upon the wedding.

'In small ways, perhaps,' replied Sophia truthfully, 'but not in the ones that really count. When you have waited for five years ... when you've lived with the fear that you'll never see the man you love again ... well, other things stop being important.'

Lady Sarre nodded. 'I can second that. Adrian's been shot twice and –'

'*Twice?*' echoed Camilla.

'Yes. The first time was on our wedding day and – '

'*Really?*' asked Gwendoline, scenting scandal. 'Who shot him?'

'The who and the why are immaterial,' replied Caroline firmly. 'What matters is that, in a single moment, I learned the kind of fear Sophie is talking about – and *she* had to live with it for years, not minutes. So, if Drusilla will forgive my presumption, I'd like you all to raise your glasses to Sophie and Christian ... a love story that has waited a very long time – not for its happy ending – but for its happy *beginning*.'

CHAPTER TWENTY

On the morning of her wedding, Sophia woke early and lay gazing at the gown draped carefully over the sofa, marvelling afresh at its perfection. Nearby on the floor, two small bags waited for the things she would need this morning – all the rest of her clothes and possessions were already at Hazelmere House. But Jingo still grinned at her from the nightstand. He would be the last item to be packed.

It was odd to realise that, after she left it today, this house would no longer be home ... and a little sad that Julia would be the only person she missed. She continued to worry about how Julia would manage – particularly during the week she and Christian would be spending at Hazelmere. But there was nothing she could do about that now. She'd tried to impress on Mama and Gwendoline the importance of allowing Julia to lipread but she hadn't much faith in them remembering to do it. Fortunately, Drusilla had promised to visit often and take Julia out for drives. It would have to do for now.

Sophia looked at the clock and sighed. It was only a little after seven and the wedding wasn't until noon but she was too wide awake and restless to stay where she was. Distant sounds told her that the servants were up and about their duties. Good. It wasn't too early to ring for a bath – and best to do it now, before someone beat her to it. Also, Drusilla had promised to come early, bringing her own maid to dress her hair. Glad that on this day of all days she didn't have to rely on Betty, Sophia got up.

A little later, whilst soaking in scented water, she reflected that, at some point, Gwendoline would turn up to inspect the gown – as if she hadn't already snooped – in order to find fault with it. A small smile curled Sophia's mouth. Since there was no fault to find, it would be interesting which of Gwen's arsenal of disparaging remarks she would choose this time.

In fact, when Sophia was barely out of the bath, it was Julia who arrived first, bubbling with excitement. Next, Betty appeared with a posy of violets and lily of the valley from

Christian. And finally, as expected, Gwendoline swept in, stared at the gown for a moment and then said, 'It's positively plain, isn't it? From what one hears about Phanie, I'd have thought she could do better.' And swept out again.

Sophie sighed, shook her head and then signed Gwendoline's verdict to Julia.

Julia's jaw dropped. 'Plain? Is she blind?'

'No. Just jealous.' And then, 'I hear a carriage. Is it Drusilla?'

Running to the window, Julia confirmed that it was, adding, 'Can I stay for a little while? I won't get in the way and it's too soon for me to change.'

'Stay as long as you like. In fact, if you fetch your things, you can get ready here.'

Julia beamed, blew her a kiss and ran off.

Seconds later and trailed by her maid, Drusilla arrived in a cascade of ruffled eau-de-nil silk to say cheerfully, 'Have you been up since dawn?'

'Not quite.'

'Butterflies?'

Sophia nodded ruefully. 'Swarms of them.'

'So long as they're excited rather than nervous. Are they?'

'Mostly.'

'Good. Well, forget them for a while and let's get started.' Then, as Julia tripped in with a pink striped *robe a l'Anglaise* over her arm, 'Please tell me Gwendoline won't be joining us as well.'

Sophia grinned. 'What do you think?'

While clad in a wrapper over corset and petticoats, Sophia was sitting before the mirror having her hair swept up into a torrent of curls, entwined with silver ribbons, Drusilla laced Julia into the pink gown. She was just about to turn her attention back to the bride when the door opened upon the Dowager who, inevitably Drusilla supposed, was severely resplendent in black figured taffeta.

'Ah – good morning, Drusilla. How kind of you to come and help.'

'It's my pleasure, ma'am. Sophie did as much for me, after all.'

'So she did.' A glance at Julia brought forth a slight frown. 'I am not entirely happy to see mourning being *completely* cast aside.'

'It's only for the day, Mama,' sighed Sophia. 'You surely didn't expect me to be married in black? And Julia's lavender gown was one of those that were dyed – so she has nothing that would even pass as half-mourning.'

'Oh, very well. With the wedding in such an out-of-the-way place, I don't suppose anyone who matters will see – or anyone at all, for that matter. Where is Gwendoline?'

'In her room, I imagine. She's enjoying Betty's undivided attention today.'

'She's probably ready by now,' said Drusilla. Then, cunningly, 'Perhaps *she* has decided upon black. She did the other evening, after all.'

Knowing that Gwendoline would bleed to death sooner than risk being outshone by her sisters again, Sophia kept her face expressionless and said nothing.

'I shall go and see,' allowed the Dowager. 'If she *is* ready, she can keep me company until it is time to leave.'

'Splendid idea,' murmured Drusilla. And briskly to her maid as Lady Kelsall sailed from the room, 'Are you finished, Ann?'

'I believe so, my lady.' The maid held up a hand mirror so that Sophia could see the back of her hair. 'What do you think, Miss?'

Sophia twisted and turned, admiring the apparently artless tumble of curls and said warmly, 'It's lovely, Ann – really lovely. Thank you.'

'Pleasure, Miss. I'll just put some finishing touches to Miss Julia, shall I?'

'Yes, please. That would be very kind.' She signed the maid's offer to Julia who beamed and immediately sat down at the dressing table.

Drusilla, meanwhile, bustled across to where the bridal gown still occupied the room's only chair. 'Time to get you dressed, Sophie. Where are your shoes?' And over her shoulder to the maid, 'Finish Miss Julia, then go and get a cup of tea, Ann. I won't need you again.' She fussed unnecessarily with Sophia's corset laces and took a great deal of interest in her shoes. Then, when the maid left the room, she dropped the under-dress over Sophia's head and, making sure that Julia was in no position to lipread, asked bluntly, 'Has your Mama told you what to expect tonight?'

'No.'

'What – nothing at all?'

Sophia shook her head, mischief dancing in her eyes. 'Thankfully, she didn't need to – not that she's aware of that, of course.'

'What is that supposed to mean?'

'That I already *know* what to expect. Well, some of it, anyway.'

'You do?' And when Sophia nodded. 'How?'

'I asked Kit ages ago.'

Drusilla's jaw dropped. She spluttered. 'You ... you ... and he *told* you?'

'Yes. Why wouldn't he?' And then, 'What's the matter, Silla?'

'I'm trying very, very hard not to imagine that conversation. And not to say ... as long as *telling* you was *all* he did?'

'Don't be ridiculous. Of course it was. Now, are you going to get me into my gown or not?'

Further conversation was suspended until Sophia stood before the mirror fully dressed. The gown, as she and Drusilla both knew, was not plain at all but a cunning deception in which the pearl grey watered silk had been allowed to be its own ornamentation. There were no frills or pleating and only a minimal trimming of narrow slightly darker ribbon on the sweeping decolletage and where the sleeves ended in drifts of silk chiffon. The gown gathered the light and played with it;

every movement made it ripple like water. In short, it was a work of genius.

* * *

In Berkeley Square, meanwhile, Christian had been ready for over an hour and, with his cravat seemingly growing tighter by the minute, regretting it.

'For God's sake, stop pacing and sit down,' said Benedict, his tone one of sympathetic amusement. 'Would a nip of brandy help?'

'Probably – but I won't have any. And I can't sit down. Doyle doesn't want me to risk creasing my coat.'

'Take if off, then. There's another half-hour or more before we need to leave.'

Deciding that sounded like sensible advice, Christian let Benedict help him out of the sable brocade and hang it over the back of a chair. Then, hauling in a shaky breath, he said, 'This is ridiculous. Why am I nervous?'

'It's traditional, I believe.'

'That's nonsense. After all, it's not as if I'm worried that Sophie may not turn up or say no when the time comes. There's nothing to be nervous about.'

But there was. Two things, in fact ... both of them related to something he longed for and feared in equal measure. His and Sophie's wedding night.

Although he'd been doing his best to ignore it, anxiety had been building for some days. Mostly it had centred on how to get through the occasion without – well, just *without*. In a rational part of his mind, he knew that he couldn't do this throughout his married life, that sooner rather than later he'd have to stop hiding ... but he couldn't face the thought of polluting their first night together with *that*. It wouldn't be dealt with quickly. Sophia would have questions – which meant he'd have to *talk* about it; and, if anything was guaranteed to destroy his ardour, it was that. So his best course, for now at least, was avoidance.

Then there was other thing. Their first night together was also Sophie's first time ever and, in certain ways, might as well be his. He wasn't a virgin, of course. There had been a handful of brief liaisons at Oxford before he met Sophie. But *after* that, he'd wanted only her and found the notion of sleeping with anyone else repellent – so he hadn't done so, not even on the Grand Tour. Then had come his three years of captivity ... and now, here he was at the age of twenty-eight with about as much sexual experience as the average sixteen-year-old. Had he *ever* known his way about a woman's body? He hoped he had – because then there was a chance of it being something one didn't forget.

He drew a long breath and, as if to reassure himself, said again, 'There's nothing to be nervous about.' And, looking at Benedict, 'Is there?'

'Nothing at all. Do you feel better now?'

'Not really.'

Mr Sandhurst walked in, immaculate in understated claret. He said, 'Are Anthony and Daniel meeting us at St. Bride's?'

Benedict nodded. 'More discreet than having two carriages setting off from here, we thought.' He hesitated and then added, 'I could be wrong ... but I suspect one or two others may also be joining us there.'

Christian eyed him sharply. 'Who, for example?'

'Oscar. Adrian and Caroline Sarre ... Adam Brandon and his wife.'

There was a long silence. Then, 'Anyone else?' asked Christian.

Benedict sighed. 'Vere might come.'

'Oh *wonderful!*' groaned Christian. 'What's the point of *us* being discreet if a carriage with a ducal crest is going to attract a crowd outside the church?'

'Oscar is supposed to make sure that doesn't happen.'

Since Christian appeared to be speechless, Gerald said, 'Just out of interest ... when was the last time Belhaven went anywhere in a vehicle that *didn't* advertise his presence?' And, when Benedict said nothing, 'Yes. That's what I thought.'

The three of them looked at each other. And then, against all expectation, Christian saw the funny side and laughed. 'You know ... I really don't care. So we'll draw attention. Does it matter? No. Only one thing matters today and that is that I'm finally, *finally* marrying Sophie. So I don't give a fig if a regimental band marches up and down outside the church. Why should I?'

Benedict grinned at Gerald.

'I think he's feeling better,' he said.

* * *

They arrived at St. Bride's to find Daniel and Anthony awaiting them in the porch. Shaking hands with Christian, Anthony said, 'There are a few uninvited guests inside.'

'Yes. Benedict warned me there might be. Belhaven?'

'Not as yet – but Oscar's not here, either, so there's still time. Shall we go in?'

Christian nodded and fell into step beside Daniel, who said, 'Nervous?'

'Not any more.'

Inside the church, Lady Kelsall's three widowed friends sat on the bride's side. Daniel and Anthony joined Lord and Lady Sarre, on the groom's. Christian greeted them all, brushed aside Adrian's apologies for turning up uninvited and went to shake hands with the Reverend Highsmith. Next to arrive were Adam and Camilla Brandon, closely followed by Sophia's mother and sisters. Lord and Lady Colwich, Christian knew, would be coming with Sophie because his lordship was to give her away. At a few minutes to noon, the organist began playing so Christian took his place at the front with Benedict beside him, thinking, *Soon. She'll be here soon*.

Behind him, the door opened again and he turned. Then, smothering a laugh and nudging Benedict, 'Guess who.'

'Do I need to?'

'No. Oscar ... and making one of his rare appearances, His Grace, the Duke of Belhaven,' agreed Christian. Then, with a brief glance across the church, 'Sophie's mother looks as if she's swallowed a fly.'

Benedict muttered something incomprehensible. But before Christian could ask him to repeat it, the organ embarked upon something stately by Handel and he knew the moment had arrived. His bride was here. He turned and stepped into the aisle to catch his first glimpse of her as, smiling widely, Drusilla tripped down the nave and slid into the pew behind the Kelsall ladies.

Then Sophia appeared on Jonathan Colwich's arm ... and everything inside Christian seemed to cease functioning. She had always been beautiful; but never, surely, quite as breathtaking as in this moment? The shimmering silver-grey gown was lovely, rendering her almost ethereal; and the slender curves inside it enticed, as powerfully as did the luxuriant, glossy, night-dark hair. But it was her face that stole the air from his lungs. The delicate colour in her cheeks, the sweetness of her smile and, above all, the love shining in those delphinium eyes ... all of them capable of stopping any man's heart for a moment.

As for Sophia, she saw a tall, well-made gentleman in black. Some might have taken that for a sign of mourning but she knew better. Not just because, years ago, she'd laughingly told him that black made him look like a romantic hero but because of the rich gold thread edging his coat and cuffs and the gold silk vest lying beneath it; gold no brighter or richer than the hair, drawn smoothly back from his brow and secured in long, black ribbons at his nape. The silver eyes rested on her face, their expression filled with everything that was already between them and everything that was still to come. And beyond all of that, she saw Kit ... steady, loving and kind.

Then she was at his side, her hand in his, and the service began.

Later, she would remember it in snatches. His fingers warm about hers; the stillness that bound them while they exchanged their vows and the odd shaft of sunlight that danced about them as they did so. And, in no time at all, it was over and they were walking out into the noise and bustle of Fleet Street.

Tilting her face up to his, she whispered, 'Did you know Belhaven was coming?'

'No. Or the Sarres or the Brandons either, for that matter.' He gestured first to the ducal carriage and then to the little huddle of interested faces across the street. 'Not quite as discreet as we'd intended. Doubtless your mother will have something to say.'

'About the most elusive duke in London turning up without warning at her daughter's wedding?' laughed Sophia. 'Her friends will never hear the last of it! As to the audience ... what can we do about that?'

'This,' replied Christian. And, pulling her into his arms, he kissed her.

As the onlookers cheered and applauded, their friends and relatives emerged from the church to gather about them, offering their congratulations. Julia hugged Sophia tightly; Caroline Sarre begged pardon for gate-crashing her wedding; and Drusilla said, 'My goodness, Sophie – *Belhaven* of all people. Wonders will never cease!'

Christian, meanwhile, finding himself shaking hands with the duke and silently hoping that his household staff could cope with some additional guests, said, 'It was good of you to honour us, sir. Will you and Oscar join us at Hazelmere House?'

'I can't speak for Oscar,' replied Belhaven, 'but, though I thank you for the invitation, I will not. However, allow me to offer both my felicitations and my apologies for attending your nuptials uninvited. I was unable to resist witnessing the culmination of the longest betrothal I believe the *ton* has ever seen.' And he sauntered back to his carriage, apparently oblivious to the stares and pointing fingers of the watching crowd.

Lord Oscar blithely accepted an invitation to the wedding breakfast.

Caroline Sarre and Camilla Brandon both demurred until Christian, fingers crossed behind his back, insisted that five surprise guests would not pose the *least* problem. And finally, everyone set off for Berkeley Square. Inside the carriage and held close in the circle of Christian's arm, Sophia said, 'Will Fallon have a fit?'

'I hope not. Fortunately, we decided on a buffet – which should make things easier. If we linger over wine in the drawing room, Fallon can oversee the necessary adjustments.' He smiled at her and drew her in for a kiss. 'We've been married for at least half an hour and I haven't yet told you how incredibly beautiful you look.'

'I noticed. But I knew you'd get around to it sooner or later.' She smiled a little shyly. 'Thank you for my dress. It's lovely, isn't it?'

'Lovely,' he agreed, 'though, as I think you know, it wasn't the dress I was complimenting. In fact, I suspect I'll like the other garments you mentioned better.'

'Oh.' She blushed a little and toyed with one of the buttons on his vest. 'Those.'

'Yes, *those*.' A glance through the window told him they were turning into Berkeley Square – which, he realised, was probably just as well. 'We're here and appear to have beaten our guests. Ah. Fallon already has the door open. Good.'

Christian jumped out of the carriage, handed Sophia down and then swept her up in his arms. She gave a startled squeak. 'Kit! What are you – ?'

'What does it look like?' he responded, carrying her up the steps and past Fallon into the hall, to an enthusiastic round of applause from the assembled staff. Then, setting her down, he said simply, 'Welcome to your new home, Lady Hazelmere.'

She laughed up at him, curtsied and then, turning a beaming smile on the servants, said, 'Thank you all so much for greeting us. But his lordship has a confession to make and I'm afraid it won't wait.'

'How is this *my* fault?' muttered Christian. And then, loudly enough for everyone to hear, 'We were ambushed at the church by uninvited guests, Fallon – five of whom will be joining the party. They are all hard on our heels even as I speak.'

'That will not be a problem, my lord.' The butler clapped his hands, issued three brief orders and the household scattered. Then, to Christian, 'Wine is waiting in the drawing room, if you and her ladyship would care to go up. You may leave everything else to me.'

* * *

The wedding breakfast went without a hitch and, in most respects, grew extremely merry. Inevitably, and at greater length than was necessary, Lady Kelsall and the widows expressed their disappointment that the duke had not chosen to join them; Gwendoline did her best to hold the attention of Lord Oscar … but, after enduring one conversation with her, he took care to make himself a moving target; and a number of guests noticed how often Mr Sandhurst and Miss Julia Kelsall gravitated towards each other.

All the usual speeches were made and the traditional toasts to the happy couple proposed and drunk. The widows were the first to show signs of leaving and, shortly after them, Lady Kelsall also rose and was about to summon her daughters when Christian waylaid her, saying, 'A brief word before you go, if I may, ma'am.'

She inclined her head and followed him into the next room, for once saying nothing.

Coming directly to the point, he said, 'I have arranged a quarterly allowance for yourself and the girls – beginning on the first of next month. Mr Sandhurst will be administering this and he'll discuss the details with you as well as answer any questions you have. Will it be convenient for you to receive him tomorrow?'

'Thank you, Christian. You are most kind. But it will be more convenient and, indeed, more *appropriate*, if you were to deal with the matter yourself.'

'I disagree,' he returned calmly, having expected this. 'You will find Gerald more than competent and he has my full authority. So … may he call on you tomorrow?' Seeing her open her mouth to argue, he added, 'Or if not, some other day in the near future? As you're aware, Sophie and I are going to Hazelmere and I'd like this in train before we leave.'

She hesitated and then, ungraciously, 'Oh, very well. Tomorrow, then.'

'Thank you. And now I must return to our guests.'

In the drawing room, meanwhile, watching Julia blossoming under Mr Sandhurst's quiet attention, Drusilla said, 'Sophie ... Julia is enjoying herself. If I offer to take her – and Gwendoline – home a little later, do you think your mother will allow them to stay?'

'Probably.' A glance across the room revealed that Gwendoline had given up on Lord Oscar and had moved on to Anthony Wendover.' Sophia sighed. 'I don't think his lordship will thank you, though. Gwen would do better if she didn't *try* so hard.'

'True. But you needn't worry about Cousin Anthony. He's armour-plated. I'll offer, then and – ah. Here's your mama. And, unless I'm mistaken, not looking best pleased.'

'You're not mistaken,' sighed Sophia. And then, 'Even today. How utterly *typical*.'

CHAPTER TWENTY-ONE

It was a further hour before everyone had taken their leave and Sophia was able to drop contentedly beside Christian on a sofa, saying, 'That was fun – but I'm glad they're gone.'

'No more so than I.' He pulled her into his lap for a kiss. 'Are you exhausted?'

'No, although – much as I love it – I shall be happy to get out of this gown.' She paused, then added, 'Unfortunately, I can't do it without help.'

Christian appeared to think about this. Finally, he said, 'I've asked Fallon to choose a suitable housemaid to substitute until you have a maid of your own. Or … I could help you myself.'

Her colour rose a little and she slid her arms about his neck, murmuring wickedly, 'Could you? It wouldn't be … too much trouble?'

'It would be my very great pleasure.' And then, 'Hussy.'

She laughed but, after a moment, said, 'You told Mama about the allowance, didn't you? And I can guess what she said.'

'Excellent. That means we needn't talk about it.' He glanced at the clock, calculating the number of hours before darkness fell and wishing he didn't have to wait until then. 'Someone should have unpacked for you, by now. And I imagine you'd like to see your rooms. Shall I show you?'

She nodded and slid to her feet. 'Please.'

Taking her hand, he led her upstairs to the suite traditionally occupied by the countess; a bedchamber, dressing closet and boudoir. They were decorated in shades of pink and cream and were looking very faded. He said, 'They haven't been used since my mother's time. I thought you might enjoy redecorating them to your own taste.'

He'd told her about the mother he'd idolised and who had died in childbed along with his baby sister the year he went to Eton. Sophia said, 'Are you sure?'

'Yes, love. The rooms need it and they're yours now. Mine are through here.' Putting an arm about her waist, he opened the connecting door. 'I only moved back into them just over a week ago, thanks to Eustace's fondness for blood-red velvet.'

She looked at the toning shades of green. 'This is lovely.'

'I like it.' Seeming to make a decision, he said, 'It's not quite four o'clock so we've time to go for a drive, if you'd like.' And when she nodded enthusiastically, 'Then here's what we'll do. Ring for a maid and change into something less festive while I do the same. Society will know soon enough that we've married but they don't need to know it today.' He dropped a kiss on the tip of her nose. 'We'll go to St James's Park ... and I'll enjoy the anticipation of acting as your ladies' maid later.'

* * *

The fresh air was invigorating and they completed their circuit of the park laughing about a conversation they'd had with an elderly gentleman who had been a friend of Christian's father and who had asked, point blank, when he was going to do his duty by both Miss Kelsall and his title.

In the end, when the old fellow had refused to let the subject go, Christian had given up and said, 'You win, sir – and you may congratulate us. We were married privately earlier today and, with the exception of a very few wedding guests, you are the first one to know.'

And he *had* congratulated them – warmly and at great length.

'Will he tell anyone, do you think?' Sophia asked as they drove home.

'Almost certainly. It will be all round White's by the end of this evening. But that hardly matters because the announcement will be in the *Morning Chronicle* tomorrow. Meanwhile, I shall tell Fallon that, between now and when we leave for Hazelmere, we are not at home to visitors no matter *who* they are. And that includes your mother, should she take it into her head to come here after having seen Gerald.'

Leaving him to speak with Fallon, Sophia drifted upstairs to the drawing-room – from which all signs of the party had vanished. Since their guests had left, awareness of Christian and the night to come had begun tingling along her nerves. Part of her was glad of this time to simply be with him; another part sizzled with mingled excitement and impatience. She wondered if he felt the same ... then ordered herself to think of something else. *Anything* else.

'Julia and Mr Sandhurst seem to get on amazingly well,' she remarked when Christian came in. 'I don't suppose he's said anything to you?'

'About Julia? No.' He looked amused. 'Sweetheart, they've only met twice. It's a bit premature to be looking for signs of romance, isn't it?'

'Well, yes. But – '

'And how many other gentlemen has Julia met?'

'None, of course.' Sophia held up a hand to stop him interrupting again. 'But they took to each other immediately. And today, they were almost inseparable.'

'I don't deny it. But even if they fell head over heels in love, your mother isn't going to consider Gerald a suitable *parti*, is she? She doesn't see the son of a good but far from wealthy family or a young man who left Oxford with a better degree than Benedict or Daniel or me. She just sees my secretary.'

'Yes. But the key is that she believes Julia is unmarriageable.'

'*Does* she?' His expression made it clear that he hadn't known that. 'Because Julia is deaf?' And when Sophia nodded, 'I see. So, at a pinch, in her eyes Gerald would do?'

'Perhaps. Probably, in fact. But I wasn't thinking about Mama. I was thinking of Julia having a chance of happiness and a family of her own. I recognise the difficulties, of course. Any gentleman who thought of marrying her would have to learn to sign, as would one or more members of their household. It's a lot to ask ... so only a man who loved her would contemplate it. And Julia *deserves* to be loved.'

Christian looked at her in silence for a long time. Finally, he said, 'You're worried about leaving her, aren't you?'

'Yes. Mama and Gwen know some very basic sign language but often can't be bothered to use it. And I've taught Dunne and the most intelligent of the housemaids enough to be able to understand simple things – such as a request for hot water, for example. But it's not *enough*,' finished Sophia angrily. 'She'll be lonely.'

'I see.' He drew her against him and dropped a kiss on her hair. 'Then, while we're at Hazelmere, we'll work out what can be done about it for the future.'

'We will?'

'Yes. Obviously the simplest solution would be for her to live here with us. But – '

She twisted round to stare at him. 'You'd *do* that?'

'Why not? Goodness knows the house is big enough. But I suspect your mother would resist that idea.'

'So would Gwen – if Julia was invited but she wasn't.'

'Which she wouldn't be. I'm sorry, love – but one has to draw the line somewhere.'

'If you didn't, *I* certainly would.' She settled back against his shoulder, enjoying the warmth and feel of his body in ways that brought the lovely, quivery sensations flooding back. 'I shouldn't have started this. We don't need to talk of these things now.'

Christian said nothing, tacitly agreeing with her. In truth, he was somewhat grateful she'd opened a conversation that offered distraction from the other thoughts and stirrings invading his mind and body. Anticipation was a steadily burning fuse and it had been lit too soon. There were several hours to be got through first.

He said, 'I've ordered supper to be served in your boudoir. I thought it might be more pleasant than the formal dining-room. How does that sound?'

'Perfect. No servants popping in and out,' she said. And blushed, realising how that might sound. 'I meant – '

'I know what you meant and I thought exactly the same.'

'Good.' Reluctantly, she moved away from him and stood up, gesturing to the carriage dress she'd worn for their drive. 'But I'm not sitting down to dine with you wearing black. Not today. So I'll go up and ring for Maisie.' A tiny laugh rippled through her. 'She's a mass of nerves and terrifyingly eager not to let me or herself down. It's a bit like dealing with an eager puppy.'

Christian also laughed and came to his feet.

'We'll get you a proper ladies' maid soon. Meanwhile ... when will it be my turn?'

'Later,' Sophia muttered, feeling her cheeks grow even hotter. 'Much later.'

'Is that a promise?'

'Yes.'

'Then tell Maisie you won't need her again today.'

* * *

Maisie helped Sophia out of the black gown and into one of periwinkle tiffany but admitted that she had no idea how to dress her hair. Sophia told her to tie it back in a ribbon and that it was of no consequence since she and his lordship would be dining privately. Truth to tell, she'd been half-tempted to wear one of the daring ensembles that Drusilla had insisted would drive any husband wild ... but decided against it because, if Kit was looking forward to taking her clothes off, the flimsy robes and wrappers didn't present much of a challenge.

Christian strolled in, formally clad but for the absence of his cravat, and carrying a flat leather box which he put down on the table beside the sofa, saying, 'You look delightful. I like your hair loose like that.'

'Good – because you'll be seeing it this way a lot,' she replied, smiling. 'But that won't matter until I need to leave the house – which, of course, I must do the day after tomorrow for our journey to Hazelmere.'

'I'll ask Gerald to find out if an agency can supply someone on a temporary basis. Then, if she doesn't suit you, we can try again after we return to London.' He broke off as a tap at the door heralded a footman with a tray containing wine and glasses. 'Thank you, John – set it down there, please. And tell Fallon to serve supper in about half an hour.' Then busying himself with the wine as the footman left, 'A toast first, I think.'

'To what, exactly?' she asked, rising to accept the glass he offered.

'Making up for lost time?' he suggested, smiling.

'Or, as was said by Caroline Sarre, to our happy beginning?'

'Ah. Yes. I like that. To both then.'

'To both,' agreed Sophia, as his glass touched hers.

Waiting until she was seated, Christian set his glass aside and, reached for the box. 'I have something for you ... a wedding gift.'

Startled, she said, 'That – that's lovely of you. But you gave me everything I could possibly want earlier today at St Bride's.'

'I could say the same but I'm glad you think so, too.' He placed the box in her hands. 'This is something to mark the occasion. Open it.'

Slowly, almost hesitantly, she did ... and then stared, seeming not even to breathe, at the necklace, bracelet and earrings lying on a bed of white velvet. Sapphires and moonstones; a complete set to match her betrothal ring.

Seeing that she was literally dumbstruck, Christian said, 'There are family jewels that traditionally belong to the countess, of course – quite a lot of them. But I wanted you to have something of your own.'

Very, very slowly, she looked up at him, her gaze a little shy and her eyes very bright. Then, setting the box on the sofa, she rose and casting her arms about his neck, mumbled, 'Thank you. It – they are b-beautiful. But I didn't expect ... *thank* you.'

'My pleasure, love.' He held her close and was conscious of a wish that darkness would fall very, very soon. Inevitably, this brought another thought to mind. 'Shall I help you put it on?' And, feeling her nod, 'Come over to the mirror so you can see.'

Standing behind her, he fastened the necklace around the base of her throat and watched her touch it with awed fingers. Then, reaching around her with both arms, he clasped the bracelet on her wrist. Sophia stood very still, less conscious of the coolness of gold and jewels on her skin than the warmth of his body against her back.

Feeling her breathing change and watching her eyes darken as she looked up from the bracelet to meet his in the mirror, Christian thought hazily, *Good. Not just me, then.* Bending his head, he trailed kisses down her neck and along her shoulder and felt the soft, unsteady breath that escaped her as she leaned into him, closing her eyes.

The first polite tap at the door seemed so far away and unimportant that he ignored it. The second tap was a little firmer and Christian awoke to the fact that their supper must have arrived. Sighing, he released Sophia and moved slightly away, murmuring, 'That was a very short half-hour.' Then he bade whoever was out there enter.

Fallon and both footmen came in bearing laden trays. He let the butler get on with dictating where and how everything should be placed while one of the footmen went around lighting candles. Then, when the trio withdrew and they were alone again, Christian surveyed the table and said dubiously, 'I'm sure I didn't order this much food. In fact, I distinctly recall asking for a *light* supper.'

Laughing, Sophia lifted the lid from a tureen of asparagus soup and another from a dish of dressed crab. Waving a hand at the rest, she said, 'We don't have to eat it all.'

'Fortunately.' He handed her into a chair, reclaimed their wine glasses and took his own seat. 'Your health, Lady Hazelmere.'

'And yours, my lord.'

For the next hour whilst sampling small portions from most of the dishes, they talked about the wedding and the unexpected – and highly uncharacteristic – appearance of Belhaven. Then they discussed their forthcoming trip to Oxfordshire and Christian told her about some of the places he wanted to show her whilst feeding her strawberries with his fingers, just to watch the way her tongue swept the juice from her lower lip.

Gradually, the light outside the windows faded, leaving them in a pool of warm candlelight ... and he found himself dwelling more on the silky sweep of her eyelashes and the curve of her throat than what either of them were saying. He rose to draw the curtains, thinking to pull himself together at the same time. It didn't work. If he didn't touch her soon, he was going to lose his mind. Gesturing to the still laden table, he said, 'Have you had enough of this?'

'Yes.' In truth, she'd had enough some time ago but had let him ply her with strawberries because the heat in his eyes sent little sparks dancing along her veins.

Crossing to pull the bell for the servants, he said, 'Perhaps one more glass of wine?'

She nodded and stood up, hovering near the table. The jumble of feelings inside her defied interpretation; excitement, mingled with a hint of nervousness and, more than either of those, eagerness for whatever came next. She watched Christian pour more wine before removing his coat. A surge of something hot and strong swept through her, driving everything else before it.

Setting their glasses down on the table by the sofa, he turned to take her hands and draw her into his arms for a kiss that was far briefer than either of them wanted. Smiling, he said ruefully, 'The servants will be here any minute.'

'Of course.' She sat decorously, her eyes never leaving his. 'The maids will come up to tend the bedchamber fires and turn down the – the beds.'

Christian's only instruction regarding the bedchambers – more specifically *her* bedchamber – had not been about either of those things. Taking the seat beside her, he said, 'But no Maisie?'

'No.' She swallowed. 'No Maisie.'

Largely in silence, they sipped their wine and tried not to look at each other while the footmen cleared the table. That done, Christian checked that no one else was lurking in the bedrooms and returned to report that all had been done for the night.

'Although,' he murmured, as he took her in his arms again, 'someone has laid out a very enticing bit of froth on your bed – all lace and ribbons and such-like.'

'Oh,' said Sophia weakly. 'Have they?'

'Mm.' He filled his hands with her hair and captured her mouth in a seemingly lazy kiss. 'I'll enjoy seeing you wear it. Later.'

Strange, barely familiar pulses throbbed inside her and the little, dancing sparks multiplied. She twined her arms about his neck and kissed him back, unaware of his hands unlacing her gown until it loosened about her and slid away. Christian kissed her hair, her eyelids and her throat while his hands strayed to newly-revealed, petal-soft skin and then, without haste, allowed his mouth to follow them. Sophia pulled the tie from his hair to run her hands through the cool silk of it before tracing the line of his shoulders and, frustrated by the impediment of his vest, fumbled blindly with its buttons. The merest ghost of a laugh shook him and he finished the job for her, then shed the vest and tossed it aside before claiming her mouth again.

Somewhere at the back of his mind was relief that he still knew how to undress a woman ... and that instinct was telling him what would please them both once he'd done so. His tongue explored the tender hollows at the base of her throat, the delicate line of her clavicle, the curve of her shoulder; and when she clung to him, sighing his name, he said, 'I love you, Sophie-Rose. I loved you from the very first moment. And always will.'

He rose, taking her with him to gather her closer and closer while his mouth tantalised hers with butterfly-light kisses. He sent her gown slithering to the floor followed, presently, by her corset. Her breath hitched and he felt the echo of it through himself; her breasts pressed against his chest, sending arousal spiralling through him. He untied the tapes of her petticoats, letting them join everything else and leaving her in only her chemise and stockings. He investigated the delicacy of her rib-cage and the curves of waist and hip, a silent groan vibrating deep inside him. Sophia tugged at his shirt, waking an unwelcome voice in his head reminding him to be careful.

He had never hated the reason for that more than he did at this moment. He ordered himself not to think about it. If he did ... if he let it in, even for an instant, it would mar the beauty of this long-awaited night; and not just for him, but possibly for Sophia, too. He couldn't – *wouldn't* – let that happen. He'd bleed to death first. Deepening the kiss, he slid his palm over and around her breast.

An arrow of pure sensation shot through Sophia's body making her tremble and give a tiny, sobbing gasp. She said helplessly, 'Oh Kit ... I want ... *oh.*' This, as he did it again and then again. 'Please.'

'Yes, love. Yes.'

Lifting her out of the discarded clothes and into his arms, he carried her into the bedchamber. It was darker there. He'd taken the opportunity to put out some of the candles and leave his dressing-robe conveniently placed. Sophia didn't seem to notice either of these small changes. She clung to him and tugged again at his shirt. Again, he ignored it.

Just for tonight, he told himself. *Tonight and perhaps tomorrow. When we're at Hazelmere ... then I'll ...* He stopped, killing the thought. To distract both her and himself, he let the shift slide part-way down her body so that when he touched her again he found her skin. The breath hissed through his teeth at the warm softness of her and the driving need to feel it with more than just his palms. She wanted his shirt gone and so, desperately, did he. *Just do it!* ordered the voice in his head. *Now!*

Christian refused to let himself think. In one fluid move, he stepped back from her, dragged the shirt up and over his head and tossed it aside. Then he closed the space between them to fold her against him ... and groaned at the sheer bliss of it.

Sophia's hands slid slowly up his chest and on about his neck to glide over hot, smooth skin. Her mouth grazed his throat and shoulder. Unable to resist the temptation, she used the tip of her tongue to taste him.

His brain melted. Lifting her to sit on the edge of the bed, he removed her stockings rather more quickly than he'd intended, leaving her clad only in her shift.

Catching sight of the pretty, lacy thing, he tossed it on top of his robe, muttering, 'Something to look forward to tomorrow.'

Then, because one of them had to go first and instinct told him that it should be him, he swiftly shed the rest of his clothes, letting her watch.

Sophia's breath caught. He was so beautiful; all lean, tailored muscle and skin, gilded by the candlelight. She held out her hands to him in urgent invitation. He smiled and accepted, joining her on the bed and simultaneously drawing her down into his arms. Then, slowly divesting her of the shift, he said hoarsely, 'Oh God, Sophie-Rose. You are so unbelievably lovely.' And kissed her.

After that, there were no more words, just soft sighs and ever more intimate caresses as they explored each other with hands and mouths. Holding his own desire under rigid control, Christian sought and unlocked the secrets of her body, treasuring each gasp and shuddering moan; discovering and learning what pleased her most until he was absolutely sure that her hunger equalled his own.

Then he managed to say raggedly, 'Forgive me, love. Just this one time.'

And with exquisite care, joined his body to hers. She went still for a moment, her eyes locked with his. He was drowning in intoxicating pleasure but he forced himself to wait … clinging to the shreds of his self-control until he felt her relax and saw her smile. Then and only then, did he resume his worship of her body, somehow finding sufficient control to ensure her ultimate pleasure before allowing himself to seek his own.

Afterwards, their bodies still one, she smiled up at him and touched his cheek with awed fingers to whisper, 'I didn't think there would be magic. But there is, isn't there?'

'Yes, my darling. For us, there is.'

When he was sure she slept, he rolled from the bed to check the fire and snuff the remaining candles. Then he slid back beside her, grateful for the cloak of darkness. He needed to be awake before her. But that was for tomorrow.

CHAPTER TWENTY-TWO

While Christian and Sophia were travelling to Oxfordshire, Benedict summoned Anthony, Daniel, Oscar and Gerald to a meeting in Dover Street.

He said, 'What with Daniel's duel and Kit's wedding, we've done nothing further with regard to Basil so it's high time we held a Council of War. He was at Sinclairs last night which means he's back from whichever bit of heather has been hiding him. As for Kit, he said they'd only stay at Hazelmere for a week. So I suggest we start moving the plan along by having a few words with whoever we decide is best placed to help. What does everyone think?'

'It makes sense,' nodded Anthony. 'If we can launch a discreet rumour about the emergence of 'new evidence', the initial steps will already be in place when Kit gets back, which means we'll be in a position to proceed.'

'Forgive me for continuing to play Doubting Thomas,' said Oscar, 'but perhaps we should first focus on those niggling little difficulties I mentioned before? Namely, how to prod Basil into trying his hand – his very *inept* hand, I might add – at burglary. And, assuming we accomplish that, how to steer him into doing it at a time of our choosing – because the kind of witnesses you want for that aren't going to turn up more than once if things don't go according to plan.'

'True,' sighed Daniel. 'And how can we be sure that, if Basil *does* decide that stealing the evidence is his best bet, he won't pay somebody to do the deed for him? In his shoes, it's what *I'd* do.'

'He won't.' It was Gerald who spoke. 'If Basil employs a house-breaker, he risks the fellow reading the evidence and then using it to blackmail him afterwards. So he won't do that. He'll have no choice but to come himself.'

'You seem very sure about that.' Oscar still sounded unconvinced.

'As much as one can be.'

'Gerald's right,' said Anthony. 'Basil may be stupid – but he's not *that* stupid.'

'I disagree,' argued Daniel. 'He's *exactly* that stupid – or he can be. If he wasn't, he'd have taken his damned coat and boots off rather than risk drowning, wouldn't he? But let's assume he recognises the blackmail risk and breaks into Kit's house himself ... do we let him find what he's come for? Will he even know where to look for it?'

'I think it's safe to assume he knows where valuable items are kept,' said Benedict. 'He lived in Kit's house for three years, after all, and during that time, he's bound to have done his fair share of snooping.' Then, to his brother, 'As to your point about how we force him to make the attempt on one particular night ... we could make it appear that Kit has briefly been called out of town. Then we accidentally let it be known when he's expected back and that as soon as he *is*, the evidence we hope everyone will by then be anticipating will immediately be made public. The combination leaves Basil no choice but to walk into our trap.'

Oscar shook his head. 'You make it sound simple – but it won't be.'

'I know that. I'm perfectly well aware that we have to think of everything that might go awry and, as far as it possible, cover all the eventualities. But we have to start *somewhere,* Oscar – unless you'd prefer us to go on sitting on our hands forever?'

'I didn't say that.'

'You may as well have done.'

'I was merely advising caution.'

'You think we're just plunging into this without due care?' demanded Benedict. And then, 'Here's an idea. If you have a better alternative, let's hear it.'

'Peace, children,' said Anthony, with a grin. 'We're all on the same side, remember.'

'*Do* you?' persisted Benedict.

Oscar's mouth curled wryly. 'No, little brother. I don't.'

'Then stop being so damned negative.'

There was a long, awkward silence. Finally, Daniel said, 'I am so glad you're here, Oscar. Before you joined our merry band, *I* was the one they always picked on. It's enjoyable watching someone else suffer.'

'Do you think,' murmured Gerald mildly, 'that we might get back to the point at issue and make a decision? I promised to keep Christian informed of developments and would like to know if there are going to be any.'

'Fine,' returned Benedict curtly. 'Are we in agreement about letting word leak out about Kit's letter from the Consulate?'

Everyone nodded.

'And who shall we trust to set it in motion?'

They all thought about this. Then Anthony said, 'Not Nicholas, I think. My vote would go to Sarre instead. And Sebastian. Both of them have been a target of what rumour can do ... and Sebastian has a greater knowledge than usual of the law.'

'I agree,' said Oscar. 'They'd also both be more subtle than Nick.'

Daniel laughed. 'I can't argue with that. Benedict?'

'Neither can I,' shrugged Benedict. 'Sebastian and Adrian, then. I'll try to arrange an opportunity to speak with them privately – and you should be there too, Gerald, as Kit's representative. Just one last question, gentlemen. Do we present the rumour to them as if it's actually true? Or do we tell them what we're really doing?'

Once again, everyone considered this. Then Gerald said, 'That would depend on how much you trust them. I can't judge because I scarcely know either of them. But if the rest of you *do* and are confident they are to be relied upon, I suggest making them privy to the truth from the outset. If you don't, they may quite reasonably resent having been kept in the dark when everything comes to light later.'

Oscar and Daniel nodded. Anthony said simply, 'He's right.'

'I know.' Benedict glanced around at them all. 'Very well. Let the games begin.'

* * *

The day after they arrived at Hazelmere, Christian awoke early and, once again, left Sophia sleeping to slip away to his own room and dress. Outside the window was the promise of a beautiful day and it helped him come to a decision. For three nights since the wedding he had managed to keep his secret but he couldn't go on with it. Not any more. Not even for one more night. Having to be constantly on his guard was beginning to feel like slow suffocation; it was destroying his peace of mind, leaving him perpetually on edge. And the lengths he had to go to in order to hide it from Sophia were already beginning to threaten his sanity. The only sensible thing, therefore, was to drag everything into the light and tell her the truth ... or as much of it as he could bear to.

However, if he was going to reveal all, he wanted to do it away from the house, out in the open and in a place he'd always loved. So he sent Doyle to ask the kitchen to prepare a picnic and then went to kiss his wife awake.

She blinked sleepily up at him, twined her arms about his neck and, yawning, said, 'Must you *always* get up at the crack of dawn?'

'It's way past dawn, sweetheart,' he grinned. 'The sun is shining out there, just waiting for us to go and enjoy it. What do you say to a picnic by the lake?'

She thought about it. 'Will you swim?'

His stomach lurched but he said, 'I might. Will you?'

'I don't know how. But after I've judged your prowess, I might let you teach me.'

'How kind.' He stepped back and yanked the covers off her. 'Up with you!'

'Beast!' she said, snatching them back and blushing a little. 'Hand me my robe before Eliza finds me without a stitch on again. Yesterday, she was quite shocked.'

He passed her the robe but said, 'She does *know* that she's on a week's trial?'

'Yes, of course.'

'Then, if she likes the cachet of serving a countess, she'd better get over her shock – or at least keep it to herself.' He drew her to her feet, dropped a kiss on the tip of her nose and said, 'Wear something simple and comfortable. I'll see you at breakfast presently.'

* * *

Having disdained the aid of a footman, Christian trudged across the lawn and through the screen of willows that bordered the lake weighed down by a picnic hamper in one hand and the armful of blankets he'd refused to let Sophia carry in the other.

'Oh!' she gasped when she got her view across the water from the sun-dappled clearing where Christian came to a halt. 'What a lovely spot.'

'I'm glad you like it,' he said, setting everything on the grass. 'It's always been one of my favourite places in the park – not very far from the house but always wonderfully private. As you may have noticed from upstairs, you can catch the gleam of water and see part of the opposite bank but this bit of the shore is quite hidden.'

Busying herself spreading out one of the blankets, Sophia couldn't help wondering if he had some particular reason for choosing this particular place. Blushing afresh, she hoped he had. She said, 'I suppose you played here as a boy?'

'Frequently. And in the school holidays, often with Benedict and Daniel.'

'Not Lord Wendover?'

'Rarely. Poor Anthony was usually ordered home to the family.' Setting the basket in the shade, he helped her with the second blanket. 'The rest of us played all the usual idiotic games boys play and returned to the house filthy, with our clothes ruined. The servants must have despaired ... my father, too. But all he ever did was tell us to enjoy ourselves while we were young and had the opportunity.'

Sophia sat down, hugging her knees. 'And after you went to Oxford?'

'The games changed. Our friendship didn't. If anything, it deepened ... and Gerald joined the circle.' He dropped down beside her. 'As you know, but for them I probably wouldn't be here now.'

She gave a slight shiver. 'Don't. I can't bear to think of that.'

'No. Neither can I.'

She gazed over the lake, the odd remoteness in his voice striking a faint chord.

The first three nights of her marriage had been a revelation. Christian had unlocked secrets contained in her body that she had never suspected were there ... and each time he made love to her was more exquisite than the one before it. And yet, afterwards, she occasionally had the feeling that he was holding a tiny part of himself back; that he was never quite as wholly overwhelmed by the passion as she was. She realised that she could be imagining it or that he might be restraining himself just a little because of her inexperience. But every now and again, she wondered.

'I can't bear remembering either,' he continued in the same flat tone, 'but unfortunately I have no choice in that.'

Sophia reached out, grasping his hand. 'I know. But it will get easier in – '

'No. It won't.' He withdrew his hand and turned his head so she could no longer read his expression. Then he said rapidly, 'I brought you here because there's something I have to tell you – to show you. It's not nice or pretty. And it's something that no one else knows or ever *will* know; not Ben or Dan or even my damned valet. So far, I've even been keeping it from *you* – but I can't go on doing that. If I did – if I even *tried* – it would gradually poison everything that is between us. Do you understand what I'm saying?'

Thoroughly bewildered, she opened her mouth on something comforting but what came out was, 'Not really, no.'

'No,' he echoed, getting to his feet and pulling off his coat. 'Of course you don't. How could you? But you will.' He set about unbuttoning his vest and went on in staccato sentences.

'When you've seen what I'm talking about, you'll have questions. I'll answer as best I can but I'd be grateful if you kept them to a minimum.' The vest followed the coat and he tugged his shirt from his breeches. Then, standing still but breathing very fast, he said, as if it was a perfectly reasonable afterthought, 'Don't be alarmed if I look as though I might vomit. I won't actually do it.'

Already alarmed, Sophia was trying to rise. She said, 'Stop, Kit. Stop it. You don't have to – '

'I do.' And dragging off his shirt, he turned his back.

She looked up at him. Just below his shoulder-blades were two narrow black rows of something she didn't recognise ... something that might have been either a sort of pattern or writing. It was elegantly and precisely drawn and not at all ugly.

'Nothing to say?' he demanded, tension in every line of his body.

She could think of half a dozen things to say but she wasn't sure which of them would be acceptable and which not. So she reached up to tug at his hand and said, 'Kneel down, please.'

He made an odd sort of sound she couldn't interpret but did as she'd asked. 'Well?'

Sophia ran gentle fingers over it, as if afraid of hurting him. He flinched at her touch as if she'd done so.

'What *is* this?'

'A tattoo.' And then, because she might not know, 'That means it's permanent.'

'Done while you were in Turkey?' And when he nodded, 'Of what, exactly?'

'Arabic script.'

'So it means something?'

'Yes.' He reached for his shirt. 'If you've seen enough, I'll cover – '

'In a minute.' She laid her hand over the tattoo again and said softly, 'You said it wasn't pretty. Actually, I think it's quite beautiful.'

He burst into harsh, bitter laughter and dragged the shirt back over his head.

'Do you now?'

'Yes.'

A tiny part of him was grateful she wasn't as appalled as he'd expected her to be but it couldn't compete with his memories or self-disgust. He said, 'Forgive me if I can't agree with you ... but you weren't there at the time. I was.'

Suddenly and with sickening clarity, she realised what he was telling her. He had not wanted this or consented to it. It had been done against his will. He had been held powerless while this was somehow written on his skin. She had no idea how that could have been done but suspected that it had probably taken time and been painful. Worse than any of that, however, was the fact that his body would always carry a reminder of what he regarded as humiliation. Tears stung her eyes and she thought, *Oh Kit. No wonder you can't bear anyone to see it or even know it exists*.

Her voice very small, she couldn't help saying, 'Did it hurt?'

'Yes.' He sat down again but at a distance, keeping his face turned to the lake. Then he said, 'I will talk about it just this one time, then never again. I was trying to escape and bribed a servant to get a message to the outside. He was caught and beaten on the soles of his feet. My punishment was this.' He jerked a hand over his shoulder. 'They used to come at night. Not *every* night, so I never knew when to expect it. I didn't know what they were doing or how long it took. And I didn't *see* what had been done to me until it was complete. Ibrahim was delighted with it. He called it a work of art. Perhaps it is. But ... not to me.'

'No. Of course not.' Sophie thought for a moment and then said hesitantly, 'Do you know what it means?'

'Oh yes.' The acid derision in those two syllables was scorching. 'It means, *There is no God but Allah, Mohammed is his messenger and I am their servant*. Except, of course, that

I'm not.' He finally turned to look at her. 'And now, if you don't mind, I'd like to consider the subject closed. Can we?'

She put her arms around him, ignoring his initial resistance.

'Yes. Thank you for – for showing me. I know you can't have wanted to.'

'I didn't.' He buried his face against her hair and, his voice rather muffled, said, 'But the alternative was spending the rest of my life never letting you see my back. And, having tried it these last three days, I realised how impossible and – and *damaging* that was going to be.' He drew a long, calming breath and mumbled, 'I thought you'd find it loathsome. Are you sure you don't?'

'Perfectly sure – if we are talking about how it *looks*.' Shifting so that he was forced to meet her eyes, Sophia said firmly, 'But there are two quite different things here ... and the one I *do* find loathsome is that it was inflicted on you against your will and in such a horrible way. It's *that* which has you convinced it's something repulsive that must be hidden away at all costs – not the tattoo itself. I can understand that. And I think you should try to do the same.'

A hint of something resembling a smile touched his mouth.

'Are you lecturing me, Sophie-Rose?'

'Well, *somebody* has to and it seems that I'm the only one who can.' She laid her palm against his cheek and added, 'One last thing before we stop talking about it. For very good reasons, you've been regarding it as an ugly, shameful secret. But no one else – your friends, for example – need ever know those reasons if you choose not to tell them. And I suspect you'd find that, like me, they merely appreciate the artistry of it.' She paused and then, attempting to inject some levity into her voice, added 'I wouldn't be at all surprised if Mr Shelbourne was actually *jealous*. And now, my lord, are you going to show off your swimming skills or not?'

He didn't answer. He didn't swim, either. He merely lay for a long time with his arms about her, staring up into the fronds of willow and blue sky beyond while he tried to assimilate what had just happened and what it meant. She hadn't been disgusted by it. She had shone a light on what had always been a very dark place; she'd called it beautiful, for God's sake, and even *touched* the damned thing – something he could scarcely bear to do himself. But the real point, he eventually realised, was that she hadn't known what it was or, more importantly, what it meant. He investigated the possibility that this would probably be equally true of other people. Some men – admittedly not usually of his class – had their bodies tattooed by choice, didn't they? No one had to know that his had been forced upon him. No one but Sophie-Rose ... who had listened to the foul and extremely abbreviated tale without either turning away or thinking any less of him. That knowledge eased something inside him. He kissed her in gratitude. Then he sat up and set about behaving as he always did.

Sophia saw precisely what was going on behind his smiles and light conversation while they ate and drank and strolled, hand in hand, around the lake. He was reassembling his usual façade and, up to a point, she was content to let him. For now.

But in their bedchamber that night were changes that proved he had spent the day thinking. He did not snuff most of the candles before even removing his vest; he didn't withdraw to his dressing-room to shed the remainder of his clothing; and he didn't make any obvious attempt to hide his back from her.

He also didn't make love to her, merely holding her quietly in his arms until she fell asleep. But in the morning, she awoke to the knowledge that, for the first time, he was still beside her ... to the promise of lazily drifting hands ... and the hope that a small degree of healing was already taking place.

* * *

In London, Benedict and Gerald – having agreed that it would be unwise for them to be seen speaking privately with Lords Wingham and Sarre – awaited them in the upstairs room of a small tavern on the fringes of Westminster. Adrian was the first to arrive and, tossing his hat on to a table, he said,

'This is all very mysterious. There's some reason we couldn't meet in one of the private rooms at Sinclairs?'

'Yes,' replied Benedict simply. 'But we'll wait for Sebastian before we get down to business.'

Adrian's brows rose.

'Sebastian's joining us?' And when Benedict nodded, 'Anyone else?'

'No. You're acquainted with Mr Sandhurst, I believe.'

'Of course. We met at Hazelmere's wedding.' Adrian held out his hand. 'You're his secretary, aren't you? I suppose he's still enjoying his bridal trip?'

Shaking hands, Gerald said, 'He is, yes – though he'll be back by – '

He stopped as the door opened on Sebastian who blinked and said, 'Adrian? I didn't expect to see you here. Not that I knew *what* to expect – and I had the devil of a job finding this place. I take it there's some reason for all this cloak and dagger business?'

'There is. But perhaps we might all sit down and take a glass of wine?' suggested Benedict, already filling glasses. And when everyone was seated, 'Gerald and I thank you both for coming, gentlemen. The cloak and dagger business was necessary for reasons which will become plain when we explain what we're hoping you will help us with. But first, you need to know *why* we're asking it. And in order to tell you, I must stress that what I'm about to say is highly confidential.'

'I think we've already gathered that,' said Adrian dryly. 'It's to do with Hazelmere, of course?'

'Yes. But mostly it's about what *really* happened in Athens.'

Sebastian and Adrian exchanged glances.

'Go on,' said Sebastian. 'We're listening.'

Benedict related the tale clearly, unemotionally and in as few words as possible. At the end of it, Adrian said coldly, 'Basil Selwyn really is unspeakably vile, isn't he?'

'Unspeakably,' agreed Sebastian. 'But why didn't Christian make this public as soon as – ' He stopped. 'Ah. No proof and the possibility that Selwyn would squirm out of it?'

'Yes. Kit knows what happened and his word would have been sufficient for a good many people. But it may not have been enough to achieve the required result.'

'Which is?' asked Adrian.

'Exposure and ruin. And we believe we have a way to make that happen ... with a little help from yourselves.'

'Tell us,' said Sebastian. 'I can't speak for Adrian, of course, but – '

'Speak for me, by all means,' invited that gentleman calmly. 'What do you need?'

Benedict looked at Gerald. 'Since a good deal of our plan was yours, perhaps you should take it from here.'

Gerald nodded and said, 'It involves subterfuge and deceit. And rumour. In short, Mr Selwyn's own weapons.'

Sebastian grinned. 'That sounds appropriate,'

'We thought so.' He explained about the 'new evidence' they had manufactured on behalf of the Consulate and how they planned to use it. At the end, he said, 'What we would like *you* to do is start a hare but without being obvious about it. And we asked you to meet us in this out-of-the-way place so no one would see the four of us together and suspect collusion.'

'That makes sense,' agreed Adrian. 'However, the kind of gossip you want doing the rounds can only have originated with one of you.'

'Yes. But there's a way that you can probably avoid being asked which of us told you. Rather than actually *telling* someone what you want them to know and pass on, I suggest you let yourselves be overheard in private conversation. Something about a letter from Constantinople and the truth finally coming out, perhaps? In the hands of the right person, that should be sufficient to set the wheels in motion. And with a bit of luck, eventually someone will come to Benedict or Daniel – or even Christian himself – and ask if it's true;

whereupon their answer will be a very sharp, *Who told you that?'*

'Thus confirming it *without* confirming it,' approved Adrian. And then, 'Yes. We can do that. Sebastian?'

'Certainly.' He paused. 'I have just one question. Why come to us for this?'

'It wouldn't have been advisable for one of us to do it,' began Benedict.

'I understand that. But why *us?* Why Adrian and me particularly?'

'Confidence in your tact and discretion, mostly.'

Adrian laughed. 'That may have been part of it but it's not the real reason, is it? You chose us because if our names end up attached to it, everyone will assume we had it from Rockliffe – who, as everyone knows, is never wrong.'

CHAPTER TWENTY-THREE

In Oxfordshire, while Christian devoted an hour each morning to estate matters with Mr Harrington, Sophia got to know both the house and Mrs Wetherby, the housekeeper. Hazelmere Court was large but not vast and comfortable rather than ostentatious. Due to his lordship's protracted absence, it had been kept in good repair but little else had been done – and, as Christian said, at least it had escaped Eustace Selwyn's fondness for red. Sophia agreed with Mrs Wetherby that the formal drawing-room and the library both required refurbishment and said that this would be their first priority when she and his lordship returned from London in the autumn.

Their duty done for the day, Christian helped Sophia rediscover her skill in the saddle after almost two years of scarcely riding at all and also began teaching her to drive. What Sophia had had in mind when she asked him to do this was learning to drive his curricle. Consequently, she wasn't very happy when he laughed immoderately at that idea and had the ancient governess cart brought out of retirement. He did, however – much to the amusement of the tenants – allow her to handle the ribbons when they went about the estate making visits.

Aware that his lordship was newly married, neighbours were delighted to meet the new countess at church but tactfully refrained from visiting, so the couple spent most of their time alone and in whatever way they wanted. This, since the weather remained exceptionally fine, inevitably resulted in long, romantic afternoons in the dappled shade beside the lake ... and finally, of Christian tempting her to join him in the water.

It began promisingly enough with him shedding every stitch he was wearing and letting her watch. The next part, however, didn't go quite so well.

Having stripped down to her shift and ignored him when he suggested that she might as well remove that as well since as soon as it got wet it wasn't going to hide anything, Sophia dipped a toe in the water and pronounced it cold.

'Only at first. You'll soon get used to it.' He held out an inviting hand and, when she stayed where she was, shook his head, saying, 'Coward.'

'I'm not a coward. I – I'm just thinking about it.'

'Oh? Well, while you do that – rather than stand about here in the buff, I'm going to swim.' He stepped into the water and waded out until it was deep enough to swim a few strokes, then flipped on to his back to float. 'Come on, sweetheart. You can learn to do what I'm doing now. It's easy. And I promise I won't let you drown.'

'I know that. I'm just … I'm just enjoying the view.'

This, as it happened, was perfectly true. Her gaze had feasted on the smooth muscles of his back, on the dark, graceful lines of the tattoo and on his taut buttocks. Now she had a splendid view of his arms and chest, sleek and gleaming with water, and glimpses of his groin which, interestingly, was *not* in the state she was accustomed to seeing in the bedroom.

'Thank you – but you're welcome to do that at any time.' He smiled lazily. 'Come into the water and you can touch as well.'

'That's very tempting … but I think I'd rather just watch.'

'You don't know what you're missing.'

'In which case I *won't* miss it, will I?'

Deciding it was time to end this game, Christian stood up and waded out to where she stood. He was still smiling so Sophia remained on the bank, admiring him – which was how she missed his intent. He left the water, was beside her in two strides and, sweeping her up in his arms, pivoted back the way he'd come.

'*No!*' Sophia squealed and struggled. 'Put me down this instant!'

He laughed and kept on walking, right into the water until her toes touched the surface – then further still until her calves were submerged.

'No – don't you dare drop me!' She clung limpet-like to his neck. 'Kit, *no!*'

He didn't drop her but he may as well have done since the result was the same. He simply sank down into the water, taking her with him until only her head was above the surface. And, still laughing while she gasped and squeaked, removed his arm from beneath her so that her feet found the bottom, saying 'There. That wasn't so bad, was it?'

'You absolute *beast!* It's cold! Let me go!'

'I *have* let you go. In case you haven't noticed, you're the one hanging on to me. Now ... stop fighting and do what I tell you. I'm going to stand behind you and hold you up under your arms. Just let your body float up.'

'It won't,' she moaned.

'It will. The water will hold you up if you relax and let it.'

'I hate you,' she muttered. '*Promise* you won't let go?'

'I promise. Lean back into my hands and trust me.'

Her first attempts weren't successful but he kept encouraging her until finally she seemed to find the knack of it and was floating with only the minimum of support.

'Well done. Just close your eyes and drift,' said Christian. And, after a few minutes, 'You're allowed to admit that you like it.'

'I don't *know* if I like it.'

'Liar.'

'Oh very well,' she huffed, trying not to laugh. 'I suppose I *might* like it.'

'Excellent. Then you don't still hate me?'

'Not as much, perhaps.'

'That's a relief. So why don't you hold my hand?'

'How can I do that? You're ...'

She stopped, opening her eyes. Christian was no longer behind her, holding her up, but floating idly several feet away. The shock propelled her into unwary movement and she promptly sank. He was there in a second, even as her feet touched the bottom. She arose spitting out water, grabbing his shoulders and clamping her legs around his waist for good measure.

'Well, *here's* a whole world of new possibilities,' he murmured seductively. And, with a sigh, 'But rather than explore them, you need to start moving or you'll get cold. Move your legs from around me.'

'Why?' she asked suspiciously.

'Because, if you're going to learn to swim, you'll need them. Hold on to my hands, let go with your legs and float on your stomach towards me.' He waited until, with reluctance, she did so. 'Good. That's right. Now kick your legs. Yes, just like that. Don't worry. I'm not going to let go of you. You're out of your depth here.' He began turning them towards the bank. 'Keep going. You're doing brilliantly. Are you sure you're not part mermaid? Those *are* legs and not a fish tail and fins?'

Sophia laughed and got a mouthful of water. 'Idiot.'

'That's old news. Just another two or three yards and you can put your feet down.' And when she'd done so and was beaming up at him, 'That's enough for today, I think. There are towels in the bag. Take off that wet shift, sit in the sun and start getting dry while I swim a length or two.'

She squeezed the water out of her hair, wrapped herself in a towel and then laid the blanket down in the sunniest spot from which she could sit and watch him. His arms arced rhythmically, propelling him swiftly to the far side of the lake, then back again. When he emerged from the water, hands raised to wring out his hair, she was reminded of something Drusilla had said of Daniel Shelbourne.

One can't deny he's a particularly fine specimen of masculinity.

Sophia couldn't resist a smug smile. In her opinion, Kit was a finer one. And he was hers. She tossed the other towel to him, saying, 'You were right. That was fun.'

'Told you so,' he retorted, blotting his hair and giving his body a somewhat cursory rub down before winding the towel around his waist. 'Are you cold? Shall I get the other blanket?'

'No. I'm fine.' She patted the space beside her. 'It's warm here.'

Seating himself with his usual grace, he offered her an oblique smile and said, 'It may surprise you to hear that you look extremely fetching right now.'

'I think bedraggled is probably closer to the mark.'

'Not from where I'm sitting. In fact ...' He turned and, taking her completely by surprise, pushed her flat then leaned down to kiss her. 'In fact, just the sight of you is warming me up at quite remarkable speed.'

Aware of what was stirring against her thigh, Sophia blushed.

'Yes. Well, *something* certainly is. But Kit ... we can't. Not here.'

'Why not? He kissed her again, then nuzzled her neck and dipped his tongue into the hollow beneath her ear. 'If there was the remotest chance of anyone seeing, do you think I'd have been cavorting around naked just now?' His hand slid between them and prised her towel away so that he could caress her breast. 'Or don't you want to?'

She did want to – that was the problem. As soon as he touched her this way, she was melting wax in his hands. 'Yes. But – '

He kissed the rest of that sentence away and his hand stroked downwards to a place that made Sophia gasp and writhe against him. She said, 'You ... you're insatiable.'

Somewhere at the back of his mind, Christian thought that sometime when he felt like talking, he should tell her that for seven years, give or take a month or two, he'd been as celibate as a monk. But right now, talking was the last thing on his mind, so he said, 'Yes. Aren't you?' And disposed of both towels so that his body and hers could communicate in other, more satisfying ways.

* * *

On the following morning, a letter – the only one since they'd come to Hazelmere – was brought to Christian at the breakfast table. He glanced idly at it, then laid down his knife and broke the seal, saying, 'It's from Gerald.'

Sophia's brows rose. 'We're returning to London in two days. What could be so urgent it can't wait until then?'

'I asked him to keep me informed about something,' replied Christian absently, already reading the letter. And then, putting it to one side with a satisfied nod, 'Not urgent at all. But interesting.' He grinned at her. 'Curious?'

'Truthfully? Yes. But don't tell me if you'd rather not.' She reached for the coffee pot and refilled both their cups. 'Must you reply – or will it wait until we go back?'

'It can wait.' He looked at her, seeming to mull something over. Then he said, 'But it concerns something that you should know about and which I haven't got around to telling you yet.'

Sophia looked back at him. 'Basil?'

'Basil,' he agreed. 'And what we intend to do about him. But I'd rather we talked about that where we can't be overheard – and Harrington will be waiting for me in the study, anyway. As soon as I'm free, let's drive to Henley-on-Thames. We could have luncheon there, then take a boat out on the river. Would you like that?'

'Does it mean I get to see you row?' she laughed. 'If so, absolutely!'

Henley, a quaintly attractive market town on the river, was less than an hour's drive away and Sophia loved it on sight. After a light meal in The Old Bell, they strolled along the waterside until they found an elderly man renting out boats by the hour. Christian paid him for twice that, handed Sophia in and then, having removed his coat and rolled up his shirt sleeves, settled at the oars. As he did so, he couldn't help recalling that, had Basil's plan succeeded, he'd currently be chained to an oar in a very different craft to this one and far, far away from peaceful Henley. A shiver went down his spine.

But, smiling at Sophia, he pushed off from the jetty and started rowing upstream. The water was moderately busy but not unduly so and he'd rowed here often as a very young man and was familiar with the currents.

Shaded by a frivolous lacy parasol, Sophia enjoyed the play of his muscles under the thin lawn of his shirt, the way the sun gilded his hair and his skill in handling the little craft. She said so.

'Practise,' he returned easily. And with a grin, 'A lot of us rowed at university. It's an elegant, gentlemanly sport, good exercise and an easy way to impress girls.'

'I doubt you needed to do anything at *all* to attract the girls,' observed his wife aridly. 'A look and a smile and I expect they fell at your feet.'

'A slight exaggeration.' Then, recalling his thoughts yesterday, he said, 'I won't deny that I had one or two ... liaisons ... while at Oxford. But none at all after I first saw you.'

She stared at him. '*Ever?*' And when he shook his head, 'You're saying you haven't ... you know ... at *all?* Not for years? No. That can't be right.'

'Yet it is.' A hint of colour, caused either by the effort of rowing or by embarrassment, touched his skin. 'Until our wedding night, I hadn't slept with a woman since I was twenty-one.' He hesitated, then added, 'Having sex with one female while wanting another struck me as tasteless – sordid, even. So I didn't.' He smiled at her. 'I thought you might like to know.'

It was several moments before she could find her voice.

'That is – I don't know. Extraordinary? Remarkable? Or ... or just *you.*' She blinked away what he suspected was a tear and whispered, 'Thank you.'

'Don't thank me. Just know you needn't worry I'll ever stray. If I felt that way when I *didn't* have you, I certainly won't be looking elsewhere now I *do.*'

A short while later, Christian spotted a suitably quiet bit of bank, pulled in and tied up the boat. Then, moving over to sit beside her, he said, 'And now, to more important matters. We'll come to Basil in a minute. First I want to talk about Julia and an idea I've had that might be a solution.'

They'd discussed Julia's situation before but never reached a satisfactory conclusion. Eyeing him hopefully, she said, 'Go on.'

'It's very simple – so simple I don't know why I didn't think of it before. Julia needs what your mother would call a paid companion ... but what this person *really* has to be is a very specific kind of friend. First and foremost, she needs to be young; someone Julia will like and laugh with. She needs to be a *hearing* person so she can go out and about with Julia – shopping, walking in the park, that kind of thing. But she has to know sign language – which would probably mean she has some experience of deafness. She would need to live in Charles Street, not merely visit for an hour or two here and there. And for all of this, she will need to be paid.' He paused, then added, 'Payment is easy. I'll gladly take care of that. But finding this unique female? Well, that's another matter. Unless this Braidwood fellow you told me about can help?'

'Yes!' said Sophia. 'I'm sure he could – he found us Miss Grayshott.'

'Might *she* be suitable?'

'She won't be available. She was betrothed to a deaf gentleman and will be married by now. But Mr Braidwood may know of some other young lady with the right skills and in need of a paid position.' She smiled at him. 'It's a brilliant idea! Well done.'

'Say that again when we've made it work.' He kissed her hair then, on a sigh, said, 'And now to Basil. I told you what he did but not how we're hoping to expose him. It's time you knew. Gerald wrote to say that they had a meeting a few days ago – ah, did I mention that Oscar Hawkridge has joined the team?' And when she shook her head, 'He gate-crashed, rather than being invited but no one except Benedict seems to mind.'

Sophia laughed. 'Sibling rivalry. I know all about that. I have Gwen.'

'So you do. As for our plan to make Basil betray himself, it's this.' And he briefly laid out what he and the others had done thus far and the use to which they intended to put it, ending with, 'Making this work by tempting Basil on to the right square is the difficult part but, between them, Benedict and Gerald apparently have some ideas on how it can be managed. Meanwhile, they've enlisted the help of Lords Sarre and Wingham.'

'To do what?'

'Discreetly allow word to leak out about the 'new evidence' I've supposedly received from Turkey.' This time, his smile contained a hard edge. 'During the next few days, it should be starting to spread. Everyone involved on my behalf will be looking out for signs that it's reached Basil. If it gets to him before we're back in London he won't be sure where the incriminating papers are – in my pocket or locked up in Berkeley Square. That puts him in something of a quandary, wouldn't you say?'

'Yes. And I hope it ruins both his appetite and his ability to sleep at night,' she replied. Then, 'You once said he doesn't know that you know. But once this starts, that will change, won't it? He'll assume the 'new evidence' has told you.'

'I would think so, yes.'

'Then you'll need to be careful. He won't confront you directly. He's too cowardly for that. But he may pay others to do his dirty work for him, exactly as he did in Athens.'

'I know.'

'So you'll be careful?' She reached across to take his hands. 'Promise me you will.'

'I promise. I didn't survive captivity and reclaim both my life and you to let Basil take those things from me again,' came the coldly purposeful reply. 'One way or another, I intend to let the world know precisely what he is and leave him with a choice between prison and exile. I'd prefer the latter for my uncle's sake. There's nothing to indicate that Eustace was complicit in what Basil did or even *knows* about it. So it seems unfair that his good name and life should be destroyed by having a son in Newgate. But that's up to Basil. All I want is never to see him again.'

* * *

In London, meanwhile, Lords Sarre and Wingham were giving serious consideration to the question of within whose earshot they should choose to be loose-lipped. This, they agreed, was critical. They wanted the word to travel in a trickle, not a flood – so none of the most obvious candidates would do.

'Not Augustus Winterton,' said Sebastian. 'One might as well put it in *The Whisperer* – the same being true of Viscount Ansford. And we'd better avoid Charles Fox, as well.'

Adrian nodded. 'Someone like Colonel Barker, perhaps? He likes being *au fait* with the current talk.'

'He does – but Lord knows how he does it since he's virtually deaf.'

'Is he? Oh. Well, not him, then.'

They both considered the matter. Sebastian suggested the Dowager Lady Swanson but neither of them could work out how to engineer an occasion when she might conceivably overhear anything they said. They sat in silence for a time staring into their wine. Then Adrian said suddenly, 'What about Jeremy Frobisher?'

Sebastian blinked. 'The Member for Middlesex? The fellow who all but lives in the reading room at White's and hogs all the newspapers? *That* Frobisher?'

'Yes. He likes to have the latest gossip at his fingertips but he's selective about with whom he shares. And he's a stickler for the facts – well known for it.'

'He's also got a ram-rod up his backside.'

'Well, yes. But people listen to him and – '

'From choice?'

'– believe what he tells them.' Adrian cast him an exasperated look. 'Think about it. He's exactly what we need. An unwitting but reliable carrier pigeon.'

Sebastian shrugged. 'Well, when you put it that way ...'

'I do. Also, we know where to find him on any given day. And the reading room at White's is just the sort of place one goes to enjoy a private conversation – even one you want someone to hear a snatch of. So ... are we agreed?'

'I suppose so. Frobisher it is, then. But please tell me I don't have to talk to him.'

'Why on earth would you? As Sandhurst suggested, we merely want him to overhear the words *'new evidence from Constantinople'*. There won't be any need to sit down for a chat.' Adrian poured them both more coffee. 'We'll do it tomorrow morning. Now, let's discuss precisely *how*.'

CHAPTER TWENTY-FOUR

Christian and Sophia arrived back in Berkeley Square at around four in the afternoon two days later. Sophia kissed her husband's cheek, summoned Eliza and, without bothering to remove her hat, set off on foot for Charles Street. Christian left Fallon dealing with luggage and, taking a handful of correspondence with him, went in search of Gerald.

Mr Sandhurst grinned at him and said, 'You look extremely pleased with yourself. Married life going well, is it?'

Actually, he looked somehow different; lighter, as if an invisible load had been removed from his shoulders. Gerald wondered what aspect of marriage to the girl he plainly adored had previously worried him.

'So far,' retorted Christian. Then, 'Thank you for your letter. Adrian and Sebastian were a good choice. Have they let the cat out of the bag yet?'

'Yesterday at White's ... to a fellow named Frobisher.'

Christian shook his head. 'I don't know him.'

'Lord Sarre calls him a stiff-rumped splitter of hairs... Lord Wingham's description is more colourful and less polite. But they agree he's the ideal man for the job.'

'Good. So now we wait, I suppose.' He sat down facing Gerald across the desk. 'Your letter said Basil is back in Town. Do we know where he went?'

'No. But it hardly matters since he only went away until the laughter died down.'

Christian nodded. 'And how was your initial meeting with Lady Kelsall?'

'Frosty. She feels she should be dealing with the organ-grinder, not the monkey.'

'Well, that's no surprise – but she'll have to get used to it.' He grinned suddenly. 'And I'm sure you'll find subtle ways of demonstrating your authority.'

'I already have. She had her dressmaker send her account here.'

'Oh dear. And you said?'

'I reminded her that she is in receipt of an allowance with which to pay such bills. Then I suggested that if she preferred *me* to take care of them, it would be a simple matter to remove the said allowance from her hands and administer it myself on her behalf.' Gerald smiled and added simply, 'She decided against that ... very quickly.'

Christian laughed. 'Yes. She would do.'

'I gather Lady Hazelmere has gone directly to Charles Street?'

'You can call her Sophia, you know. She'd probably prefer it.' And when Gerald made no reply, 'But yes, she did – though less on her mother's account than on Julia's. Speaking of which, did you see Julia at all while we were away?'

'Very briefly whilst waiting for her ladyship to receive me.'

'And how did she seem?'

'A little less bubbly than previously. But that is natural, surely? She'd be missing La— her sister.' And, as if unable to help himself, muttered, 'The other one is no company for her at all.'

'I know. And Sophie and I hope to remedy that with the help of a fellow named Braidwood who runs a school for the deaf and dumb in Hackney. In fact, if there's nothing you and the others need me for, I'd like to try setting that in hand tomorrow.'

'Aside from transferring the Consulate forgeries from Dover Street to here, there isn't anything you can do now but wait. Benedict and the rest of them are keeping their ears to the ground for the progress of our rumour – which, if their lordships are right about Mr Frobisher, should be slow and steady, thus allowing talk to build up naturally and become widespread.'

'I'd like to know when there's some sign it's reached Basil.'

'As would we all – and now you're back, you'll be kept informed of everything anyone knows or *thinks* they know as soon as it happens,' came the calm reply. 'Benedict said to tell you that he and Daniel will be at Sinclairs this evening, if you returned today and felt inclined to join them.'

Christian shook his head and stood up.

'I won't go out tonight – just a quiet supper with Sophie. But if she feels up to presiding over what, in essence, will be a bachelor dinner, I'd thought of inviting our little band – and that includes you – to dine with us tomorrow evening.' He smiled suddenly. 'She knows everything now, so she may as well be part of the Grand Plan.'

* * *

Returning shortly after Christian had bathed and changed, Sophia met him on his way downstairs and said, 'I didn't mean to be so long. But Mama is – is – oh, I don't know *what* she is. And Gwen is worse. I could murder the pair of them.' Then, 'I'm sorry. If you give me an hour to take a bath and recover my temper, I'll stop fuming.'

He pulled her against him for a comforting hug.

'Take as long as you need, sweetheart – and fume as much as you want. I'll have dinner set back an hour and wait for you in the library. Yes?'

'Yes. Thank you.'

'You'll have to stop thanking me for every little thing. It might go to my head.'

She laughed, felt better and went on her way smiling at his nonsense.

When she joined him, clad in pewter satin trimmed with black, the shadows had cleared from her eyes and she was herself again. Cuddling up to him on a sofa, she said, 'Mama did not see any need for Julia to have a *companion* – I was forced to call it that – until I said that you would pay for it. Then I could see her thinking of all the ways such a person might be useful to her personally. Gwen, of course, merely complained about Julia getting what she sees as preferential treatment.'

'And Julia herself? What does she think?'

'I explained it all to her just as you explained it to me and for a little while I don't think she could believe it. Then she put her arms round me and burst into tears.'

'Ah. I take it that means she liked the idea – not just that she's had a miserable week?'

'She *loved* it. She saw all the things it would make possible and thinks you're the kindest, most wonderful brother in the whole world. So I told her that when we go to see Mr Braidwood, she can come with us. Is that all right?'

'It's absolutely fine, love. And I thought we'd go tomorrow.'

'As soon as that?'

'Yes. Why not? I've no other calls on my time. But I'll want a favour in return.'

'Name it.'

'Would you mind if I invited my friends for dinner tomorrow?'

'Of course not. I don't know why you're asking.'

'To be polite. And would you do us the honour of joining us at table yourself? It would be Benedict, Daniel, Anthony, Oscar and Gerald – who, by the way, is going to insist on addressing you by your title unless you tell him otherwise.'

'I make that two favours,' Sophia pointed out. 'Three if I include Gerald.'

'Well, that's husbands for you. Always taking advantage. Will you? Please?'

'If you'd like me to.'

'I would,' he replied, taking the opportunity to kiss her. 'Very much.'

* * *

Julia fizzed with excitement all the way to Hackney – at the prospect, Sophia explained to Christian, of perhaps meeting some of her former classmates again. Then, leaning forward to hide her face from Julia and without signing as she spoke, 'What I don't think she realises is that, even if any of them are still there, many of them may be speaking rather than signing by now.'

'They will?' He stared at her, plainly astonished. 'But if *they* could be taught to speak, why wasn't Julia?' And then, reading her bleak expression and reaching out to take her hand, 'Oh. I'm so sorry. I didn't know that.'

'Neither did we until Mr Braidwood told us,' she replied bitterly. Then, sitting back, summoning a smile for Julia's benefit and signing once more, 'He's a remarkable man. All the methods used at the academy are ones he developed himself since taking on Charles Sherriff as his first pupil.'

'Sherriff the miniaturist?' asked Christian. And when she nodded, 'Good Lord!'

'And *he*,' finished Sophia, simply, 'has the same condition as Julia. So you see …?'

'I do. Very clearly. And I'm looking forward to meeting your Mr Braidwood.'

They were admitted to the academy by a smiling young woman who returned Julia's greeting with one of her own, accepted Christian's card and showed them into a comfortable office. Five minutes later, a tall, grey-haired gentleman walked in, checked on the threshold and said, 'Miss Kelsall – Miss Julia. This is an unexpected pleasure!' And to Christian, 'Forgive me, my lord. I am somewhat confused.'

Extending his hand and finding it taken in a firm grip, Christian said, 'Perfectly understandable, sir. Miss Kelsall is now Lady Hazelmere and we are here, as you may imagine, on her sister's behalf. But first, allow me to thank you for making the time to see us without an appointment. I appreciate it.'

'You are most welcome.' Just as Sophia did, he began signing as he spoke. 'I'm always happy to see my former pupils. Julia, my dear … and prettier than ever. How are you?'

She beamed at him and her hands flew in answer. Laughing a little, Sophia said ruefully, 'Kit, she's telling him why we're here, what we want – everything. It's all flooding out like a spring tide. Ought I to stop her?'

'Why? This is about her, after all – so let her talk.'

Braidwood gave him a brief, approving glance – though whether on account of his own words or whatever Julia was telling him, Christian wasn't sure. But eventually, she stopped signing to gaze hopefully at Braidwood who said with some amusement, 'Well, now young lady ... perhaps I might offer your sister and his lordship a seat while we discuss this properly?'

She laughed and nodded enthusiastically.

When they were all seated, Braidwood said, 'So, my lord ... let's see if I understand this correctly. You're looking for a permanent companion for Julia. A young woman who is not herself deaf but has signing skills and is of an age to be more than merely a paid employee. Is that it?'

'It is. May I speak bluntly?'

'By all means.'

'Well then, my wife has always been Julia's only real companion but, as of a week and a half ago, she no longer lives in the family home. This wouldn't be a problem if her mother and other sister were different ... but unfortunately they're not. Although Sophia and I would happily have Julia live with us, Lady Kelsall is very unlikely to agree to it. So we thought perhaps a young lady such as you describe – one who could also become Julia's friend and *confidante* – could be a solution. We're here in the hope you might be able to help us find her.'

Braidwood nodded. 'I will certainly do what I can – although it may take a little time. Unless ...' He stopped, frowning, and then stood up, saying, 'Will you excuse me for a few minutes?' And left the room.

Julia swung round to Sophia and asked what Christian had said. Sophia shrugged and replied that it was pretty much the same thing Julia had told Mr Braidwood herself. Then she wanted to know where he had gone and Sophia said, 'He didn't say. Try to be patient, Julia. The chances of Mr Braidwood producing anyone at all today – let alone someone suitable – are virtually zero. You know that.'

Christian waved his hand to attract Julia's attention and, when she looked at him, said, 'After we leave here, shall we go for tea and cakes on Bond Street?'

She beamed, nodded, and blew him a kiss.

Sophia said something with her hands which made Julia shake her head, laughing.

'What did you say?' Christian asked.

'I told her to stop flirting with my husband,' she replied. 'And you're as bad.'

He laughed and blew a kiss back to Julia just as Mr Braidwood returned. Immediately, all the younger girl's focus shifted, her face bright with hope.

Signing as he spoke, Braidwood said, 'I must stress that what I'm about to say is only a possibility since the young lady in question isn't here in the school or even in London. She was never a pupil here but, like yourself with Julia, Lady Hazelmere, she attended with her older brother. He quickly learned to speak and lip-read with exceptional fluency and therefore stopped needing an interpreter a long time ago. In fact, he recently joined my staff here as a tutor. His family is respectable but large and by no means wealthy, resulting in the sister I spoke of being sent to live with an elderly aunt in Middlesex. However, young Mr Gardiner believes that a paid position, should she be fortunate enough to obtain one, would be very welcome.' He eyed Christian enquiringly. 'What do you think, my lord? Does any of this sound like something worth pursuing?'

'Yes.' Christian looked first at Sophia and then at Julia. When both of them nodded, he turned back to Braidwood and said, 'Would it be possible to meet her brother?'

'Just what I was about to suggest.' He pulled the bell and, when the young woman who had admitted them appeared, said, 'Fetch Mr Gardiner please, Susan.'

A few minutes later, a large, raw-boned young man entered the room. 'Sir?'

'These are the people I told you about, Colin – Lord and Lady Hazelmere and her ladyship's sister, Miss Julia Kelsall,' said Braidwood. 'They would like to speak to you about your sister.'

Colin turned, bowed awkwardly and, in an uninflected voice, said, 'What did you want to know, my lord?'

'Your sister's age and name, perhaps?' suggested Christian.

'Jane is nineteen, my lord.' He looked at Julia so she could lip-read, apparently scouring his brain for something useful to say. 'She's quite clever. She likes reading and sewing and ... dogs.'

Julia smiled and signed, 'I like those things, too. But, though I'd love to have a dog, Mama has never allowed it.' Then, cunningly Sophia thought, since Julia was well aware that Christian couldn't understand, 'I shall ask my new brother, the earl, to change her mind.'

Colin grinned, signed, 'Good luck.' And then addressing Christian said, 'Was that all, my lord?'

'Not quite. Mr Braidwood believes that Miss Gardiner might perhaps consider a position with my sister. Do you think he's right?'

'Yes, sir. She would jump at such a chance. I could write to her, if you wish.'

'And to your parents as well, if you would be so good.' Christian produced two visiting cards and handed them to him. 'Enclose those with your letters so that your sister and your parents will know who I am and where to find me. You may also tell all of them than they are at perfect liberty to write to me directly. However, I must stress that I am offering no guarantees as yet. From our point of view – and I imagine also from that of your sister – everything depends on whether she and Julia like each other.'

Colin nodded. 'I understand, my lord. That is most reasonable. But I thank you on Jane's behalf for the opportunity.'

Christian smiled, held out his hand and when the younger man, though plainly startled, took it, said, 'Then we are in agreement and I look forward to hearing from your sister when she's had time to consider the matter and consult with your parents.'

When Colin had gone, Christian turned to Mr Braidwood and said, 'That young man is deaf?'

'Profoundly so from birth,' came the reply. 'Much can be done, as you have seen.'

'Yes. I'm very impressed, sir. Would a donation to the school be in order?'

Braidwood smiled wryly. 'Very much so, my lord. When I first began working with the deaf and mute in Edinburgh I took only boarding pupils whose parents could pay the necessary fees. Nowadays, I'm also taking some special cases who can't – so, in effect, any contribution your lordship makes would be sponsoring these.'

'Expect to hear from my secretary, then.' He held out his hand again. 'I'm pleased to have met you, Mr Braidwood. And thank you.'

CHAPTER TWENTY-FIVE

That evening, Lords Benedict and Oscar Hawkridge, Baron Wendover, the Honourable Mr Shelbourne and Mr Sandhurst joined the Earl and Countess of Hazelmere in Berkeley Square.

Sophia welcomed them all with a dazzling smile and said, 'I'm so pleased you were all able to come tonight despite such short notice. It's a special occasion for Kit and me – our very first party. And though it may be a small one, you are the guests we would both most want to be here.'

'Please tell me you weren't including Oscar in that,' murmured Benedict, bowing over her hand. 'He's a latecomer, an interloper and, most of the time, the prophet of doom.'

She laughed. 'Surely not?'

'*Absolutely* not,' said Oscar, elbowing his brother out of the way. 'He's just jealous of my superior looks and charm. It's very sad.'

'Ignore them,' advised Anthony, bowing in his turn. 'The rest of us do.'

And Daniel, taking her hands in a warm clasp, said, 'I hope Kit's suitably appreciative of his good fortune. If he's not, I'm your man.'

'Find a lady of your own,' said Christian, drawing Sophia away, 'if you can. This one's taken.'

Looking around at them all and feeling suddenly and unexpectedly emotional, Sophia said, 'Please don't let the fact that Kit is married change anything between all of you and him. You are always welcome in this house and need not wait for an invitation. I – I'm just grateful that Kit has such good friends. And I would like it if you could regard me as an honorary sister ... and call me Sophie, please. You, too, Gerald.'

Mr Sandhurst looked faintly embarrassed.

'I appreciate you saying so but I'm not sure that would be –'

'If you won't, I shall be forced to call you Mr Sandhurst – which seems ridiculous when you *live* here,' she retorted firmly. And to Christian, 'Tell him, Kit.'

'I already did. I suspect you'll just have to let him get used to the notion gradually.' And, with a grin as he passed around glasses of wine, 'The difficulty is that he's got some very old-fashioned, starchy ideas.'

'No, I haven't,' objected Gerald. 'And I'm standing right here, you know.'

'So you are. Now have a drink and relax.'

Conversation over dinner was lively and touched on everything except Basil Selwyn. Christian talked about Braidwood's academy and explained why he and Sophia had gone there. Daniel thought he had *mostly* lived down the duel. And Anthony said he'd had a third offer for his sister Charlotte's hand and once again she would have none of it.

Finally, Oscar told them that Belhaven had plunged into one of his even more than usually reclusive phases, studying Plato's tetralogies ... at which point Benedict groaned, 'Stop. Have mercy and just *stop* before someone asks what a tetralogy is and – '

'They explore the levels of the soul. Menexenus, Clitophon and Timaeus, for example.'

'And you answer in words none of us understand,' finished Benedict. Then, to the company in general, 'This is why I quit the ducal mansion in favour of Dover Street. Vere tosses those sort of names about at breakfast, in between Oscar pontificating about Thermopylae or some such. It's maddening – worse than being back at Oxford.'

Everyone laughed. Daniel remarked that, in his opinion, all conversation at breakfast ought to be banned; Anthony told him to be grateful he only had *one* sister and then, smiling at Sophia, 'Do yours chatter non-stop?' And coming to an abrupt halt, flushed and said hurriedly, 'I'm so sorry. That was stupid. Please forgive me.'

'There's nothing to forgive,' she replied cheerfully. 'Julia talks as much as anyone – she just does it differently. And Gwendoline makes sure we don't eat in silence. I wish she didn't.' Then, deciding that this was as good a time as any to withdraw, she stood up, saying, 'I'll leave you to your port, gentlemen – and please don't feel you have to hurry. I shall have tea in the drawing-room and – '

'No.' Christian also rose. 'We'll take port in the library and you'll have your tea there with us. Thus far, we've avoided the main subject for discussion but we all know what – or rather *who* – it is. So we'll get to that now. And from this point on, Sophie-Rose, you'll be part of it.'

When the tea tray had been brought in and Christian had supplied all the gentlemen with a glass of either port or brandy, everyone found a comfortable seat and Anthony said, 'Can I open the meeting by asking what progress, if any, has been made by our rumour?'

Daniel grinned. 'Firstly, according to Nick Wynstanton, Rockliffe's heard it.'

'Of course he has,' nodded Benedict. 'Frobisher probably just *told* him. And I'd guess that, if Rockliffe asked him where he'd got that little nugget, he probably told him that, too – in which case the duke will certainly speak to Adrian and Sebastian.' He glanced quickly at Christian, 'Don't worry. They'll confirm the rumour but that's all.'

'I know. If they weren't to be trusted, you and Gerald wouldn't have trusted them.' And to Daniel, 'You said 'firstly'. There's more?'

'Yes. Adam Brandon took me to one side at the *Salle* this morning to ask if it was true that fresh information regarding Kit's disappearance had come to light,' finished Daniel. 'I asked who'd told him that and he said Rainham had mentioned it.'

'Plato notwithstanding, Vere's heard it, too,' volunteered Oscar. 'Though *how* he has, since he's barely set foot through the door during the last week, is a complete mystery.'

'So,' said Christian thoughtfully. 'It's arriving in all the right quarters. It should reach Basil in another day or two – if it hasn't already.'

'As of last night, it hadn't,' Anthony said. 'He was at Sinclairs with those idiot friends of his, apparently without a care in the world and enjoying a run of luck at the Hazard table. But for what it's worth, my money is on Eustace hearing it first. He's a regular at White's, as are the fellows with whom he usually associates. Someone is bound to ask him what he knows about it.'

There was a brief silence into which, finally entering the conversation, Sophia said, 'That would be extremely helpful, don't you think?'

Six pairs of eyes locked upon her. Then, smiling, Christian said simply, 'Yes.'

'Why?' began Daniel. Then, 'Oh. Eustace will come to the horse's mouth, won't he?'

'If that means me, I believe so – though I take exception to your choice of phrase.'

'As do I,' added Sophia, firmly but with laughter glinting in her eyes. 'As for Eustace … he won't rely on hearsay. He'll want to know, beyond any doubt, that it's true.' And to Christian, 'How much will you tell him?'

'That the Consulate has finally located the dragoman who escorted me from Athens. The story he tells is … unexpected. Shocking, in fact. So much so, that the unfortunate fellow is in a great deal of trouble over it.' Christian shrugged. 'Something along those lines, anyway.'

'And when Eustace demands details?' asked Oscar.

'I refuse to give any. The matter remains strictly between myself and my man of law while we consider how best to proceed.'

'The implication that there's something to be done *here* should be enough to scare Basil witless,' remarked Daniel. 'Good. So … what happens next?'

'The forgeries we made are now lodged in the strong box here. It's over there,' he gestured vaguely to a corner of the room, 'concealed behind what look like several rows of books on the genealogy of all the crowned heads of Europe. It's where money and some of the Hazelmere jewels are kept. Basil will know that. I imagine he'll also know where to find the key. So this room is where we have to lure him and where I will appear to confront him alone.'

'Splendid choice, if I may say so.' Oscar looked up at the narrow gallery that garlanded the room, giving access to the topmost shelves. 'Your witnesses can lurk there unseen. I assume that pretty little spiral isn't the *only* way to get up there?'

'It isn't. There's a door connecting to an upstairs corridor.' Christian rose in order to begin refilling glasses. 'Are there any other questions?'

'Not a question as such,' said Anthony thoughtfully. 'Just an idea I had. We'd decided that Basil could be tempted here on the night of our choosing if he believed that you were from home, Kit – which means Sophia being away as well. But, that way, he'd have to break in at night and the house would still be full of servants, at a loose end and liable to pop up anywhere. So I wondered if there might not be a better way.'

'Such as what?' asked Benedict.

'Some sort of function with numerous people coming and going and which keeps the servants wholly occupied?'

'You mean like a ball?' said Sophia, aghast. 'We can't. We're in *mourning!*'

'No, of course not a ball,' said Anthony hastily. 'But perhaps a charity event? In support of the academy for the deaf you were talking of earlier? And not even held inside the house but across the street in Berkeley Square gardens?'

Everyone considered this. Finally, Oscar said, 'That's not such a bad idea. Basil would think it an easy matter to slip in unnoticed – which it would be if we weren't expecting him.'

'True as that may be,' observed Sophia, 'we would have to fix a date well in advance. We'd have to pray for good weather. And the whole thing would require a *massive* amount of organisation.'

'Yes,' agreed Christian slowly. 'But it's not impossible. We don't need to set a date more than a week ahead if – '

'Of course we do!' She stared at him as if he'd gone mad. 'How *else* are we to send out invitations?'

'We don't. Instead, we advertise it and …make an admission charge at the gate?' No one argued so he went on.

'As for the weather, we can protect against rain by erecting pavilions all around the gardens. And for organisation ... in addition to ourselves, Drusilla Colwich, Caroline Sarre, Cassandra Wingham and probably half a dozen other ladies would be happy to lend a hand – even Gwendoline and your mother.' He watched her pull a face. 'I know. But it would be in two very good causes, wouldn't it? Finally, if we make it sound impromptu, no one will mind if it's a bit haphazard.'

'And while we ladies are finding ways of parting the guests from their money and arranging supper and goodness knows what else, what will all of *you* be doing?'

Christian grinned and spread his hands expansively. 'Everything else. Pavilions, lanterns in the trees, tables for food and drink, stalls from which to sell things.'

'From which to sell *what* things?' demanded Sophia. Then, very firmly, 'I'm sorry Kit, but I don't think you've the remotest idea of the difficulties of making this happen. And doing it inside a *week*, for heaven's sake? We'd need a miracle.'

'Or alternatively,' said Gerald, speaking for the first time and holding up a folded newspaper, 'you could engage Osbert Sutton at the Marylebone Gardens to do it for you. According to the *Morning Chronicle*, he offers a full, tailor-made service.'

Everyone stared at him. Sophia said, 'He does?'

'Yes.' And reading from the newspaper, '*Vauxhall and Ranelagh in the grounds of your own home? We bring the complete pleasure garden experience to a place of your choosing – every eventuality and requirement catered for. Nothing is impossible! Contact Sutton & Company for further information.*' He stopped and looked up. 'One can only conclude that the downward slide at Marylebone continues. However ... what do you think?'

Sophia bathed him in a wide, admiring smile.

'It's brilliant, Gerald – the perfect answer! And tomorrow, you and I will go and set the wheels in motion with Mr Sutton. The rest of you,' she sniffed, waving a dismissive hand at the other gentlemen, 'are no longer needed.'

Colouring a little, Gerald turned to Christian and murmured, '*You* are. At least, I assume you're to bear the cost of it ... and, if so, perhaps you might wish to reconsider the generous donation to Mr Braidwood's academy that you discussed with me earlier?'

'No. Let it stand,' replied Christian. 'The Berkeley Square Pleasure Garden event isn't purely for the academy. It's camouflage for what *else* we'll be doing.'

* * *

Late the following afternoon, Sophia all but danced into the library where Christian was attending to some long overdue correspondence. She said, 'It's done – and it's going to be marvellous! A miniature Vauxhall just across the street. There will be music, a temporary dance floor, jugglers and acrobats ... little rotundas, a Chinese pavilion, lights in the trees – even a small firework display. And Mr Sutton's people will take care of advertising the event. The only thing they *won't* be taking over completely is serving food and wine. Mr Sutton will provide some additional footmen for that but we'll put Fallon in overall charge so that our own servants are seen to be busy.' She collapsed on to a sofa. 'We've set the date for a week today. Will that be satisfactory, do you think?

'I don't see why not. And if you're satisfied, then so am I,' he replied, crossing to sit beside her. 'But please don't tell me what it's all going to cost until I have a large brandy on hand in case I faint.'

She laughed but said, 'It isn't going to be cheap. However, if it achieves the desired result with regard to Basil and makes a few pounds for the academy it will be worth it.'

'Undoubtedly.' He put his arm about her and felt her nestle against his shoulder. 'Forgive me, sweetheart ... but I've agreed to dine at Sinclairs this evening with Benedict and Daniel. We'll find out if there's anything new. But mainly it's time I gave men who have heard our rumour the chance to look me in the eye instead of gossiping behind my back. It will be interesting,' he added dryly, 'to see how many actually *do*.'

'Might Eustace be there?'

'He *might*, I suppose – though it's not one of his usual haunts. But if and when he's got something to say to me, he won't do it in a public place. He'll come here.'

* * *

While Christian, Benedict and Daniel dined at Sinclairs, Eustace Selwyn was sitting down to dinner at White's with his old friend, James Cunningham – and about to have his appetite ruined.

Mr Cunningham waited until the food had been served and then, helping himself to some slices of duck, said, 'Have you heard what's being said of your nephew?'

Mr Selwyn's fork paused half-way to his mouth. He thought, *Hell. What has Basil done now?* But he said calmly, 'No. Something new, is it?'

'Apparently. There's a whisper going around that information – some say evidence – has reached him from Turkey regarding his mysterious disappearance. Just that. Not a word to suggest what it is.'

The small flicker of relief that whatever this was, it wasn't Basil's work, died very fast – slain by the premonition that it could be much, much worse. Eustace forced himself to eat what was on his fork and asked if Mr Cunningham knew where the rumour had started.

'Hard to say. Frobisher's name has been mentioned – as has Rockliffe's – so there's a good chance there's some truth in it.' He took a mouthful of duck and chewed. Then, 'It's odd, though.'

'What is?'

'Well, if there *is* new information about what went on abroad three years since, it would have gone to young Hazelmere personally, wouldn't it? Yet he was out of Town on his bridal trip until a couple of days ago and, by then, the talk was already circulating.' He cut another piece of meat. 'It makes one wonder, doesn't it?'

'Yes,' agreed Eustace bleakly. 'It certainly does.'

He didn't know how he managed to endure the rest of the evening without either fidgeting or snapping Cunningham's head off. But finally they bade each other good night and Eustace was able to take a hackney back to Maddox Street, only to learn that Basil was still out. Grimly, he left instruction with the butler for his son to be sent to join him in the drawing-room as soon as he returned ... and then, pouring a large glass of brandy, he sat down to wait.

Basil came in at a little after one in the morning and in a very good mood. The luck he'd found the other night at Sinclairs was still with him and, tonight, he'd had a similarly successful evening at a discreet little place off Wardour Street. Just a few more sessions like this, he thought, and the worst of his money troubles would be significantly eased.

He could well have done without being told that his father was waiting to see him but it didn't completely ruin his mood and he sauntered into the drawing room with a smile which lingered even after he saw Eustace's expression.

He said, 'Not had a good evening, Father?'

'That is one way of putting it. Sit down.'

'All right. Just let me get a – '

'Sit *down!*'

Basil flinched and sat. 'What on *earth* is the *matter* with you?'

'Since you're so cheerful, I take it you haven't heard the latest rumour.'

'If you mean the one about Lottie Hailsham and the – '

'No. I mean the one about Christian having received new information connected with his disappearance; information sent to him from Turkey.'

Basil's mouth opened, then closed again. He lost a little of his colour and all of his *joie de vivre*. He said feebly, 'What? But how could –?' Then stopped, trying to gather himself. 'Well, I've no idea what that might be. As far as *I* know, there's nothing to discover. I've said it until I'm *sick* of saying it.'

'So you have.'

'What else are people saying?'

'Nothing other than that, as far as I know.'

'Oh. Then it's probably just all talk and no substance.'

'I'm reliably informed it comes with Rockliffe's name attached to it.'

Basil started to feel sick. He said, 'That doesn't prove it isn't – '

'It's good enough for most people to think it true.' Eustace stared balefully at his son. 'As you say, we've been over this ground often enough – but I have never been wholly convinced that nothing untoward happened between the two of you in Athens. If I'm right about that – '

'You're not!'

'Perhaps. But if I *am*, the only saving grace has been that, since he did nothing about it, Christian was either ignorant of it or prepared to overlook it. However, that may no longer be the case.' Eustace drained his glass and stood up. 'Tomorrow, I intend to find out.'

'How?' Basil also rose, trying to hide his rising panic. 'How does one ever prove or disprove a rumour?'

'One goes to the person who must be the source of it.'

'Christian?'

'Yes.'

'But you can't believe *him*. He – he's probably just having his own back for me nearly marrying Sophie.'

'If it were someone else, I might think so but Christian is too intelligent to play those kind of games. And even if he were not, why do so now? He and Sophia Kelsall are married and, judging by the gossip surrounding their discreet nuptials, happily so. If he wanted to '*have his own back*', as you put it, why wait until now instead of doing it when you were giving him ample provocation?' Eustace took a couple of steps as if intending to leave the room; then, turning, he said, 'And there's one other thing. If whatever is in his possession *did* come from Turkey, it's a written document – and can therefore be presented as evidence, should it be necessary. Think about it.'

CHAPTER TWENTY-SIX

On the following morning, Lord and Lady Hazelmere were still at the breakfast table when the butler informed his lordship that Mr Selwyn had called and wished to speak with him urgently.

Christian and Sophia exchanged glances. Then, tossing his napkin aside, Christian said, 'Show him to the library, Fallon. I'll be there shortly.'

Fallon bowed and withdrew.

When the door closed behind him, Sophia said, 'He's heard, then.'

'So it would seem ... and is close to panicking, if calling here at such an hour is any indication. Good. Let us hope that Basil is in the same state.' Finishing the last of his coffee, he stood up. 'The trick now is to add a little fuel to the fire without giving too much away. Wish me luck.' And he left her.

He found his uncle pacing restlessly by the window. But as soon as he entered the room, Eustace said bluntly, 'What's this I hear about new information from Turkey concerning your ... disappearance?'

'I suppose that would depend on what you've been told.' Christian gestured to a chair. 'Shall we sit?'

With an impatient sound, Eustace took the offered seat. 'Exactly what I've just said. Is it true?'

Quite without haste, Christian sat facing him and nodded. 'Yes.'

'And?'

'And what?'

'Where did it come from?'

'As you've just said yourself, Uncle, it came from Turkey.'

Eustace almost ground his teeth. 'I *meant*, from *whom?*'

Christian subjected him to a level stare. 'Does that matter?'

'Of course it matters! It's a question of whether it can be relied upon. Can it?'

A hesitation, a tiny shrug ... and then, 'Yes.'

Sucking in a breath, Eustace waited for Christian to elaborate and, when he didn't, asked if it had come from the fellow who had held him captive.

'Ibrahim? No. Oddly enough, after being threatened with the wrath of God by Daniel Shelbourne and Anthony Wendover, Ibrahim and I haven't stayed in touch.'

There was silence for a few moments. Then, 'So it came from Constantinople?'

'Yes.'

'From the Consulate?'

'Again, yes.'

'And?'

Christian's brows rose. 'I'm at a loss to understand your interest, Uncle.'

'You're my nephew. Of *course* I'm interested.'

'Forgive my saying it ... but you didn't appear so at the time.'

Eustace's colour rose. 'That is untrue. I – *we* – did our best.'

'That isn't how it looked. But we won't argue. It's water under the bridge, after all.'

'Not as far as the Consulate is concerned if they've written to you. There must have been some reason for that.'

'There was.' Christian sighed and then said, 'When their initial enquiries into how I ended up in Tekirdağ didn't bear fruit, I assumed that was the end of the matter from their point of view.'

'But it wasn't?'

'Apparently not. Enquiries continued to be made after my departure.'

'With what result?'

'You know ... this inquisition of yours is becoming very tiresome.' Christian stood up. 'I am at a loss to understand both *it* and what should bring you here at such an early hour. But if you *must* know, they were merely keeping me informed.'

'Of what?'

'Of recent progress.'

Eustace almost ground his teeth. 'There has been some?'

'So they say. They finally found the witness they'd been searching for and were able to persuade him to … cooperate. And this has – '

'A witness to what?'

'How I came to end up in Ibrahim's palace,' came the impatient reply. 'And that's quite enough, Uncle. No more questions. For the time being, the details of this remain strictly between myself and my man of law while we decide how best to proceed.'

Surging to his feet, Eustace echoed, 'Proceed? From *here?*'

'Certainly from here.' Christian's tone clearly said, *Where else?* 'And now I'm afraid I must ask you to excuse me. Sophie wishes to hold a charity gala for the school for the deaf which helped her younger sister – and she wants to do it next week, so we are both extremely busy just at present.' He pulled the bell for Fallon. 'Ah. Before you ask – no, we have *not* forgotten that we are in mourning, so the event will be held in Berkeley Square gardens rather than here in the house. Perhaps you and Basil might buy tickets?'

* * *

'Well?' prompted Sophia as soon as he returned to the breakfast parlour.

'He wanted chapter and verse. He didn't get it, of course. I merely told him that the Consulate has found someone who knows how I ended up in Ibrahim's palace.' Christian smiled crookedly 'He's frightened.'

'You think he knows?'

'No. If he did, he'd have asked different questions. But he certainly suspects there's something *to* know. I think he's had doubts ever since I got back … and has probably asked Basil about it before. He's never quite been satisfied with the answer but been able to shut his eyes to it. Until now.'

Seeing the trouble in his eyes, Sophia rose and crossed to put her arms about him.

'Don't let yourself feel guilty about this. It isn't your fault. It never was.'

'I know. But it's not really Eustace's fault either.'

'No – but you're not responsible for what his son did. And what else can you do? Allow Basil to go unpunished for stealing three years of your life – and mine, for that matter? For hoping you'd *die*? Letting him off scot-free to spare Eustace?'

Christian sighed. 'No. I can't go that far.'

'And neither should you. What we need now is for Eustace to go home and pass his fear on to Basil by telling him that you have written proof of ... something,' she said bracingly. And then, struck by a new thought, 'I wonder ...'

'What?'

'If Basil were to be frightened enough to finally tell his father the truth, do you think Eustace would share it with you?'

This was a possibility Christian had never previously considered. He did so now and eventually, drawing a long, slow breath, said, 'I don't know. He might, I suppose ... if he believed that doing so might persuade me to keep it in the family.'

'Which it could,' said Sophia simply, 'if the price of your silence was Basil quitting England.' And smiling up at him, 'But you didn't need me to tell you that, did you?'

* * *

In Maddox Street, Basil's nerves were at full stretch. He'd barely slept, tormented by the prospect of exposure and what might come of it. He tried telling himself that it wouldn't happen; that Christian couldn't *know* – no one could; and that whatever information he'd received – assuming there actually *was* some – wouldn't be able to prove anything. But this no longer worked as well as it had in the past and his mind ran around in circles, trying to formulate a way out, should disaster strike.

The morning got worse when he learned his father had left the house at a time when most people were still at breakfast. If Eustace had gone to Hazelmere House at such an hour, it was as good as *telling* Christian that he feared the current rumour might come home to roost.

Kit will find a way to make use of that – a way to make everything worse, he thought. Then, *What if they* have *found that thrice-blasted dragoman? It ought to be impossible – a chance in a million. But what if they* have? *What the hell am I going to do then?*

Unable to face a cup of coffee, let alone food, Basil paced the drawing-room for what felt like hours, waiting for his father to return. And when he heard the front door open, followed by Eustace's step in the hall, he snatched up the previous day's *Morning Chronicle* and threw himself into a chair in an attempt to look relaxed.

Eustace entered the room, checked briefly on the threshold and then, shutting the door behind him, said coolly, 'You are up unusually early, Basil. Is there any reason for that?'

'No, not at all. Why should there be? And you were up and out even earlier – though it's a devil of a time to go visiting.'

'Normally, yes. But not today. I imagine you don't need to ask where I have been.'

Tossing the newspaper carelessly aside and demonstrating his indifference with a yawn, Basil said, 'No. I suppose not. But I doubt if the newly-weds were thrilled to receive you so early in the morning.'

'I did not see her ladyship. As for Christian … he was civil enough.' Eustace took the chair facing his son and said flatly, 'Don't overdo the display of nonchalance. The mere fact that you've left your bed to sit here waiting for me to return tells its own story. You want to know what I found out.'

'Not as much as you want to tell me,' muttered Basil. 'Go on, then. Spit it out.'

'You really do have a way with words, don't you?' He paused and then said simply, 'The rumour that Christian has received a communication from Turkey is true. It is a letter from the Consulate in Constantinople.'

'Saying what? Or wouldn't he tell you?'

'Saying that they have found a witness they've been searching for.'

'A witness? To what?'

'How Christian vanished from the outside world and ended up in a Turkish governor's palace.'

Basil felt suddenly very cold. His vision darkened around the edges and there was a faint buzzing in his ears. For one nasty moment, he thought he was going to pass out. He hauled in a breath and then another ... and finally managed to say, 'So how did he?'

'He didn't tell me that – neither did I ask.'

'Why the hell *not?*' And then, when his father's brows rose, 'I mean, that was the whole point, wasn't it?'

Face and voice equally grim, Eustace said, 'No. I didn't ask because Christian made it clear that he'd said as much as he was going to. And I'd already learned what I wanted to know. Namely, that he *does* have new information; that it is in writing; and that, since he's been discussing the matter with his lawyer, he intends to take action of some sort.'

Dread began clawing at Basil's gut. Unable to trust his voice, he remained silent.

'Nothing to say?' asked his father.

Mutely, he shook his head.

'And you're quite sure there's nothing you'd like to add?'

Clearing his throat, he said, 'Such as what?'

'Such,' snapped Eustace, coming to his feet, 'as what *really* happened in Athens. I have never been wholly convinced that nothing did and I'm not about to become so now. But perhaps it's as well that I don't know because, if whatever piece of monumental stupidity you committed is going to blow up in your face, at least I will be able to plead ignorance.' He swung away towards the door and then, looking back, 'Think it over, Basil – and think very carefully. You have a few days' grace. Christian and his bride are planning to hold some charity event in the gardens of Berkeley Square next week – so nothing is likely to happen before then. But after it, I suspect the axe may fall.'

And he walked out.

For a long time after he had gone, Basil stayed where he was, paralysed by a mixture of shock and panic. For several minutes, he couldn't move, couldn't think … could barely breathe. But eventually his brain resumed its function by saying none too helpfully, *A witness. They found a witness and he talked. Who? The bloody dragoman? Or the slaver he sold Kit to?* And then, *If it's the slaver, I'm safe. He'd never have heard my name. Why would he? But if it's the dragoman … oh God. If it's the dragoman, Kit knows everything and I'm finished.*

He dragged himself out of the chair and across the room to pour a large brandy from the decanter. Then, downing half of it in one gulp, he sat down again and tried to force his brain to work. There *must* be a way out of this; a way to stop whatever evidence Kit had from being made public. There just *had* to be a way … and he had to find it. Fast.

* * *

Next day, while the household was being turned upside down with preparations for what Christian was privately calling *One Night Only in Berkeley Square*, he tracked Sophia to the library where she and Julia were sitting amidst a small heap of rosettes they were making out of coloured ribbon. He almost asked what the rosettes were for, before deciding he'd probably prefer not to know and, waving a letter at them, said, 'Miss Gardiner has written to me.'

'Who?' asked Sophia vaguely. And then, differently, 'Oh. Miss Gardiner. Of course! What does she say?'

'Basically? She says yes. She is extremely interested in the position with Miss Kelsall and honoured to be considered. She is currently back at her parents' home in Holborn and would be most happy to attend for an interview at any time to suit us.'

Smiling, Sophia clapped her hands, translated for Julia and said, 'The sooner, the better, then. Tomorrow?'

He nodded. 'Fine. I'll send John with a note telling her that our carriage will collect her at eleven.'

'If she's honoured at merely being considered, she'll be *overwhelmed* by that.'

'Well, we can't have a nineteen-year-old girl taking a hackney half-way across London, can we?' he asked, temporarily distracted by the rosettes. 'It's no good. I have to ask. What are those for?'

'Everyone who attends will get one. There are four colours, each representing a team because Daniel has suggested – '

'Stop. If Daniel has persuaded you to go along with one of his mad ideas, I'd rather not know what it is. Just tell Julia about tomorrow, will you? She has to be here.'

* * *

Jane Gardiner was indeed overwhelmed – first by the earl's smart carriage, then by the imposing house in what must surely be one of London's finest squares and finally by the stately butler who instructed a maid to relieve her of her hat and cloak. She was also regretting the small, shaggy dog of indeterminate breed that she'd somewhat impulsively brought with her. By the time a very beautiful and elegantly-dressed lady appeared, she was half-inclined to flee. But the lady smiled warmly and came towards her, hand outstretched, saying, 'Thank you for coming, Miss Gardiner – I'm Lady Hazelmere, Julia's sister, and I'm *very* happy to meet you.'

Jane accepted the proffered hand, managed to drop a curtsy and whispered, 'Thank you, my lady. It – it was very kind of you to send the carriage. You needn't have.'

'My husband thought otherwise and I agreed.' Sophia began drawing the girl across the hall with her, then stopped, seeing the dog and, on a note of laughter, added, 'Oh. Who is this?'

'That's Hamish, ma'am. It seemed like a good idea to bring him,' she stammered, colouring fiercely. 'But I p-probably shouldn't have. I'm so sorry.'

'Don't be.' Sophia stooped to pet the little animal who panted and licked her hand. 'Julia will be as delighted to see him as to meet you, I'm sure.'

'But what about his lordship? Won't he mind?'

'Not at all. At present, he's in the square's gardens with a couple of his friends overseeing – or more likely interfering – with the preparations for something due to take place there on Friday. But he will join us later, I'm sure, *and* tell you what is going on across the street. First, however, you and Hamish must come and meet Julia before she bursts with excitement.'

Under this gentle flow of words, Jane relaxed enough to say, 'Please, my lady ... I've been told that what Miss Julia needs is a companion and friend. Is that right?'

'It is *exactly* right. Now that I am married, she has no real company at home. Neither my mother nor other sister can sign, so she has no one to talk to. And though she can spend as much time as she wishes here, it isn't an answer. Do you see?'

'I do, my lady. Completely.'

'Good. Come, then. Let's see how the two of you get on.'

As soon as the door opened, Julia was half-way across the room, only to come to a halt, smiling uncertainly. Sophia signed, 'Meet Miss Jane Gardiner, Julia.' And then moved back, waiting to see what each girl would do.

Julia took a couple of small steps, then stopped again.

Jane smiled, curtsied and signed, 'Hello. It's lovely to meet you.'

Her smile widening, Julia replied that it was a pleasure for her, too. She began to hold out her hand and then stopped, eyes widening, when she noticed the dog.

'My brother said you like dogs but don't have one of your own ... so I thought I'd introduce you to mine,' signed Jane. And speaking as well, 'Sit and shake hands, Hamish.'

Hamish sat and raised a paw. Julia dropped to her knees, took the paw in one hand and ruffled his ears with the other. Then, looking up, she signed quickly, 'He's so clever!'

'Not really,' replied Jane, ruefully. 'His only other talent is finding a nice cushion to sleep on when no one's lap is available. But he's very affectionate. You can pick him up if you want to. He won't mind.'

Very, very carefully, Julia gathered the little dog in her arms and stood up. Hamish licked her chin, making her giggle.

From her place near the door and deciding that her presence wasn't necessary, Sophia slipped out unnoticed.

Almost an hour later, Christian and the Hawkridge brothers returned from the gardens looking mildly dishevelled but extremely pleased with themselves. Catching them *en route* for the drawing-room, Sophia blocked their path and said, 'Don't go in there – Julia and Miss Gardiner are making friends. I'll have coffee sent to the library.'

Waving Benedict and Oscar onwards, Christian said, 'You left them alone?'

'Yes. They're fine. When I listened outside the door ten minutes ago, they were running about, laughing – probably chasing the dog.'

He stared at her. 'What dog?' And then, 'Miss Gardiner brought her *dog?*'

'Yes.' Twinkling up at him, she said, 'His name is Hamish.'

He grinned at this but said, 'Will she do?'

'She's just what we need. She was a bundle of nerves when she arrived – but she struck exactly the right note with Julia. Do you want to meet them now or later?'

'Now, I think. Wait. Them? You're going to introduce me to the dog?'

'Yes. He shakes hands.'

Two pink-cheeked young ladies stopped in their tracks when the door opened, thus allowing Hamish to make a dash for freedom. Christian swooped on him, shut the door with his foot and, looking the dog in the eye, said, 'Hamish, I presume?'

'I'm so sorry, my lord,' mumbled Jane as she hastened towards him. 'We were playing and he's a bit – a bit over-excited. I'll keep hold of him till he calms down.'

'Why?' Christian set Hamish on the floor, where he promptly sat down to scratch an ear. 'He's doing no harm. How old is he?'

'Just over a year.'

'Still a puppy, then.' He strolled towards the girl, smiling. 'How do you do?'

'V-Very well, my lord,' she stammered, unprepared for the earl's stunning good looks. 'Thank you f-for this chance.'

'You are quite welcome. Do you think you might enjoy keeping Julia company?'

'Oh *yes*, my lord.' She smiled at Julia and briefly signed something which sent the younger girl all but dancing over to kiss Christian's cheek. 'If she and you and her ladyship think I'd suit, that is.'

'There seems little doubt of that.' He looked briefly at Sophia who nodded in response to his unspoken question. 'I'll speak with you before you go home, Miss Gardiner. But for now, we will leave the two of you – and Hamish, of course – to continue getting acquainted. Tell Julia to ring for more tea, if you want it.' Glancing at the severely depleted tray, he added, 'And cakes. And if she hasn't already done so, ask her to tell you what will be taking place in the gardens on Friday. Since I wrote to Mr Braidwood about it, I imagine your brother already knows.'

Once back in the hall, he slid an arm about Sophia's waist and said quietly, 'You're right. From the little I've seen, she'll do very well. She and Julia already seem well on the way to becoming friends.'

'They do. So the only real question is whether Miss Gardiner and Hamish come as a pair? And, if so, what on earth Mama is going to make of it?'

* * *

Joining Oscar and Benedict in the library and accepting the cup of coffee that Christian poured for her, Sophia said, 'How are things going across the road?'

'Extremely well,' said Benedict. 'Mr Sutton has a very efficient team – and fortunately the weather has cooperated thus far.'

'They've built the pavilions, a rotunda for the musicians, laid the surface for dancing and are currently working on your Chinese grotto,' added Oscar. 'Everything seems to be on schedule. The only thing that is giving them a headache is where to set up the firework display so that it won't present a hazard. But I daresay they'll work something out.'

'Half the servants in the square have been over to see what's happening,' Christian told her. 'I suspect the neighbours are sending them – rather than be seen gawking themselves.'

'No one's complained, have they?' Sophia asked him quickly. 'When we visited everyone to explain the idea, no one objected. But I suppose now it's happening outside their door, with wagons coming and going all the time, some of them may feel differently.'

'Since nearly every household in the square has already purchased tickets, I don't think we'll be hearing complaints. Or not until the fireworks set everyone's dogs barking, anyway.'

'And speaking of dogs,' murmured Oscar, 'having obliquely offered the bait, what are the chances of Basil taking it, do you think?'

'We can but hope,' replied Christian. 'By now he'll know there's written evidence here in the house that could damn him. I'd guess his first reaction will be panic … and his second, to somehow get his hands on it. From there, it should be a short step to how and when he might be able to do that.' He shrugged. 'If he doesn't make an attempt on Friday, there's nothing we can do.'

'So we go ahead as planned,' said Benedict. 'And it's time we stopped debating the question of witnesses and made a decision. Just one of us – we can't *all* be there. But we need a couple of others; gentlemen who are both impartial and influential – which creates a slight problem in that we somehow have to persuade them to help without revealing what they'll be helping *with*.'

'Vere,' said Oscar simply. 'I'll talk him into it. You know he can't resist a mystery. And my other suggestion would be Rainham.'

'Why him?' asked Christian.

'I just have an odd feeling that there's more to him than meets the eye.'

'Talk to Belhaven first and then we'll see,' said Christian, coming to his feet. 'And now I'd better find out if Julia wants to keep Miss Gardiner. Coming, Sophie?'

'You don't need me. She can lip-read, remember?' Sophia reached for a biscuit. 'And when she's said yes – which she will – and you're agreeing terms with Miss Gardiner, don't forget to ask about Hamish. Forewarned and all that.'

* * *

'Let me check that I understand this correctly,' said the Duke of Belhaven that evening. 'You want me to hide in Hazelmere's library in order to eavesdrop on a conversation between his lordship and someone you won't name but who is presumably his unspeakable cousin and who may or may not turn up. Is that right?'

Oscar nodded uneasily. His brother was many things but stupid wasn't one of them.

'Yes. I know it sounds bizarre ... but will you? It will be worth it, I promise you. And you won't be alone.'

'How comforting. Who else will be there?'

'Anthony Wendover and, hopefully, Viscount Rainham.'

'Ah.' The duke's eyes narrowed. 'Rainham. Yes. Are we there to witness a crime or prevent one?'

'A cross between the two. What is it about Rainham that made you think that?'

There was a long silence until, ignoring his brother's question, Belhaven asked one of his own. 'Is it serious?'

'Yes.'

'Then I suggest you also permit me to have a word with the Earl of Alveston. Don't ask why. Suffice it to say that his lordship has a very long arm and powers which would undoubtedly surprise you.'

CHAPTER TWENTY-SEVEN

Much to Sophia's relief, the day of the charity gala dawned dry and warm and looked set to remain so. Mr Sutton's men arrived early with all the things that couldn't be put in place until the day itself; chairs, tables, long trestles for the food and, of course, the fireworks. Lanterns were hung in trees and bushes; snowy linen and quantities of cutlery and glassware arrived; additional, smartly-liveried footmen were given their orders by Fallon; and, with military discipline, the kitchens of Hazelmere House completed the numerous dishes that comprised the Grand Buffet.

Mr Braidwood was bringing four of the academy's students to mingle with the guests, handing out leaflets outlining the school's work and answering questions. Colin Gardiner would escort his sister so that she could be introduced to Lady Kelsall. Over two hundred tickets had already been sold and a footman was to be stationed at the main gate to deal with last-minute customers.

The gardens were scheduled to open at eight o'clock. At five, exactly as promised, Mr Sutton informed Lord and Lady Hazelmere that the preparations were now complete and invited them to come and see for themselves. Although, throughout the last week, Christian had visited the gardens on a daily basis, he had given instructions that the household staff were to be kept out unless they had a reason to go there. And by her own choice, Sophia had forbidden herself to take even the tiniest peep at what was going on behind the screen of greenery. So now Christian rang for the butler and, when he appeared, said, 'Assemble the troops, Fallon. We're going in.'

And drawing Sophia's hand through his arm, 'Ready?'

'Yes!' she said, virtually dancing with impatience. 'Let's go.'

Leading the procession, Mr Sutton said, 'Everything will look quite different later when the lanterns are lit. Four of my men will remain here to do that when the time comes and also for security. Perhaps you would wish to have a ceremonial opening, my lord?'

'Why not? But I believe that honour should go to her ladyship,' replied Christian. And softly to Sophia, 'It's your turn. I've been having fun all week.'

'I noticed,' she retorted. And then, entering the gardens and getting her first glimpse of the transformation, 'Oh! It's lovely, Mr Sutton – you've worked wonders!'

'Thank you, my lady. But as I said, you won't see the full effect until dark.'

Around them, footmen and maids went in different directions exclaiming over the pretty pavilions, the linen-covered tables, each with a coloured glass lantern waiting to be lit and the exotic Chinese grotto. Then the drift of music caused everyone to stop talking and listen.

'The ensemble arrived a little while ago,' explained Mr Sutton, 'and wished to hold a brief rehearsal. Perhaps, when they have done so, they might wait inside the house with their instruments until ten minutes before opening time?'

'Certainly,' said Sophia. 'They shall have a comfortable room for their own use where they can be served a light supper. And the footmen you supplied will sit down to a meal with our own staff.'

'Thank you, my lady. They will appreciate it, I'm sure.'

Christian beckoned Fallon and said, 'Give them a few more minutes and then herd them back inside, please.' And, to Sophia, 'Well, love? Are you pleased?'

'Pleased? I'm delighted! This could become an annual event.'

He winced and murmured, 'Don't get your hopes up, Sophie-Rose. Mr Sutton hasn't presented his account yet.'

* * *

After that, time flew by. Sophia gave last minute instructions to the staff before going upstairs to prepare for the evening. Although she knew she ought to wear black, she had chosen a gown of mid-grey and dark-violet shot silk which she hoped would pass muster by lantern-light – particularly if she didn't add anything but a simple strand of pearls.

By the time she was ready to go down, it was almost half past seven. The light was fading and, across the street in the gardens, lanterns were being lit. Sophia stood for a moment, enjoying the magic of it. Then she went in search of Christian.

She found him in the library and he wasn't alone. Daniel Shelbourne, Anthony Wendover and Lord Rainham were there, along with all three Hawkridge brothers and a gentleman she didn't know.

Curtsying to the duke, the viscount and the stranger, she bade them good evening but wasn't sure what else she could safely say if the third gentleman wasn't party to the plot.

'Introduce me, Belhaven,' he said. 'Lady Hazelmere and I have not met.'

'No? My apologies. My lady, allow me to present my friend the Earl of Alveston.' And leaning a little closer, added conspiratorially, 'He is here, like Rainham and myself, to witness the proceedings. Did Oscar not mention it?'

'Not to me.' Offering her hand, she smiled at the earl. 'But thank you for agreeing to help, my lord. Did I interrupt some last-minute plotting?'

'Something like that,' agreed Alveston gravely. 'I understand that your husband has someone looking out for the Selwyn gentlemen?'

'Numerous people,' she replied. 'If they come, he'll know.'

'Excellent,' said Belhaven. And to Lord Alveston, 'That means you and I need not spend the *entire* evening in hiding.'

'You want to join the party outside?' Sophia teased, knowing he didn't.

'Perish the thought – although I may be moved to make a donation. His lordship and I would much prefer to pass the time over a game of chess with a glass of claret until our presence is required.'

'I'm sure we can arrange that,' she told him, amused. And to Rainham, 'And is that what *you* will be doing to pass the time, sir?'

'By no means. I intend to spend a little time in your pleasure gardens with my wife.'

'Vivian's here?'

'Not yet. She's coming with Adam and Millie Brandon.' He grinned at her. 'I'm fairly sure virtually *everyone* you know will be here tonight.'

'Oh? Well, that's good news for the academy.'

Christian emerged at her side, saying, 'You'll have to excuse us, gentlemen. Some other guests have arrived and we should join them. But my thanks to all of you for helping later – if later *happens*, that is.' Then, to Sophia, 'Your mother and sisters are here – as are Braidwood and the Gardiners.'

'Jane hasn't brought Hamish with her, has she?' asked Sophia quickly. 'I'll need to choose the right time to break *that* bit of news to Mama.'

'She hasn't. But Fallon's put them all in the drawing-room.'

'*All?* Oh dear. That's a bit awkward.'

'Isn't it?'

The scene in the drawing-room was *definitely* awkward. Lady Kelsall and Gwendoline stood stiffly to one side ... Julia and the Gardiners to the other; and, between the two, Mr Braidwood. After a brief, exchanged glance, Christian and Sophia sailed into action – he to Braidwood and the Gardiners, she to her mother and sister.

'You're early, Mama – how lovely!' And without giving her ladyship a chance to speak, 'Have you met Miss Gardiner yet? No? Then let me introduce you.' She beckoned the two girls, aware that Christian was shaking hands with Mr Braidwood and Colin Gardiner. 'This is Miss Gardiner, Mama – the young lady who will be Julia's companion. Jane ... my mother, Lady Kelsall and my other sister, Gwendoline.'

Jane smiled, curtsied and murmured a 'good evening'. Neither Kelsall lady did any of those things. Sophia swallowed a sigh and hoped that Julia had found an opportunity to warn Jane of the kind of welcome to be found in Charles Street. Julia signed something and Jane said, 'Julia asked me to tell you that the younger gentleman talking to his lordship is my brother. The older one is Mr Braidwood who owns the academy.'

'Really?' said Lady Kelsall in a tone which suggested she didn't need to know that.

'So you'll be living with us?' demanded Gwendoline of Jane.

'Yes. Lord Hazelmere has suggested that I take up my position next week.'

'Lord Hazelmere,' remarked the Dowager, 'takes a great deal upon himself.'

'And pays for it,' interposed Sophia sweetly. 'Let us not forget that.'

A glance at the clock informed her that it was five minutes to eight and a second one through the window, that a little crowd had formed outside the gate to the gardens. Turning, she called, 'Forgive us, everyone – but it's time, so Kit and I must go. Please feel free to follow, if you wish.' And softly, to Christian, 'Did *you* know Lord Alveston was joining the witness team?'

'Not until Oscar mentioned it half an hour ago. Belhaven's suggestion, seconded by Rainham, apparently.'

It wasn't only the drawing-room guests who shadowed their steps. Mr Shelbourne and the two younger Hawkridge brothers did the same, all three looking rather serious.

'What's the matter with them?' whispered Sophia. 'Regardless of what happens in the library, *outside* is just a party. They're supposed to look as if they're *enjoying* themselves.'

'They think I may need protection though I've no idea why. Basil's hardly going to shoot me in front of a couple of hundred people, is he? And even if he tried, he'd either miss or kill somebody else by mistake. He's always been a terrible shot.'

They walked through the front door to a ripple of applause and the crowd parted to allow them access to the gate. Christian bowed and handed her the key; Sophia smiled at him, slid it into the lock and turned it. Then, as he pushed the gate open, she said clearly, 'Welcome, everyone. The Berkeley Square Pleasure Garden is now officially open.'

* * *

Within the hour, the gardens were already busy and people were still arriving. Music was tempting dancers on to the floor. Footmen with trays of wine winnowed skilful paths between strolling guests, jugglers and a man on stilts. The Chinese grotto was a huge success with the younger people, and older ones enjoyed the comfort of the pavilions. Braidwood's students mingled with the guests, distributing their leaflets and sometimes being detained in conversation; Mr Sutton's fellows continued to man the gate and sell tickets to those who didn't have one; and Mr Sandhurst (who, Christian noticed, was spending most of his time with Julia and Jane) occasionally collected money from them.

The buffet supper was to be served at ten o'clock and it had been arranged that, just before it, Mr Braidwood would make a short speech of thanks to everyone for supporting the event and hinting that donations to the academy were always welcome.

As the hour approached Christian became increasingly aware that his uncle and cousin hadn't so far put in an appearance. He was confident that, short of donning a wig and false nose, there was no way Basil could be in Berkeley Square without him knowing. It was why he'd firmly vetoed the idea of making the evening a masquerade. And he'd taken every possible precaution. Aside from Benedict, Daniel, Oscar and Gerald all keeping watch inside the gardens, he'd got two grooms who knew Basil patrolling the perimeter outside.

Damn, he thought. *Have we completely miscalculated? If Basil hasn't worked out that tonight is his best chance of slipping into the house unseen, perhaps he hasn't thought of stealing the evidence either. And if that's so, I've got a duke, an earl and a viscount waiting in the wings for something that isn't going to happen ... and no back-up plan.*

Across the street, he could see relays of footmen taking trays of food from the maids and carrying them to the buffet tables. In fifteen minutes or less, he himself was supposed to introduce Braidwood for his speech. Deciding that, if necessary, Sophia could deputise for him, he sped off to warn her – just in case.

* * *

Outside the south end of the gardens, Basil lurked in the shadows, watching the activity at Hazelmere House. Originally, he'd considered briefly joining the party … but later he'd realised the folly of letting himself be seen. It would be much the best thing if no one knew he was anywhere near Berkeley Square tonight.

A fellow engaged in trying to light his pipe bumped into him, nearly causing him to jump out of his skin. Muttering, 'Blimey, mister. Didn't see you there,' he wove drunkenly on.

Basil took a steadying breath and waited for his nerves to settle. As he watched, two ladies followed a footman up the steps – presumably *en route* for the ladies' retiring room. There were a great many servants around this evening. He'd sooner not be seen by any of them but tried to comfort himself with the knowledge that it wouldn't be a disaster if he was because they'd just assume he was a guest at the party. And he had no intention of going in through the front door. He'd need to pick the right moment, of course, but his preferred route was a side door that opened on to the terrace. He'd used it quite a few times while he and his father had lived in the house … and he still had the key in his pocket.

Activity around the front steps was lessening. The maids disappeared back inside and the only footmen Basil could see weren't wearing Hazelmere livery, which meant they were extra hands hired for the evening who wouldn't know him.

Everything will be fine, he told himself, aware that he was sweating and his hands weren't quite steady. *All I have to do is get to the library and out again without being seen while everybody, including my damned cousin, is busy with guests. It will be fine.*

He decided to give it another few minutes, then saunter casually across the road and into the house as if he had a perfect right to be there.

* * *

The drunk with the pipe – more usually Christian's head groom – also waited, slouching against the railings as if half-asleep. But the instant Basil moved, he was at the gate and telling the footman there to get Lord Hazelmere.

'But they're having supper,' began the footman. 'I can't – '

'Yes, you bloody can. Tell him Jim said he's here and on his way in. *Go!*'

The footman ran. A minute later, Christian was at the gate, saying, 'Where?'

'Gone round to the side, milord. Now you know, I'll go and keep an eye out.' And he shot off across the road.

Christian turned to find Gerald at his side, with Daniel two steps behind him. He said, 'He's on his way in. Gerald, get Belhaven and the others into position.'

Gerald went off at a run.

'Daniel, tell Benedict and Oscar. Ask Oscar to stay with Sophie and keep her out here at all costs. You and Benedict follow me. I'll be giving Basil time to get to the library and open the strongbox before entering the library myself from the drawing room. But once I have, you guard that door and tell Benedict to guard the one from the hall so no one else comes in and Basil doesn't get out before I'm finished with him.' Then he was striding in the wake of both his groom and his cousin.

* * *

Basil slid inside the house and remained where he was for a few moments, straining his ears. What sounds he could hear were some distance away, probably in the kitchens and servants' hall. Now they'd got the food laid out, in all likelihood most of them would take the opportunity to sit down for a few minutes and take a breather before the next onslaught.

Nobody will be above stairs while everything is still going on outside, he assured himself, *so getting to the library should be easy. After that, all I need is just five minutes to get the damned letter from the strongbox and make sure it's what I'm looking for – I can read it properly later. Then I'll be on my way.*

At the foot of the stairs, he waited again to listen before starting to climb. The library doors stood open and two lamps had been left alight but the room was silent and empty. Basil shut the doors behind him and crossed to the ornate desk where the key to the strongbox had always been kept in a concealed drawer. He hoped that Christian hadn't decided to put it somewhere else; if he had, it could be anywhere and there would be no way of finding it. But no. The drawer opened as easily as it always had ... and the key lay in its usual place. He let out a relieved breath. So far, so good. Now to open the box.

The panel hiding it looked like a dozen or more hefty tomes on genealogy. Basil knelt, flicked the catch and opened it wondering, not for the first time, why whoever had installed it had put it at floor level instead of somewhere more convenient. Not that it mattered. It was the work of a moment to turn the key and snap the door open.

As it always had, the strongbox contained a large quantity of money and several velvet cases in which reposed numerous pieces of family jewellery. But lying on top of these was a slim buff folder of papers and it was this that Basil, his heart hammering in his chest, reached for. Coming to his feet, he turned to look at it in the light of the lamp on the desk.

Consulate Correspondence, it said helpfully.

He opened it to glance at the top sheet ... and then froze, staring. It wasn't in English. It wasn't even written in a recognisable alphabet. It was a page full of loops and lines and curls which Basil dimly supposed must be Turkish. He rifled through the other two pages – and found them the same.

For a moment, his brain seemed to stop working. Then, numbly, *What use is this? Who the hell can read it? Can Kit? And it could say anything or nothing. It might not be a witness statement at all. It could be a sodding fairy tale for all anyone knows.*

He was so completely poleaxed by his discovery that he didn't hear the connecting door to the drawing-room open ... and therefore the first thing he knew of Christian's presence was his voice saying quietly, 'Is this what you were looking for, Basil?'

CHAPTER TWENTY-EIGHT

Christian strolled unhurriedly towards his cousin, holding up a second folder and reminding himself of the importance of getting this right. Although the document in his hand contained the truth, it had not come from the Consulate in Constantinople; and a forgery was of no use whatsoever except as a tool to force Basil to confess. Unless he could make that happen, everything he and his friends had done in preparation for tonight would be wasted. Nothing could be proved beyond doubt and Basil might go free. Christian couldn't and *wouldn't* let that happen. He prayed that, after this, he would never have to see his cousin's face again.

Basil opened his mouth but no sound came out. He glanced wildly about the room as if considering flight, took a couple of steps in the direction of the hall and then hesitated.

'Very wise. That way, your path lies through Benedict Hawkridge. The other door has Dan Shelbourne behind it. So ... it's just you and me, Cousin.'

Shaking his head as if to clear it, Basil said stupidly, 'You – you were expecting me.'

'Obviously.' Tapping the folder in his hand, his smile faint and far from friendly, Christian said, 'This is the English translation of the one you're holding. I'd let you read it if I could trust you not to throw it in the fire. But I can't, can I? A pity ... because it tells a very interesting story.'

Basil's heart slammed against his ribs. Attempting to brazen it out, he said, 'I don't know what you're talking about.'

'Of course you do. If you didn't, you wouldn't be here, burgling my library.'

'I'm not. I just – I came to get something I left behind when you threw us out.'

'If that was true, why creep in like a thief?' And when Basil began interrupting, 'Stop. Don't strain your powers of invention or my credulity. You're here to steal the information I recently received from Turkey because you're frightened your name is in it. Actually, if you're honest, you *know* your name is in it and in what context – thus you can't risk it being made public. And you *certainly* can't risk me handing it over to Sir John Fielding at Bow Street.'

'*Bow* Street?' Basil tried to sneer but it sounded more like a yelp. 'You're talking nonsense! Fielding won't give a rap what anyone's saying in Turkey.'

'You think not?' Christian opened the folder and read aloud from the topmost sheet.

'*This being the sworn statement, of Yusuf Zeytin, dragoman, formerly of Athens; witnessed and signed in the presence of Huseyin Demir and Sir Henry Yardley of the Constantinople Consulate.*' He looked up. 'Do I really need to go on? After all, you already know what Mr Zeytin has to say, don't you?'

'No.' Basil felt sick. He wanted to leave but Hawkridge and Shelbourne weren't going to let him. 'If Zeytin's the fellow who left Athens with you, I scarcely exchanged two words with him. Somebody recommended him and I sent him to you. That's it.'

'Not quite. Not at all, in fact.'

'It *was*, I tell you! If he said anything else – if he's tried to make what happened *my* fault – he's lying. He hadn't done his job properly, had he? He'd lost a – a client, for God's sake. *You.* Of course, he'd lie to hide that.'

'That's a nice try. It might even work with other people. But not with me. I was there, remember.'

'Well, *I* wasn't. And I haven't the faintest idea what Zeytin did after you left Athens. He was paid to get you to Constantinople. If he did something else, it's not my fault.'

Christian could feel the old, familiar rage start to burn inside him and resolutely forced it aside. Very slowly and deliberately, he said, 'You're wasting your breath, Basil. I know. I've *always* known.'

Basil stared blankly at him. 'Wh-What?'

'You heard. How I ended up in Ibrahim Pasha's home was never a mystery to me. I knew exactly how it had happened – and lived with that knowledge every day of the three years I spent there.'

Staring at him, horrified, Basil managed to croak, 'I – I've no idea what you're talking about. There's nothing *to* know!'

'Is that what you've been telling yourself all this time? And what you've been telling your father?' Christian advanced a couple of steps and perched on the corner of the desk. 'Did it never once occur to you that I might know what you'd done? Didn't my attitude towards you from the instant I came back make it *obvious* that I knew? Why else do you think I wouldn't have you in my house?' He paused as if waiting for an answer and then, once more gesturing with the folder, 'I didn't need this to *tell* me what you did, Cousin. I only needed it to prove that you *did* it. So you can continue denying it until you run out of breath for all the good it will do you. It won't change the fact that I know – or that now, thanks to the Consulate, I can make sure everyone else knows, too.'

Basil stared at him, white-faced and sweating. He said, 'What do you want?'

Christian took his time about answering, aware that this was the moment he'd been waiting for. Then, keeping both face and voice under rigid control and with the merest hint of a shrug, he said, 'To hear you admit it.'

'*What?*'

'I want to hear you say it. I want you to look me in the face and admit what you did and why you did it and what you hoped the result would be.' He gave a contemptuous laugh. 'But you won't, will you? You won't ... because you still think you can lie your way out of it, just as you've always done.'

'It isn't *me* who's lying!' said Basil desperately. 'It's that bastard, Zeytin. Whatever he's told them in Constantinople – whatever he told *you* – it's lies. All of it.'

'No.' Christian shook his head. And then, in a tone dripping with contempt, he said, 'Be a man for once, Basil. It will be a novel experience for you but ...you never know, you might get to like it. Be a man and admit what you did.'

'Admit to *what,* for God's sake? What the hell am I accused of?'

'You don't need me to tell you that. I doubt you've forgotten.' Christian had always known that wringing a confession out of his cousin wouldn't be easy; and he was equally aware that he couldn't prompt him – that the words had to come from Basil himself. 'But you just can't do it, can you? Even as a boy, you could never own up to little things like a broken ornament. You'd do anything – *say* anything – that would enable you to squirm your way out of trouble. And you're still doing it.' He paused, wondering how much further he had to take this before Basil lost both his temper and what little sense he possessed ... and whether his own self-control would last long enough for it to happen. So he said derisively, 'You're a coward, Cousin. You always have been.'

Patchy colour suffused Basil's otherwise white face.

'How dare you? I don't have to take that from you!'

'But you *are* taking it, aren't you? You're standing there and letting me say anything I choose. And why? Because you haven't an ounce of backbone – or if you do, it's made of jelly. And you're also apparently too stupid to see that things can't possibly get any worse for you than they already are.'

'Hurling insults at me won't – '

'Have I not made it plain enough yet? It isn't *possible* to insult you.'

Basil threw the useless folder he still held down on the desk and swung away towards the door. He said, 'I'm not going to listen to any more of this. I'm leaving.'

'I wouldn't advise it – but you can try,' said Christian coldly. And watched his cousin stop dead. 'I'm not the only one who knows what you did. My wife and my friends do, too – so neither Benedict nor Daniel will mind hurting you. But we're straying from the point. I'm still waiting for your confession ... and you won't get safe passage out of this room until I have it.'

Hands clammy and perspiration trickling down his back, Basil hesitated, considering his options, none of which were promising.

Wanting more than anything to be done with this and unsure how long he could continue to control the sick rage boiling inside him, Christian said, 'Perhaps a few words from Mr Zeytin will jog your memory.' And reading, '*The man Selwyn paid me to take his cousin, the earl, to Constantinople. He asked many questions about the dangers along the way. When I told him about them, he said he'd pay extra if I would ...*' He stopped. 'If he would *what*, Basil? Say it. Say it and I'll let you leave.'

There was a long, airless silence. And then, his face contorting with rage and hate, Basil's nerve finally broke and he shouted, 'If he *didn't* get you to Constantinople, damn you! If he lost you somewhere along the way – somewhere you couldn't get back from. He said that would be easy because there were plenty of slavers between Greece and Turkey. Any one of them would buy you from him and sell you to the galleys. He said nobody ever came back from that. But he said dealing with slavers was chancy so it would cost extra for him to take the risk. Satisfied now? Is that what you wanted to hear?'

Christian's heart gave a single, hard thud. He searched for some sense of triumph but could only find weariness in the knowledge that this was almost over. He nodded. 'Go on.'

'What more do you want? What more *is* there?'

'Why you did it, perhaps?'

'*Why?* Why do you *think?*' demanded Basil bitterly. 'Christian, the golden boy – always everybody's favourite and held up as a shining example to me all my life. Christian, the perfect student, the perfect son – the perfect sodding nephew. You were born with every single advantage for no better reason than that your father was ten minutes older than mine. Why *wouldn't* I seize an opportunity to get rid of you? So when I had one, I took it. You were supposed to disappear for good. But that didn't happen, did it? *Oh* no. God knows how, but *you* ended up in a comfortable palace as some Turkish fellow's pet.'

'That's one way of looking at it. As to how I escaped the galleys ... both Zeytin and the slave-master knew that, as an educated foreigner, I'd fetch a better price elsewhere. They *also* saw an opportunity and took it.'

'Well, it worked out nicely for you, didn't it? You didn't come back looking half-starved and ill-treated – so the worst that happened was that you weren't allowed to leave. You fell on your feet, the same as you always do. *Hell!* I wouldn't be surprised if you didn't actually enjoy yourself!'

Christian laughed, the sound jarring and bitter.

'*Enjoy* myself? Enjoy being deprived of every part of my identity, of being reduced to *no* one? Enjoy knowing that escape wasn't possible and that, with every passing day, my chances of rescue got smaller? Here's what captivity does to you, Basil. It stops you hoping. It stops you thinking of home. And eventually it even stops you *remembering* because it's too painful. *That* is how much I enjoyed it.' He stopped, breathing rather hard. 'You stole three years of my life – but that isn't all you wanted, is it? I was meant to die, chained to an oar, so that what had been *my* life could become *yours*. Admit it.'

'All right – I admit it. I didn't care if you lived or died so long as I never saw you again.' Basil headed for the door to the hall. 'You asked for the truth and you have it – so call your guard dogs off. I'm leaving.'

'No,' said a voice from above. 'You are not.'

Basil swore and whirled around, his frantic gaze raking the gallery.

There was a moment of acute silence. Then Lord Alveston appeared, followed by His Grace of Belhaven. Starting down the spiral stairs, the earl said, 'I have just heard you confess to attempted murder, Mr Selwyn – and to the various lesser crimes it was meant to make possible and, indeed, *did* make possible for three years. Lord Hazelmere might be willing to let you walk away from that, sir, but *I* am not.'

Wild-eyed, Basil turned from where Lords Rainham and Wendover had joined Belhaven on the gallery and stared instead at Christian. 'You – you *bastard!*'

'Perhaps. But don't they say it takes one to know one?' Leaving Basil stranded in the centre of the room as all four witnesses converged on him, Christian opened the doors so Benedict, Daniel and Gerald could join them.

'It's done?' asked Benedict, briefly squeezing his shoulder.

'It's done,' agreed Christian, sounding drained. 'Mostly, anyway. I ought to get back to the party I'm supposed to be hosting ... and Sophie will be worried. But I can't do that yet. First, I need to have a word with Lord Alveston and finish things here, so can you –?'

'Yes,' said Benedict. 'I'm on my way.' And left.

Looking terrified, Basil was being held in place by Rainham while Alveston said, 'If you are wise, Mr Selwyn, you will stay silent until asked to speak. Bluster and excuses will not help you now.' And, crossing to Christian, 'An appalling affair, my lord. I shall take charge of it from this point and tomorrow you and I should discuss the various ways in which it can be handled. For now, however, Mr Selwyn must be held in custody for obvious reasons. Rainham ... take him to Wilfred Street and tell whoever is on duty to secure him.'

'If you need any help,' offered Mr Shelbourne cheerfully, 'just say the word.'

'With *him?*' asked Rainham. 'Hardly. But you might explain to Vivian for me and make sure Adam and Millie Brandon are still here and will take her home.'

'Of course.' With a grin and a nod, Daniel followed in Benedict's wake.

Lord Alveston offered his hand first to Christian and then to both Belhaven and Anthony, murmuring, 'I'll bid you good evening, gentlemen. It has been most ... enlightening. Ah. Just one thing more, Lord Hazelmere. May I take the Consulate correspondence with me?'

'If you wish, sir – but it has served its purpose.'

The earl's eyes narrowed. 'Meaning what precisely?'

Christian hesitated, shrugged and then, seeing no help for it, said, 'Those pages tell the truth ... but they didn't come from Constantinople.'

'Oh dear,' said Alveston. 'Please don't say anything further.'

'No, my lord. I wasn't about to.'

* * *

A short while later, when Belhaven had also left, Christian found Sophia with Oscar, Benedict, Daniel and Vivian Rainham while the pleasure gardens went on in full swing around them. The instant she saw him, Sophia rose and went to take his hand, saying softly, 'Was it horrible?'

'Yes.' He was only just beginning to realise quite *how* horrible and how contaminated it had left him feeling. 'But it's over now – or will be after I meet Lord Alveston tomorrow. He is very ... efficient. And intimidating.'

Catching his last words, Vivian said wryly, 'You have no idea. However, I understand that Mr Selwyn is now on his way to Wilfred Street.'

'Yes – although I'm not sure where, or more pertinently *what*, that is.' He glanced at his friends and added, 'We'll have a post-mortem later. Right now, I'm going to stroll the gardens with my wife.' Once away from the others, he said, 'I'm sorry I dashed off with scarcely a word and left you to deal with everything. Were there any problems?'

'No. And of *course* you had to go. We both knew that.' She squeezed his arm, knowing he needed a few minutes to recover from whatever the last hour had cost him. 'Mr Braidwood left a little while ago because, although the young students have had a wonderful evening, it was time they were in bed. He apologised for not taking his leave of you but asked me to tell you that he's been promised a number of donations and is extremely grateful to you both for tonight and the opportunity it provided for him. As for the Gardiners, they are still here somewhere. Jane and Julia have been largely inseparable – accompanied by Gerald, I might add, until you needed him.'

'Yes. I noticed ... and suspect you may have been right about that.'

'I *was* right about it,' she said firmly. Then, 'This evening's been a huge success, you know. A few people have left but most are staying for the fireworks.'

Christian pulled out his watch. 'They are due to begin any time now. Good. I'm glad it's been a success and that our guests have enjoyed themselves but ...'

'But now you want them to go home?'

'Yes. I'm sorry.'

'Don't be. I want the same – '

She broke off with a gasp as the first of the fireworks tore the sky with a bang and a shower of red and green, swiftly followed by a cascade of silver. All around the garden, conversations died and people stopped to stare upwards with exclamations of pleasure. Laughing, Sophia leaned against Christian and felt his arms close about her. She sensed that some of the tension she felt in him was beginning to ease and that his mind was slowly recovering from wherever it had been. He had wanted tonight; *needed* it, even. But he hadn't enjoyed it. So she leaned against his warmth and let him watch starbursts of colour filling the sky without any need to either think or speak.

* * *

Having already told Fallon to bring the household staff out to watch the firework display and let them enjoy the gardens themselves for a little while before clearing away things which must be brought inside, Christian and Sophia bade the last of their guests good night and retired to the library. Benedict, Oscar, Daniel and Gerald were all there, listening to Anthony's abbreviated account of what had taken place earlier. But when Christian appeared, he broke off to say, 'Well done, Kit. There was a moment or two when I thought Basil was going to hold his nerve ... but you won in the end.'

'Not because of anything *I* said,' admitted Christian wryly. 'I won because he didn't dare leave through either door, knowing Benedict and Daniel were the other side of them.'

'Perhaps. But I particularly liked the moment when you remarked that, if he *had* a backbone, it was made of jelly,' grinned Anthony, 'and followed it up by saying that it wasn't possible to insult him.'

This made everyone laugh but Christian. Then Daniel said, 'When Basil finally confessed, what was the reaction upstairs?'

'Rainham looked murderous, Alveston disgusted and Belhaven completely unsurprised,' came the concise reply. Then, 'So ... what happens next, Kit?'

'I suspect that will be up to Alveston – who is clearly more than just an earl.'

'As Rainham is more than merely a viscount,' added Oscar. 'And I wouldn't be a bit surprised if Adam Brandon isn't another of the same ilk – whatever that is. Interesting, isn't it? One wonders what the bond is.'

'One also gathers that we're not meant to know anything about it,' remarked Benedict. 'However ... returning to the original question?'

Oscar grinned, shrugged and subsided.

'As you know, I'm to meet Alveston – though whether at his home or at Wilfred Street, I don't know.' Christian found Sophia's hand and held it because it helped to keep at bay the things he didn't want to think about yet. 'Unfortunately, he asked for the so-called Consulate papers which meant I had to admit they wouldn't be very useful.'

'So he knows we forged them?' asked Daniel.

'Yes. As does Belhaven who was there at the time. But since the word 'forgery' was never mentioned, there's a chance that part will be discreetly forgotten.' Christian thought for a moment and then said, 'Regarding tomorrow's meeting, Alveston mentioned discussing various alternatives which I assume meant solutions for dealing with Basil other than a trial for attempted murder. Oh God.' He stopped in response to a sudden thought. 'I have to tell Eustace.'

'*Someone* has to tell Eustace,' agreed Sophia, 'but it need not be you. In fact, in my opinion, it *shouldn't* be you.'

'I'll do it,' volunteered Gerald. 'Tomorrow, while you're meeting the earl. As for where that will be, he'll presumably send a note. But it's almost certainly going to be Wilfred Street – wherever that is – because Basil is there and Alveston will want to question him.'

'Well, I hope he doesn't expect me to help with that,' muttered Christian, draining his glass and holding it out to Daniel, who appeared to have taken charge of the decanter. 'I'd hoped never to have to so much as *look* at Basil again.'

'And perhaps you won't,' said Benedict. Then, 'I don't know if Alveston will allow it ... but, if he does, do you want company tomorrow?'

'Yes.' He said it without thinking. 'God, yes. You'll come?'

'Of course. Any of us would. You know that.'

'Yes.' Christian looked around at the men who had stood by him throughout all this and more. 'No one ever had better friends. And I'm grateful – truly I am. But – '

'That didn't need saying,' said Daniel. 'And gratitude has no place here.'

'I disagree. But though I understand you all wanting to celebrate our victory, I ... can't. Not yet. So could we please talk about something else for a little while?'

'Certainly,' agreed Oscar promptly. 'The pleasure gardens of Berkeley Square, for example. This is one evening that won't be forgotten in a hurry – in fact, you and Sophia may even have set a fashion. Time will tell. But it was an enormous success which everybody thoroughly enjoyed.'

'Mama didn't,' contradicted Sophia cheerfully. 'She said it was vulgar and so was a good deal of the company and what on *earth* possessed us to sell tickets at the gate? As for Gwendoline, she enjoyed herself until all the eligible gentlemen vanished and – '

'*I* didn't vanish,' protested Oscar. 'As ordered, I remained glued to your side.'

'Exactly – much to Gwen's annoyance. So she and Mama left, dragging poor Julia with them.' She cast a mischievous glance in Gerald's direction. 'It was very kind of you to look after Julia and Jane. I'm sure they appreciated it.'

Flushing slightly, Gerald said, 'Young Gardiner was assisting Mr Braidwood. And with so many people – some of whom were strangers – I didn't think the young ladies should be left alone. It was no hardship to keep an eye on them.'

'And none for them either,' she replied. 'I'm sure they enjoyed your company.'

* * *

Later, when they were finally alone, Christian lay holding Sophia's hand and staring up at the silk tester. After a while, feeling the air about them thick with something she couldn't identify, she said softly, 'What is it?'

'What is what?'

'The thing you are thinking but can't make up your mind to say.'

He turned his head to look at her. 'You always know. How *is* that?'

'It's a mystery. Now ... are you going to tell me?'

His gaze returned to the tester and it was a long time before he spoke. But finally he said, 'Was I wrong to do it this way? Involving Alveston, for example? Was it really necessary to force Basil's confession within earshot of a man like him?'

'You know it was. All of *us* knowing would never have been enough. Basil had to condemn himself before someone whose impartiality wouldn't be questioned. You did what you had to do to get justice.'

'Did I? All along, I've admitted to myself that it was revenge I wanted. And that's not quite so noble, is it?'

She turned, propping her head on her hand so she could look at him.

'You're doubting your motives?'

'Yes. Aren't you?'

'No. Not for a minute.' She laid a hand against his cheek. 'Look at me.' And when, reluctantly, he did so, 'And now listen. He couldn't be allowed to get away with it, Kit. He wanted you *dead*, for heaven's sake! He wanted to steal your life for himself ... and he almost managed to do it. But for your friends, he *would* have done it. That isn't just unforgivable – it's downright wicked. And can you name even *one* thing you ever did to deserve it?'

He sighed and shifted restlessly.

'Nothing ... deliberate. I was too good to be true, apparently. And he came very close to saying even his own father preferred me to him. That can't be right, can it?'

Actually, Sophia thought it probably could. That, deep down, Eustace might have looked at both his son and his nephew and recognised which of them was the better man. But she said, 'It's ... unlikely. However, even if it's true, it doesn't excuse what Basil did. Nothing can do that. And since your return, he's continued trying to do you harm through malicious rumours and gossip and the like.' She paused. 'Did it never occur to you that, in time and if he wasn't stopped, he might go further than that?'

A faint frown creased his brow. 'No. Not really.'

'Well, *I* thought it. And I'm not prepared to lose you again.'

'Nor I you, Sophie-Rose. Nor I, you.' He hesitated and then added, 'I hadn't expected it to get out of my control tonight – but it has. Yes, I want Basil gone; but not dead or in prison – just gone. I'm not sure how much say I'll have in that now.'

'Lord Alveston won't disregard your opinion. He can't. You are the injured party, after all. Tell him what you want to happen and why. He'll listen to you.' She smiled down at him and stroked his hair back from his brow. 'And if he doesn't, he can listen to *me* instead.'

The shadows vanished from his eyes and he laughed.

'Sebastian Wingham once told me that his wife is part Valkyrie. I'm beginning to understand what he meant.' He drew her into his arms. 'I'm also beginning to wonder why I'm lying here with you worrying about tomorrow. It will take care of itself, won't it? One way or another.'

'Yes. You've done all you could. So ... time to let it go, at least for tonight.' She pulled him down so that his head rested against her breast, sensing that what he needed now above all things was peace. 'Stop thinking, Kit. Stop thinking and just let me hold you. It will be tomorrow soon enough.

CHAPTER TWENTY-NINE

A note from Lord Alveston arrived when they were at breakfast and was swiftly followed by Benedict.

'Wilfred Street,' announced Christian, passing his lordship's letter to Sophie and pushing the coffee pot in Benedict's direction. 'He's given directions and asks me to be there at ten.'

'This isn't a request,' said Sophia. 'It's more like an order.'

'Yes. I'm trying to disregard that. Are you still coming, Benedict?'

'Why else do you think I'm up and dressed at such an hour?'

'Thank you.'

'No need for that. Last night was a joint enterprise and there's no reason today should be different. Have you decided how you want to play it?'

'I suspect that very much depends on Alveston. But I know how I want it to end.' Christian pushed his chair back, stood up and went to kiss his wife's cheek. He said, 'Don't stay at home worrying about me and what's happening. Go shopping or something. Take Julia with you.'

'Yes. I think I might,' she smiled, knowing that she wouldn't.

'Ask her if she likes Gerald,' suggested Benedict slyly.

'Are you still at school?' sighed Sophia. 'Or do you think *I* am?'

'Ouch,' said Christian. 'And on that note, let's go.'

* * *

The address given in Alveston's letter turned out to be an unremarkable house in a dingy street on the fringes of Westminster. The door was opened by a young man with freckles and a ready smile who looked from Benedict to Christian and back again, saying, 'Lord Hazelmere?'

'I'm Hazelmere. This is Lord Benedict Hawkridge.'

An unconcerned nod greeted this information.

'Yes. Goddard said you might bring someone. If you'd just wait here for a minute, gentlemen, I'll see if he's ready for you.'

Staring at each other under raised brows, Christian and Benedict both mouthed, *Who's Goddard?*

Then the young fellow was back and leading them to a comfortable office occupied by Lord Alveston, Rainham and a bespectacled gentleman to whom, although he looked vaguely familiar, neither Christian nor Benedict could put a name.

All three rose to bid the visitors good morning and Alveston introduced the third man as, 'Roger Falconer, our legal expert. He's here to listen, make notes and perhaps ask the occasional question for the sake of clarity. He will share his opinions with me later. As for Rainham, I asked him to attend this meeting as a result of a brief conversation we had last evening and because his insight is occasionally useful. But if you prefer to discuss the matter privately, Hazelmere, he need not stay.'

'Since there's very little his lordship doesn't already know, I see no reason for him to leave,' said Christian. 'Just one question ... who is Goddard?'

Without lifting his head from something he was writing, Falconer grinned and murmured, 'Oh dear.'

Alveston and Rainham exchanged a pained glance and Rainham bellowed, '*Geordie!*'

There was a sound of running feet and then the freckled face appeared around the door. 'Sir?'

'How did you refer to me when our visitors arrived?' asked Alveston.

Geordie thought about it and then, groaning, said, 'Oh.'

'Oh,' agreed the earl. 'Did you forget what I said or just not listen?'

'I – it was just habit, sir. You're *never* Lord Alveston when you're here so – '

'Except this morning.'

'Yes, sir,' came the gloomy reply. 'Except this morning. I'm sorry.'

'Mm. Another three months on the door, I think.' And when Geordie opened his mouth to protest, 'Go. Now.'

When the door closed again, Rainham said, 'That's a bit harsh, isn't it?'

'Is it? Talent's no use if he can't keep his wits about him.' Alveston turned back to his guests. 'This house is home to a small and very discreet government department of which I am section chief; and since we don't use titles here, I'm generally known as Goddard. In order to avoid any possibility of having to share that information with you and to ask *you* not to share it elsewhere, I would have preferred to hold this meeting at my home. Unfortunately, at some point we shall need to speak to Mr Selwyn – and he is currently detained below stairs.' His lordship's gaze became exceedingly acute. 'Am I making the position plain?'

Benedict merely nodded. Christian said, 'Extremely so, my lord.'

'Good. And now to business. Last evening, I heard Mr Selwyn confess to what, in essence, was attempted murder. Lord Hazelmere ... perhaps you would be good enough to relate the sequence of events from your point of view.'

'If I must.' His posture rigid and his jaw tense, Christian said, 'After some weeks in Athens, I felt it would be a pity not to see Constantinople since we were so close. Basil disagreed and wanted to start for home, so we eventually decided that I would travel to Turkey and he would await me in Palermo. Because of language difficulties and local customs, I needed a dragoman. Basil volunteered to find one ... and a day or so later, he introduced me to Yusuf Zeytin.'

'He was Turkish, I presume?' queried Rainham.

And when Christian nodded, Falconer said, 'May I ask if it was you or your cousin who made the necessary arrangements with him?'

'Basil. Until we left Athens, I'd barely spoken with Zeytin ... but he was pleasant enough and seemed to know what he was doing.'

'And then?' prompted Alveston.

'We set off in a small ship – something similar to a caravel – to cross the Aegean. On the third day out of Athens when we must have been about half-way to the Dardanelles, we pulled in at one of the islands; to take on fresh water, Zeytin said.' He paused and then added tonelessly, 'Only that wasn't the real reason.' He stopped again, his expression strained. 'How much detail do you want?'

'Everything that is relevant – nothing that isn't,' replied the earl. 'Take your time.'

Christian took several long, slow breaths and began again.

'There was a second ship there, a larger one than ours. Zeytin said the captain was a friend of his and suggested that, while the water was being loaded, he and I go and take a glass of the local spirit with him. I saw no reason to refuse … so we went. Although he smiled a lot, the other captain didn't speak English so the two of them spoke Turkish with Zeytin translating from time to time. But something about the way the rest of the crew were looking at me began to feel … odd. Wrong, even. So I told Zeytin I'd return to our vessel, leaving him to be sociable.' This time, the pause was a long one. 'The next thing I knew, I was face down on the deck and someone was putting manacles on my wrists.'

Benedict swore softly. Rainham said, 'You'd no idea what was happening?'

'My first thought was kidnap for ransom; that I'd be left there while Zeytin sailed back to Athens and got money from Basil – except I realised that wasn't going to work because Basil was no longer *in* Athens.' He gave a strange, bitter laugh. 'Stupidly, I thought that was the worst of it. But then they hauled me upright and Zeytin explained that his friend, Captain Kartal, was a slave-trader … and that my cousin had paid him to hand me over to one such. Specifically, he said, one who would sell me to the galleys so that I'd never be seen again.'

'Is that *precisely* what was said,' asked Falconer, 'or an approximation of it?'

'It's precise. I had it going round and round in my head for three years.'

'Thank you, sir. That is helpful. Please go on.'

'Zeytin and Kartal decided against the galleys because they knew that, in the right market-place, an educated man such as myself was worth far more than a galley slave. So they haggled, struck a deal and money changed hands. During it, I heard the name of Ibrahim Pasha for the first time. Zeytin told me to count myself lucky. I'd have a more comfortable life in Tekirdağ than chained to an oar. Then he left.'

When he stopped speaking, an almost suffocating silence filled the room. Finally, his voice low and furious, Benedict said, 'Lord Alveston ... will you give me ten minutes alone with Basil Selwyn?'

'No.'

'Five?'

'Again, no – though I sympathise.' The grey gaze rested on Christian. 'So ... putting all this in a nutshell ... on the instructions of Basil Selwyn, you were sold, first to a slaver and then to this man, Ibrahim, who held you captive for three years?'

'Yes.'

'And, if asked, you would swear to this under oath?'

'Again, yes.'

Alveston nodded. 'Then let us move on. How were you treated during those years?'

'Aside from not being allowed outside the grounds? Well enough, compared to some of the other places I might have ended up.'

'No ill-treatment?'

Something shifted behind Christian's eyes. 'Not the sort of thing you mean.'

'And what do you think that is?'

'Being chained up somewhere? Beatings? Starvation?'

'So ... none of those.' Then, thoughtfully, 'But something else, I suspect.'

It wasn't a question. Feeling Benedict's eyes upon him, Christian pressed his lips together and said nothing.

Alveston tried again. He said, 'You need not be specific, merely – '

'Good. Because if I haven't even shared it with my friends – the men without whom I wouldn't be sitting here today – I'm certainly not going to tell *you*,' snapped Christian.

'Merely confirm that there *was* something,' finished the earl quietly. 'Which, by implication, it seems you have now done. Thank you, my lord. I am aware this has been difficult. But a clear picture of the results of Mr Selwyn's actions will help me make a suitable determination regarding his future. Rainham ... bring him up to join us, will you?' And as the viscount nodded and left the room, 'While we wait, is there anything further you wish to add?'

'Yes. I don't believe my uncle knows what Basil did. If I'm right ... and if Basil goes to prison, his father's life will be almost equally destroyed. Although I'm not particularly close to Eustace, I'd prefer to avoid responsibility for that if at all possible.'

'A generous sentiment and one which does you credit,' came the non-committal reply. Then, 'I shall be interested to see if your cousin's attitude has changed at all since last evening. Some remorse and less spite would help his cause.'

'Don't expect either. He'll be frightened and sorry his sins have found him out as I imagine do most of those who fall into your hands, my lord. But Basil has never been very good at seeing where his best interest truly lies. If he was, he wouldn't be in this mess and I'd have been spared three years of – of what I described in rather too much detail last night.'

'You regret making those admissions?'

'Yes. It was not the time or place. Neither did it serve any useful purpose.'

'I disagree,' said Benedict, speaking for the first time. 'Anthony told us what you said. It explained a lot about your state of mind when we got you back. Knowing it *then* might have made us better able to help you.'

'You helped enough.'

'Did we?'

The words, *But not enough for you to trust us with the worst of it*, hung unsaid in the air.

And then the door opened and Rainham hauled Basil inside.

Not unnaturally, he looked somewhat the worse for wear and, in addition to uncombed hair and rumpled clothes, a bruise was blossoming on his jaw. Seeing Alveston contemplate this beneath raised brows, Rainham shrugged and said smoothly, 'He had a slight disagreement with a door. But no real harm done.'

Basil opened his mouth as if to deny this but closed it again when Rainham's fingers bit into his shoulder, shoving him into a chair.

'Very wise,' murmured Alveston. 'Impetuous accusations are rarely helpful. Now ... Lord Hazelmere has related what befell him after leaving Athens. Nothing in that mitigates or materially changes your confession of last evening. But if you have anything to add that might count in your favour, this is your opportunity to say so. You will be given a fair hearing.'

Basil stared sullenly at the carpet beneath his feet for several minutes before eventually mumbling, 'What I said last night, was only said because Christian wouldn't let me leave without having to fight my way out. *I* didn't tell the dragoman to lose him on the journey or give him to a slaver – that was Zeytin's own idea. He must have come up with it when I asked what the dangers of journeying to Turkey would be. And he knew I was leaving Athens myself so I'd probably never find out what he'd done.'

'That isn't what you said last night,' remarked Rainham. 'You said you'd paid the dragoman to make sure your cousin never got to Constantinople. He told you how it could be done but claimed it would cost more due to the risks involved in dealing with slavers.' He surveyed Basil over folded arms. 'I'm surprised you fell for that – since the fellow would be *selling* Lord Hazelmere to the slaver, not making a gift of him. However, I can only deduce that money was no object as long as you got what you wanted.'

'That's a very good point,' observed Benedict. 'Is that how it was, Basil?'

'*No!* You're twisting everything – talking as if I planned it!'

'And didn't you?'

'*No*, I tell you. Look ... you're all making it sound worse than it was.'

'How, exactly, *could* it be worse?' asked Rainham idly. 'And last night you were all but boasting about how clever you'd been.'

'That would be right,' murmured Benedict. 'He never *did* know when to keep his mouth shut. But here's what probably happened. He had what he thought was a sudden flash of inspiration in Athens – and acted on it. Was that it, Basil?'

'I don't have to answer to you, Hawkridge.'

'Perhaps not. But you do have to answer to *me*,' Alveston informed him. 'And nothing you have said so far helps your case.'

'Judge and jury, are you?' demanded Basil belligerently. 'I don't think so.'

'Then think again. Here in this office, as far as you are concerned, I am both.'

'If that's so, I want a lawyer. And I'm saying nothing more until I have one.'

Falconer laid down his pen and said mildly, 'It *is* his legal right, sir.'

'I know that – and we'll get to it later. Meanwhile, listen to me carefully, Mr Selwyn.

Whatever the outcome of today, there is scant chance that you will go free. But I have the authority to decide between sending you first to Newgate and then for trial ... or to a less public but no less permanent alternative. Your attitude here will decide which is more appropriate – and, so far, you are not inclining me in your favour.'

Silence fell as five pairs of eyes rested inimically on Basil.

Finally, addressing him for the first time, Christian said, 'Does my uncle know?'

Basil twitched. 'What?'

'Have you told Eustace what you did? Does he know any of this?'

'No.' He looked around at his accusers. 'He won't even know where I am.'

'By now, he will. Since I had to be here, Gerald Sandhurst will have explained the situation. So not only will your father know *where* you are, he'll also know *why*.'

'You bastard,' growled Basil. 'Enjoying this, are you?'

'Not particularly. If I have to look at you much longer, I may well vomit.' And to Alveston, as he came to his feet, 'If you've no further questions for me, I'm leaving. Let me know the outcome when you've decided what it's to be.'

'No. I need you to remain a little longer, sir – so please sit down. However, since it appears that he has nothing useful to add, I believe we can dispense with Mr Selwyn's presence for now. Rainham; take him away, please. And don't let him walk into any doors on the way.'

'I'll try not to, sir.'

Grinning, Rainham took a firm grip on Basil's arm and hauled him from the room.

When the door closed behind them, Alveston said, 'Just to be clear, Hazelmere ... you said earlier that you'd prefer to spare Eustace Selwyn the ignominy of his son's public trial and subsequent imprisonment. Is that still the case?'

'Yes. But that doesn't mean I want Basil to escape punishment. I don't.'

'Good. Because, even if you did, I would be extremely reluctant to allow it.'

'Sir,' interposed Falconer quietly. 'If I might remind you of the conversation we had regarding – '

'Unnecessary. I was just coming to that,' returned Alveston impatiently. And to Christian, 'As you know, the fact that the so-called Consulate papers did not actually *come* from the Consulate makes them useless as evidence in court; but sworn statements from myself and the other gentlemen who heard Mr Selwyn's confession would be sufficient to obtain a conviction – hence your somewhat risky strategy of last evening. However, you want this handled discreetly and, fortunately, I have both the authority and the means to do so.' He paused and then, sighing, said, 'I told you that this is a little-known government department. Our most common function is to make embarrassing situations go away – mostly those affecting Royalty, the government or other prominent figures. Consequently, there is a system in place which enables us to make such undesirables as come to our notice ... quietly disappear.'

Christian frowned at him. 'What are you saying?'

'I am saying that there is a secure facility in a location known only to myself and Lord North. We call it the Retreat and its current population comprises sixteen gentlemen and seven ladies. Some come from exalted backgrounds and their sins encompass everything between serial bigamy and insurrection. Since they are not the usual sort of criminals, they are not locked in cells. They are comfortably housed, each with his or her own private room and there are common areas both inside and out where they may mix with each other. However, they are not allowed to be idle. As far as is practicable, the Retreat is required to be self-sufficient. Food has to be grown and cooked; clothes have to be laundered, rooms cleaned and so forth. Everyone, without exception, has to lend a hand and, in return, they are allowed every illusion of freedom save one. No one who is sent there ever leaves.' He paused as Rainham re-entered the room and then added, 'If you wish it and for the sake of his father, I am prepared to offer your cousin a place there.' He stood up. 'I will hold him here until noon tomorrow – no longer than that; time for you to consider the matter and for Mr Selwyn's father to visit him and be given the option I've just laid before you. After that, with your agreement, I shall send him on his way.'

* * *

On Benedict's suggestion, he and Christian left Wilfred Street for an hour spent in a quiet tavern where, as he put it, they could wash the nasty taste from their mouths with a tankard or two of ale. For a long time, Christian said nothing about their visit to Alveston's office and when he did, it was merely to remark on what appeared to be the earl's double life.

'And not just his, either,' agreed Benedict. 'Aside from Rainham and possibly also Adam Brandon, it makes you wonder how many *other* gentlemen we know have a whole different identity.'

'Not very many, I imagine. He said it was a small department, didn't he? And the more people involved in something like that, the harder it is to keep it secret.'

'True.' Benedict thought for a moment and then said, 'I haven't *entirely* worked out what we're allowed to tell the others and what we're not. Since we're not supposed to mention Alveston's other persona or that he heads a government department, how do we explain the extent of his authority and the existence of the secret prison?'

'You're talking about Daniel and Anthony and Gerald – all of whom we trust,' returned Christian, a little impatiently. 'So we tell them everything but stress it must go no further. Speaking for myself, I'm not letting Basil make me start hiding the truth from my friends.'

Sitting back, Benedict debated whether to say what was on his mind or not. Then, because Christian had just given him the ideal cue, he looked up and said gently, 'But you're already doing that, aren't you?'

Christian met his gaze for a moment and then looked away, flushing slightly.

'Yes. And I'm sorry. But that is something I can't talk about.'

'Can't – or won't?'

'Won't, probably.' He toyed with his tankard, turning it around in circles. 'If you *must* know, it's ... to me, it's humiliating. Degrading, even.'

'Also, unless I'm mistaken, the cause of your nightmares?' And when Christian nodded, 'Do you still have them?'

'No, thank God. Not at all since the wedding.'

'That's good. And does Sophie know whatever it is you won't tell us?'

'Yes.'

'Well, that's something I suppose. And was *she* ...?' He stopped, unsure which word to use.

'Disgusted? No. I thought she would be. But she ... surprised me.'

'So might we, Kit,' said Benedict. 'So might we. Think about that, will you?'

Christian stared into the half-empty tankard as though there were answers at the bottom of it. He thought, *He could be right. The five of us don't judge each other. We never have. Their reaction might not be so very different to Sophie's and she calls it a medal for survival, not a badge of shame. And whereas I still can't bear to glimpse the bloody thing in the mirror, she even* kisses *it, for God's sake.* At some other time, he might have seen the potential humour in that. Instead, he merely thought, *But my friends are a different matter. They are more likely to feel sorry for me ... and there's been more than enough of that already.* A frown touched his eyes as a new notion occurred. *On the other hand, how long do I want to continue being a coward about this? It's never going away, is it? And how long can I go on hiding it? Sooner or later, someone will see it. All it would take is some sort of accident requiring my shirt to come off and the secret is out. Is that a risk I really want to take? Wouldn't it be better to grasp the nettle and just* show *them?*

He said slowly, 'All right. But I'm not going through it more than once, so I want to tell all of you at the same time and somewhere private. And right now, I need to go home to Sophie.' A brief pause and then, 'If you, Anthony and Daniel are free to take pot luck with us this evening, we can hold a *'thank God it's over'* dinner.'

CHAPTER THIRTY

Back in Berkeley Square, Christian saw that Sutton's men were still busy removing traces of last night. Leaving them to get on with it, he walked into the house and hadn't even removed his hat when Fallon said, 'Mr Selwyn is here, my lord. Mr *Eustace* Selwyn. He has been here for two hours or more.'

'*How* long?'

'Two hours, my lord. He won't go. Both her ladyship and Mr Sandhurst have assured him that you will call on him when you are able to do so – but he insists on waiting and refuses to leave until he has seen you.'

Wishing he'd come straight home after the meeting with Alveston, Christian laid his hat aside and stripped off his gloves. 'Where is he?'

'In the library with Mr Sandhurst.'

'And my wife?'

'The drawing-room, my lord.'

'Thank you. I'll see her ladyship first but you can tell Mr Sandhurst and my uncle that I'll join them directly.'

He found Sophia pacing to and fro in front of the hearth while, around her, two abandoned novels and a half-written letter bore witness to her inability to settle to anything. As soon as she saw him, she said, 'Thank goodness! Fallon has told you?'

'Yes.' Putting an arm around her, he kissed her cheek. 'I could have come home sooner than this and am sorry I didn't. However ... what has Eustace said to you?'

'Not a great deal. Gerald called on him as planned and he had no sooner come back than Eustace appeared hard on his heels. Fallon told him you weren't here; Gerald and I told him the same. He believed none of us. In the end, Gerald took him out to the mews to prove your phaeton was missing. He believed us *then* – but instead of leaving, he said he would wait and he's been here *hours*.'

'And thoroughly upset your day, by the looks of it.'

'That's of no consequence. Kit, he's almost distraught – understandably, under the circumstances – so one can't help feeling sorry for him. Will what you can tell him help?'

'No – though it could be worse. And I've half a mind to leave the full story to Alveston.' He paused, kissed her again and said, 'I'll tell you everything presently but I'd better see Eustace before he barges in here. It's a pity I can't speak to Gerald privately first but there'll be no chance of that.'

And he went out.

In the library, with Eustace prowling restlessly around him, Gerald had been trying to complete the accounts from the previous night's party. But as soon as Christian appeared, he gathered up his papers and slipped out just as Eustace said, 'And about time! Where the *hell* have you been till now?'

'As I'm sure Gerald told you, I was summoned to a meeting with Lord Alveston at an office in Westminster; 27 Wilfred Street, if you wish to go there yourself – as I presume you will since it's where Basil is being held.'

'Has he been charged?'

'In effect, yes.'

'With what? I know what Sandhurst said but I want to hear it from you. What is my son being charged with?'

'Attempted murder. Mine.'

'Oh God.' Eustace stared at him, then collapsed into a chair clutching his head. He was pasty white and breathing unevenly. 'It's true, then.'

'Yes. Unfortunately.' Christian crossed the room and came back with a glass of brandy. Putting it in his uncle's hands, he said, 'Drink that and take a moment. If it helps at all, I'm aware you had no idea what he'd done.'

Downing the drink in two swallows, Eustace looked up at him and said wearily, 'You always knew, didn't you? Right from the beginning.'

'Yes. The dragoman Basil employed told me to my face what he'd been paid to do – and what the result was intended to be.'

'Yet you waited until now to have your revenge.' He gave a bitter, shaky laugh. 'They say it's a dish best eaten cold, don't they?'

'They do. Revenge or justice ... what you call it doesn't change anything.'

'You prefer justice?'

'I'd *like* to say that's what it was but I don't know how true it is. As for why I waited ... the only evidence of what Basil did was my word. In the event that it proved insufficient, I needed him to confess before witnesses. And last night he did so – hence the involvement of Lord Alveston.'

'And Belhaven and Rainham,' added Eustace bitterly. 'You were making damned sure he'd never talk his way out of it, weren't you?'

'Yes.' Christian drew a long breath, loosed it and said, 'Basil robbed me of three years of my life, Uncle ... and if his plan had succeeded I'd be dead. In my shoes, what would *you* have done? Better yet, if the positions had been reversed and I had done to Basil what he did to me, what then? Would you have swept it all under the carpet for the sake of the family and let me go unpunished? I don't think so.'

'No. Probably not.' Eustace leaned back against the chair and shut his eyes. 'I always suspected there was something but, when I asked, he always denied it. And even my imagination would never have come up with what you say he actually *did*.' Opening his eyes again, he said, 'What will they do with him?'

'I think you should ask Alveston that question. For what it's worth, I'm not out to claim my pound of flesh and his lordship knows it.'

'What does that mean, exactly?'

'It means I told him I'd prefer to avoid a public trial and everything that entails.'

A tiny glimmer of hope lit Eustace's eyes. 'Did he listen?'

'Yes. And he's prepared to offer an alternative which he'll explain to you. If you can accept that, then so will I.'

For a few moments, there was silence. Then Eustace said, 'I was about to ask why you'd spare Basil a trial. But of course you won't want the family name dragged through the mud and plastered all over the newspapers and scandal sheets.'

'That is one reason, certainly.' He chose not to point out that it wasn't the main one.

'But let's be very clear on one thing. Basil has brought this on himself and will pay for what he did. If he had behaved differently upon my return, there may have been a time when I might have let it go and not looked for redress. I'm not sure. But he *didn't* behave differently, did he? He continued trying to injure me with his lies and rumours and insinuations. And, as my wife has pointed out, he might eventually have gone further. So here we are.'

'Yes. Here we are.' Eustace stood up. 'Will I be permitted to see him?'

'Of course. And, as I said, Alveston wants to speak with you.'

'Then I'll go.' He started towards the door, then stopped and looked back. 'I suppose I should thank you.'

'No, Uncle. It's Basil who should thank me. But he won't.'

* * *

Gerald was in the drawing room with Sophia and, as soon as Christian walked in, he rose, saying, 'I'm sorry. I tried to make him see sense – to go home and wait until – '

'It wasn't your fault. The conversation he and I just had was inevitable. And at least it's behind us. He's off to Wilfred Street to see Basil and hear what Alveston has to say.'

'Is there going to be a trial?' asked Sophia hesitantly. 'I know it isn't what you want ... but Lord Alveston might see it differently.'

'Lord Alveston,' said Christian flatly, 'is section chief of a government department – with all the discretionary powers that go with it. So no, Basil will not face trial. He'll be sent to what his lordship describes as a 'secure facility' where the inmates are free to move around, rather than locked in cells, but from which there will be no coming back.'

'And you are satisfied with that?' asked Gerald.

'Yes. It may sound too kind but it spares Eustace and means I'll never see Basil again. And though in some senses it may *sound* kinder than he deserves, it's still captivity. When it gradually sinks in that he's going to be kept there for the rest of his days, he's going to understand all the helplessness and hopelessness I tried to describe last evening ... along with the knowledge that nobody is ever coming to rescue him. I find that singularly apt.' An odd smile curled his mouth. 'The punishment may not completely fit the crime. But it's close enough.'

'So it's over,' said Sophia with satisfaction. 'Good.'

'Yes. Ah. Sophie ... promise you won't hit me?'

'Why? What have you done?'

'Invited Benedict, Anthony and Daniel to dine this evening – you too, Gerald. And don't say you won't join us. Thanks and a moment to enjoy finally being able to put this whole thing behind us are in order, don't you think?'

'If you say so. But now, since there's peace in the library, I'm going to balance the books from last evening. Excuse me.' And with a small bow for Sophia, he left them.

Crossing to ring for Fallon, she said, 'You couldn't tell me we're hosting a dinner party tonight when you first came home?'

'I had other things on my mind. Sorry.' In truth, the main thing he'd been thinking of hadn't been Basil so much as what he'd let Benedict lure him into agreeing to. 'But it's just our friends and I *did* call it pot luck – so there's no need for the kitchens to go to a great deal of trouble.'

'Since the staff have barely finished clearing away after last night, that's just as well,' she replied. And when the butler appeared, 'Please convey his lordship's apologies to Cook, Fallon, and tell her that we shall be six for dinner this evening.'

'Very good, my lady.'

'Apparently the gentlemen will be happy taking pot luck.'

A pained expression crossed his face. 'But Cook will not be happy serving it.'

'Quite. That's what I thought. Thank you, Fallon.' And when he had gone, sitting beside Christian in order to take his hand, 'Did you have to see Basil this morning?'

He nodded. 'And answer questions I'd rather not have answered. But as you said, it's over now. And I suppose the end justifies the means.'

'Did Lord Alveston say *why* he knows of this comfortable prison?'

'Yes. He told Benedict and me several things he'd have preferred not to and which we were told not to repeat ... but we'll break that embargo this evening, then forget we ever knew.'

'It sounds rather cloak and dagger.' Sophia leaned against his shoulder. 'I noticed that you didn't mention Lord Oscar earlier. Is he not invited?'

'Not tonight, no. I have reasons for wanting it to be just *us* this evening.'

She twisted her head to look up at him. 'Oh?'

'I've let Benedict persuade me to do something I don't want to do and will probably regret.' And on a long, slow breath, he told her.

* * *

Gathering in the drawing-room for pre-dinner sherry, Anthony, Daniel and Gerald listened to Christian's brief account of what had taken place in Alveston's office that morning. At the end of it, Daniel said, 'Am I alone in thinking that, even with the *'everyone has a job to do'* rule this so-called prison sounds too good for Basil?'

'No,' replied Benedict. 'I think the same. But it *is* a prison and he'll never leave it ... so it's as good a solution as any. And a trial would stir up a storm of notoriety that will affect Kit and Sophie as much as it would Eustace.'

'And which we don't want,' said Christian firmly. 'Imagine Basil digging and hoeing or mopping floors, Daniel. I guarantee that you'll feel better.'

There was a ripple of laughter into which Anthony said, 'Did Lord Alveston give no clues at all as to where it is?'

'No. Only he and the Prime Minister know that. But I did wonder if the place being mostly self-sufficient is about more than keeping costs down and the inmates occupied but also to do with its location.' Christian shrugged. 'A remote island, perhaps? That would make escape extremely difficult, if not impossible.'

'And somewhere with terrible weather?' suggested Daniel. 'All right. Maybe Basil *isn't* getting off as lightly as I originally thought.'

'I still haven't got over discovering that both Alveston and Rainham have a sort of undercover existence,' said Sophia. 'I wonder if it ever involves anything dangerous? And whether Vivian Rainham knows about it?'

'She knows,' nodded Daniel. 'When I told her that Rainham was taking Basil away under arrest, she didn't need to ask where he was taking him *to*.'

'Might I suggest that we stop speculating about what goes on in Wilfred Street?' asked Benedict mildly. 'Kit and I aren't supposed to know anything about it, let alone be telling the rest of you. And I suspect that Lord Alveston will not be pleased if one of us inadvertently lets something slip out. Personally speaking, I'd sooner not annoy a man who has the power to lock me up with a mixed bag of undesirables and, in all likelihood, give me the room next to Basil Selwyn's.'

'An excellent point,' agreed Anthony. 'Let's change the subject.'

Conversation over dinner, in which Sophia took little part, centred largely about the success of the previous evening's charity event and how much it had raised for Braidwood's academy. Gerald said that he didn't yet have a fully accurate final figure as yet but all the indications were that it would be in the region of three thousand pounds.

'On top of which,' he said, 'Braidwood has also been promised personal donations from a number of quarters – Belhaven, Sarre and Amberley, to name but three.'

'You can add Rockliffe to that list,' said Anthony. 'I met him at White's this morning and he said that, although he and the duchess didn't attend the party, he is always willing to support a good cause.'

'Might that include bailing me out when the cost of last night lands me in debtors' prison?' murmured Christian wryly. Then, in response to Sophia's expression, 'I'm joking, love. *This* time, anyway. But please don't get any similar ideas for a while.'

'I'll try not to,' she agreed. And went back to toying with her apple tart whilst worrying about what he intended to do later.

She was proud of him for deciding to trust his friends with what she suspected he still thought of as a shameful secret … but she hadn't forgotten what it had cost him to reveal it to *her* and didn't think he'd find tonight any easier. On the other hand, his reasons for his decision made perfect sense. It was bound to come to light sooner or later; how on earth he'd managed to keep it from his *valet* for so long was a minor miracle! And she had every faith in his friends' reactions. They wouldn't find the tattoo repulsive any more than she did – because it simply wasn't. Perhaps they would find a way of convincing Kit of that.

By the time they left the table and decamped to the drawing-room, Christian was edgy with nerves. He thought, *Why the hell did I agree to this? Damn Benedict for making it about trust!* He knows *I trust him – as I do all of them. But that doesn't necessarily mean I have to tell them every single thing, does it? The truth is, I don't have to do it at all – let alone this evening. And if I must, do I really have to show them? Wouldn't just telling them be enough? Surely they don't need to actually* see *it.*

But he forced himself to behave normally, pouring port or brandy for the gentlemen and taking the opportunity, when Fallon brought the tea tray in, to tell him they didn't wish to be disturbed.

For a little while, Daniel made the others laugh with a tale about a carriage race which had been cut short by both vehicles losing a wheel inside the first half mile.

But all too soon, there was a lull in the conversation and, grimly telling himself to just bite the bullet and get it over with, Christian downed his brandy in one swallow and said jerkily, 'Today I was asked whether I suffered ill-treatment in Tekirdağ. I said no. But Alveston pressed it and I – I ended up refusing to tell *him* something I hadn't even told my friends. Benedict has opinions about that. The rest of you probably do, too. So I'll rectify the omission now.'

And taking off his coat, he began unbuttoning his vest.

CHAPTER THIRTY-ONE

Anthony, Daniel and Gerald all stared at him in wordless surprise. But Benedict, with alarm bells clanging inside his head, stood up, saying quickly, 'Kit – stop. I'm sorry. I ought not to have said anything. You don't have to do this – so just stop.'

Christian didn't reply and he didn't stop. The vest followed the coat and he moved on to his cravat. Sophia sat very straight, holding his eyes with her own and sending him all the love and encouragement of which she was capable. When he tugged his shirt from his breeches and hesitated briefly, breathing rather hard, she said softly, 'Bravo, my love. Bravo.'

He gave a small, bitter laugh, dragged the shirt off ... and turned his back.

For what seemed a very long time, no one spoke. Then, rising from his chair and walking over for a closer look, Daniel said, 'Is that a *tattoo?*' And when Christian grunted an assent, 'Good Lord! It's remarkable.'

'It is,' agreed Benedict. Having, for a horrible moment, expected something far worse, he was having difficulty finding his voice. 'It's intricate and elegant. But ... done without your consent, I gather?'

'Yes.' Christian reached for his shirt. 'It was a punishment. Have you seen enough?'

'Not quite,' said Anthony, almost apologetically. 'It's Arabic script, of course. But what does it mean?'

"*There is no God but Allah and Muhammed is his messenger, as I am his faithful servant,*" muttered Christian. 'It's meant to give the impression I converted. I didn't.'

'Well, no one but you need ever know the intention behind it,' remarked Gerald. 'And Benedict is right. In its way, it's quite beautiful.'

'That's what *I* said.' Rising, to lay her hands over Christian's where they were clenched on his shirt, Sophia smiled up at him. 'You see? It isn't so terrible.'

'I agree,' said Daniel enviously. 'It really isn't. *I* want one.'

'There!' she whispered. 'I *knew* he'd say that.'

This time, though still no more than a huff of breath, his laugh was almost real. Stepping back and pulling his shirt back on, he said, 'No, Daniel. You don't. Trust me.' Shoving the shirt roughly back into his breeches and shrugging into his vest, he said, 'Will somebody please pour me another drink?'

Benedict did so and handed him the glass, saying, 'I'm sorry, Kit. But I'm sure I speak for us all when I thank you for trusting us enough to share this. We know how hard you found it and we understand why. But please *try* to believe that we're not lying when we say it's neither shameful nor repulsive because it isn't.' He paused briefly. 'Then again ... the tattoo itself isn't the problem, is it? The *problem* is how you got it.'

'Yes.'

'You said it was a punishment. For what?'

Christian took a hefty swallow, then said, 'Trying to engineer a way out. The only thing I managed to hide from them was my signet ring. I bided my time until I had a few words of Turkish, then used it to bribe a servant who acted as a courier between Ibrahim and Constantinople. I told him he could keep the ring if he just took word about me to the Consulate.' He stopped, stared into his glass and then said, 'He was caught and bastinadoed. It's possible he may never have walked again. Two days later, I was held face down by a couple of eunuchs while the tattooist set to work on my back.'

'How?' asked Daniel. And quickly, 'Don't tell us if you'd rather not.'

'I'll tell you if it means we can have done with it. Does it?'

'If that's what you want, of course.'

'Well, then. It was done in instalments over what seemed a very long time but was probably no more than two or three weeks. They use a special dye made, amongst other things, from soot and then tap it into your skin with various sized needles. Scabs form over the treated area and they waited for those to fall off before starting the next part. It's painful ... and if you're unlucky, it can become infected.' He glanced at Daniel and, 'Do you still want one?'

Daniel grimaced. 'Possibly not.'

'Wise choice.' And to Sophia who had grown rather pale, 'I'm sorry. I deliberately didn't tell you any of that before and shouldn't have done so now.'

'Yes, you should,' she replied fiercely. 'If you could endure having that done to you, *I* can endure hearing about it.'

For almost a minute, he said nothing before words seemed to burst out of him,

'During the whole time it was going on, I was confined to my rooms. They'd removed the mirrors so, until it was finished, I'd no idea what they were doing to me. And for weeks after I came back, I dreamed about them doing it. That incessant damned tapping, coupled with pain. Even this week – when Sutton's fellows were knocking hooks into the trees for the lanterns – it all came back. And last night when Basil said I'd *enjoyed* my captivity I wanted to put my hands around his throat and choke him. In some part of myself, I still do. But I *will* put it behind me. If I don't, you might as well have left me there.' He stopped as abruptly as he'd started, then mumbled, 'Sorry. Can we *please* talk about something else?'

'By all means,' replied Benedict smoothly. 'What are your plans now that the business of Basil has been resolved? The Season's virtually over and people are already leaving Town. So will you stay here or get away from everything for a time?'

'We'll do whatever Sophie wants,' For her sake, he managed a crooked smile. 'You didn't have either the wedding or the bridal trip you deserved. I can't do anything about the wedding. But if there's somewhere you'd like to go, all you need do is say the word.'

'There wasn't anything wrong with our wedding,' she retorted. 'I enjoyed it. As for somewhere I want to go ... one day, I'd like you to take me to Florence.'

He lifted her hand to his lips. 'With pleasure, love.'

'Thank you. But for now, when I'm satisfied that Jane has settled in with Julia, all I *really* want is to go back to Hazelmere for a few weeks. I think we both need peace ... and time alone with each other.' She sent a dazzling smile across the room and added, 'Not that you won't all be welcome to visit, of course. Just not immediately.'

'Is that a polite way of telling us it's time to go home?' grinned Daniel.

'By no means. I think that what all of us need now – especially Kit – is something to make us laugh. So ...' She thought for a moment and then said, 'Yes. I challenge each of you to describe just *one* of the silly things you got up to at Oxford – and the sillier, the better. Benedict; you can go first.'

* * *

Much later, lying in bed, naked but for the sheet lying across his lap and still smiling from time to time as he watched Sophia brushing out her hair, Christian said lazily, 'That was a good idea of yours. I haven't thought of some of those tales for years – such as the time Daniel had to flee his would-be mistress's house in such a hurry he didn't have time to put on his breeches. The sight of his bare backside descending from a balcony is probably one of the funniest things I've ever seen.'

She smiled at him in the mirror but said, 'I'm fairly sure Anthony and Gerald felt he shouldn't have told that particular tale while I was present.'

'They're right. He shouldn't have. But you didn't mind?'

'No. I wanted to see you laugh ... and you did.' She paused. 'I was so very proud of you tonight.'

'Thank you. But you know, don't you, that I couldn't have done it without you? If I hadn't had *your* reaction to hold on to – both from the first time and every day since then – I wouldn't have had the courage to go through with it.'

'Yes, you would. Deep down, you trusted Benedict and the others to react exactly as they did because doubting them would have been an insult to the friendship you all share. Even *I* knew how they'd behave and I know them much less well than you do.' She paused and gave a tiny laugh. 'Though after this evening, I've learned a few things.'

'That's one way of putting it.' He fell silent for a time, marvelling, as he sometimes did, at how well she understood him. Then he said, 'Do you truly want to go to Hazelmere?'

'Yes. I truly do. It was good for us there and, as I said, I think we need it.' Laying down the brush, she rose and crossed to clamber up beside him. 'But first there's Julia to consider.' Toying absently with his fingers, she said, 'Jane Gardiner is the perfect answer but Mama isn't going to make her life easy; and I *still* haven't told her about the dog.' She paused and then added, 'I don't suppose you'd do it for me?'

He groaned. 'Well, clearly *one* of us has to.'

She beamed at him. 'Thank you.'

'I'll expect to be rewarded. However ... after that?'

'I'd like to see how things go for a few weeks. Jane may not confide in me – but Julia will. And if she says that Mama is treating Jane like an extra chambermaid and trying to get rid of poor Hamish, I'll step in. With your agreement, I'll remind her that you are paying Jane's wages and will continue to do so. *Then* I'll add that, if the arrangement isn't working out, Julia had better come and live here with us – in which case the allowance you make Mama will naturally be reduced.'

Christian stared at her and murmured, '*Definitely* a Valkyrie. You even scare me.'

'That's useful to know. But would it be all right with you if I did that?'

'Yes. But if it becomes necessary, wouldn't you rather Gerald or I did it?'

'You, perhaps. But not Gerald.' Laughter danced in her eyes. 'Just in case, you know.'

He shook his head at her. 'You don't give up, do you?'

'Not if I can help it.' She leaned against his shoulder. 'I suppose we can expect another visit from Eustace tomorrow.'

'Possibly. And a note from Alveston, seeking my written agreement to Basil being packed off to wherever it is. I'll give it, of course. Presumably Eustace has already done so and also had Basil's personal effects made ready to travel with him.'

'Do you think Basil has been told yet?'

'I don't know. And I've thought about him as much as I'm going to.' He leaned back against the pillows and then, recalling something that had sprung to mind earlier, sat up again. 'Excuse me for a moment, will you?'

He got up and, pulling on his chamber robe, left the room. Sophie wondered where he was going that made the robe necessary, then shrugged at the realisation that, very unusually, and for the second night in a row, she was wearing a nightgown. Last night, she had known he simply needed to be held. Tonight ... tonight, the only thing she was sure of was that laughter shared with his friends had banished the shadows caused by what had come before it.

Christian returned carrying a small, unframed canvas. Shedding the robe, he settled back beside her and said, 'I found this in a little shop in Florence and bought it because it reminded me of you. I couldn't quite bring myself to part with it before ... but now I have the *real* you, I thought we could get it framed and you might like to have it.'

She looked at the portrait. It showed a beautiful lady whose waving golden hair was partly covered by a gauzy veil. Soulful golden-brown eyes were set beneath slender arched brows; the soft pink mouth wore a gently compassionate smile and there was the merest hint of a cleft in her perfect chin.

Without taking her eyes from it, Sophia said, 'Kit ... she's lovely. Exquisite, in fact. But she doesn't look like me – or, at least, *I* don't look like *her*.'

'I disagree – though in my opinion, you outshine her. No, don't argue. Just tell me whether or not you like her.'

'Yes. How could I not? Do you know who painted it?'

'Well, that's the interesting part. To begin with, I don't believe this is a copy; in fact, I'm almost certain it isn't. But as to the artist, I've no idea. The man who sold it to me didn't know either, though he said the style suggests the fifteenth century so the artist *may* have been one of the many patronised by the Medici. I meant to try to learn more once I got home ... but you know how that turned out; and since I came back, there hasn't been time. However, I considered asking Adam Brandon if his brother would take a look at it.'

'Leo Brandon? The portraitist?'

'Yes. I haven't met him but apparently he studied in Italy so he may be able to make an educated guess. We could leave it with him while we're at Hazelmere.' He took the portrait from her and placed it on the night stand. 'But for the time being, she'll have to remain a mystery. And right now, I am thinking of other mysteries entirely.'

'You are?'

'Yes. For example, this garment you're wearing … I am unfamiliar with it.'

'It's called a nightgown,' Sophia told him helpfully.

'I think I knew that much.' He tugged lightly at one of the pink silk bows. 'These are pretty. Do they do anything?'

'Perhaps. Why don't you find out?'

'That's a good idea.' He undid one of them and gave a satisfied smile when the gown fell open at the shoulder. 'Aha! Cunning.' He moved on to the other side and then slid his hand lightly down as far as her hip before beginning to gather up the soft material in his fingers. 'But there does seem to be a great deal of it and it's somewhat in the way. Do you mind if I get rid of it?'

'Not at all. In fact, I think you should.'

'Excellent.' Sitting up, he removed the nightgown in two quick tugs and tossed it overboard. 'Success. Now … where was I?' He turned, sliding his thigh between hers and his hand around her hip, then slowly upwards over her ribs to her breast. 'Ah yes. I remember now.'

* * *

As things turned out, it was mid-August before they departed for Hazelmere.

It took four weeks for Sophie to be satisfied that Mama was no longer behaving in a way likely to make Jane pack her bags – and a further two before she was convinced that this happy state of affairs would continue when she herself was no longer nearby. But eventually Julia assured her that, in addition to becoming accustomed to Jane's presence in the household and to recognise the benefits of it, Mama had even grown reconciled to Hamish, Sophia felt that it was safe for herself and Christian to leave Town. An added factor in this was that Gerald had taken to calling regularly in Charles Street and often accompanied the girls on their daily walks with the dog. He was even, Julia told Sophia with obvious delight, trying to learn sign language.

Once at Hazelmere, they were both kept busy – Christian with estate matters and Sophia with the house. Together, they visited every family on the estate, received and returned calls from their neighbours and held two small dinner parties. But throughout the fine days of September they still found time to take picnics at the lakeside and Sophia learned to swim … naked, as Christian always did. Then, when the chill of October put an end to this pleasure, they discovered new ones inside the house … and somewhere along the way tacitly decided to remain at Hazelmere through Christmas and the turn of the year.

* * *

During his first week in the place laughingly called the Retreat, Basil thought he was in Purgatory. By the time November arrived and he'd been there for three months, he decided it was actually hell. He still didn't know exactly *where* he was and it seemed none of the other residents did either. He knew it was an island – and a small one, at that, because he'd walked around it; twice, in fact, looking without success for a way to leave. He knew it was cold and bleak; that the wind howled almost constantly and the rain came sideways. But the weather was by no means the worst of it.

His room was adequate rather than luxurious and there were scarcely any real servants – only burly fellows there to keep order and see that the rules were followed. But his first appalling taste of what the future held was learning that, if he wanted a bath, he had to use the bathing room near the kitchen, fetch the water himself, dispose of it afterwards and leave the bath clean for whoever used it next. When he objected to this, he was told that the Retreat didn't supply valets or skivvies and that residents were responsible for clearing up after themselves. He was further informed that, like everyone else, he would a spend part of each day *working* ... and handed a broom with which to sweep the corridors.

The discovery that his fellow prisoners were not gutter-scum was a relief. At least, there were occasionally cards in the evening and some conversation – though he quickly noticed that no one spoke of why they were there. And he'd been cheered to learn that there were women there, too ... until he found out that the women's wing was strictly off-limits and the door to it locked every night at nine.

In the early weeks before the weather worsened, he was sent to help dig over the vegetable patch and blistered his hands sawing logs for the fires. And throughout it all, he rained down curses on Lord Alveston for sending him to this hell-hole and on his father for not finding a way to stop him doing it. But his blackest thoughts were reserved for Christian – but for whom he'd still be free. Christian who shouldn't have come back ... shouldn't even be *alive* ... and shouldn't have everything which had so nearly, so *very* nearly, been his.

It was when the snow came that Basil finally began to look into the future and find it terrifying as any nightmare. Unless he could find a way off this God-forsaken rock, he was going to end up like Prince Leopold, scion of some minor principality and now in his seventies, who had been at the Retreat for thirty-two years.

They're not going to let me out, are they? he realised with a sudden sense of panic. *It's true what the others say. No one leaves. Ever. I'm never going to be free. I'll never laugh with old friends at the club or ride in the park or marry. Hell, I may never even have a woman in my bed again.'* His insides turned icy as the true reality of his situation hit him. *The months and years will pass just like these last ones have and the only thing that will change is that I'll get old. I'll grow old on this bloody rock; I'll die without ever living ... because the only alternative is to jump off a cliff.*

And he wasn't desperate enough to do that ... or brave enough, either. Not yet, anyway; or probably, he suspected with a rare flash of self-knowledge, not ever.

* * *

At Hazelmere, letters came from Julia and from Christian's friends who, with the exception of Gerald, had also left London for the country. Then, around the middle of November, Sophia broached the idea of holding a house party at Christmas.

'Nothing too grand,' she said. 'Just family and close friends, I thought.' And ticking names off on her fingers, 'Mama, Gwendoline and Julia; Jane, too of course, unless she wants to spend the holiday with her family. And perhaps you might consider inviting your uncle?'

Christian sighed. 'Yes. With Basil gone, I suppose it's up to me attempt some kind of reconciliation. And Eustace needn't come if he doesn't want to. So ... who else?'

'Drusilla and Jonathan ... Gerald – again, unless he has other plans. Not that I think he *will* have if he knows Julia is to be here.'

He shook his head at her. 'You really think something will come of that?'

'Yes. I suspect the only things holding him back are Mama's likely attitude and Julia not being quite eighteen yet. However, going back to the question of Christmas ... we'll be making up baskets for all the estate families, of course, and I also wondered if we might hold a party for the children.'

'All this in addition to inviting a houseful of guests?' he teased.

'Yes. Shall we?'

Christian laughed. 'Why not? Everything you've mentioned, sweetheart – and all the things that you haven't thought of yet but doubtless will. However, with Christmas only just over a month away, don't be too disappointed if some of the people you'd like to be here have already made other plans.'

'I know – and wish I'd thought of it earlier. But it isn't too late. I'll send invitations out tomorrow and hope for the best.'

'I'll remind you of that,' he said lazily. Then, 'Have you realised that, aside from this being our first Christmas together, it will also be *my* first in over five years?'

'Yes – and that's why I want to make it an especially good one,' she told him, her face bright with enthusiastic determination. 'Boughs of holly, kissing balls and a Yule log; wassailers, spiced wine and every kind of festive delicacy that Cook can think of. And most important of all, those of your friends who are closer than brothers. Benedict, Daniel and Anthony; three gentlemen without whom you and I wouldn't be sharing this very precious Christmas – or, indeed, anything at all.'

EPILOGUE

The first batch of replies to the invitations arrived within the week. Acceptances came from Lord and Lady Colwich, Sophia's mother and sisters and also from Jane Gardiner and Gerald. Next came a letter from Eustace, thanking Sophia for the invitation but sending his regrets; he had, he said, already agreed to join some old friends in Bath for the festive season.

Benedict also accepted. *Oscar's off to Paris*, he wrote, *and Vere has a constitutional dislike of what he calls the 'enforced jollification' of Christmas, so spending it with you and Kit will be a great pleasure.*

Anthony wrote to say that he couldn't get to Hazelmere in time for Yule but would join them before New Year, if that would be acceptable. Charlotte, the sister he'd begun to think would never marry, was finally betrothed to a neighbour she'd known all her life. *And Mama is insisting on holding a St Stephen's Day ball in honour of it*, he explained. *And to make sure it's watertight*.

Sophia laughed but said, 'He must be delighted.'

'Yes. Two sisters settled, two more to go. So ... who haven't we heard from yet?'

'Daniel. But he's sure to come, isn't he?'

A week went by before Daniel's letter arrived.

I'm sorry, he wrote. *I delayed replying in the hope that circumstances might change – but they haven't. My father had a riding accident; he suffered a head injury and has yet to regain consciousness. It's been several days and, as you may imagine, my mother is frantic. Obviously, I won't be able to join you for Christmas but I wish you and your guests all the compliments of the season and will write again when I know more.*

'Oh dear. Poor Daniel,' said Sophia. And then, 'His father remaining unconscious for so long doesn't bode well, does it?'

'No. I wouldn't think so.' Laying Daniel's letter aside, Christian said, 'I'll write to him and send word to Anthony and

Benedict so they'll write as well. If the worst happens, he'll need support. I know *I* did.'

'It won't be as bad for Daniel, surely? You weren't even twenty-one and inheriting an earldom.'

'A *wealthy* earldom,' he pointed out. 'Daniel is older than I was, yes. But if his father dies, he'll become Viscount Reculver and inherit responsibility for an estate that hasn't shown a profit in years. So he'll need all the help he can get.'

* * *

A week later, with no further news from Daniel, Christian received a letter that had nothing at all to do with their Christmas party.

'Ah. Finally,' he said. 'Word from Leo Brandon regarding the portrait.'

'Really? What does he say?'

Christian read rapidly through the closely-written page and then handed it over to her. 'Read it for yourself. It's no wonder it has taken a while. He's been extremely thorough.'

I apologise for the delay, Leo had written. *I had certain suspicions when I first saw the lady but didn't want to speak prematurely without seeking to get them confirmed by a couple of gentlemen better-placed than I to make a determination. The expert I consulted here in England thought I was right but couldn't be positive - so I made a copy of the painting and sent it to a collector in Florence who is familiar with the Medici art collection. He, I'm delighted to say, is quite certain that my first thoughts were correct.*

We believe that the portrait was painted by one Sandro Botticelli, an artist under the patronage of Lorenzo the Magnificent during the Renaissance. I understand that much of his work was allegorical or mythological in nature; lush, beautiful and often featuring nudes. But in the 1490s, Lorenzo died, Florence fell under the spell of a charismatic preacher named Savonarola and public taste turned deeply Puritanical. Paintings were burned as a result – and not just ones by Botticelli. It's impossible to know how many masterpieces were lost. But it seems that, for this and other reasons, Botticelli died impoverished, his work largely eclipsed by artists such as Michelangelo and Raphael. These days, even his name has been forgotten – a great pity, in my opinion. But there seems little doubt that your lady is an early Botticelli Madonna; and should you ever wish to sell her, I hope you will come to me first.

Sophia looked up from the letter and said, 'It's a sad story, isn't it? And hard to believe that a man who painted like that could be so completely forgotten.'

'Yes. But clearly politics and religion played their part in that – not to mention some serious competition.' He grinned suddenly. 'Still, at least now we know something about the portrait ... and it's interesting that Leo Brandon covets it. I'll write, thanking him and telling him that he can enjoy our Madonna until just before Christmas when Gerald will collect her and bring her to us here.'

* * *

On the evening before the first of their guests were due to arrive, Sophia reached a decision about something she had been thinking over for the last fortnight. In the drawing room after dinner, she crossed to sit on Christian's lap and put her arms about his neck, saying, 'This is the last evening we shall have completely to ourselves for a while.'

'It is. Are you regretting it?'

'Not a bit. I'm looking forward to seeing everyone and celebrating Christmas. But there's a particular gift I want to give you now while we're still alone.'

'You do? That sounds intriguing.'

'Yes.' She paused. 'Not so much the *actual* gift, you understand ... more the promise of it.' Another pause while she toyed with his hair. 'In about seven months' time, I think.'

She felt the breath leave him. He said, 'Do you mean – are you – will we – ?'

'Yes. You're going to be a father.'

'Oh God, Sophie-Rose.' His arms tightened around her and it was several seconds before he spoke. Then, 'That – that's – I don't know what to say. Our very own *baby?* It's wonderful. And terrifying. And next to yourself, the very best gift you could give me.'

'As to that, it's not all my own work, is it? You deserve *some* of the credit.'

He gave an unsteady laugh. 'Thank you for recognising it.'

'You're welcome. And you'll be a marvellous father. I know you will.'

'I – I hope so. I'll certainly *try* to be. God, Sophie ... you've knocked me sideways. I don't know why I'm shocked. I shouldn't be. Lord knows, we've been ... well. But this?' Laying a hand on her stomach and talking to the bump that wasn't yet there, he said gently, 'Who are you, little one? A lovely girl with eyes like your Mama's, perhaps.'

'Or a handsome, kind-hearted little boy like your Papa?' countered Sophia.

'Boy or girl ... whichever you are, you are welcome,' promised Christian. 'And whoever you *become*, you will be loved. Always.'

Author's Note

Unusually, I have taken one slight liberty in *The Shadow Earl*. Thomas Braidwood's Academy for the Deaf and Dumb in Hackney – the first school of its type in Britain – actually opened in 1783, rather than 1780 when my story is set.

However, Braidwood had been working with the deaf and dumb (these days, this condition is called deaf-mute) in Edinburgh since 1760 when Charles Shirreff, the miniaturist, had been brought to him as a child to be taught to write. Having developed methods he found to be successful, Braidwood continued with this work. He taught sign language and lip-reading – the former being recognised as the foundation of what would become British Sign Language.

The Botticelli portrait purchased by Christian in Florence crept into the story for two reasons. One is that I love Botticelli's work. The other is that I recently learned something about him that I hadn't known and that I find frankly incredible.

Christian would have visited the Uffizi Gallery in Florence on his Grand Tour – but he wouldn't have seen paintings by Botticelli because there weren't any.

There is no single, clear reason to explain why the artist died impoverished and already fading from memory. Between 1478 and 1490, he produced some of his most famous paintings; *Mars and Venus*, *Primavera* and *The Birth of Venus*. In 1481, he was painting the walls of the Sistine Chapel in Rome. And in the turbulent 1490s, when the Medici were exiled and Savonarola was convincing Florence to repent because the world was about to end, Botticelli became a disciple of Savonarola himself. He changed his style to suit the times and devoted much of the decade to illustrating Dante's *Divine Comedy*. Yet seemingly in no time at all after his death, his work had been eclipsed by that of Raphael and Michelangelo and even his name lay forgotten.

But where it becomes incredible – at least to me – is that Botticelli *stayed forgotten for three centuries*. He was finally rediscovered by the Pre-Raphaelite Brotherhood in the middle of the 19th century. Now, thanks to them, the Uffizi Gallery has five rooms devoted to Botticelli and there are at least six of his paintings on display at the National Gallery, London.

~ * * ~ * * ~

Thank you for reading **The Shadow Earl**. I hope you've enjoyed it. A brief review on the marketplace where you bought it would be appreciated by me and helpful to other, future readers.

Stella Riley
May, 2023

Printed in Great Britain
by Amazon